DEMONIC SECT ELDER AND THE GREAT WAR

DEMONIC SECT ELDER AND THE GREAT WAR

Kalzara

All rights reserved. No part of this publication may be reproduced, stored in a retrieval system, or transmitted in any form or by any means electronic, mechanical, photocopying, recording, or otherwise without prior written permission from Podium Publishing.

This is a work of fiction. Names, characters, places, and incidents are either products of the author's imagination or used fictitiously. Any resemblance to actual events, locales, or persons, living, dead, or undead, is entirely coincidental.

Copyright © 2026 by Kalzara

Cover design by Dalia and Sam

ISBN: 978-1-0394-7155-9

Published in 2026 by Podium Publishing
www.podiumentertainment.com

DEMONIC SECT ELDER AND THE GREAT WAR

CHAPTER ONE

Dusty's stomach growled loudly as he jogged behind the group of Nascent Soul cultivators, his breathing already coming in short puffs despite them barely having traveled half a li from their camp. In his right hand, he clutched a half-eaten spiritual rooster leg, the golden meat still steaming from the fire he'd hastily prepared before they'd set out.

"Could you . . . maybe slow down a bit?" he called out between bites, trying not to sound too pathetic. The other disciples were practically gliding across the rough terrain while he stumbled over every root and rock.

Senior Brother Caelum glanced back with that patient expression he always wore when dealing with Dusty's limitations. Even with his recent breakthrough to Origin Realm, Caelum never acted superior about it. "We're maintaining a steady pace, Junior Brother. The mission parameters require us to reach the supply depot before sunset."

"Right, right," Dusty panted, taking another bite of his rooster leg. The spiritual meat helped replenish his qi, but it couldn't fix his terrible cardiovascular fitness. "Just give me a moment to—"

"Eat while moving," suggested Yi Ziming, one of the Nascent Soul disciples from the main sect. His tone wasn't unkind, but there was an edge of impatience there. "We can't afford delays. Not with the war escalating."

The war.

Even a month after it had officially begun, Dusty still couldn't quite believe they were living through it. The conflict between the demonic sects, primarily the Black Rose Sect and their recently allied Black Heart Sect, and the three major righteous sects had started with border skirmishes and escalated into something none of them had expected.

It wasn't the grand, apocalyptic battle everyone had feared, though.

Instead, it had settled into a strange pattern of raids, supply line attacks, and territorial disputes. The righteous sects would strike at a demonic outpost, the demonic sects would retaliate against a righteous trading convoy, and so on. Like a deadly game of tag that nobody wanted to end.

"Any word from the scouts about enemy movement in this sector?" asked Lan Ming, another Nascent Soul disciple, who specialized in earth-based techniques.

Caelum shook his head, his hand unconsciously moving to rest on the hilt of Starforge. "Intelligence suggests the Pure Soul Sect has been pulling their forces back from this region. Either they're consolidating for a major push elsewhere, or they're trying to draw us into overextending."

Dusty listened to the tactical discussion while focusing on not tripping over his own feet. This was exactly the kind of thing he'd never wanted to be involved in. Strategy, warfare, life-and-death decisions; he just wanted to cultivate peacefully, maybe open a spiritual cuisine restaurant someday. Live a quiet life.

But Boss Morvran had been insistent. "Boy needs experience in real combat situations," his master had declared. "Can't spend his whole life hiding behind roosters and cooking fires."

Easy for him to say. Boss Morvran was built like a boulder and could probably arm-wrestle an Origin Realm cultivator. Dusty was built like . . . well, like someone who enjoyed food a little too much and avoided physical exercise whenever possible.

"Senior Brother Caelum," he ventured as they crested a small hill, "do you really think this mission is necessary? I mean, it's just a supply depot. Surely they'll abandon it once they realize we're coming."

Caelum's expression grew more serious. "That's exactly why we need to hit it before they can relocate everything. Intelligence reports indicate they're storing formation materials there, the kind used for large-scale barrier arrays. If they manage to establish fortified positions in this region . . ."

He didn't need to finish. Even Dusty understood what that meant. Fortified positions meant the war would drag on longer, claim more lives, create more opportunities for everything to spiral completely out of control. Which explained why they had sent Senior Brother Caelum, one of the most powerful Origin Realm cultivators from the sect.

"Besides," Yi Ziming added with a slight grin, "think of it as advanced training. Better to learn combat in a controlled raid than when an enemy kicks down your front door."

Dusty supposed that made sense, but it didn't make him feel any better about the whole situation. He took another bite of rooster leg, savoring the way the spiritual energy flowed through his meridians. At least his cultivation was progressing well. The breakthrough to Core Formation had been surprisingly smooth, probably thanks to Boss Morvran's unconventional but effective teaching methods.

The Way of the Cock wasn't the most dignified cultivation path, but it worked. Dusty could feel the accumulated power of dozens of spiritual roosters flowing through his core, each one adding to his strength and resilience. It was a strange feeling, knowing that his power came from . . . well, eating a lot of chickens.

"You know," Lan Ming said, "my cousin joined the Heavenly Light Sect about six months before all this started. Wonder if I'll run into him at some point."

"Hopefully not on a battlefield," Caelum replied quietly.

That sobered the mood considerably. The reality of the war was that many of them had friends, acquaintances, even family members on the opposite side. The divide between righteous and demonic cultivation had never been absolute; plenty of people had connections across factional lines.

Which reminded Dusty of something far more painful than the prospect of facing strangers in combat.

He'd been trying not to think about it, but the conversation about divided loyalties brought the memory rushing back: that terrible day, three weeks ago, when Sect Master Slifer had summoned all the disciples to the main courtyard for an emergency announcement. Dusty remembered standing in the crowd, still confused about why everyone looked so grim. The sect master had appeared on the elevated platform, his usual composed demeanor replaced by something colder, more dangerous.

"I'm sure many of you have noticed that my disciple Nomed has been absent from recent gatherings," Slifer began. "Some of you may have assumed he was away on a special mission, or perhaps in closed-door cultivation."

A chill ran down Dusty's spine. Nomed was his best friend, the person he had grown up with, the one who'd helped him adjust to sect life, who'd shared meals and cultivation insights and stupid jokes about their masters' quirks.

"The truth," Slifer continued, *"is that Nomed was never truly one of us. He*

was an infiltrator, a demon working for the righteous sects to gather intelligence and sabotage our operations from within."

The courtyard erupted in shocked murmurs, but Dusty felt like the world had gone completely silent. Nomed? His Nomed, who got excited about new techniques and worried about whether he was progressing fast enough in his cultivation? The same Nomed who'd spent hours helping Dusty understand the basics of qi circulation?

"Evidence recovered from his quarters confirms his true allegiance," Slifer said as he produced a collection of communication talismans and coded documents. "He had been feeding information to our enemies since before the tournament. The attack on the Sealed Realm portal, the subsequent escalation of hostilities, all of it was facilitated by intelligence he provided."

Dusty stared at those documents, his mind refusing to process what he was hearing. It had to be a mistake. Someone had planted those things, or maybe they were talking about a different Nomed entirely.

But then Sect Master Slifer explained how they'd discovered the deception, how certain mission failures and security breaches finally made sense in context, and Dusty's last hopes crumbled.

His best friend had been lying to him. For months. For years. For over a decade. Maybe for the entire time they'd known each other.

"Junior Brother Dusty?"

Caelum's voice snapped him back to the present. The group had stopped walking, and everyone was looking at him with concerned expressions.

"Sorry," Dusty mumbled, realizing he'd been standing motionless in the middle of the path. "Just . . . thinking about stuff."

"The Nomed situation?" Caelum asked gently.

Dusty nodded, not trusting his voice. Even a month later, it hurt to think about. Not just the betrayal itself, but all the questions it raised. Had any of their friendship been real? Had Nomed actually cared about him, or was Dusty just a useful idiot to maintain his cover?

"I know it's difficult." Caelum patted his shoulder. "Betrayal by someone you trusted . . . it changes how you see everything."

"Did you ever suspect?" Dusty asked. "I mean, looking back, were there signs I should have noticed?"

Yi Ziming shifted uncomfortably. "That's not really a productive line of thinking, Junior Brother. Infiltrators are trained to blend in perfectly. If it was obvious, they wouldn't be very good at their job."

"Besides," Lan Ming added, "the fact that you trusted him completely just proves you're a good friend. Don't let his deception make you cynical."

Dusty appreciated their attempts to make him feel better, but it didn't really help. The worst part wasn't even the strategic damage Nomed had caused, though that was serious enough. It was the personal betrayal, the knowledge that someone he'd cared about had been using him the entire time.

"We should keep moving," Caelum said after a moment. "We're still on schedule, but we don't want to cut it too close."

They resumed their journey, but the conversation had shifted to lighter topics. Apparently, Lan Ming was having trouble with a formation array he was designing, and Yi Ziming had recently discovered a new tea blend that enhanced meditation. Normal everyday concerns that seemed almost surreal given the context of their mission.

Dusty found himself thinking about how strange it was to be discussing tea preferences while traveling to raid an enemy supply depot. War wasn't like the stories made it seem: all dramatic speeches and glorious battles. Mostly it was just ordinary people doing violent things because their leaders had decided it was necessary.

"There," Caelum said suddenly, pointing toward a cluster of buildings visible through the trees ahead. "Target confirmed. Looks like the intelligence was accurate."

Dusty squinted at the distant structures. They looked disappointingly normal, just wooden buildings with a few guards visible around the perimeter. No dramatic fortifications or arrays of deadly traps. Almost anticlimactic, really.

"Remember the plan," Caelum continued in a low voice. "Yi Ziming and Lan Ming take the perimeter guards quietly. I'll handle the depot commander if he's present. Junior Brother Dusty, you stay in the rear and provide support as needed."

Translation: stay out of the way and try not to get killed. Dusty was perfectly fine with that arrangement.

They moved closer, using the forest cover to mask their approach. Dusty's heart was beating faster now, adrenaline mixing with fear in his bloodstream. This was really happening. He was about to participate in an actual combat operation.

The attack itself went smoothly at first.

Yi Ziming and Lan Ming killed the outer guards with a single strike, while Caelum advanced toward the main building, his sword remaining sheathed but ready.

Dusty hung back as instructed, watching the proceedings with a mixture of admiration and anxiety. His seniors made it look so easy, so professional. Maybe the mission would be over without any real violence.

Then everything went wrong at once.

A tremendous spiritual pressure descended on the area like a crushing weight, making Dusty's knees buckle and his vision blur. This wasn't the scary presence of a Nascent Soul cultivator or even the terrifying aura of an Origin Realm expert.

This was Ascendant-level power, raw, overwhelming, almost transcendent.

"A trap!" Caelum shouted as his composure finally cracked. He drew Starforge in a motion almost too fast to follow. "Everyone behind me, now!"

Dusty stumbled toward the group's leader, his rooster leg forgotten as it fell from nerveless fingers. The spiritual pressure was so intense he could barely think, let alone move properly.

A figure materialized above the depot buildings: a middle-aged woman in pure white robes. Her hair floated around her head as if she were underwater, and her eyes blazed with righteous fury.

"Demonic scum," she spat. "Did you really think you could raid Pure Soul Sect holdings without consequences?"

Yi Ziming and Lan Ming had retreated to flank Caelum, their faces pale but determined. Even with one of the most talented Origin Realm experts on their side, against an Ascendant cultivator, their chances were essentially zero, but they'd apparently decided to make a stand anyway.

"Master's emergency protocols," Caelum said quietly as he reached into his storage ring with steady hands despite the hint of fear in his eyes. "I'm not going to let any of you die here."

He pulled out a simple-looking jade talisman, no larger than his palm. To Dusty's untrained senses, it didn't seem particularly special, just a flat piece of stone with some inscribed characters.

The Ascendant cultivator raised her hand and spiritual energy coalesced around her palm in preparation for an attack that would probably vaporize all of them instantly.

"Final Judgment of the Pure Soul," she whispered, her voice taking on an otherworldly resonance.

A beam of white light erupted from her hand, aimed directly at their group.

Dusty had time for exactly one thought: *This is how I die. At least it'll be quick.*

And it was at that moment that Caelum crushed the talisman.

A ghostly figure materialized between them and the incoming attack, translucent but clearly recognizable as Sect Master Slifer. The apparition was massive, easily nine times the size of a normal person, and radiated power that made even the Ascendant cultivator's aura seem weak by comparison.

The ghostly Slifer raised one hand almost casually, and the beam of concentrated light struck its palm and dispersed harmlessly, like water hitting a mountain.

"Impossible," the Ascendant cultivator breathed, her confident expression replaced by shock and growing fear. "An apparition shouldn't be this powerful!"

The ghostly figure didn't speak. Instead, it clenched its raised hand into a fist and punched forward through the air.

Dusty felt the shock wave pass over him like a physical thing, ruffling his robes and making his ears pop. The punch itself seemed to transcend normal space. One moment the ghost was striking at empty air, the next moment the Ascendant cultivator's body exploded in a shower of gore that painted the surrounding trees crimson.

What had been a dignified figure in pristine white robes became an unrecognizable splatter of flesh and bone fragments scattered across a fifty-meter radius.

A moment later, a panicked spirit form, the cultivator's soul, separated from its destroyed physical vessel and fled toward the horizon at incredible speed. Even in her terror, she was apparently smart enough not to stick around and see what else the ghostly sect master might do.

The silence that followed was deafening.

Dusty stared at the spot where the Ascendant cultivator had been standing, his mind struggling to process what he'd just witnessed. An Ascendant, someone who could level mountains and split seas, had been defeated so thoroughly it wasn't even a fight.

The ghostly figure of Sect Master Slifer turned toward them, and for a moment Dusty felt the weight of that gaze. Even as a projection, even through what was obviously just a protective talisman, there was something in those eyes that spoke of power beyond comprehension.

Then the figure nodded once, a simple acknowledgment that somehow managed to convey approval, reassurance, and a mild warning all at once, and faded away like morning mist.

The oppressive spiritual pressure vanished with it, leaving only the normal sounds of wind through trees and Dusty's own rapid breathing.

"Well," Yi Ziming said after a long moment, his voice slightly hoarse. "That was educational."

Lan Ming was staring at the empty space where their attacker had been. "I've heard stories about emergency talismans from powerful cultivators, but I never imagined . . ."

"Master is stronger than anyone knows," Caelum said quietly as he sheathed Starforge with hands that only trembled slightly. "Much stronger."

Dusty nodded mutely, still too shaken to speak. He'd known intellectually that Sect Master Slifer was powerful—you didn't become the leader of a major sect without serious cultivation—but seeing even a projection of that power in action was something else entirely.

It also raised uncomfortable questions about what kind of person he was learning under, what kind of sect he'd joined. Someone who could casually destroy an Ascendant cultivator with a projected technique... What did that make them?

"Mission parameters have changed," Caelum announced, his leadership instincts reasserting themselves. "We secure what we can from the depot and withdraw immediately. If they had one Ascendant watching this place, they might have others."

The others nodded and moved to comply, but Dusty found himself lingering for a moment longer, staring at the spot where the ghostly figure had stood.

What have I gotten myself into? he wondered, not for the first time since joining the sect.

But as he watched his seniors efficiently loot the abandoned depot, as he thought about Boss Morvran's genuine care for his development, as he remembered all the small kindnesses he'd received from fellow disciples, Dusty realized something important.

Whatever else Sect Master Slifer might be, whatever power he possessed, he used it to protect his people. The talisman hadn't been given to them for conquest or aggression; it was emergency protection, a way to keep his disciples safe when they were in over their heads.

Maybe that was enough. Maybe in a world where wars broke out over philosophical differences and old friends turned out to be enemy spies, having someone powerful on your side wasn't the worst thing that could happen.

Dusty picked up his dropped rooster leg, brushed off the dirt, and took another bite. The spiritual meat tasted the same as always, but somehow the world felt a little more complicated than it had that morning.

Still, he thought as he hurried to catch up with the others, *at least I'm on the winning side.*

CHAPTER TWO

Slifer sat behind the massive obsidian desk in his newly renovated sect master chambers, staring at a stack of reports that seemed to grow taller each day. The sunlight filtered through the tall windows and cast long shadows across detailed maps of the surrounding territories. Red pins marked recent skirmishes, blue ones showed supply routes, and yellow indicated neutral settlements caught in the crossfire.

A month. It had been exactly one month since the so-called Great War had begun, though calling it "great" felt like an overstatement. What they were experiencing was more like an extended series of tactical raids and border disputes than the apocalyptic conflict everyone had initially feared.

He picked up the latest intelligence report from Morvran, scanning the neat handwriting that detailed the previous week's activities. The Heavenly Light Sect had struck three of their outer supply depots, making off with formation materials, spiritual artefacts, and spiritual herbs. In retaliation, the Black Heart Sect had ambushed a Pure Soul Sect convoy, capturing two elders and a dozen disciples. The White Tiger Sect seemed content to focus their aggression on the smaller demonic organizations, systematically dismantling rogue cultivator groups that had allied themselves with the Black Rose Sect.

The pattern was obvious to anyone paying attention. This wasn't random warfare; it was coordinated harassment designed to wear down the demonic sects' resources and morale. Each attack targeted something specific: supply lines, communication networks, recruitment efforts, or territorial control. Someone with strategic knowledge was orchestrating these strikes.

Slifer suspected he knew who that someone was, though he lacked concrete proof. Lady Chi had demonstrated her ability to manipulate minds during their confrontation at the sect. If she could control three sect masters simultaneously, coordinating their military strategies would be child's play. The question was why she was taking such a measured approach instead of launching an all-out assault.

The answer probably lay in the limitations of her power. Mind control on that scale had to be exhausting, even for someone of her cultivation level. She was likely pacing herself, building up momentum while gradually weakening their defenses. It was a smart strategy, frustratingly so.

"Master?" Morvran's voice interrupted his thoughts as the large man entered the chamber carrying a fresh pot of tea. "The latest casualty reports from the border outposts."

Slifer accepted the tea gratefully, noting how Morvran's usually immaculate appearance showed signs of strain. Dark circles under his eyes, a slight tremor in his hands when he thought no one was looking. The constant state of alertness was wearing on everyone.

"How many this time?" Slifer asked, dreading the answer.

"Seventeen wounded, three dead. All from the eastern checkpoint that got hit two nights ago." Morvran's voice remained steady, but Slifer could hear the underlying frustration. "The White Tiger Sect used some kind of coordinated beast attack. War panthers and steel-wing hawks working together. Our disciples managed to drive them off, but . . ."

"But the coordination was too sophisticated for wild beasts," Slifer finished. "They had human handlers."

"Exactly. Which means the White Tiger Sect is committing more resources to these raids than we initially calculated."

Slifer leaned back in his chair, processing the implications. The White Tiger Sect specialized in beast taming and physical cultivation. If they were deploying trained war beasts for border harassment, it suggested they were preparing for something larger. War beasts required significant time and resources to train properly. You didn't waste them on minor raids unless you were testing enemy defenses for a major offensive.

"Have we heard anything from our allies?" he asked.

"The Black Heart Sect reports similar pressure on their northern borders. Three attacks this week, all targeting their alchemical facilities. They're requesting additional defensive formations." Morvran paused to consult his notes. "The Wandering Sword Sect has offered to provide intelligence on righteous sect movements, but they want guarantees that we won't drag them into direct confrontation."

Slifer nodded absently. The smaller sects were walking a careful line, wanting to benefit from alliance with stronger powers while avoiding the worst consequences of open warfare. It was a reasonable position, but it left the major demonic sects bearing most of the burden.

"What about recruitment efforts?"

"Surprisingly successful. Word of your . . . encounter with Lady Chi has spread through the cultivation world. Many smaller clans and rogue cultivators see alignment with us as protection against righteous sect aggression." Morvran's expression grew thoughtful. "Though I suspect some of them are more interested in the legendary treasures they've heard we possess."

That made sense. Slifer's collection of System-provided artifacts had developed quite a reputation over the past months. Every time he used one in public—the Divine Azerion Ark, various protective talismans, the mysterious pills that could heal the fatally wounded—rumors spread and grew in the telling. By now, half the cultivation world probably believed he had access to an entire treasury of Immortal Realm artifacts.

The irony wasn't lost on him. His actual power level remained embarrassingly low compared to his reputation. Without the System's support, he would still be a Core Formation cultivator struggling to maintain relevance in a world of Ascendant Realm elders and Half-Step Immortal Realm monsters. But perception was often more important than reality in the cultivation world. As long as people believed he was an unstoppable force, they would act accordingly.

A soft chime from his desk drawer interrupted his thoughts. The sound was barely audible, designed to alert him without drawing attention from anyone else in the room. Slifer's hand moved casually to the drawer and retrieved what appeared to be an ordinary jade communication token. To Morvran's eyes, it would look like he was checking routine sect business.

In reality, the token was connected to the emergency talismans he had given his disciples. Each talisman could create a projection of his power when activated, providing a last resort for life-threatening situations. The downside was that each use drained a significant number of his Karmic Credits.

The token's surface glowed with soft golden light, indicating an active emergency. A quick mental check through his Disciple Management interface showed the alert was coming from Caelum. His most reliable student was in danger somewhere, facing something powerful enough to require divine intervention.

Slifer closed his eyes and extended his consciousness through the spiritual connection to the activated talisman. The process was always disorienting, like trying to see through someone else's eyes while maintaining awareness of his own body. The world shifted, and suddenly he was standing in a different place entirely.

The projection manifested in a rugged landscape dotted with sparse vegetation and rocky outcroppings. Mountains rose in the distance, their peaks shrouded in mist. This looked like the borderlands between the Black Rose Sect's territory and the neutral zones to the south.

Three figures stood in a loose formation near a pile of rubble that might once have been a building. Caelum was on one knee, blood trickling from a cut above his left eye, his hand pressed against what looked like a serious wound in his side. Behind him, two other disciples—Slifer recognized them as Yi Ziming and Lan Ming from the main sect—were attempting to maintain defensive positions despite obvious exhaustion. And cowering behind a boulder was Morvran's disciple, Dusty.

Facing them was a middle-aged woman in white robes. Her spiritual pressure radiated outward like a physical force, causing the air to shimmer around them. The aura was unmistakably Ascendant Realm, probably mid-stage based on its intensity. Her dark hair floated around her head as if she were underwater, and her eyes blazed with righteous fury.

"Demonic scum," she was saying. "Did you really think you could raid Pure Soul Sect holdings without consequences?"

Ah. So, she was guarding an outpost. Slifer made a mental note to review the operational parameters for disciple assignments. Sending Core Formation and Nascent Soul students against Ascendant opposition was the kind of mistake that got people killed, even if they were led by the sword prodigy Caelum himself.

The woman raised her hand, spiritual energy coalescing around her palm in preparation for an attack that would probably vaporize all four disciples instantly. Her technique was already forming: Final Judgment of the Pure Soul, a signature move of the Pure Soul Sect that Slifer recognized from intelligence reports.

He didn't hesitate. The projection's hand moved almost casually, and the beam of concentrated light that erupted from the woman's palm simply stopped. The attack struck his ghostly palm and dispersed harmlessly.

The Pure Soul Sect cultivator's confident expression transformed into shock, then growing fear as she realized what she was facing. "Impossible," she breathed. "An apparition shouldn't be this powerful!"

Slifer didn't bother to respond. Instead, he made his projection clench its raised hand into a fist and punch forward through the air. The strike caused the Ascendant cultivator's body to explode in a shower of gore.

The woman's spirit form separated from her destroyed physical vessel and fled toward the horizon at incredible speed, apparently smart enough not to stick around and see what else the ghostly sect master might do.

The projection nodded once at the four disciples before fading away.

Slifer opened his eyes back in his chamber and immediately felt the drain on his resources. The emergency talisman had cost him nearly two thousand Karmic Credits, a significant expense but worth it to save four disciples and send a message to the Pure Soul Sect. More importantly, it would reinforce his reputation as someone who protected his people.

"Master?" Morvran was looking at him with concern. "You seemed . . . distant for a moment."

"Just checking on our forward positions," Slifer replied smoothly. "It appears the Pure Soul Sect has escalated their tactics. They sent an Ascendant to attack one of our scouting parties."

Morvran's expression darkened. "How many casualties?"

"None, thanks to some timely intervention." Slifer stood and moved to the large window that overlooked the sect's main courtyard. Below, disciples went about their daily training routines, practicing forms and sparring under the watchful eyes of their instructors. The sight was reassuring in its normalcy, a reminder that life continued even during wartime.

"This changes things," he continued. "If they're willing to deploy Ascendant cultivators for border raids, it means they're preparing to escalate significantly. We need to adjust our defensive posture accordingly."

"Should I recall our forward teams?"

Slifer considered the question carefully. Pulling back their scouts would improve their safety, but it would also blind them to enemy movements. On the other hand, losing experienced disciples to overwhelming force served no strategic purpose.

"Recall the Core Formation teams. Replace them with Nascent Soul groups, and make sure each team has emergency communication methods." He turned from the window to face Morvran directly. "I want to know about any Ascendant-level movement in our territory within a few seconds of detection."

"Understood. What about offensive operations?"

That was the crucial question. So far, their side had been primarily reactive, responding to righteous sect aggression rather than initiating conflicts. It was a defensive strategy that minimized their losses but also ceded the initiative to their enemies. Lady Chi and her puppet sect masters could choose when and where to strike, forcing the demonic sects to spread their defenses thin.

"We need to shift the dynamic," Slifer said after a long pause. "Right now, they're controlling the pace and location of conflicts. We're always responding, never acting."

He moved to the large map on his wall, studying the positions marked with various colored pins. The righteous sects had been systematically probing their defenses, testing response times and identifying weak points. It was textbook military strategy: gather intelligence, identify targets, then strike with overwhelming force at the most vulnerable positions.

"The problem is that we're fighting their kind of war," he continued. "Conventional military tactics favor the side with superior numbers and resources. The righteous sects have both."

Morvran nodded thoughtfully. "What kind of war should we be fighting?"

"The kind where our advantages matter more than our disadvantages." Slifer tapped the map at several key locations. "We have better intelligence networks, more flexible command structures, and access to techniques they can't predict or counter. We should be hitting targets they don't expect, using methods they can't defend against."

The strategy was sound in theory, but implementation would be challenging. The righteous sects had spent centuries developing defenses against demonic cultivation techniques. Their formations, protective arrays, and combat doctrines all assumed they would be facing enemies who used soul attacks, poison, mental manipulation, and other traditional demonic methods.

But Slifer had access to System-enhanced abilities that didn't follow conventional rules. And then there were his protagonist-like disciples: Caelum's space manipulation, Amelia's purification-based attacks, Hughie's probability-defying luck. These weren't traditional demonic techniques. They were entirely new forms of power that existing defenses weren't designed to handle.

"I want you to coordinate with the other demonic sects," he told Morvran. "Set up a meeting with their leadership. It's time we started working together more effectively."

"The other sect masters have been requesting such a meeting for weeks. They're concerned about the lack of unified command structure."

Slifer grimaced. He had been avoiding those meetings because they inevitably led to discussions about strategy, tactics, and resource allocation; topics where his actual knowledge was embarrassingly limited. Leading a single sect was manageable because he could delegate most decisions to competent subordinates. Commanding a multi-sect alliance required expertise he simply didn't possess.

But avoiding the issue wasn't working. The righteous sects were clearly coordinating their efforts, while the demonic side remained fragmented and reactive. If he wanted to win this war, or at least avoid losing it catastrophically, he needed to accept responsibilities that made him deeply uncomfortable.

"Schedule it for tomorrow evening," he said finally. "All sect leaders, plus their top military advisors. We need to start acting like allies instead of neighbors."

Morvran made notes on his ever-present tablet. "Should I prepare briefing materials on our current defensive positions and resource allocations?"

"Yes, but keep the details vague. Share enough information to enable coordination but not enough to compromise our security if there are information leaks." Slifer paused, considering additional precautions. "And make sure the meeting location has anti-surveillance formations. I don't want Lady Chi eavesdropping on our planning sessions."

The mention of their mysterious enemy reminded him of another pressing concern. Lady Chi's ability to manipulate minds made conventional intelligence gathering extremely difficult. How could they trust any information that came from righteous sect sources? How could they verify that their own people hadn't been compromised?

"Have we made any progress on developing countermeasures against mental manipulation?" he asked.

"Grand Elder Lydia has been working with the Formation Hall to create protective arrays, but progress is slow. The techniques being used are beyond our current understanding." Morvran's expression grew troubled. "We've tested the prototypes on volunteers, but they either provide insufficient protection or interfere so severely with normal thinking that they're impractical for daily use."

That was frustrating but not entirely unexpected. Mental protection arrays were notoriously difficult to create because they had to distinguish between hostile intrusion and normal cognitive function. Too little protection and the enemy could still influence the user's thoughts. Too much protection and the user became incapable of making complex decisions.

"What about the Void Being Aura?" Slifer asked. His own resistance to Lady Chi's mental attacks had come from that ability. If they could replicate that effect . . .

"We've studied the technique extensively, but it appears to be tied to specific bloodline characteristics that can't be easily transferred." Morvran hesitated before continuing. "Grand Elder Lydia did suggest that you could potentially share the protection through direct spiritual contact, but the process would be... intimate."

Slifer winced. The idea of forming spiritual connections with dozens of sect members was both exhausting and uncomfortably personal. Spiritual contact of that depth would give both parties access to each other's memories and emotions. It was the kind of vulnerability that made his skin crawl. And with his true identity and power level, it was not something he could risk.

"In that case, keep working on the formation-based approach."

A knock at the chamber door interrupted their conversation. "Enter," Slifer called, settling back into his chair to maintain the appearance of casual authority.

The door opened to admit a young disciple in the black and red robes of an Inner Sect messenger. The boy looked nervous, probably intimidated by being in the sect master's presence. He bowed deeply before speaking.

"Master, urgent message from the southern border. Elder Magnus requests immediate consultation regarding enemy movement."

Slifer accepted the sealed message tube, noting the multiple security seals that indicated high-priority intelligence. Breaking them revealed a single sheet of paper covered in Magnus's precise handwriting, along with a detailed sketch that made his blood run cold.

The sketch showed a formation array of massive proportions carved into the ground across several mountain peaks. The symbols were unfamiliar, but the overall pattern radiated malevolent purpose. According to Magnus's notes, righteous sect forces had been constructing this array for at least two weeks, working under heavy guard in a previously uninhabited region.

"What does it mean?" Morvran asked, reading over his shoulder.

Slifer studied the sketch more carefully, trying to match it against formation patterns he had learned from the System's knowledge implants. The central symbol looked familiar, something related to binding or containment. The outer rings appeared to be power amplification matrices, designed to channel massive amounts of spiritual energy into whatever the central formation was supposed to accomplish.

"I think," he said slowly, "they're building a trap."

All of the border raids, the systematic probing attacks, the gradual escalation of force—it had all been designed to drive the demonic sects into a specific response pattern. Lady Chi had been herding them like livestock, positioning their forces exactly where she wanted them.

And now she was ready to spring whatever trap she had been preparing.

"Send immediate recall orders to all forward positions," he ordered. "Emergency withdrawal, maximum speed. And get me a communication link to the other sect leaders. We need to warn them before—"

The chamber suddenly went dark as every formation in the building failed simultaneously. Through the windows, Slifer could see similar darkness spreading across the entire sect compound. Emergency lighting flickered on a moment later, but the main defensive arrays remained offline.

"Master," Morvran's voice was tense in the dim light. "The primary spiritual vein just went dead."

Slifer closed his eyes and extended his spiritual sense to examine the sect's infrastructure. The damage was extensive and precisely targeted. Someone had severed the connection between their spiritual vein and the formation network, cutting power to everything except the most basic life-support systems.

It was the kind of sabotage that required intimate knowledge of their defensive systems and access to heavily protected areas. The work of someone trusted, someone with authority to move freely through restricted zones.

Someone like Nomed.

The pieces fell into place with sickening clarity. His newest disciple, the one who had seemed so grateful and loyal, had been perfectly positioned to cause maximum damage at the worst possible moment. He must have planned this before he left for the Sealed Realm.

"Morvran," he said quietly. "Activate the emergency communication array. Send a priority message to all allied sects: 'Trust no one. The enemy is among us.'"

Outside, the first explosions began.

CHAPTER THREE

The ground shook beneath Slifer's feet as another explosion rattled the sect's outer defenses. Through the tall windows of his chambers, orange flames painted the night sky in violent strokes. The acrid smell of burning formations and scorched earth drifted through the air, carrying with it the metallic tang of spilled blood.

So it begins.

Slifer closed his eyes and took a deep breath. In his previous life, the closest he'd come to warfare had been playing strategy games in his basement. Now he stood at the center of what could become a realm-spanning conflict, with thousands of lives hanging in the balance. The weight of responsibility sat heavy on his shoulders, but there was no time for self-doubt.

A soft chime echoed in his mind, and the familiar blue interface materialized before his eyes.

Ding!
Urgent mission detected.
New Mission: Defend the Black Rose Sect
Repel the coordinated assault by the three major righteous sects. Minimize casualties among your disciples and sect members. Discover the source of the enemy coordination.
Reward: 100,000 Karmic Credits, Special Defensive Array Upgrade
Failure: Complete sect destruction, disciple death, mission chain termination
Warning: This appears to be a coordinated assault. Enemy forces include multiple Ascendant Realm cultivators. Extreme caution advised.

One hundred thousand credits. The System was offering more than he'd ever seen for a single mission, which meant the danger was proportionate. Slifer dismissed the interface and moved toward the door. The explosions were getting closer.

"Morvran!" he called out.

His right-hand man appeared instantly, somehow managing to look composed despite the chaos erupting around them.

"Master, the outer perimeter has been breached in three locations," Morvran reported. "The attacking forces include disciples from all three major righteous sects. Conservative estimates put their numbers at over two thousand cultivators."

"Ascendant participation?"

"Confirmed. We've detected at least two distinct Ascendant auras approaching from different directions. Grand Elder Wyatt is coordinating our defensive formations, but . . ." Morvran hesitated, which was unusual for him.

"But what?"

"The attacking patterns suggest perfect intelligence about our defensive layouts. They're striking at precisely the right locations to cause maximum damage with minimum effort. Someone has provided them with detailed information about our sect's vulnerabilities."

Slifer's jaw tightened. It was probably Nomed.

Another explosion, much closer this time. The windows rattled in their frames, and dust rained down from the ceiling. Slifer could hear shouting from the courtyards below, the clash of weapons against spiritual energy, the screams of the wounded and dying.

"Where is Master Caelum?" Morvran asked.

"Returning from an assignment. We're on our own." Slifer moved to his desk and began pulling out various jade slips and communication talismans. "Send immediate recall orders to all disciples currently on missions outside the sect. Emergency protocols. And gather Hughie, Amelia, Fenlock, and Val in the main courtyard. We need our strongest defenders here."

"At once, Master."

As Morvran departed, Slifer took a moment to assess their situation. Without Caelum's sword cultivation prowess, they were missing their most reliable combat asset. The other disciples were formidable in their own ways, but facing coordinated Ascendant-level opposition would push them beyond their limits.

Think, Slifer. What advantages do you have?

His disciples weren't just powerful cultivators; they had protagonist-like qualities that made them unpredictable in combat. Hughie's ridiculous luck could turn impossible situations around. Amelia's soul techniques were devastating against unprepared opponents. Fenlock's sound cultivation was perfect for battlefield control. And Val . . . Well, a recently broken-through Origin Soul dragon was worth an entire squad of elite cultivators.

But would it be enough?

Slifer made his way through the corridors of the sect, noting how many disciples and elders were already mobilizing for combat. The death warriors, Morvran's rescued orphans, moved in formations, their black armor gleaming as they took up defensive positions. Outer Sect disciples hurried past carrying weapons and supplies, their faces grim but determined.

The Black Rose Sect had been his home for over a year now. These people had accepted him, served him, looked up to him as their supreme elder and now sect master. He'd reformed their practices, improved their cultivation methods, and tried to guide them toward a more righteous path. The thought of watching it all burn because of one traitor's betrayal filled him with cold fury.

The main courtyard was in controlled chaos when Slifer arrived. Disciples rushed back and forth carrying wounded from the outer defenses. Emergency medical stations had been set up near the eastern wall, where several healers worked frantically to stabilize injuries. The air crackled with defensive formations being powered up to maximum strength.

"Master!" Hughie's voice cut through the noise. Slifer's disciple approached at a run, his usual easygoing demeanor replaced by focused intensity. Behind him came Amelia, her eyes already beginning to show hints of purple flame. Fenlock followed, his gentle features set in uncharacteristic hardness.

"Where's Val?" Slifer asked.

"Here!" the young dragon's voice piped up from behind a pile of supply crates. She emerged in her baby form, but Slifer could see the barely restrained power radiating from her compact frame. Her golden eyes held an eager gleam that suggested she was looking forward to the coming battle.

"Good. Listen carefully, all of you." Slifer gestured for them to come closer, speaking in a low voice that wouldn't carry to the other disciples. "This isn't a random attack. The righteous sects have been fed intelligence about our defenses by a traitor within our own walls. They know exactly where to strike for maximum effect."

Amelia's eyes flared with purple fire. "Nomed?"

"Yes, but that's not important right now. What matters is that we're facing a coordinated assault by potentially thousands of cultivators, including multiple Ascendants. Our goal isn't to win a decisive victory; it's to hold them off long enough to identify their true objectives and force them to withdraw."

"You want us to fight defensively?" Hughie asked, frowning. "That doesn't sound like us."

Slifer almost smiled despite the circumstances. His disciples had developed quite the reputation for aggressive tactics. "Sometimes the best offense is a good defense. But I'm not asking you to simply hold positions. I want you to be unpredictable. Use your unique abilities to create chaos in their ranks. Make them question their intelligence, doubt their plans."

He turned to each disciple individually. "Hughie, I want you mobile. Use your transformations and that impossible luck of yours to hit their rear formations. Create diversions, rescue trapped allies, and generally be a thorn in their side. Don't get pinned down in prolonged fights."

Hughie nodded, cracking his knuckles. "I can do that."

Next, Slifer faced Amelia. "I want you to target their officers and coordinators. Use your soul techniques to disrupt their command structure. But be careful; they'll likely have prepared defenses against mental attacks after your reputation spread."

"Let them try," Amelia replied, her voice carrying an undertone that suggested her ghoul transformation was already beginning. "I have new techniques they haven't seen yet."

"Fenlock." Slifer turned to his gentlest disciple. "I know combat isn't your preference, but your sound cultivation is perfect for battlefield control. I want you coordinating with our defenders and using your techniques to enhance communication and disrupt enemy formations. Can you handle that?"

Fenlock straightened his shoulders. "For the sect, Master, I'll do whatever is necessary."

"And Val." Slifer looked down at the young dragon, who was practically vibrating with excitement. "I want you in your full dragon form, but don't engage the Ascendants directly. Focus on their support formations, supply lines, and escape routes. Make them realize they're not fighting just another sect; they're fighting a dragon's lair."

Val's grin revealed teeth that were already beginning to sharpen. "Can I eat the ones I defeat?"

"Within reason," Slifer finally answered.

Another explosion shook the courtyard, this one close enough that Slifer felt the pressure wave in his chest. Dust and debris rained down from the defensive walls, and several disciples stumbled. In the distance, he could see the glow of fires spreading across the sect's outer buildings.

"Master." Grand Elder Wyatt appeared at Slifer's shoulder, his face grim. "The enemy has broken through the eastern wall. We have confirmed Ascendant cultivators leading the assault. At least two, possibly three. Our formations are holding, but they won't last much longer under this kind of pressure."

Slifer nodded. "Deploy the disciples as discussed. Coordinate with the grand elders for overall defense, but give them tactical autonomy. They know their abilities better than anyone."

As his disciples scattered to their assignments, Slifer found himself alone with his thoughts for a moment. The sounds of battle were getting closer: the clash of weapons, the roar of spiritual techniques, the cries of wounded and dying cultivators from both sides.

This is it. The moment where all those System cards and that careful planning either pay off or get everyone killed.

A tremendous roar echoed across the sect grounds as Val transformed to her full dragon size. Even from the main courtyard, Slifer could see her massive form rising above the outer buildings, her scales gleaming like burnished gold in the firelight. Her wings could spread wide enough to cast shadows over entire courtyards, and her presence alone would likely give the attackers pause.

Good. Let them wonder exactly what they'd gotten themselves into.

"Death warriors, form ranks!" Morvran's voice carried across the courtyard. The black-armored fighters took up positions along the defensive walls and key chokepoints. Each one was a rescued orphan who owed their life to the sect, and their loyalty was absolute. They might not be the most powerful cultivators, but they were disciplined and fearless.

Slifer made his way to the central command platform that had been hastily erected in the middle of the courtyard. From here, he could observe the entire battlefield and coordinate the defense. Communication talismans crackled with reports from various sections of the sect.

"Eastern wall reports heavy casualties. Requesting immediate reinforcement."

"Southern approach compromised. Enemy Nascent Soul cultivators have breached the outer formations."

"Northern sector is holding, but we're running low on defensive treasures."

Each report painted a picture of a coordinated, professional assault. This wasn't a spontaneous attack driven by righteous indignation. Someone had planned this operation carefully, timing it for maximum impact when key defenders were away from the sect.

Lady Chi. It had to be . . .

A flash of purple light from the eastern section caught his attention. Amelia had engaged someone significant; her soul techniques were blazing like a miniature star. Almost immediately, he heard the distinctive howl that

DEMONIC SECT ELDER AND THE GREAT WAR 25

meant Hughie had activated one of his transformations. The sounds of battle from that direction intensified dramatically.

Good. Keep them off-balance.

A communication talisman at his elbow crackled to life. "Master, this is Fenlock. I'm coordinating with the defenders at the main gate. The enemy appears to be probing for weak points rather than committing to a full assault. I think they're waiting for something."

Waiting for what? Slifer frowned. If they had such detailed intelligence about the sect's defenses, why weren't they pressing their advantage?

Unless . . .

"All units, be advised," Slifer said into his own communication talisman. "This may be a probing attack designed to gather additional intelligence or draw out our strongest defenders. Do not commit to extended engagements unless absolutely necessary."

But even as he gave the order, Slifer realized they might not have a choice. The attacking forces were systematically dismantling their outer defenses, and each breach brought them closer to the sect's vital areas. The residential quarters where non-combatant disciples sheltered. The libraries containing irreplaceable cultivation knowledge. The spiritual gardens that had taken decades to cultivate.

The sound of approaching footsteps made him turn. Grand Elder Lydia approached, her robes stained with blood and her face drawn with exhaustion.

"Sect Master, we're receiving wounded faster than we can treat them. Many of the injuries appear to be from techniques specifically designed to be difficult to heal. Lingering curses, spiritual poison, soul damage. This isn't random violence; someone has prepared specifically to fight against our sect's capabilities."

"Do what you can, Grand Elder. If we can't save everyone, focus on those who can return to the fight quickest."

Grand Elder Lydia nodded and hurried back toward the medical stations. Slifer watched her go, feeling the weight of command pressing down on him. Every decision he made could mean the difference between life and death for his people.

A new sound joined the chaos of battle, a deep, thrumming note that seemed to resonate in the bones. Fenlock was using his sound cultivation to coordinate the defenders, and the effect was immediate. Slifer could see sect members moving more efficiently, communicating more effectively, their attacks becoming more synchronized.

That's my boy.

The communication talismans erupted with new reports.

"Val has cleared the eastern approach! Enemy forces are in full retreat from that sector!"

"Hughie has disrupted three separate assault teams. The southern advance has stalled!"

"Amelia has eliminated two enemy commanders. Their coordination in the western section is breaking down!"

His disciples were performing exactly as hoped. Their unique abilities were creating chaos in the attackers' carefully laid plans. But Slifer knew this was just the opening phase. The real test would come when the enemy adapted to their tactics.

As if summoned by his thoughts, a new spiritual pressure descended on the sect. This one was different from the Ascendant auras he'd detected earlier: deeper, more refined, carrying an almost divine quality that made the air itself seem to thicken.

Half-Step Immortal.

The pressure was coming from directly above, and when Slifer looked up, he saw a figure descending from the night sky like a falling star. Brilliant white light surrounded the newcomer, so bright it was difficult to look at directly. But Slifer forced himself to observe because he recognized the spiritual signature.

Ace. Sect Master of the Heavenly Light Sect. The most powerful righteous cultivator in the mortal realm.

The figure touched down in the sect's main courtyard, and the white light around him gradually faded to reveal a man who looked to be in his early thirties. His white hair gleamed like moonlight, and his blue eyes held the kind of power that could reshape landscapes. His white robes were immaculate despite the journey, and they seemed to glow with their own radiance.

But it was what happened to the sect members around him that truly demonstrated Ace's overwhelming power. Every disciple, elder, and death warrior within a hundred meters simply stopped. Not frozen by technique or spiritual pressure, but dead. Their life force had been drained so completely that they hadn't even had time to scream.

Slifer felt his blood run cold as he stared at the circle of corpses surrounding the Heavenly Light Sect Master. This wasn't combat; it was casual annihilation. A demonstration of power so absolute that mortal cultivators were less than insects before it.

Ace's blue eyes swept across the courtyard until they found Slifer standing on the command platform. When their gazes met, the sect master smiled. It was a cold expression, empty of warmth or mercy.

"Sect Master Slifer," Ace said. "I believe we have much to discuss."

CHAPTER FOUR

Slifer stared at the blue-eyed cultivator who had just descended from the sky like some divine messenger of judgment. Ace stood amid the circle of corpses, his pristine white robes untouched by the carnage around him, radiating the kind of casual power that made reality itself seem fragile.

The acrid smell of burned formations mixed with the metallic scent of blood in the air. Slifer could hear the distant sounds of battle throughout the sect grounds, his disciples and elders fighting desperately against the coordinated assault. But here, in this moment, everything felt suspended in time.

"You want to discuss something?" Slifer kept his voice level, though his mind was already racing through his available options. The System interface flickered at the edge of his vision, showing his remaining Karmic Credits and available cards. "Then perhaps you could explain why three righteous sects decided to attack my home in the middle of the night."

Ace tilted his head slightly, those unsettling blue eyes never leaving Slifer's face. "Attack? I prefer to think of it as pest control. The demonic sects have grown too bold, too dangerous. Your recent... activities have forced our hand."

"My activities?" Slifer took a step forward, careful not to make any sudden movements that might provoke an immediate fight. The dead disciples around Ace served as a reminder of what happened to those who underestimated the Heavenly Light Sect Master. "I've been working to reform the demonic sects, to find peaceful coexistence between our paths. If that threatens you, perhaps the problem isn't with my activities."

A cold smile played at the corners of Ace's mouth. "Reform? You've been gathering power, absorbing other sects, positioning yourself as some sort of demonic emperor. Did you think we wouldn't notice? Did you think we would simply allow you to continue building your empire unchallenged?"

The accusation stung because it wasn't entirely wrong. Slifer had taken control of multiple sects and had been consolidating power across the demonic cultivation world. But his motivations weren't conquest for its own sake. He was trying to create something better, to guide these sects away from their worst impulses.

"And what about Lady Chi?" Slifer asked, watching Ace's expression carefully. "The woman who's been manipulating your sect masters, pulling their strings like puppets. Did you think I wouldn't notice that either?"

For the briefest moment, something flickered across Ace's features. Confusion? Recognition? But it vanished so quickly Slifer almost thought he'd imagined it.

"I have no idea what you're talking about," Ace said, his voice carrying the ring of absolute certainty. "There is no Lady Chi. There is no manipulation. The decision to eliminate the demonic sects was made by rational, clear-minded leaders who recognized a growing threat."

Slifer studied the man's face, searching for any sign of deception. Either Ace was an incredible actor, or he genuinely believed what he was saying. Which meant Lady Chi's mental manipulation might be even more sophisticated than Slifer had realized. She wasn't just controlling actions, she was editing memories, rewriting perceptions of reality itself.

"You're being used," Slifer said quietly. "Someone is playing you like a chess piece, and you don't even realize it."

Ace's eyes hardened. "Enough games. I came here to end this personally, to ensure there would be no doubt about the outcome. You've killed too many good cultivators, corrupted too many souls. Tonight, your reign of terror ends."

The spiritual pressure that erupted from Ace's body was like being caught in the path of a collapsing mountain. The very air around them began to crack and distort under the weight of his power. Slifer felt his knees buckle as the overwhelming force pressed down on him from all sides.

This was Half-Step Immortal Realm cultivation at its peak. Ace wasn't just powerful, he was approaching the threshold between mortal and divine. Each breath he took seemed to draw energy from the very fabric of reality.

The System had warned Slifer this day might come and prepared him for the possibility of facing opponents whose power dwarfed his own. Everything depended on timing, strategy, and a healthy dose of luck.

"Last chance to surrender," Ace said, raising his hand. Golden light began to coalesce around his palm, forming into what looked like a miniature sun. "I'll make it quick."

"I'll pass," Slifer replied, and he activated the Critical Block Card just as Ace's attack launched.

The golden beam that erupted from Ace's palm could have vaporized a mountain. It struck Slifer dead center, and the brilliant light washed over everything in a wave of searing heat. The remaining structures in the courtyard simply ceased to exist, reduced to less than ash in an instant.

But when the light faded, Slifer stood exactly where he had been, completely unharmed. The Critical Block Card had absorbed the attack entirely, its protective barrier flickering once before dissolving.

Ace's eyes widened slightly. "Interesting. But that won't work twice."

He vanished from sight, moving faster than Slifer's eyes could track. Only his spiritual sense warned him of the incoming strike from behind. Slifer spun and pulled out a Reflection Barrier Card as Ace's fist approached his head with enough force to shatter stone.

The barrier shimmered into existence just in time. Ace's punch connected with the reflective surface and bounced back toward him with equal force. The Heavenly Light Sect Master twisted in midair, barely managing to deflect his own reflected attack with his other hand.

Slifer didn't waste the opening. He activated his Phase Ability and became translucent and intangible as he moved through the space where Ace had been standing. But the man was already gone again.

Then he appeared above Slifer with both hands raised. Twin beams of golden light lanced down. Slifer rolled to the side as the attacks carved molten furrows in the ground where he'd been standing. The heat was incredible, making the air shimmer and dance.

Ace landed, his pristine white robes somehow still spotless despite the violence. "You have some interesting defensive techniques. But defense alone won't save you."

This time he didn't bother with ranged attacks. Ace rushed forward, his body wreathed in golden flames that made him look like a living star. His speed was terrifying as he closed the distance between them in a heartbeat.

Slifer activated another Critical Block Card as Ace's flaming fist approached his chest. The card flared and dissolved as it absorbed the impact. But the follow-up elbow strike came too fast. Slifer threw himself backward, and the attack passed close enough that he felt his robes singe.

He hit the ground hard, then rolled to avoid Ace's descending foot stomp that cracked the stone beneath it. A quick mental count showed he was burning through his defensive cards faster than he'd hoped. At this rate, he'd be out of protection long before Ace ran out of energy.

Time to change tactics.

Slifer pulled out a Thunderous Wrath Card as he came to his feet. Lightning gathered around his form, crackling with violent energy. He thrust his hand forward and sent a bolt of electricity toward Ace's chest.

The attack struck true, but Ace barely flinched. His golden aura absorbed most of the lightning's power, dispersing it harmlessly into the air around him.

"My turn," Ace said calmly.

He gestured with one hand, and the air itself seemed to condense into dozens of golden spears. They hung suspended for a moment before launching toward Slifer from every conceivable angle.

Slifer activated his Void Piercer technique and sliced through space to appear behind Ace. But the man had anticipated the move and spun around with a backhand that Slifer barely ducked under.

The spears curved in mid-flight, following Slifer's new position. He was forced to use another Critical Block Card, and the projectiles dissolved against its protective barrier.

"You're running out of tricks," Ace observed, his tone almost conversational despite the deadly combat. "I can sense your desperation."

Slifer didn't bother responding. He was too busy calculating odds and possibilities, trying to find a way to turn this fight around. Ace was right about one thing: his defensive cards wouldn't last forever. But he still had a few surprises left.

The Siren's Call amulet hung around his neck, taken from the late Grand Elder Darius. It was an Immortal-level mental attack artifact, powerful enough to affect even Ascendant cultivators. The question was whether it would work on someone at Ace's level.

Only one way to find out.

Slifer activated the amulet and felt its insidious power reach out toward Ace's mind. For a moment, the blue-eyed cultivator's expression went blank, his movements faltering.

Then his eyes blazed brighter, and golden fire erupted from them as he shook off the mental intrusion.

"Nice try," Ace said. "But my will has been tempered in the fires of countless battles. Your petty mind tricks won't work on me."

Slifer couldn't help but smile at the irony of that statement.

Ace raised both hands above his head and golden energy gathered between his palms. The power building there was enormous, enough to level half the sect.

"Final Radiance," Ace intoned. "Let this light purge the darkness from this realm."

The attack that descended was less of a technique and more of a natural disaster. A pillar of golden fire wider than a building crashed down on Slifer's position, obliterating everything in its path.

But Slifer was no longer there. He'd activated his Dimensional Slide technique and stepped through space to appear at the edge of the courtyard. The sight that greeted him was sobering. Where he'd been standing was now a perfectly circular crater, the stone melted and fused into glass.

"Impressive mobility," Ace acknowledged, turning to face Slifer's new position. "But you can't run forever."

This time Slifer was ready for him. As Ace launched himself forward, Slifer activated the Heaven's Wrath Card he'd been saving. The sky above them darkened as storm clouds gathered with supernatural speed.

Lightning, far more powerful than anything Slifer could generate naturally, crashed down on Ace's position. The Heavenly Light Sect Master raised his hands and golden barriers formed above him to deflect the electrical assault.

But the lightning was just a distraction. While Ace was focused on the sky, Slifer used a Soul Fire Card and sent invisible flames directly at his opponent's spiritual core.

Ace stumbled and his golden aura flickered as the soul attack struck home. For the first time in the fight, he showed signs of actual pain, his perfect composure cracking slightly.

"Clever," he admitted, rubbing his chest where the soul fire had hit. "I underestimated your arsenal."

"You underestimated a lot of things," Slifer replied, pulling out his most powerful remaining card. The Binding of Eternal Servitude was an Immortal-rank artifact, capable of imprisoning even Half-Step Immortal cultivators. He'd been hesitant to use it, knowing he might need it later, but the situation was desperate enough to warrant the expense.

Ace seemed to sense the danger. His golden aura exploded outward, the power washing over everything like a tidal wave. "Whatever you're planning, it won't be enough. I am the strongest cultivator in this realm. I have dedicated my entire existence to the pursuit of power and righteousness. I will not be defeated by a pretender hiding behind borrowed strength."

The golden energy reached its peak as Ace's form became so bright that it was painful to look at directly. He was preparing something massive, a final attack that would end the fight once and for all.

Slifer didn't give him the chance to complete it.

He activated the Binding of Eternal Servitude Card, and its power erupted outward in chains of pure spiritual energy. They wrapped around Ace before he could react and bound his arms to his sides, then dragged him to his knees.

The golden light around Ace flickered and died as the chains constricted. He struggled against them, his face contorting with effort, but the Immortal-level binding held firm.

"Impossible," Ace breathed, staring down at the chains in shock. "This level of power . . . What kind of demon are you?"

"Not a demon. Just someone who's tired of war," Slifer said quietly. He approached the bound cultivator carefully, ready to activate another defensive card if needed. "Someone who's tired of watching good people die for the ambitions of those who manipulate them from the shadows."

Ace's eyes met his, and for a moment, Slifer saw something beyond the fanatical certainty that had driven the attack. Confusion. Doubt. The barest hint of recognition that something was wrong with the situation.

"The war will continue without me," Ace said, his voice strained but still defiant. "You've won this battle, but you cannot win them all. The righteous sects will not rest until every demonic cultivator is purged from this realm."

"Maybe," Slifer acknowledged. "But they'll have to do it without their strongest champion."

He activated the imprisonment function of the binding chains. Ace's form began to fade as he was drawn into the spiritual prison where he would remain until Slifer chose to release him. It was a merciful fate, all things considered. The man had killed dozens of Slifer's disciples without hesitation. But he was more useful alive than dead.

As Ace disappeared completely, the sounds of battle throughout the sect began to change. The coordinated attacks were faltering, the righteous sect forces pulling back as word spread of their leader's defeat.

Slifer looked around at the devastation, at the crater where Ace's final attack had struck, at the scattered debris of what had once been a peaceful courtyard. The cost of this victory had been high, and he suspected it was only the beginning.

In the distance, he could see his disciples rallying, pushing back against the retreating attackers. Caelum's starlight sword carved through the darkness, while Amelia's purple soul flames drove back a squad of Pure Soul Sect elders, and Val's roar shook the heavens as she pursued fleeing enemies.

The immediate threat had passed, but Slifer knew Lady Chi was still out there somewhere, still pulling strings, still manipulating events toward some grand design. Tonight's battle had been a victory, but the war was far from over.

He pulled out a communication talisman and sent word to all his disciples and allied sects. The righteous forces were retreating for now, but they would regroup, adapt, come back stronger. The demonic sects needed to be ready for whatever came next.

As the last of the attackers disappeared into the night, Slifer stood alone in the ruins of his courtyard, already planning for the battles to come. The game Lady Chi was playing was far from finished, and he intended to be ready for her next move. But first, he needed to find out if she really was the true culprit, and that required interrogating his new prisoner.

CHAPTER FIVE

The familiar blue interface materialized before Slifer's eyes. His breathing was still heavy from the intense confrontation, but seeing the System notification brought a welcome sense of relief.

> *Ding!*
> Mission Complete: Defend the Black Rose Sect
> Coordinated assault repelled. Casualties among disciples minimized. Source of enemy coordination discovered.
> You have gained 100,000 Karmic Credits. The Special Defensive Array Upgrade is now unlocked.
> Additional Rewards:
> Imprisoned Half-Step Immortal cultivator: 15,000 Karmic Credits
> Defeated coordinated assault without sect destruction: 10,000 Karmic Credits
> Total Karmic Credits Earned: 125,000

Slifer's eyes widened at the numbers. One hundred and twenty-five thousand credits. It was more than he'd ever possessed at one time. The weight of what he'd just survived began to sink in as he dismissed the interface and looked around at the devastation.

The main courtyard was completely unrecognizable. What had once been an elegant space with carefully maintained gardens and ornate pathways was now a crater-filled wasteland. Chunks of stone and twisted metal from defensive formations littered the ground. The acrid smell of burnt spiritual energy hung heavy in the air.

"System," Slifer muttered under his breath, "show me that defensive array upgrade."

> Special Defensive Array Upgrade available: Celestial Guardian Formation Protects against attacks up to Immortal Realm. Auto-activates when sect is threatened. Draws power from sect's spiritual veins.
> Cost: 50,000 Karmic Credits
> Accept upgrade?

Slifer didn't hesitate. "Yes."

The moment he confirmed the purchase, he felt a subtle shift in the sect's spiritual atmosphere. Deep underground, formation lines that looked more ancient than the sect itself began to form. The spiritual veins that fed the sect's power began humming with new energy, and Slifer could sense protective barriers forming at the very edges of the sect's territory.

A soft golden glow emanated from key points around the sect as the new formation integrated itself with the existing defensive structures. It was invisible to most observers, but Slifer could feel its presence like a warm blanket settling over everything he considered his domain.

"Master!" Morvran's voice called out as the large man hurried across the rubble-strewn courtyard.

"Morvran." Slifer nodded, genuinely relieved to see his right-hand man intact. "Report. How bad are our losses?"

Morvran pulled out a jade slip and consulted it grimly. "Could have been much worse, Master, but we still paid a price. Twenty disciples dead, seventy-three injured with varying degrees of severity. Most of the casualties came from the initial breach when they overwhelmed our outer defenses."

Slifer's jaw tightened. Twenty lives lost because someone had used his sect as a battleground. The faces of the disciples he'd seen training just that morning flashed through his mind. Young men and women who'd looked up to him for protection, who'd trusted that joining the Black Rose Sect meant safety.

"The death warriors?" he asked.

"Six lost, twelve wounded. They held the eastern wall longer than anyone had a right to expect." Morvran's voice carried a note of pride mixed with grief. "Boss, they died protecting the sect. Every single one of them fought to the last breath."

The death warriors' loyalty to the sect was absolute, born from genuine gratitude rather than fear or ambition. Losing even twelve of them felt like losing family members.

"What about the grand elders?"

"Grand Elder Wyatt took some injuries, but he'll recover. Grand Elder Lydia exhausted herself healing the wounded, but she's stable. The others . . ." Morvran hesitated. "Grand Elder Tenzin didn't make it, Master. A group of righteous sect disciples cornered him near the library. By the time reinforcements arrived, it was too late."

Slifer closed his eyes briefly. Tenzin had been an old-school demonic cultivator, but he'd also been one of the few grand elders who'd genuinely supported Slifer's reforms. His death was both a personal loss and a political complication.

"The attackers?"

"Complete rout once you defeated their leader. Most fled the moment they saw the Heavenly Light Sect Master imprisoned. We captured about thirty disciples and killed roughly twice that number. The rest escaped in the confusion."

Before Slifer could continue questioning Morvran, the sound of running footsteps echoed across the courtyard. A young Outer Sect disciple came sprinting toward them, his face pale with panic and exhaustion. Slifer recognized him as one of the messenger disciples who handled communications within the sect.

"Sect Master! Sect Master!" The boy skidded to a halt and dropped into a hasty bow, his words tumbling out in a rush. "Your quarters, Sect Master! Someone broke into your quarters during the battle!"

Slifer felt a chill run down his spine that had nothing to do with the night air. "What do you mean, broke in?"

"The guards were called away to defend the outer walls," the disciple explained, still breathing heavily. "When they returned, they found your chambers . . . Master, everything's been torn apart. Furniture overturned, storage containers emptied, even your private study has been ransacked."

"Was anything taken?" Slifer asked, though he suspected he already knew the answer.

"That's just it, Master. The guards can't find anything missing. Whoever did this, they weren't after your treasures or cultivation resources. They were looking for something specific."

Slifer and Morvran exchanged glances. The pieces of a larger puzzle were starting to fall into place, and Slifer didn't like the picture they were forming.

"Come on," Slifer said, already heading toward his living quarters. "I need to see this for myself."

The walk through the sect revealed the full extent of the damage. Defensive walls had been reduced to rubble in several places. Buildings that had stood for centuries were now missing roofs or entire walls. Disciples moved through the wreckage like ghosts, some tending to wounded comrades, others salvaging what they could from the destruction.

But what struck Slifer most was the atmosphere. Despite the devastation, there was no sense of defeat among his people. If anything, they seemed more determined than before. The attack had been intended to break the Black Rose Sect's spirit, but it appeared to have had the opposite effect.

"Sect Master," a young female disciple called out as they passed. "Thank you. Thank you for protecting us."

Similar words followed them as they walked. Disciples who had witnessed Slifer's overwhelming victory over Ace weren't seeing him as just their sect master anymore. He'd become something more: a protector who could stand against the most powerful cultivators in the realm and emerge victorious.

The irony wasn't lost on him. These people were looking at him with the kind of reverence usually reserved for legendary heroes, and he was just a middle-aged man from another world who'd gotten lucky with a mysterious System. But their faith in him was real, and that made the responsibility he felt even heavier.

When they reached Slifer's quarters, the extent of the intrusion became immediately apparent. The elegant wooden doors hung askew on their hinges. Through the opening, Slifer could see furniture scattered across the floor, scrolls and books strewn everywhere, and what looked like the remains of several expensive decorative vases.

"The guards discovered it about two minutes ago," the messenger disciple explained. "They've been standing watch but haven't touched anything, waiting for your orders."

Slifer nodded and stepped inside, Morvran close behind him. The destruction was thorough but not random. This wasn't the work of vandals or opportunistic thieves. Someone had methodically searched every possible hiding place in his chambers.

His sleeping area had been completely torn apart. The bed had been moved away from the wall and the mattress sliced open, its contents scattered. Even the floorboards had been pried up in several places, as if someone was checking for hidden compartments.

The study was worse. Every scroll had been unrolled and examined before being tossed aside. Books lay open with their pages ruffled, indicating someone had shaken them to see if anything was hidden inside. His desk had been pulled apart piece by piece, and even the ink stones had been cracked open.

"They were very thorough," Morvran observed grimly. "And they knew what they were doing. This isn't random destruction; someone was looking for something very specific."

Slifer moved through the wreckage, his mind racing. What could Lady Chi have been searching for? She'd obviously used the massive assault as a distraction, keeping everyone's attention focused on the battle while she conducted her real mission here in his private chambers.

But what could she possibly want from him? He'd killed Darius, yes, but that was months ago. If she'd wanted simple revenge, she could have attacked him directly, but then again, she did try that, and it had failed spectacularly. But what was so valuable that she'd orchestrated this elaborate scheme involving mind-controlled sect masters, a coordinated assault by thousands of cultivators, and sacrificed Ace, the most powerful cultivator in the realm, as a distraction?

Whatever she'd been looking for, it had to be incredibly valuable. More valuable than Ace's life, which was saying something.

Slifer continued his inspection, checking his storage areas and cultivation resources. True to the messenger's report, nothing seemed to be missing. His jade slips containing cultivation techniques were scattered but present. His collection of spiritual stones had been dumped out and sorted through, but none were gone. Even his treasures were still in their proper containers, just moved around during the search.

"This doesn't make sense," he muttered. "If she went to all this trouble, why didn't she take anything?"

"Maybe she did find what she was looking for," Morvran suggested. "Something you wouldn't immediately notice was missing?"

Slifer considered that possibility. What did he possess that would be worth this kind of effort? His mind went through his various System-provided items, but most of those were stored in his personal inventory space, inaccessible to anyone else.

Having had no success in finding out the truth, Slifer decided it was time to talk to his new prisoner.

The bound form of Ace materialized in his mind. The Heavenly Light Sect Master was still trapped in the spiritual prison, completely at Slifer's mercy. If Lady Chi was connected to his sect, if she'd been manipulating him, then Ace might have answers—assuming he was even aware of the manipulation.

"Morvran," Slifer said, turning back to his aide. "I need you to prepare a secure interrogation chamber. Something with multiple layers of protective formations."

"The old questioning cells beneath the main hall should suffice. Grand Elder Lydia had them reinforced last month." Morvran's expression grew curious. "May I ask who you intend to interrogate?"

"Our guest from the Heavenly Light Sect. It's time I had a conversation with Sect Master Ace."

The walk to the underground chambers gave Slifer time to think. If Ace was under Lady Chi's mental control, then simply asking questions wouldn't work. Mind control techniques, especially at the level Lady Chi seemed capable of, could make someone genuinely believe false information or block access to crucial memories.

But the System Shop had solutions for almost every problem, assuming he was willing to pay the price.

The interrogation chamber was a sterile, windowless room carved from solid stone. Protective formations covered every surface, designed to contain even Ascendant-level spiritual techniques. A single chair sat in the center of the room surrounded by binding arrays that could restrain cultivators far beyond Slifer's own level.

He pulled out the Binding of Eternal Servitude Card and carefully released just enough of its power to manifest Ace in the physical realm while keeping the spiritual chains intact. The Heavenly Light Sect Master appeared in the chair, his white hair disheveled and his blue eyes unfocused.

"Where am I?" Ace asked, his voice hoarse. He tested the spiritual chains binding him, but they held firm. "What is this place?"

"The Black Rose Sect," Slifer said, taking a position across from the bound cultivator. "You attacked my sect alongside Lady Chi. I want to know why."

Confusion flickered across Ace's features. "Lady Chi? I don't know anyone by that name." His eyes narrowed as he focused on Slifer. "You're the one who imprisoned me. I remember our battle, but after that . . ." He frowned and pressed a hand to his temple. "The memories are unclear."

Slifer studied the man's expression carefully. Either Ace was an exceptional actor or the confusion was genuine. "You don't remember working with a woman who controls plants and minds? Red eyes, black hair, claims to be the lover of someone named Darius?"

"I've never heard of this Lady Chi," Ace insisted. "And I would hardly work with a demonic cultivator. My sect stands against everything they represent."

The certainty in Ace's voice was troubling. If Lady Chi's mind control was sophisticated enough to completely erase memories rather than just implant false ones, then Ace might genuinely believe what he was saying. Standard interrogation techniques would be useless.

"Tell me about the last few weeks," Slifer said. "What led you to attack my sect?"

Ace's brow furrowed in concentration. "The righteous sects received intelligence about increased demonic activity. Reports of sect takeovers, forced conversions—the usual expansion patterns we've seen from your kind. My fellow sect masters and I agreed that swift action was necessary to prevent . . ." He trailed off, his expression growing troubled.

"To prevent what?" Slifer prompted.

"I . . . I'm not certain. The memory feels wrong, like looking at a reflection in disturbed water." Ace shook his head. "This shouldn't be happening. My cultivation includes mental fortification techniques. No one should be able to affect my memories."

Now they were getting somewhere. Slifer activated the Insight skill, focusing on Ace's spiritual patterns. What he saw was disturbing: threads of foreign spiritual energy wrapped around the man's consciousness like parasitic vines. The mental control was still active, maintaining its hold even now.

"Your mind has been compromised," Slifer said bluntly. "Someone has been manipulating your thoughts and memories, probably for weeks or months. They used you as a weapon against my sect while you remained unaware."

Ace's eyes blazed with indignation. "Impossible. I would know if someone was controlling me. My will is absolute."

"The best mind control makes the victim believe they're acting freely," Slifer replied. "What's the last clear memory you have? Something you're completely certain about?"

The silence stretched as Ace searched his memory. Gradually, his expression grew more troubled. "I . . . There are gaps. Decisions I made that don't align with my usual reasoning. Meetings I can't quite recall the details of."

Slifer could see the realization dawning in Ace's eyes. The proud, powerful cultivator was beginning to understand that he'd been nothing more than a puppet, his legendary strength turned against innocent people.

"Who would do this to me?" Ace whispered, more to himself than to Slifer.

"Someone with a personal grudge against me, apparently." Slifer accessed his System interface and scrolled through the available cards and techniques. "The question is whether I can break the control without damaging your mind in the process."

Several options appeared in the Shop, but most were either too expensive or carried significant risks. Mental manipulation at this level required delicate handling; one wrong move could leave Ace a drooling vegetable.

Finally, he found what he was looking for.

Name: Mind Liberation Technique
Rank: Heaven

> Description: Safely removes all forms of mental control, compulsion, and memory manipulation. Restores original memories and personality.
> Warning: May cause severe psychological trauma as suppressed memories return.
> Cost: 45,000 Karmic Credits

Forty-five thousand credits was a significant expense, but if Ace could provide information about Lady Chi's plans and capabilities, it would be worth the cost. And if the man was truly innocent of his recent actions, then Slifer had an obligation to free him from the mental control.

"I'm going to attempt to break the mental bindings," Slifer said. "Fair warning: this might be unpleasant. Suppressed memories have a tendency to return all at once."

Ace looked up at him with something approaching gratitude. "Why would you help me? I attacked your sect. Your disciples died because of my actions."

"Because you weren't in control of those actions," Slifer replied simply. "And because whoever is responsible for this needs to be stopped."

He purchased the Mind Liberation technique and felt the knowledge flow into his mind. The process was complex, requiring precise manipulation of spiritual energy to unweave the foreign control threads without damaging the underlying consciousness.

Slifer placed his hand on Ace's forehead and channeled the technique through his fingertips. Golden light began to emanate from the point of contact, flowing over Ace's head and down through his body. The spiritual threads became visible as dark lines against the golden radiance, writhing as the technique worked to dissolve them.

Ace's body went rigid, his eyes rolling back as the suppressed memories began to return. His mouth opened in a silent scream as weeks or months of controlled actions flooded back into his consciousness.

The process took nearly an hour. Slifer maintained the technique despite the drain on his spiritual energy, watching as the dark threads slowly dissolved. Finally, the last of the foreign control crumbled away, leaving Ace's mind clear for the first time in who knew how long.

The Heavenly Light Sect Master slumped forward in his chair, gasping for breath. When he finally looked up, his eyes held a mixture of horror, rage, and crushing guilt.

"What have I done?" he whispered, staring at his hands as if they were stained with blood. "The things I said, the orders I gave . . . How many people died because of my actions?"

CHAPTER SIX

Slifer watched as the most powerful cultivator in the mortal realm sat slumped in his chair, blue eyes staring at hands that had killed dozens of innocent disciples just hours earlier. The silence stretched between them, heavy with the weight of returned memories and crushing guilt.

"The mind control was thorough," Slifer said quietly, settling into a chair across from Ace. "You couldn't have known what you were doing."

Ace's laugh was bitter, devoid of any warmth. "Couldn't I? The techniques I used, the orders I gave . . . Somewhere deep down, didn't part of me enjoy the power? The ability to simply destroy anything that opposed me?"

"That wasn't you speaking," Slifer replied firmly. "I've seen real mind control before. It doesn't just puppet your actions; it corrupts your thoughts and makes you believe the twisted impulses are your own. The fact that you're horrified now proves your true nature."

The Heavenly Light Sect Master closed his eyes and pressed his palms against his temples. "I remember fragments now. Moments where I questioned orders that seemed too extreme, too brutal. But then there would be this . . . pressure in my mind, and suddenly the orders made perfect sense. Like someone else's voice becoming my own thoughts."

Slifer leaned forward, genuinely curious about how such sophisticated mind control worked. In his old world, mental manipulation was purely theoretical, something from fantasy novels. Here, it was terrifyingly real, and he needed to understand it if he was going to protect himself and his people.

"Tell me about when it started," he said. "How did you first encounter this Lady Chi?"

Ace's expression grew distant, his eyes unfocused as he accessed memories that had been suppressed for weeks or possibly months. "It was over six weeks ago. I was returning from a routine inspection of our outer territories when she appeared. Just . . . materialized in front of me like she'd stepped out of thin air."

"What did she look like?" Slifer asked, though he already knew from their previous encounter.

"Beautiful," Ace said without hesitation. "Devastatingly so. Long black hair with red eyes that pierce your soul."

Slifer nodded. The description matched perfectly with the woman who had attacked his sect, though he was interested to hear Ace's perspective on their encounter.

"She introduced herself as Lady Chi and was seeking information about recent demonic sect activities. Said she represented certain interests in the Immortal Realm." Ace's voice grew flat, mechanical, as if he was reciting facts rather than recalling personal experience. "I agreed to speak with her. That was my first mistake."

"She was powerful?"

"Beyond anything I'd ever encountered," Ace admitted, a trace of his previous fear bleeding through. "When we spoke, I felt like I was sitting across from a sleeping dragon. Every movement was controlled, every word chosen with precise intent. But she seemed reasonable, concerned about the same threats I was monitoring."

Slifer could imagine the scene. Lady Chi was clearly a master manipulator, skilled at presenting herself as an ally before revealing her true nature. The fact that she'd managed to fool someone as experienced as Ace spoke to both her abilities and her patience.

"When did you realize something was wrong?"

Ace was quiet for a long moment, his brow furrowed in concentration. "Looking back, there were signs from the beginning. She knew things about me that weren't public knowledge. Personal details about my cultivation methods, my sect's internal politics, even my private thoughts on other sect leaders. But at the time, I rationalized it as excellent intelligence gathering."

"And the actual control?" Slifer pressed gently.

"That came gradually," Ace said, his voice growing harder. "She would make suggestions during our conversations. Small things at first: adjustments to patrol routes, changes in training emphasis, modifications to our diplomatic stance with the demonic sects. Each suggestion seemed logical.

Beneficial, even. I began implementing her recommendations without questioning them."

Slifer could see the insidious nature of the manipulation. Rather than immediately enslaving Ace's mind, Lady Chi had slowly introduced her influence, making each step seem like the victim's own idea. It was a much more sophisticated approach than simple mental domination.

"The suggestions became more frequent, more specific," Ace continued. "Within a week, I was regularly seeking her counsel on major decisions. Within two weeks, I couldn't make important choices without first considering what she would advise. By the third week . . ."

"By the third week, you weren't making your own decisions at all," Slifer finished.

Ace nodded grimly. "The worst part is that I felt grateful to her. She was helping me become a better leader, making decisions that strengthened my sect and positioned us advantageously against our enemies. Or so I believed."

"When did she give you the order to declare war on my sect?"

The question hung in the air like a drawn blade. Ace's eyes met Slifer's, and for a moment, the full weight of recent events passed between them.

"A month ago," Ace said. "She appeared in my private chambers at midnight. I remember being startled by her sudden presence but not alarmed. By then, her visits felt natural, expected. She told me that intelligence had confirmed the Black Rose Sect was preparing a major offensive against all righteous sects."

Slifer kept his expression neutral, though internally he was cataloging the lies. His sect had been focused on defense and internal reform, not aggression. The news that they were being targeted by the righteous sects had been a huge shock to him.

"She said the demonic sects had formed an alliance under your leadership," Ace continued. "That you were gathering power to launch a coordinated assault that would devastate the righteous cultivation world. The evidence she presented was compelling: forged documents, altered communication records, testimony from supposed defectors."

"And you believed all of this?"

"Completely," Ace said with disgust. "More than believed it; I was outraged by it. She had convinced me that you were a threat to everything I'd spent my life protecting. The idea of preemptive action seemed not just reasonable, but morally necessary."

Slifer could see how the manipulation had worked. Lady Chi had taken Ace's genuine desire to protect his people and twisted it into a weapon against innocent targets. It was psychological warfare of the highest order.

"But that wasn't the real reason for today's attack, was it?" Slifer asked. "You said the assault was meant to be a distraction. What was she actually after?"

Ace's expression grew puzzled, as if he was accessing memories that didn't quite fit together properly. "That's where things become strange. The night before the attack, she visited me again. This time, she seemed different: more intense, more focused. She gave me very specific instructions about the timing and targets of the assault."

"What kind of instructions?"

"The attack was to begin at exactly midnight and focus primarily on your outer defenses and main buildings," Ace recalled. "But I was to avoid your personal quarters until the very end. When I asked why, she said it was to prevent you from escaping before justice could be served."

Slifer frowned. That didn't sound like someone trying to kill him efficiently. If Lady Chi had wanted him dead, ordering Ace to target his quarters immediately would have been the logical strategy.

"Did she say anything else about specific objectives?"

"Yes," Ace said slowly, his voice taking on a troubled tone. "She mentioned that during the chaos of battle, certain items needed to be . . . acquired. Personal effects that could be used as evidence of your crimes. At the time, it made sense to me. Now . . ."

"Now you realize she was planning to steal something from my quarters while I was distracted fighting you," Slifer concluded.

"What could she have wanted badly enough to orchestrate such an elaborate deception?" Ace asked. "The risk was enormous. If her manipulation of me had been discovered, if the attack had failed, she would have made enemies of every major sect in the realm."

Slifer thought back to the state of his chambers after the battle. Everything had been torn apart, searched with methodical thoroughness. But nothing had been taken—at least, nothing he'd noticed missing.

"She was looking for something specific," he said. "Something she believed I possessed. Did she ever mention what it might be?"

Ace concentrated, his eyes distant as he sifted through layers of manipulated memories. "There was something . . . A technique she mentioned needing components for. Something about creating a connection across great distances."

"What kind of components?"

"Personal items," Ace said, his voice gaining certainty as the memory solidified. "Hair, blood, clothing worn close to the skin. Things that carried the target's spiritual essence." His eyes widened as understanding dawned. "She was planning some kind of curse technique."

The pieces clicked together in Slifer's mind. Lady Chi had orchestrated the entire war as an elaborate theft operation, using the chaos of battle to steal materials for a long-range curse attack. It was both brilliant and terrifying in its scope.

Curse techniques were among the most feared abilities in the cultivation world. Unlike direct attacks that required physical proximity, curses could strike across any distance, through any defense, as long as the caster possessed a strong enough spiritual connection to their target. Personal materials like hair or blood provided that connection.

The fact that Lady Chi was willing to go to such lengths suggested she had been studying curse techniques specifically designed to harm or control him. Given her demonstrated mastery of mind control and plant manipulation, Slifer didn't want to imagine what she might be capable of with a direct spiritual link to his essence.

"This is worse than I thought," he muttered as he access his System interface while maintaining the conversation. "Curse techniques are nearly impossible to defend against through conventional means."

The System Shop materialized before his eyes, invisible to Ace. Slifer quickly navigated to the defensive categories, searching for items that could protect against curse-based attacks. The prices were substantial, but given the stakes, he couldn't afford to take chances.

Several options appeared in the catalog.

Spiritual Ward Talisman	Rank: High Earth	Cost: 15,000 Karmic Credits
Karmic Shield Pendant	Rank: Low Heaven	Cost: 35,000 Karmic Credits
Essence Barrier Ring	Rank: Mid Heaven	Cost: 50,000 Karmic Credits
Soul Fortress Technique	Rank: High Heaven	Cost: 75,000 Karmic Credits

Slifer grimaced at the prices. Even with his recent credit gains, spending that much on a single defensive item would severely impact his resources. But looking at Ace's haunted expression and remembering the casual way Lady Chi had killed his disciples during their first encounter, he knew the investment was necessary.

He selected the Karmic Shield Pendant. The description indicated it could deflect curse attacks up to Immortal Realm level by redirecting the spiritual energy back toward the caster. It seemed like the most practical option as it was not just defensive, but potentially offensive if Lady Chi tried to curse him.

Ding!
Purchase successful.

> 35,000 Karmic Credits deducted.
> Current balance: 90,570 Karmic Credits

The pendant materialized in his storage space, a simple silver disc inscribed with complex protective runes. He discreetly slipped it around his neck under his robes while Ace was still lost in troubled memories.

"The other sect masters," Slifer said, drawing Ace's attention back to the present situation, "Ming Yue and Feng Lei. They're still under her control, aren't they?"

Ace nodded grimly. "Almost certainly. The three of us have been coordinating closely for weeks, following what we believed were joint strategic initiatives. If she was controlling me, she was undoubtedly controlling them as well."

"Which means they're probably planning follow-up attacks right now, wondering why you haven't reported back."

"Worse than that," Ace said, his voice heavy with dread. "We had contingency plans in place. If one assault failed, the others were authorized to escalate using increasingly extreme measures. Ming Yue has access to forbidden techniques from the Pure Soul Sect archives. Feng Lei commands beast armies that could devastate entire regions."

Slifer felt a chill that had nothing to do with the underground chamber's temperature. Lady Chi wasn't just manipulating individual sect masters; she was orchestrating a campaign that could plunge the entire realm into chaos. And with him having disrupted her primary plan, she would likely push her remaining puppets to even more desperate measures.

"We need to free them," he said. "The Mind Liberation technique I used on you should work on others."

"But the process requires direct physical contact and sustained spiritual energy channeling. Getting close enough to Ming Yue or Feng Lei without them killing us first would be . . . challenging." Ace sighed.

"What if we approached them openly? You could claim that you escaped and request a meeting to plan the next phase."

Ace considered this but shook his head. "Lady Chi is too clever for simple deception. She would have methods to verify my continued loyalty, ways to detect if the mental control had been broken. The moment she realized I was free, she would either flee or trigger some kind of failsafe in the other sect masters."

Slifer leaned back in his chair, contemplating their options. They were facing an enemy with Immortal Realm power who had demonstrated mastery of mental manipulation, combat techniques, and strategic planning. She had already successfully controlled three of the most powerful cultivators in the realm and was likely preparing backup plans in case her primary strategy failed.

But they did have some advantages.

Ace's knowledge of Lady Chi's methods and the other sect masters' likely locations would be invaluable. Slifer's System abilities provided options that conventional cultivation couldn't match. And Lady Chi didn't know that her control over Ace had been broken, which gave them a brief window of opportunity.

"There's something else," Ace said suddenly, his expression troubled. "During our meetings, Lady Chi sometimes mentioned being on a timeline. She spoke of needing to complete her objectives before 'they' realized what she was doing. I don't think she's working alone, but at the same time, I don't think she's allowed to be here."

This was news to Slifer. The idea that Lady Chi might have backing from other Immortal Realm beings was deeply unsettling. It suggested that the current crisis might be part of a larger power struggle beyond the mortal realm's understanding.

"Did she say who 'they' were?"

"No, but she was clearly concerned about discovery. Several times she mentioned needing to finish her work and 'return before the others grow suspicious.' It sounded like she was operating without permission from her superiors."

So, Lady Chi was a rogue agent of some kind, pursuing her own agenda while trying to avoid detection by her peers. That information might prove useful, but it also suggested that even if they defeated her, there might be consequences from whatever organization she belonged to.

"We need to act quickly, then," Slifer decided. "If she's working on a deadline, she'll escalate her timeline now that her primary plan has failed. The other sect masters are in immediate danger, and through them, their sects and territories."

Ace nodded, rising from his chair. Despite the trauma of his recent experiences, the Heavenly Light Sect Master was clearly ready to fight. "What do you propose?"

"We work together," Slifer said simply.

CHAPTER SEVEN

Lady Chi materialized from the earth near the twisted grove where she had established her temporary sanctuary, her robes still pristine despite the violent encounter at the Black Rose Sect. The ancient trees around her seemed to wither slightly as she passed, their leaves curling and browning from the dark energy that clung to her like a second skin.

She had been careful this time. So very careful.

No grand entrances, no dramatic confrontations in front of witnesses. She had slipped in like shadow, struck at the sect's defenses, and retreated the moment that insufferable man had begun to counter Sect Master Ace's attacks. The memory of her previous battle with the fool still burned in her mind. The humiliation of being outmaneuvered by a mere Half-Step Immortal cultivator ate at her pride like acid.

"Clever little worm," she muttered, her voice carrying a note of grudging respect mixed with pure venom. "But cleverness alone will not save you from what is to come."

Lady Chi settled onto a throne of living wood that had grown from the ground at her approach, its bark weaving together to form armrests and a high back, while thorns sprouted in decorative spirals along its surface. She had always preferred the aesthetic of controlled growth and beautiful decay.

The real problem, she knew, was not Slifer's cunning or his mysterious defensive abilities. It was this accursed realm itself.

In the Immortal Realm, she could have ended this farce with a single thought. Her true power could reshape landscapes, bend the minds of entire populations, and command forests that stretched beyond horizons. Here, in this cramped mortal prison, she was forced to operate with a fraction of her abilities with her cultivation suppressed to Half-Step Immortal by the very fabric of reality.

It was maddening.

Every technique she attempted felt sluggish, every manipulation of spiritual energy met with resistance from the realm's limitations. She was a dragon forced to fight as a snake, an ocean compressed into a puddle. The indignity of it made her jaw clench until her teeth ached.

"Darius, my love," she whispered to the empty air, her fingers tracing patterns on the wooden armrest. "I failed you last time. But I swear by the deepest roots and highest branches, I will not fail you much longer."

She closed her red eyes and allowed herself a moment to remember Darius with his confident smile, his ambitious plans, his absolute devotion to power and to her. He had been magnificent in his cruelty, elegant in his pursuit of strength. When news of his death had reached her through their soul bond's final echo, something fundamental had broken inside her chest.

The mortal who had killed him would pay. Not quickly, not cleanly, but slowly and with the full understanding of what he had taken from her.

Lady Chi opened her eyes and reached into the folds of her robes, then withdrew a small silk pouch. Inside were the fruits of her careful infiltration of the Black Rose Sect Master's quarters. A few strands of white hair caught on a comb, a piece of fabric torn from a robe, a droplet of blood scraped from their last encounter.

Personal materials. The foundation of any proper curse.

She had spent centuries perfecting her understanding of curse techniques, studying the ancient arts that even most Immortal Realm cultivators considered too dangerous or distasteful to pursue. There was something beautifully poetic about using an enemy's own essence against them, turning their strength into weakness, their life force into the instrument of their destruction.

The blood was the most potent component, as it still carried traces of his spiritual signature despite the time that had passed. The hair held memories of growth and vitality. The fabric had absorbed his natural energy over months of wear. Together, they formed a connection that transcended distance and defensive formations.

Lady Chi rose from her throne and moved to a clear patch of ground where moonlight filtered through the canopy above. With delicate movements, she began arranging the materials in precise patterns, her fingers leaving trails of dark qi that seemed to absorb the light around them.

"Ancient spirits of vengeance," she began, her voice taking on the ritual cadence she had learned in the deepest archives of the Immortal Realm. "I call upon the bonds that tie all living things, the threads of fate that connect predator to prey, the roots that drink deep from the soil of retribution."

The materials began to glow with an unhealthy crimson light as she continued the chant, the words flowing in the old tongue that predated most cultivation methods. Each syllable carried weight, bending the spiritual energy around her into increasingly complex patterns.

"By hair that held his thoughts, by blood that carried his strength, by cloth that knew his form, I weave the path of his undoing."

The curse technique was not like the crude hexes that mortal cultivators sometimes employed. This was high art, a symphony of spiritual manipulation that would bypass any conventional defense. It would not kill him quickly, but rather eat away at his foundation, corrupt his spiritual energy, and turn his own cultivation against him from within.

She raised her hands above the glowing materials as dark energy coiled around her fingers like living serpents. "Let weakness grow where strength once dwelt, let doubt poison where certainty ruled, let pain bloom where comfort sheltered."

The words came faster now, each phrase building upon the last in a crescendo of malevolent intent. The very air around her seemed to thicken, reality bending under the weight of the work she was performing. Small animals in the surrounding forest fled from the oppressive aura that radiated outward from her position.

"By the bond of enemy blood, by the law of spiritual resonance, by the authority granted to me by powers beyond mortal comprehension, I bind this curse to the one called Slifer!"

She brought her hands together with violent force, and dark lightning crackled between her palms as she completed the technique. The materials on the ground burst into flame that burned black and cold, consuming themselves in seconds while sending tendrils of malevolent energy spiraling upward into the night sky.

Lady Chi smiled as she felt the curse take hold, racing through the spiritual connections she had forged toward its intended target. This was not some crude assassination attempt that could be blocked or reflected. This was inevitable decay and patient corruption that would eat away at him from within until nothing remained but empty flesh.

She waited, counting her heartbeats as the technique traveled through the metaphysical space between them. One beat. Two. Three.

Then something went wrong.

The curse slammed into an obstruction she had not anticipated, a barrier that felt fundamentally different from the defensive techniques he had used in their direct confrontation. It was not merely blocked but turned, twisted, and sent racing back along the same spiritual pathways that had carried it forward.

Lady Chi's eyes widened in shock as she felt her own curse technique returning to her, carrying with it all the malevolent energy she had invested in its creation. She threw up her hands instinctively and wove a hasty protection around herself.

"Severing Lotus Shield!" she cried, pouring her qi into a defensive technique that created layers of spiritual barriers around her body.

The returned curse struck her defenses with the force of her own hatred, dark energy clawing at the lotus petals of light that surrounded her. Most of the malevolent force was turned aside, but tendrils of corruption seeped through the gaps in her hastily constructed protection.

Pain lanced through her spiritual channels as her own technique attacked her cultivation, seeking the very foundations she had intended to corrupt in her target. She gasped and doubled over as agony shot through her meridians like liquid fire. Her perfect skin showed the first signs of withering where the curse energy touched her, fine lines appearing around her eyes and at the corners of her mouth.

Lady Chi forced herself to straighten, drawing on reserves of will that had been forged in the crucible of Immortal Realm politics. The damage was not severe, but it was deeply personal. Her own technique, perfectly crafted and charged with genuine hatred, had been used against her.

What kind of defensive ability could accomplish such a thing? A simple reflection technique might turn back a direct energy attack, but this curse had operated through spiritual connections and metaphysical principles that should have made such a reversal impossible.

"Impossible," she hissed through gritted teeth, tasting blood on her lips. "No cultivator in this realm should possess such capabilities."

She examined herself carefully, probing the damage with delicate touches of her spiritual sense. The corruption was fighting against her natural regeneration, creating a stalemate that left her weakened but not crippled. It would take time and effort to purge completely, time she did not want to spend.

More concerning was the implication of what had just occurred. If Slifer could turn her curse techniques against her, then many of the subtler approaches she had been considering were also compromised. Direct assassination through poison, spiritual manipulation through intermediaries, even attacks on his disciples or sect members might all be vulnerable to similar reversals.

Lady Chi began to pace around the clearing, her mind racing through possibilities and contingencies. The twisted trees swayed as if moved by a wind that touched nothing else, responding to her agitation. Thorns pushed through the bark in spiraling patterns that matched the frustrated energy radiating from her form.

Perhaps she had been approaching this entire situation incorrectly. She had assumed that because Slifer was merely a Half-Step Immortal cultivator in a lower realm, he would be vulnerable to the same techniques that worked on others of his supposed level. But clearly, there was more to him than met the eye.

"Some kind of treasure, perhaps," she mused aloud, pressing her fingers against her temples where a persistent ache had begun to throb. "An artifact from a higher realm, or maybe a protective formation built into his very foundation."

The more she considered it, the more it seemed likely. No natural talent could account for the abilities he had displayed. The casual way he had reflected her plant attacks, the immunity to her mental influences, and now this impossible reversal of a properly constructed curse. He had to be carrying something that granted him these protections.

Which meant she needed a different approach entirely.

Lady Chi stopped pacing and looked up at the starlit sky above, her red eyes reflecting the distant lights like fragments of burning coal. The pain from her rebounded curse was already beginning to fade as her Immortal constitution dealt with the foreign energy, but the memory of it would remain.

She had tried direct confrontation and been repelled. She had attempted subtle curse work and been injured by her own techniques. Every conventional approach seemed to fail against whatever protections he possessed.

But there was one option she had not yet explored.

"If I cannot strike at you directly," she whispered to the night air, her voice carrying across the grove like a promise of doom, "then I will tear apart everything you value until you have no choice but to face me without your precious defenses."

His disciples. His sect. His allies and resources. She would corrupt them all, turn them against him, or simply destroy them one by one until he stood alone and vulnerable. Even the most powerful artifacts had limitations, and she doubted his protections extended to everyone around him.

The thought brought the first genuine smile she had felt since receiving news of Darius's death.

Lady Chi raised her face toward the heavens, her red eyes blazing with hatred. The stars seemed to dim slightly as she spoke, as if the universe itself was reluctant to witness the oath she was about to make.

"I swear by the deepest roots that drink from the world's foundation, by the highest branches that touch the realm beyond realms, by the eternal cycle of growth and decay that governs all existence." Her voice carried a resonance that made the air tremble. "I will not return to the Immortal Realm until the killer of my beloved Darius lies dead at my feet."

The words echoed through the grove with the weight of absolute conviction, binding her to the mortal realm until her vengeance was complete. It was a dangerous oath, one that would prevent her from retreating to safety if the situation became untenable, and could even draw the attention of the "others," but she was beyond caring about such risks.

Thunder rumbled overhead despite the clear sky, as if the heavens themselves acknowledged her declaration. Lady Chi smiled at the sound, her fingers already beginning to weave new patterns in the air as she planned her next move.

The direct and subtle approaches had both failed, but she was far from finished.

CHAPTER EIGHT

"What do you need from me?" Ace asked.

The directness of the question caught Slifer slightly off guard. In his previous life, he'd dealt with plenty of people who claimed they wanted to help but then spent hours making excuses or setting conditions. Ace, despite everything he'd been through, was cutting straight to the practical matters.

"First, we need to free your sect," Slifer replied. "If Lady Chi controlled you for weeks or months, she likely has her hooks in other key members of the Heavenly Light Sect as well. How many of your elders and disciples might be compromised?"

Ace's expression grew troubled. "Potentially dozens. I've been giving orders based on her guidance for so long that anyone who questioned them would have been . . . dealt with. She was very thorough in helping me identify and eliminate sources of resistance within the sect."

The admission hung heavy in the air. Slifer could see the weight of it settling on Ace's shoulders, but the man didn't break down or retreat into self-pity. Instead, he straightened and began speaking in a more tactical tone.

"My first elder, Lu Pan, has been increasingly concerned about some of my recent decisions," Ace continued. "He's questioned several of my orders in private, which means he's likely not under direct control. If anyone in the sect can be trusted, it would be him."

"What about your other leadership?" Slifer asked.

"More difficult to assess. Elder Yulan has been enthusiastically supportive of every decision I've made lately, including some that should have troubled her based on her past behavior. Either she's been compromised, or she's developed an unhealthy degree of blind loyalty."

Slifer nodded. The Heavenly Light Sect was the most powerful righteous organization in the realm, with thousands of disciples and dozens of elders. If Lady Chi had managed to compromise even a fraction of their leadership structure, rooting out the controlled individuals would be a massive undertaking.

"You can't do this alone," Slifer said. "Even with your power level, trying to identify and free potentially dozens of mind-controlled allies is a recipe for disaster. You need backup, and it needs to be someone you can trust absolutely."

"I trust you," Ace replied without hesitation. "After what you've done for me, I would welcome your assistance."

Slifer felt a moment of panic at the suggestion. The idea of walking into the headquarters of the most powerful righteous sect in the realm, surrounded by potentially mind-controlled cultivators who would recognize him as a demonic sect leader, seemed like an excellent way to get himself killed.

"I appreciate the confidence, but I think I can offer you something better," Slifer said carefully. "One of my disciples would be perfect for this kind of mission."

He was thinking of Hughie, of course. The young man's protagonist-level luck stat had gotten them out of impossible situations before, and his transformations could provide the kind of unpredictable combat advantage they might need. More importantly, Slifer had a growing suspicion that protagonists possessed some kind of natural resistance to mental manipulation, though he had no concrete evidence to support the theory.

"You would trust one of your disciples with this?" Ace asked, sounding genuinely surprised.

"Hughie has proven himself capable of handling dangerous situations," Slifer replied. "And he has certain . . . unique advantages that might prove useful when dealing with Lady Chi's influence."

The truth was that Slifer desperately needed Ace to remain free of Lady Chi's control, but he also couldn't afford to have the man attempt this mission without some kind of protection. Hughie's luck might be exactly what they needed to tip the odds in their favor.

"I would be honored to work with one of your disciples," Ace said formally. "Though I should warn you, the Heavenly Light Sect can be . . . unwelcoming to those from demonic organizations."

"Hughie can handle himself," Slifer said with more confidence than he felt. "But I'll make sure he has the proper protection."

He opened his System interface while Ace waited patiently. The Shop's defensive category had several items designed to protect against mental attacks, though most were expensive. His recent victory over Ace had netted him some credits, but he needed to be strategic about his spending.

After a few minutes of browsing, he found what he was looking for.

Name: Mind Fortress Talisman
Rank: Mid Heaven
Description: Creates impenetrable mental barrier against all forms of mind control, illusion, and psychic attack up to Immortal Realm level.
Duration: 72 hours
Cost: 25,000 Karmic Credits

The price made him wince, but the description was exactly what they needed. He purchased two talismans and felt his credit balance drop significantly.

"I have something that should help," Slifer said, producing the two jade medallions from his storage space. "These will protect both of you from Lady Chi's mental attacks for the next three days."

Ace examined the talisman with his spiritual sense, his eyebrows rising as he detected the profound protective formations embedded within the jade. "This is . . . incredible. The complexity of the formations alone suggests master-level craftsmanship. Where did you acquire such treasures?"

"I have my sources," Slifer replied evasively. "The important thing is that they'll keep Lady Chi from regaining control over you, assuming she tries."

"She will try," Ace said with certainty. "Once she realizes I've broken free, she'll want me back under her influence as quickly as possible. My sect is too valuable a resource for her to abandon easily."

Slifer nodded. That aligned with his own assessment of the situation. Lady Chi had spent considerable time and effort establishing her network of controlled cultivators. She wouldn't give up on the Heavenly Light Sect without a fight.

"How long do you think it will take to identify and free the compromised members of your sect?" Slifer asked.

Ace considered the question seriously. "If we're thorough, possibly several days. The Mind Liberation technique you used on me requires direct contact and sustained concentration. Each person we free will need individual attention, and we'll need to be careful not to alert those still under her control."

"Three days should be enough, then," Slifer said, gesturing to the talismans.

"But you'll need to work quickly. I don't know how long it will take Lady Chi to realize what's happening and respond."

"Understood." Ace pocketed his talisman and stood from his chair. "When can your disciple be ready to depart?"

"Give me an hour to brief him and gather supplies," Slifer replied. "This isn't the kind of mission where you want to be unprepared."

Ace nodded and moved toward the door, then paused. "Slifer, I want you to know that regardless of what happens between our sects in the future, I will not forget what you've done for me today. The debt I owe you cannot be easily repaid."

"Just focus on freeing your people," Slifer said. "We can worry about sect politics after Lady Chi is dealt with."

After Ace left, Slifer remained in the chamber for several minutes, organizing his thoughts. The next few hours were going to be crucial, and he needed to make sure everything went according to plan.

He activated his Disciple Management interface and located Hughie's status. His young disciple was currently in the sect's training grounds, apparently working on his transformation techniques with some of the death warriors. His loyalty remained at a solid ninety percent, which was reassuring.

Slifer sent a mental summons through the interface, requesting Hughie's immediate presence in his quarters. Within minutes, he heard rapid footsteps in the corridor outside.

"Master?" Hughie's voice came through the door, slightly out of breath from what had probably been a sprint across the sect grounds.

"Enter," Slifer called.

Hughie stepped into the chamber, his usual carefree expression replaced by alert attention. Despite his sometimes reckless nature, the young man had learned to recognize when situations were serious.

"I have a special mission for you," Slifer began without preamble. "It's dangerous, it's important, and I need someone I can trust absolutely to handle it."

Hughie straightened, his eyes brightening with interest. "Whatever you need, Master. What's the mission?"

"You're going to accompany Ace, the Sect Master of the Heavenly Light Sect, on an infiltration mission to free his sect from mind control," Slifer explained. "Lady Chi has been manipulating their leadership for weeks, possibly months. Your job is to help Ace identify and liberate the compromised individuals."

Hughie's expression grew thoughtful. "The same Lady Chi who attacked our sect?"

"The very same. Which is why this mission is so dangerous." Slifer produced the second talisman and handed it to Hughie. "This will protect you from her mental attacks for three days. Do not remove it for any reason, and do not let anyone else handle it."

Hughie examined the jade medallion with the kind of reverence most cultivators reserved for Immortal artifacts. "This must have cost a fortune, Master. Are you sure you want to spend resources like this on me?"

The question caught Slifer off guard. In his previous life, most people would have simply accepted expensive gifts without questioning the cost. Hughie's concern for his master's resources spoke well of his character development.

"Your safety is worth more than spirit stones," Slifer said simply. "Besides, this mission is crucial to stopping Lady Chi's plans. If we can free the Heavenly Light Sect from her control, we'll have the strongest righteous sect in the realm as an ally instead of an enemy."

"What about Sect Master Ace?" Hughie asked. "Can we trust him? I mean, he was literally trying to kill us a few hours ago."

It was a fair question, and one that Slifer had been wrestling with himself. Ace's transformation from enemy to ally had been dramatic, but was it genuine? The man had seemed sincere in his remorse and determination to make amends, but years of reading web novels had taught Slifer to be suspicious of convenient character reversals.

"Ace's mind was being controlled," Slifer explained. "The technique I used to free him should have broken Lady Chi's influence completely. His actions since then suggest he's genuinely committed to stopping her."

"But you're not completely certain," Hughie said perceptively.

Slifer sighed. "No, I'm not completely certain. Which is another reason why I'm sending you with him. If something goes wrong, if he's still compromised somehow, your luck and your transformations might be the only things standing between you and disaster."

Hughie blinked in surprise.

"Don't worry, you'll be fine," Slifer continued as he moved to his storage area and began pulling out additional supplies. "Take these emergency rations, healing pills, and communication talismans. If the situation turns bad, activate the teleportation talisman. Don't try to be heroic."

"Master," Hughie said hesitantly, "what will you be doing while I'm gone?"

It was the question Slifer had been dreading. The truth was that he couldn't just sit in his sect waiting for reports. Lady Chi's network extended to at least three major sects, possibly more. Even if Hughie and Ace successfully freed the Heavenly Light Sect using the technique and the talismans he had given them, that still left the Pure Soul Sect and the White Tiger Sect under her influence.

"I'll be planning our next moves," Slifer said carefully. "This war isn't going to be won by playing defense."

Hughie looked like he wanted to ask more questions, but he simply nodded and secured the supplies in his own storage ring. After receiving final instructions about maintaining contact and exercising caution, he departed to meet Ace at the sect's main gate.

Slifer watched from his window as the two figures disappeared into the distance, Ace's golden aura and Hughie's more subdued spiritual presence gradually fading from his perception. Only when they were completely gone did he allow himself to relax slightly.

That relaxation lasted exactly thirty seconds.

A sudden crushing pain exploded through his chest, as if someone had reached into his ribcage and squeezed his heart with iron fingers. Slifer gasped and doubled over. His spiritual energy fluctuated wildly as something foreign and malevolent coursed through his meridians.

The curse.

Lady Chi's parting gift was finally manifesting, and the agony was beyond anything he'd experienced even during his worst tribulations. Every breath felt like inhaling molten metal, every heartbeat sent waves of corruption through his spiritual channels.

But then the Karmic Shield Pendant around his neck blazed with silver light, and the pain began to recede. The curse met the pendant's defensive matrix and was systematically unraveled, and its malevolent energy was redirected back toward its source. Within moments, the agony had faded to a dull ache, then disappeared entirely.

Slifer straightened slowly, his breathing returning to normal. The pendant had saved his life, exactly as advertised. But the experience had driven home a crucial point: Lady Chi wasn't done with him. She would keep trying different approaches, different attacks, until she found something that worked.

Which meant he couldn't afford to remain passive.

Sitting in his sect waiting for Lady Chi to make the next move was a losing strategy. She had the initiative, the network, and apparently access to techniques that could strike across vast distances. Every day he delayed was another day for her to consolidate power and eliminate potential threats.

He needed to go on the offensive.

The question was how. Lady Chi's location remained unknown, and even if he could find her, a direct confrontation had already proven risky. But her network of controlled cultivators was more vulnerable. The sect masters were powerful, but they were also predictable. They had territories, resources, and routines that could be exploited.

Slifer moved to his desk and spread out a detailed map of the cultivation world. Red pins marked the locations of the major righteous sects, while blue pins showed demonic territories. The Heavenly Light Sect was marked in the eastern mountains, already being handled by Hughie and Ace. That left the Pure Soul Sect in the southern valleys and the White Tiger Sect in the northern plains.

The Pure Soul Sect was probably the better target. Their territory was closer to his own, their leadership structure was more centralized, and their reputation for mercy might make them less likely to execute him on sight. The White Tiger Sect, in contrast, was known for their aggressive beast-taming techniques and their tendency to shoot first and ask questions later.

But attacking either sect would be incredibly dangerous. Even if their leadership was compromised, they still had thousands of disciples and dozens of elders who weren't under Lady Chi's direct control. Walking into their territory as a known demonic sect leader would be suicide.

Unless he brought adequate backup.

Slifer reviewed his available disciples through the management interface. Caelum was returning from his mission at the Pure Soul outpost. Fenlock was working on building confidence with his sound cultivation. Amelia was somewhere in the sect, probably traumatizing junior disciples with her "training methods." Val was napping in the beast chambers after her earlier excitement.

None of them were ideal choices for infiltrating a righteous sect. Amelia's reputation for sadistic torture would make any negotiation impossible. Fenlock was too gentle for the kind of operation this might become. Val, despite her power, was still essentially a child and would be difficult to control in a tense situation.

That left Caelum, assuming he returned soon. The young man had proven himself capable of restraint and tactical thinking. His breakthrough to Origin Realm had given him the power to handle serious threats, and his recent conversion to the righteous path might help smooth over any initial hostility from Pure Soul Sect members.

Plus, Slifer admitted to himself, he genuinely enjoyed working with Caelum. The disciple's steady competence and loyalty made him an ideal partner for complex operations.

A soft chime from his communication array interrupted his planning. Slifer activated the formation and felt a familiar spiritual signature requesting connection.

"Master?" Caelum's voice came through clearly, despite the distance. "Thanks to you, we've completed our mission and we're ready to return. Should we come back immediately, or do you have other orders?"

The timing was perfect, almost suspiciously so. Slifer wondered if this was another manifestation of protagonist luck at work. Though, in this case, it would be his own rather than Hughie's.

"Return as quickly as possible," Slifer replied. "I have a new mission that requires your specific skills."

"Understood, Master. I should be back within the hour."

The connection ended, leaving Slifer alone with his maps and his plans. An hour would give him time to finalize his strategy and prepare the necessary resources for their infiltration of the Pure Soul Sect.

He was still working on the details when footsteps in the corridor announced Caelum's arrival. His disciple knocked politely and waited for permission before entering.

"Master," Caelum said, offering a formal bow.

"I have a more urgent situation that requires your attention," Slifer said, looking up from his maps.

Caelum straightened, his expression growing serious. "What do you need, Master?"

"Pack light, bring your sword, and prepare for a potentially dangerous infiltration mission," Slifer replied. "We're going to free the Pure Soul Sect from Lady Chi's control."

Caelum's eyes widened slightly, but he simply nodded. "How long should I prepare for?"

"Assume several days minimum, possibly longer depending on how things develop." Slifer stood and began gathering his own equipment. "This isn't going to be a simple operation, Caelum. We're walking into the heart of a major righteous sect, and we won't know who we can trust until we're already inside."

"I understand the risks, Master," Caelum replied steadily. "When do we leave?"

Slifer looked at his disciple's calm, determined expression and felt a surge of confidence. Whatever challenges they might face at the Pure Soul Sect, he couldn't ask for a better partner.

"Give me thirty minutes to finish preparations," Slifer said. "Then we're going to show Lady Chi that two can play at the manipulation game."

CHAPTER NINE

Mei Lin sat cross-legged on her meditation cushion, trying to focus on the Tranquil Heart Sutra that had always brought her peace. But today, like every day for the past month, the words felt hollow in her mind. The gentle morning light filtered through the windows of her modest quarters in the inner disciple pavilion, casting the same warm patterns across her wooden floor that had comforted her for the past three years.

Everything looked the same. Everything felt completely different.

She opened her eyes and stared at the small altar against the far wall, where a stick of jasmine incense burned steadily. The sweet smoke should have calmed her thoughts, but instead it reminded her of the funeral rites they'd held for Senior Brother Wu last week. And Senior Sister Liu the week before that. And the seven other disciples who had died in what the elders called "righteous combat against the demonic threat."

Mei Lin didn't understand any of it.

The Pure Soul Sect had always been different from the other righteous sects. While the Heavenly Light Sect focused on overwhelming power, and the White Tiger Sect emphasized martial dominance, the Pure Soul Sect taught harmony. Balance. The preservation of life rather than its destruction. Their techniques were designed to purify corruption, to heal the wounded, to bring peace to troubled souls.

Elder Jinghua used to tell them during lessons that their sect's greatest strength was their ability to see the good in others, even those who had lost their way. "A pure soul recognizes that beneath every demon lies a person who simply needs guidance back to the light," she would say, her kind eyes twinkling as she spoke. "Violence should always be our last resort, used only when all other options have been exhausted."

Mei Lin had taken those words to heart. She'd spent years learning the Cleansing Palm technique not to harm others, but to purify the dark qi that sometimes infected wounded cultivators. She'd studied the Soul Soothing Hymns to calm beasts driven mad by spiritual imbalances. Every technique she knew was designed to heal, to help, to preserve life.

So why were they suddenly at war?

A soft knock at her door interrupted her troubled thoughts. "Come in," she called, grateful for the distraction.

The door slid open to reveal Junior Sister Yun, a Foundation Establishment disciple who always seemed to have ink stains on her robes from her calligraphy practice. Today was no exception—blue ink decorated her right sleeve, and her usually neat bun was askew.

"Senior Sister Mei Lin," Yun said, bowing politely. "Elder Yao has called a morning assembly. All inner disciples are to gather in the main hall immediately."

Mei Lin's stomach tightened. Morning assemblies had become far too common lately, and they never brought good news. "Did he say what it was about?"

Yun shook her head, but her expression was troubled. "No, but . . ." She glanced around nervously, then stepped closer and lowered her voice. "The other junior disciples are saying that more elders went missing last night. Elder Tian and Elder Wei haven't been seen since yesterday evening."

The words hit Mei Lin deep. Tian had been one of the most vocal opponents of the war when it began. During the first emergency council meeting a month ago, he'd stood up in front of everyone and questioned why the Pure Soul Sect was abandoning its peaceful principles. Elder Wei had supported him, arguing that they should be seeking diplomatic solutions rather than preparing for battle.

Within a week, both had been reassigned to "special missions" that took them away from the sect. Now they were missing entirely.

"Have you heard anything about Elder Jinghua?" Mei Lin asked quietly.

Yun's face fell. "Still no word. It's been two weeks since she left for her 'meditation retreat.'"

Elder Jinghua had been Mei Lin's favorite instructor, the one who'd first taught her about the sect's peaceful philosophy. She'd also been one of the strongest voices against the war, spending hours in the library researching historical precedents for peaceful resolution of sect conflicts. The day before her sudden departure, she'd seemed excited about something she'd discovered in the ancient texts. Then she was gone, leaving only a brief note about needing time for "deep contemplation."

Mei Lin stood up and smoothed her plain white robes. The Pure Soul Sect had always favored simple clothing, no elaborate designs or expensive materials that might suggest spiritual pride. But lately, even getting dressed felt strange. Everything about their daily life continued as normal while the very foundation of what they believed seemed to be crumbling.

The walk to the main hall took her past the Memorial Garden, where stone markers honored disciples and elders who had died in service to the sect. Mei Lin paused, looking at the twelve new stones that had been added in the past week. Each one represented someone who had died fighting in this war that nobody seemed able to explain properly.

She remembered when the garden had been simply called the Peace Garden, a place for quiet reflection and meditation. The markers had been rare additions usually honoring those who had died of old age or cultivation accidents. Now they were being added every few days.

"Senior Sister?" Yun's voice brought her back to the present. "We should hurry."

The main hall buzzed with nervous conversation as disciples filed in. Mei Lin found her usual spot among the other inner disciples, noting how many familiar faces were missing. Some were away on missions, others had been injured and were still recovering, and too many were represented by the new stones in the Memorial Garden.

Elder Yao stood at the front of the hall, his expression grim. He'd aged noticeably in the past month, his beard showing new streaks of gray and his eyes carrying a weariness that hadn't been there before. Behind him stood Elder Fan and Elder Zhou, two of the few remaining council members who hadn't been sent away or gone missing.

"Disciples of the Pure Soul Sect," Elder Yao began, his voice carrying easily through the hall despite its subdued tone. "I bring news from the front lines of our righteous struggle against the demonic threat."

Mei Lin winced at the formal language. Elder Yao had never spoken that way before the war began. He'd been known for his gentle manner and thoughtful words, often beginning assemblies with reminders about the sect's peaceful principles.

"Our forces have achieved a significant victory against a Black Heart Sect outpost in the western valleys," he continued. "Seven enemy cultivators have been eliminated, and their corruption has been cleansed from the region."

A few disciples cheered, but the sound felt forced and uncomfortable. Mei Lin noticed that many others looked as conflicted as she felt. Celebrating the deaths of fellow cultivators, even demonic ones, went against everything they'd been taught.

"However," Elder Yao said as his expression grew even more serious, "this victory came at a cost. Senior Brother Ma and Senior Sister Feng were both injured in the battle and are currently receiving treatment. Additionally, we have received intelligence that suggests the demonic sects are planning a coordinated assault on righteous territories." He paused, scanning the assembled disciples. "Effective immediately, all inner disciples at Core Formation or above will be assigned to defensive positions around our territory. Foundation Establishment disciples will continue their training with increased focus on combat techniques. Qi Refining disciples will assist with logistics and support."

Mei Lin felt her heart sink. Combat techniques. Defensive positions. Everything about their current path felt wrong, but questioning it directly had become dangerous. Too many elders who'd raised concerns had disappeared.

"Elder Yao." A brave inner disciple named Liu Gang spoke up from the front row. "With respect, many of us are struggling to understand how this war serves our sect's principles. Are we certain that violence is the only solution?"

The hall fell silent. Elder Yao's expression tightened, and for a moment, Mei Lin thought she saw fear flicker across his face before it was replaced by stern resolve.

"Brother Liu, these are challenging times that require difficult decisions," Elder Yao replied carefully. "The sect master and the remaining council have determined that the demonic threat to our realm is too great to address through peaceful means alone. Sometimes, preservation of life requires us to take lives."

The answer felt rehearsed, like something he'd been told to say rather than his own thoughts. Mei Lin remembered Elder Yao from her first year at the sect, when he'd spent an entire lesson explaining why their healing techniques were more valuable than any combat skill.

"But what about our negotiations with the Black Rose Sect?" another disciple asked. "I heard they've been trying to reform their practices."

Elder Yao's jaw clenched. "Any such rumors are unsubstantiated. The Black Rose Sect remains a dangerous threat to all righteous cultivators. There will be no negotiations with demonic cultivators under any circumstances."

Something about his tone made Mei Lin think of the way people spoke when they were repeating orders they didn't fully believe. She thought about

Sect Master Ming Yue, who had always been gentle and diplomatic, known for his ability to find peaceful solutions to conflicts between sects. The sudden shift to an aggressive war stance seemed completely contrary to his character.

The assembly continued with tactical assignments and training schedules, but Mei Lin found it hard to focus. She kept thinking about all the changes that had happened so quickly. One day, they'd been a peaceful sect focused on healing and purification. The next, they were mobilizing for war against cultivators who might simply need guidance rather than destruction.

After the assembly ended, Mei Lin walked slowly back to her quarters, lost in thought. The outer disciple courtyard bustled with activity as younger students practiced their forms, but even their training had changed. Where they once learned flowing movements designed to channel healing energy, now they drilled sharp, aggressive techniques meant for combat.

She passed the library, where she'd spent countless hours studying the philosophical texts that formed the foundation of their sect's beliefs. The building looked the same from the outside, but she knew that many of the books Elder Jinghua had been researching were now "restricted"—available only to the council and select senior elders.

The Garden of Contemplation, once a favorite spot for quiet meditation, now housed weapon racks and training dummies. The gentle sound of the meditation fountain was often drowned out by the clash of practice swords and the shouts of combat instructors.

Even the daily meal schedule had changed. Where they once had gathered three times a day for communal dining and discussion, meals were now rushed affairs focused on efficient energy consumption rather than fellowship. The conversations that did occur centered on missions, tactics, and enemy movements rather than philosophical insights or spiritual growth.

Mei Lin reached her quarters and slid the door closed behind her, grateful for the quiet. She moved to her small writing desk and pulled out her personal journal, a habit she'd maintained since joining the sect. Reading her entries from before the war felt like looking into another world.

"Third month, spring season: Elder Jinghua taught us about the Harmony of Opposing Forces today. She explained how righteousness and darkness can exist in balance, with each serving to define and strengthen the other. The key is not to destroy darkness, but to understand it and guide it toward light. I think I'm finally beginning to grasp why our sect focuses on purification rather than elimination."

That entry was from just two months ago, but it might as well have been from another lifetime. Now their entire focus seemed to be on elimination rather than purification, destruction rather than understanding.

She flipped to a more recent entry.

"The assembly today focused entirely on combat readiness. Elder Yao announced new requirements for all disciples to learn offensive techniques. When Junior Brother Kao asked why we couldn't use our purification methods to help the demonic cultivators instead of fighting them, Elder Yao grew angry and dismissed the question. Since when does our sect punish curiosity about peaceful alternatives?"

The pattern was clear when she looked at it written out. Every week brought new restrictions, new aggressive policies, new disappearances of anyone who questioned the direction they were heading. It was as if their entire sect had been taken over by people who looked like their leaders but thought completely differently.

A soft knock interrupted her reading. "Come in," she called, quickly closing the journal.

To her surprise, Senior Brother Han Li entered. He was one of the few remaining inner disciples who'd been at the sect longer than her, a quiet and thoughtful man who specialized in the sect's traditional purification techniques.

"Sister Mei Lin," he said quietly, glancing around her room before closing the door behind him. "May I speak with you privately?"

She nodded, gesturing for him to sit on the meditation cushion across from her desk. His expression was troubled, and she noticed he kept glancing toward the door as if worried about being overheard.

"I wanted to ask," he began in a low voice, "if you've noticed anything . . . strange about the elders lately?"

Mei Lin felt her heart rate increase. This was exactly the kind of conversation that seemed to lead to people being assigned to dangerous missions or mysterious retreats. But she was tired of pretending everything was normal.

"What do you mean?" she asked carefully.

Han Li leaned forward, his voice barely above a whisper. "I've been watching them during assemblies and training sessions. Sometimes they speak and act exactly like they always have. But other times . . ." He paused, struggling to find the right words. "Other times, they seem like completely different people. Their mannerisms change, their speech patterns shift, even their spiritual signatures feel different."

She'd noticed the same thing but hadn't dared to voice it. "Like they're being controlled somehow?"

"Exactly." His relief at her understanding was visible. "And it's not just the elders. Some of the senior disciples who were initially opposed to the war have started speaking and acting differently too. They use the same phrases, the same arguments, as if they're all reading from the same script."

Mei Lin thought about Elder Yao's rehearsed responses during the assembly. "Do you think it's some kind of technique? Mind manipulation?"

"I don't know," Han Li admitted. "But I've been thinking about what Elder Jinghua was researching before she disappeared. She'd been studying historical accounts of large-scale mental influence techniques. Apparently, there are methods that can affect multiple people simultaneously, making them believe that foreign thoughts and motivations are their own."

That sounded terrifying. If someone was controlling their sect's leadership, making them believe that war was necessary when their natural inclination would be toward peace, then everything they were being asked to do was based on manipulation rather than genuine wisdom.

"Who would do such a thing?" Mei Lin asked. "And why?"

"I have theories," Han Li said grimly. "But they're dangerous to voice. All I know is that we need to be careful. The people we trusted to guide us may not be themselves anymore."

After he left, Mei Lin sat in the growing darkness of her room, not bothering to light the oil lamp. Her world felt like it was falling apart, but at least she wasn't alone in noticing the wrongness of everything happening around them.

She thought about her family back in River Stone Village, simple farmers who'd been so proud when she'd been accepted into the Pure Soul Sect. They'd sacrificed to pay for her initial training materials and travel expenses, believing they were investing in their daughter's spiritual development and their village's future protection.

What would they think if they knew she was now being trained to kill other cultivators? Her parents had specifically chosen the Pure Soul Sect over other options because of its reputation for peaceful wisdom and healing arts. They'd wanted her to become someone who could help their community during disasters or spiritual crises, not a warrior in a sect war.

The evening meal bell rang across the sect grounds, but Mei Lin didn't feel hungry. Instead, she returned to her meditation cushion and tried once again to focus on the Tranquil Heart Sutra. The familiar words usually helped center her thoughts and connect her to the deeper principles of their cultivation path.

"Let the soul find peace in understanding. Let the heart find strength in compassion. Let the mind find clarity in acceptance of truth."

But tonight, even the sutra felt hollow. How could she find peace when everything around her had become chaotic? How could she practice compassion when she was being trained to destroy rather than heal? How could she accept truth when she suspected that everything she was being told was based on lies?

The night grew deeper, and Mei Lin finally lit her oil lamp to chase away the shadows. She tried to focus on routine tasks—organizing her few possessions, reviewing cultivation notes, planning her schedule for tomorrow's training sessions—but her mind kept returning to the central question that plagued her: how had everything changed so quickly and dramatically?

Mei Lin was deep in these troubled thoughts when she noticed something strange happening near the corner of her room. The air itself seemed to be . . . shifting somehow. Not moving like normal air currents, but actually bending and twisting as if reality was being folded.

She stood up slowly, her heart beginning to race. This wasn't any technique she'd ever learned or heard described. The distortion grew more pronounced and created what looked almost like a tear in the fabric of space itself.

Then, impossibly, the tear widened into an oval opening that revealed . . . somewhere else entirely. Through the gap, she could see part of what looked like a study or library, with bookshelves and a large wooden desk visible in the background. Warm light spilled through the opening, completely different from the cool oil lamp glow in her own room.

Mei Lin grabbed the nearest object that could serve as a weapon, a bronze incense burner from her altar, and backed against the far wall. Her cultivation was at the Late Core Formation level—respectable for an inner disciple—but whatever technique could create portals between spaces was far beyond her understanding or ability to counter.

Two figures stepped through the impossible opening.

The first was an elderly man with flowing white hair and a magnificent white beard that reached nearly to his waist. His robes were simple but well-made, black with red trim in a style that Mei Lin didn't recognize. Despite his age, he moved with the grace of someone whose body had been perfected through decades of cultivation. But what truly caught her attention was the aura that surrounded him.

Demonic qi.

Not the weak, tainted energy that Outer Sect demons might possess, but the deep, powerful corruption that spoke of centuries spent walking the darkest paths of cultivation. The air around him seemed to writhe with malevolent potential, and his presence made every protective formation in her chambers flicker with strain.

The demonic energy was so potent that her own spiritual defenses activated automatically, creating a thin barrier of pure qi around her body. But even through her defenses, she could feel the wrongness of his presence pressing against her consciousness.

This was what Elder Jinghua had warned them about in theoretical lessons: a truly powerful demonic cultivator whose very presence could corrupt the spiritual balance of everything around them. The kind of enemy that righteous sects had been founded to combat.

The second figure was much younger, probably only a few years older than herself. He had the kind of handsome features that would make any young woman's heart skip a beat, with sharp cheekbones and intelligent dark eyes. His robes were also black and red, but they were clearly of higher quality than the older man's simple garments. A sword hung at his side, and the way he carried himself suggested both martial skill and noble bearing.

More importantly, he radiated the clean spiritual energy of a righteous cultivator. His aura carried traces of light qi and star essence, techniques that were typically associated with the most pure-hearted sword cultivators. The contrast between his righteousness and his companion's obvious demonic nature was jarring and confusing.

Mei Lin's legs gave out, and she slumped against the wall, still clutching the incense burner with trembling hands. Her mind raced through every protective technique she'd ever learned, but she knew they would be useless against someone radiating this level of power.

The portal snapped closed behind them and trapped her in her own room with two complete strangers, one of whom felt like he could destroy her with a casual thought.

The old man's eyes met hers, and for a terrifying moment, she expected to see the cruel satisfaction or predatory hunger that the texts described as typical of powerful demons.

Instead, she saw something that confused her even more than his presence in her room: he looked genuinely surprised to see her and slightly embarrassed about the circumstances of their meeting.

"Please don't scream," the old man said quietly, raising his hands in what was probably meant to be a peaceful gesture.

But Mei Lin could barely hear him over the sound of her own thundering heartbeat. The demonic qi emanating from him was so intense that it made her skin crawl and her spiritual channels ache. Every instinct she possessed was screaming at her to run, to fight, to call for help, to do anything except sit frozen against the wall like a cornered rabbit.

The young sword cultivator took a step forward, and she noticed that he seemed completely unaffected by the dark energy radiating from his companion. Either he was protected by some powerful defensive technique, or he was also a demonic cultivator despite his righteous appearance.

"Master," the young man said quietly to the old man, "perhaps we should have chosen a different approach."

The old man nodded, looking genuinely apologetic. "You're absolutely right, Caelum. This isn't how I intended for this to go."

Mei Lin's mind struggled to process what was happening. These two strangers had appeared in her room through an impossible portal, bringing with them an aura of demonic power that should have been setting off every alarm formation in the sect. Yet somehow, no one seemed to notice. No elders were rushing to investigate. No defensive arrays were activating.

Which meant that either their concealment abilities were beyond anything she could comprehend, or something was very wrong with the sect's protective systems.

The terrifying thought struck her that this might be connected to all the other strange changes happening around them. If someone was controlling their elders' minds, manipulating their decisions and making them act against their natural instincts, then perhaps the same force had compromised their defenses.

She stared at the old man, trying to reconcile his grandfatherly appearance with the waves of dark power emanating from him. This was exactly the kind of scenario that their war preparations were supposedly meant to address: a powerful demonic cultivator infiltrating their sect.

But if he meant immediate harm, why was he standing there looking embarrassed instead of attacking? And why did his companion seem more concerned about startling her than about potential resistance?

Nothing about this situation matched what she'd been taught to expect from demonic sect invasions.

CHAPTER TEN

Slifer could see the terror in the young woman's eyes, and he immediately realized his mistake. The demonic qi radiating from his Demonic Devourer Dragon Bloodline was leaking out uncontrolled and filling the small room with an oppressive aura that would be overwhelming for anyone below Origin Realm.

He mentally cursed himself for the oversight. After spending so much time around his disciples and other powerful cultivators, he'd grown careless about suppressing his bloodline's natural emanations. But this girl was just a Core Formation cultivator; no wonder she looked like she was about to faint from spiritual pressure.

Slifer closed his eyes and focused inward as he drew the rebellious bloodline energy back into his core. The Demonic Devourer Dragon Bloodline had a mind of its own sometimes and constantly sought to absorb and process demonic qi from the environment. But it also projected its own dark energy as a side effect, which marked him as clearly demonic to anyone with spiritual senses.

The suppression technique he'd developed over the past weeks required careful balance. Too little control and he'd overwhelm everyone around him. Too much and he'd cut off access to the bloodline's abilities entirely. He found the middle ground by wrapping layers of neutral qi around the darker emanations until they were barely detectable.

The change was immediate. The oppressive weight in the room lifted, and the young woman's breathing became less labored. Her spiritual defenses stopped flickering desperately, and some of the color returned to her face.

"Better?" Slifer asked gently, opening his eyes.

She nodded shakily, though she still clutched that bronze incense burner like it would protect her from two cultivators who could travel through dimensional portals. Slifer found her determination oddly endearing. She was clearly outmatched by several cultivation realms, but she hadn't run or screamed for help. That showed either courage or good instincts about when noise would only make things worse.

"Please don't hurt me," she whispered, finally finding her voice. "I don't know what you want, but I'm just an inner disciple. I don't have anything valuable."

Slifer felt a pang of sympathy. The girl reminded him of his own disciples when he first met them: young, earnest, and completely unprepared for the complexities of the cultivation world. But unlike his disciples, this one seemed genuinely innocent. There was no hidden agenda in her spiritual signature, no carefully concealed darkness or ambition. Just fear and confusion.

"We're not here to hurt you," he said, keeping his voice as calm and grandfatherly as possible. "In fact, we're here to help your sect. Though, I realize appearing in your room through a portal probably wasn't the best way to start that conversation."

Caelum stepped forward. "My name is Caelum, and this is my master. We've come here because we believe your sect leadership is being controlled by an external force. We want to free them from that control."

The young woman's eyes widened at Caelum's words, and Slifer noticed something shift in her expression. The terror was still there, but now it was mixed with something else. Recognition, perhaps. Or hope.

"Controlled how?" she asked, her voice growing stronger.

Slifer let Caelum take the lead on this conversation. His disciple had a natural talent for inspiring trust, and his righteous cultivation would be more reassuring to a Pure Soul Sect member than anything Slifer could offer.

"Mental manipulation," Caelum explained, crouching down to her eye level to appear less threatening. "We believe someone with powerful mind control abilities has been influencing your elders, making them act against their natural instincts and principles. Have you noticed any strange changes in their behavior recently?"

The bronze incense burner slipped from her fingers and clattered to the floor. "You know about that?" she breathed. "But how could you possibly . . . I thought I was going crazy. Everyone else seems to accept the changes, but they felt so wrong."

Slifer exchanged a glance with Caelum. They'd found exactly what they were looking for: someone who had noticed the manipulation but hadn't been affected by it themselves. This young woman could be their key to understanding how extensively Lady Chi's influence had spread through the sect.

"What changes have you observed?" Slifer asked, settling into a cross-legged position on the floor to make himself seem less imposing. "Please, be specific. Any detail could be important."

She hesitated for a moment, clearly still processing the situation. Then the words came pouring out as if she'd been desperate to share her concerns with someone who would listen.

"Everything changed about a month ago. Our sect has always been peaceful, focused on healing and purification rather than combat. But suddenly, we're at war with the demonic sects, and anyone who questions it disappears or starts acting like a completely different person. Elder Jinghua was researching historical accounts of mind-control techniques, and then she vanished. Elder Tian and Elder Wei spoke out against the war, and now they're missing too." She paused, wrapping her arms around herself. "But the worst part is how the remaining elders speak. Sometimes they sound like themselves, but other times they use exactly the same phrases, the same arguments, as if they're all reading from the same script. And their spiritual signatures feel different during those moments."

Slifer nodded grimly. Lady Chi's control was more extensive than he'd initially realized. She wasn't just manipulating a few key leaders; she was systematically replacing the sect's entire command structure with puppet versions of themselves.

"What's your name?" Caelum asked gently.

"Mei Lin," she replied automatically, then seemed to realize she was having a civil conversation with two intruders who had appeared through a magical portal. "I still don't understand who you are or why you're here. How do I know you're not the ones controlling our elders?"

It was a fair question, and Slifer appreciated her logical thinking despite her fear. "Because if we were the ones controlling your sect, we wouldn't need to sneak in through your bedroom window," he said with a slight smile. "We'd already know where to find your sect master."

"Besides," Caelum added, "I can sense that your spiritual nature is pure and uncorrupted. If you've been resisting the influence that's affecting your elders, it means you have strong natural defenses against mental manipulation. Trust those defenses now; do we feel like enemies to you?"

Mei Lin studied them both carefully, and Slifer could see her evaluating their spiritual signatures with surprising skill for someone of her cultivation level. After a long moment, some of the tension left her shoulders.

"No," she admitted. "You feel... different. Complicated. But not evil." She paused, then added quickly, "Though, the demonic qi earlier was terrifying."

"My apologies for that," Slifer said sincerely. "I have a... complex cultivation background. But I promise you that my intentions toward your sect are peaceful. I want to free your people from whatever's controlling them."

"Then you really think our elders are being manipulated?" Hope crept into her voice. "It's not just me imagining things?"

"Definitely not imagination," Slifer confirmed. "We've encountered this kind of mental control before. It's subtle but powerful, designed to brainwash victims completely."

Mei Lin's face crumpled with relief. "I thought I was losing my mind. Everyone else seemed to accept the changes so easily, but they felt fundamentally wrong. Our sect would never choose war over peaceful solutions unless something was forcing that choice."

"And that's exactly why we need your help," Slifer said, leaning forward slightly. "We need to locate your sect master and any other key leaders who are being controlled. If we can break the mental manipulation at its source, the rest of your sect should return to normal."

"But how can I possibly help you with something like that?" Mei Lin asked. "I'm just an inner disciple. I don't have access to the leadership areas or special intelligence about their locations."

Caelum smiled reassuringly. "You'd be surprised how much an observant inner disciple notices. You've already demonstrated that you're more aware of the situation than most of your sect's members. We need someone who knows the normal patterns and can identify what's changed."

Slifer could see the conflict in her expression. She wanted to help, but she was also terrified of the consequences if they were wrong or if they failed. He decided to address her fears directly.

"Mei Lin, I know this is asking a lot. We're strangers who appeared in your room, and you have no reason to trust us. But think about what happens if nothing changes. Your sect continues down this path of war and violence that goes against everything you believe in. More of your fellow disciples die in battles that serve someone else's agenda. And eventually, whoever is controlling your leaders will have no more use for the Pure Soul Sect at all."

The words hit home. He could see her thinking about all the friends she'd lost, all the changes that had made her sect unrecognizable. When she looked up again, her expression had hardened with resolve.

"What do you need me to do?"

"Just information for now," Slifer said. "Where would your sect master most likely be at this time of day? What's the normal security around the leadership areas? And are there any patterns you've noticed about when the controlled behavior is strongest?"

Mei Lin thought for a moment. "Sect Master Ming Yue usually spends evenings in the Celestial Harmony Pavilion, either in meditation or meeting with the remaining council members. It's in the center of the sect grounds, heavily protected by formations and guarded by Origin Realm elders." She paused, her brow furrowing in concentration. "As for patterns . . . the controlled behavior seems strongest during official assemblies and decision-making sessions. But sometimes, usually late at night or early in the morning, some of the elders seem more like their old selves. Like whatever's influencing them has to focus its attention elsewhere periodically."

That was valuable intelligence. If Lady Chi's control required active concentration to maintain, then she might be vulnerable during moments when her attention was divided. Slifer filed that information away for later use.

"The Celestial Harmony Pavilion," he mused. "How would someone reach it without triggering the general alarm formations?"

"There are servant passages that connect most of the major buildings," Mei Lin said slowly. "They're less heavily monitored because they're supposed to be for cleaning staff and food delivery. But I don't know the exact layout, and they might have changed the security protocols since the war preparations began."

Slifer nodded. It wasn't perfect, but it was more information than they'd had when they arrived. "That's helpful. Now, we need to move quickly before whoever is controlling your sect realizes we're here. Is there anything else you think we should know?"

Before Mei Lin could answer, Slifer felt a subtle shift in the spiritual atmosphere around them. His enhanced senses, boosted by the Demonic Devourer Dragon Bloodline, picked up the faint activation of detection formations throughout the sect grounds.

"We've been noticed," he said quietly, standing up. "Caelum, it's time to move."

His disciple nodded as his hand instinctively moved to rest on Starforge's hilt. "How much time do we have?"

"Minutes at most," Slifer replied, already calculating their best route to the Celestial Harmony Pavilion. "They know something's wrong, but they probably don't have our exact location yet."

Mei Lin scrambled to her feet, her face pale but determined. "If you're really here to help, then I'm coming with you. I know this sect better than you do, and if you're right about the mind control, then you'll need someone who can identify which elders are still themselves."

Slifer started to object; taking a Core Formation cultivator into what was likely to become a serious battle was asking for trouble. But Caelum caught his eye and shook his head slightly.

"She's right," his disciple said. "And we don't have time to argue. If the Pure Soul Sect leadership is being controlled, they'll send their strongest fighters to stop us. We need every advantage we can get."

Before Slifer could respond, the sound of approaching footsteps echoed through the corridor outside Mei Lin's quarters—multiple sets of feet moving with the coordinated pace of trained cultivators rather than panicked disciples.

"They've found us faster than expected," Slifer muttered as he quickly reviewed his options. Fighting their way through the entire sect would defeat the purpose of their mission, but they needed to reach the sect master before the controlled elders could coordinate a proper defense.

"There's a window," Mei Lin whispered urgently, pointing to the paper screen that covered her room's only external opening. "It leads to the roof of the auxiliary building. From there, we can reach the servant passages without going through the main corridors."

Caelum moved to the window and carefully parted the screen to look outside. "Clear for now, but I can sense multiple Origin Realm auras converging on this building. Master, we need to split up."

Slifer understood immediately. Caelum was suggesting that he stay behind to delay their pursuers while Slifer and Mei Lin made their way to the sect master. It was tactically sound, but it meant leaving his disciple to face multiple Origin Realm opponents alone.

"Can you handle them?" Slifer asked, though he already knew the answer. Caelum had grown tremendously in power and skill, and his Starforged Sword Bloodline gave him abilities that could surprise even experienced elders.

"Long enough," Caelum replied with quiet confidence. "Go. Free their sect master and this all stops."

The footsteps in the corridor were getting closer, and Slifer could hear muffled voices discussing search patterns and security protocols. They were out of time for elaborate planning.

"Mei Lin, can you keep up?" he asked, moving toward the window.

She nodded, though he could see fear warring with determination in her expression. "I'll manage."

Slifer helped her through the window first, then followed her onto the roof tiles of the adjacent building. The night air was cool and clear, with enough moonlight to navigate by but not so much that they'd be easily spotted from the ground.

Behind them, he heard the sound of Mei Lin's door being forced open, followed by Caelum's calm voice saying something about peaceful discussions. Then the distinct sound of Starforge being drawn from its sheath, and the sharp crack of spiritual techniques colliding.

"This way," Mei Lin whispered, leading him across the rooftops toward a cluster of buildings in the center of the sect grounds. "The servants' entrance to the Celestial Harmony Pavilion is through that kitchen complex."

They moved quickly but carefully, staying low to avoid being silhouetted against the sky. Slifer could hear the sounds of battle intensifying behind them as more elders joined the fight against Caelum. His disciple was holding his own, but Origin Realm cultivators weren't opponents he could face indefinitely.

The kitchen complex was mostly dark, with only a few windows showing the dim light of banked cooking fires. Mei Lin led him to a small door that was partially concealed by decorative bushes, then produced a key from somewhere in her robes.

"Servants' quarters," she explained quietly. "I helped in the kitchens during my first year, so I still have access."

The interior corridors were narrow and utilitarian, clearly designed for efficiency rather than appearance. Mei Lin moved through them with confidence, leading him past storage rooms and preparation areas toward the main complex where the sect's leadership resided.

They emerged into a more elegant hallway lined with paintings and decorative alcoves. The spiritual pressure here was noticeably different: multiple powerful auras in close proximity, all carrying the subtle wrongness that Slifer had learned to associate with Lady Chi's mental influence.

"The sect master's private chambers are through that archway," Mei Lin whispered, pointing toward an ornate entrance flanked by carved pillars. "But there are usually guards . . ."

She trailed off as they approached the archway and found it completely unguarded. The absence of security was more ominous than any number of posted sentries would have been. Either the guards had been called away to deal with the disturbance Caelum was creating, or they were walking into a carefully prepared trap.

Slifer extended his spiritual senses and immediately located the sect master's presence in the chambers beyond. Ming Yue's spiritual signature was strong and stable, but it carried the same tainted quality as the other controlled elders. Lady Chi's influence was definitely at work here.

"Stay behind me," he instructed Mei Lin. "If this goes badly, run back the way we came and find somewhere to hide until morning."

She nodded, though he could see her hands shaking slightly. The girl had courage, but she was still just a Core Formation cultivator about to witness a confrontation between much more powerful forces.

Slifer pushed through the archway and entered the sect master's chambers. The room was elegantly furnished in the Pure Soul Sect's traditional style: simple lines, natural materials, and soft lighting that promoted meditation and peaceful contemplation. Under normal circumstances, it would have been a sanctuary of calm wisdom.

Tonight, it felt like entering a spider's web.

Sect Master Ming Yue sat in meditation posture at the center of the room, her eyes closed and her breathing steady. She appeared to be in deep cultivation, completely unaware of their presence. But Slifer could sense the layers of spiritual technique wrapped around the woman's consciousness like invisible chains.

"Sect Master Ming Yue," Slifer greeted, stepping into the center of the room.

The woman's eyes opened, and Slifer immediately saw the telltale signs of mental control. Ming Yue's gaze was focused but somehow distant, as if she was looking through Slifer rather than at him. When she spoke, her voice carried the same rehearsed quality that Mei Lin had described in the other elders.

"Demonic Sect Master," Ming Yue said, rising smoothly to her feet. "You have violated the sanctity of the Pure Soul Sect. Surrender now, and your death will be swift."

CHAPTER ELEVEN

Slifer looked at the sect master standing before him, her eyes carrying that distant quality he'd seen before in controlled cultivators. Ming Yue had been known throughout the cultivation world as a voice of reason, someone who sought diplomatic solutions before resorting to violence. Now she was threatening to execute him on sight.

This was going to be complicated.

"Sect Master Ming Yue," Slifer said carefully, keeping his hands visible and non-threatening. "I'm not here to fight. Lady Chi has been manipulating your mind, making you believe things that aren't true. If you'll just let me—"

He didn't get to finish the sentence.

Ming Yue moved faster than his eyes could track. One moment she was standing across the room, the next she was directly in front of him with her palm extended toward his chest. White light erupted from her hand in a concentrated beam that would have punched straight through his sternum and out his back.

The Critical Block Card activated automatically.

The beam struck an invisible barrier inches from Slifer's chest and simply stopped. Not deflected or absorbed, just stopped, as if the attack had hit an immovable wall built into the fabric of reality itself. The white light spread across the barrier's surface like water hitting glass, then dissipated harmlessly into the air.

Ming Yue's eyes widened slightly. The first crack in her demeanor.

She spun away from him in a graceful motion, her white robes flowing around her like water. Her hands came together in a complex series of seals, and suddenly the air in the chamber began to shimmer with spiritual energy.

Dozens of white lotus flowers materialized in the space between them, their petals glowing with purification qi.

"Lotus Garden of Cleansing Light," she whispered.

The flowers exploded outward in all directions. Each petal became a razor-sharp projectile infused with purification energy designed to scour away corruption from both body and soul. In the Pure Soul Sect's traditional usage, this technique was meant for healing, for burning away spiritual poison and dark qi to restore a cultivator's natural balance. Against someone the user perceived as demonic, it was effectively a shotgun blast of holy fire.

Slifer stood perfectly still as hundreds of glowing petals converged on him from every angle. Another Critical Block Card triggered and created a spherical barrier that caught every single petal before it could reach him. The petals hit the invisible shield and burst into motes of white light that drifted slowly toward the ceiling like dying embers.

"This is exactly what I'm talking about," Slifer said, trying to keep his voice calm and reasonable. "You're using your sect's healing techniques as weapons. Does that sound like something you would normally do?"

Ming Yue didn't respond. She was already moving again, her hands tracing patterns in the air that left trails of glowing white qi. The spiritual energy in the room began to condense around her in visible waves, responding to her will with the precision of someone who had spent centuries mastering their cultivation.

The floor beneath Slifer's feet cracked. Roots made of pure white light erupted from the broken stone, then wrapped around his ankles and climbed up his legs with alarming speed. They constricted like living things, and he could feel the purification energy trying to burn through his defenses.

He looked down at the glowing restraints, then back up at Ming Yue. Another Critical Block Card activated, and the light-roots simply ceased to exist. One moment they were there, the next they were gone, snuffed out of existence by the card's absolute negation.

Ming Yue's expression finally showed something beyond that distant control. Frustration flickered across her pretty features before being replaced by cold determination.

She thrust both palms forward, and a massive wave of white fire rolled across the chamber toward him. The flames weren't hot in the traditional sense, but they radiated spiritual purity so intense that it would burn away anything tainted by demonic cultivation. Furniture caught in the wave's path didn't ignite; it was simply erased as it was consumed by the purifying force.

The wave hit Slifer's position, and another Critical Block Card activated. The white fire parted around him like water around a stone, flowing to either side and scorching the walls behind him. The elegant paintings turned to ash. The decorative scrolls crumbled to nothing. The carefully maintained meditation mats were reduced to memory.

When the flames cleared, Slifer was standing in the exact same spot, completely unharmed.

"You're destroying your own chambers," he pointed out, gesturing at the ruined room around them. "I don't think the real Ming Yue would appreciate this."

She didn't acknowledge his words. Her hands moved through another series of seals, faster this time, and Slifer felt the spiritual pressure in the room suddenly intensify. The air itself became thick with power as Ming Yue drew on deeper reserves of her cultivation.

"Sanctified Judgment," she intoned.

A massive construct of white light materialized above her: a gigantic sword at least six meters long and radiating enough spiritual power to make Slifer's hair stand on end. The weapon hung in the air for a moment, its edge sharp enough to cut through space itself.

Then it fell.

The sword descended with the weight of a collapsing mountain. Slifer could actually see the air compressing beneath it, could feel the floor beginning to buckle from the sheer spiritual pressure bearing down on the chamber.

A Critical Block Card activated simultaneously.

The sword struck the invisible barrier and stopped. The impact sent a shock wave through the entire building. Windows shattered throughout the pavilion. Disciples outside stumbled and fell from the sudden spiritual pulse. The massive sword pressed down against the barriers, trying to force its way through, but the card's absolute defense held firm.

After a moment, the construct shattered into a million fragments of light that rained down across the destroyed chamber.

Slifer stood amid the falling sparkles, his robes settling back into place, not a single hair out of position. He was starting to feel genuinely bad about how one-sided this was becoming. Ming Yue was giving everything she had, drawing on techniques that probably took years to master, and his System-provided cards were negating them with the casual ease of someone swatting away flies.

Ming Yue landed in a crouch about five meters away, breathing harder now. For the first time, Slifer could see the exertion starting to show. Sweat beaded on her forehead despite the cool night air. Her hands trembled slightly as she formed another seal.

"Soul Purification Wave," she said.

This attack was different. Instead of physical force or elemental energy, she sent out a pulse of pure spiritual pressure aimed directly at his consciousness. It was the kind of technique that bypassed external defenses entirely and struck at the cultivator's inner self.

Slifer felt it wash over him like a wave of warm water. It probed at his mind, seeking dark thoughts or corrupted intentions to burn away. But his Void Being Aura acted as a natural barrier against mental intrusions. The attack simply couldn't find purchase on his consciousness.

He sighed. This wasn't working. Ming Yue could keep attacking him all night, and his cards would keep protecting him, but they were just going through the motions. She was under mind control. She genuinely believed she was fighting a demonic threat to her sect. Defeating her through overwhelming power wouldn't solve anything.

Plus, he was burning through Critical Block Cards at an alarming rate. Each one cost credits he could not afford to waste. At this rate, he'd use up his entire defensive stockpile before the night was over, and he still had to deal with the White Tiger Sect situation.

Slifer pulled up his System interface while Ming Yue prepared another attack. The Shop materialized before his eyes, invisible to everyone else in the room. He quickly navigated through the various categories, looking for something that would work.

He needed to restrain her without causing permanent harm. Something that would hold an Ascendant-level cultivator long enough for him to use the Mind Liberation technique. The problem was that most binding techniques in the Shop were either too weak to hold someone of her cultivation level or too expensive to justify using.

Ming Yue raised her hands above her head. A sphere of white light began forming between her palms, growing larger and more intense with each passing second. The spiritual pressure was building again, this time to levels that made the previous attacks look like warm-up exercises.

Slifer's eyes finally landed on something that might work: Temporal Stasis Field. Heaven Rank. Could freeze a target in time for up to ten seconds. The description noted it was particularly effective against cultivators who relied on movement and technique activation. Cost: eight thousand Karmic Credits.

He winced at the price but clicked purchase anyway. A small jade token materialized in his storage space.

"Final Lotus Bloom," Ming Yue announced.

The sphere between her hands had grown to the size of a house. It contained enough purification energy to level several city blocks. This was clearly meant to be a finishing move, the kind of technique you only used when absolutely certain of victory.

She hurled it at him with both hands.

The massive sphere of light filled his entire field of vision. There was no dodging something that large in an enclosed space. Three more Critical Block Cards activated to shield him from the incoming attack.

The sphere struck his barriers and exploded.

White light consumed everything. The walls of the chamber simply ceased to exist, vaporized by the overwhelming spiritual energy. The roof collapsed inward. Slifer felt the floor beneath him crack and fall away as the explosion carved a massive crater into the building's foundation.

When the light finally faded, Slifer found himself standing at the bottom of a smoking pit that had once been an elegant meditation chamber. Debris rained down around him. The entire Celestial Harmony Pavilion had been effectively destroyed, with only a few supporting pillars still standing.

Ming Yue stood at the crater's edge, breathing heavily. Her white robes were scorched and torn. Blood trickled from the corner of her mouth where she'd bitten her lip. She looked down at him with that same distant expression, but Slifer could see the confusion behind it. Nothing she'd thrown at him had worked. Not even her ultimate technique.

"I don't understand," she said quietly. "What are you?"

Before she could recover enough to attack again, Slifer activated the Temporal Stasis Field.

A ripple of distorted air spread out from him, moving faster than thought. It reached Ming Yue in an instant, and suddenly she just stopped. Completely stopped. Her hair, which had been settling after the explosion, froze in midair. The dust particles around her hung motionless. Even the blood on her lip ceased its downward flow.

She looked like a statue carved from flesh, perfectly preserved in that moment of confusion and exhaustion.

Slifer quickly scrambled up the side of the crater. Ten seconds wasn't much time. He pulled out the small vial containing the Mind Liberation technique he'd used on Ace. The process required direct contact and sustained concentration. He placed his hand on Ming Yue's forehead, feeling the warmth of her skin beneath his palm.

The technique activated.

Golden light flowed from his fingertips and spread across her face and down through her body. Slifer could sense the foreign spiritual threads wrapped around her consciousness: Lady Chi's mind control, far more sophisticated than he'd expected. The threads weren't just compelling obedience; they'd been carefully woven into Ming Yue's thoughts to make her genuinely believe that her actions were her own natural responses.

He began the delicate process of unweaving them. Each thread had to be carefully dissolved without damaging the underlying consciousness. It was like performing surgery while wearing oven mitts; one wrong move and he could cause permanent damage to her mind.

The temporal stasis wore off after about ten seconds, but by then the Mind Liberation technique had established enough of a foundation to continue. Ming Yue's eyes went wide as sensation returned to her body. She tried to speak, to move, but the golden light held her in place as it worked through her mental defenses.

Slifer could feel her panic rising as suppressed memories began flooding back. Weeks of being manipulated, decisions she'd made that went against everything she believed in, orders she'd given that had sent her disciples into unnecessary danger. All of it came rushing back at once.

"I know this is overwhelming," Slifer said quietly, maintaining the technique. "But you need to let it happen. The alternative is staying trapped forever."

The last of Lady Chi's control threads dissolved. Ming Yue gasped, and Slifer pulled his hand away as the golden light faded. For a moment, she just stood there at the crater's edge, her eyes unfocused as she processed what had just happened.

Then her legs gave out.

Slifer caught her before she could fall, lowering her gently to a sitting position on the broken ground. Ming Yue stared at her hands, turning them over slowly as if seeing them for the first time. Tears began streaming down her face.

"What have I done?" she whispered. "The orders I gave . . . the disciples I sent into danger . . . Oh ancestors, what have I done?"

"It wasn't you," Slifer said firmly, sitting down beside her. "You were being controlled. None of those decisions were really yours."

"But I believed they were," she replied, her voice breaking. "I thought I was protecting my sect. I thought the demonic sects needed to be eliminated. I sent so many of my students to fight and die for a lie."

Slifer didn't have a good response to that. He'd been on the receiving end of Lady Chi's manipulation attempts, and even with his Void Being Aura protecting him, her mental techniques had been frighteningly effective. Ming Yue had been exposed to that influence for weeks without any protection at all.

"How long?" Ming Yue asked. "How long was I . . . like that?"

"Based on what we know, probably about a month. Maybe longer."

She closed her eyes, fresh tears spilling down her cheeks. "A month. Thirty days of my life where I wasn't myself. Thirty days of decisions made by someone else wearing my face."

Slifer sat with her in silence for a moment, letting her process. Around them, he could hear shouts and running footsteps as Pure Soul Sect disciples converged on the destroyed pavilion. They'd need to deal with that soon, but first he wanted to make sure Ming Yue was stable enough to help.

"The woman who did this to you," he said. "Her name is Lady Chi. She's an Immortal Realm cultivator who came to the mortal realm, and she's been using mind control to manipulate the leaders of major sects."

Ming Yue opened her eyes and looked at him properly for the first time. "Why? What does she want?"

"Revenge, mainly. She's angry about the death of someone named Darius, and she's been orchestrating this entire war to get back at the person who killed him."

"This whole war . . ." Ming Yue's voice trailed off as the implications sank in. "The skirmishes, the raids, the disciples dying on both sides. All of it was her?"

"Not all of it directly, but she's been pulling the strings. Making you and the other sect leaders believe the conflict was necessary."

Ming Yue looked down at the smoking crater that had been her personal meditation chamber. "I destroyed my own home fighting you. I nearly killed you because I genuinely believed you were a threat."

"To be fair, I am technically a demonic cultivator," Slifer said. "Though, I've been working on reforming that whole system."

She actually laughed at that, a short, bitter sound. "Reforming demonic cultivation. Of course you are. Because why would anything make sense anymore?"

Slifer pulled out the Karmic Shield Pendant he'd purchased earlier and handed it to her. "This will protect you from Lady Chi trying to regain control. Keep it on at all times until we've dealt with her permanently."

Ming Yue took the pendant with trembling hands and fastened it around her neck. "Thank you. I don't . . . I can't even begin to express . . ."

"Just focus on recovering for now," Slifer said. "We still have more sect leaders to free from her control, and I'm going to need your help to do it."

She nodded slowly, wiping away tears. "The Heavenly Light Sect Master and the White Tiger Sect Master. They're both under her influence too?"

"That's what we believe. Ace from Heavenly Light has already been freed; he's helping us track down the controlled cultivators in his sect. But Feng Lei from White Tiger is still compromised, and we don't know how many others might be affected."

"This is going to start a panic," Ming Yue said. "When word gets out that sect leaders' minds were being controlled, that we've been fighting a war based on manipulation . . ."

"Which is why we need to move quickly and carefully. Can you stand?"

She nodded, and Slifer helped her to her feet. Her legs were still shaky, but she managed to maintain her balance. Around them, the sounds of approaching disciples were getting closer.

"Sect Master!" A young man in Pure Soul Sect robes appeared at the crater's edge, his eyes widening at the destruction. "We heard the explosion, we thought—" He stopped, staring at Slifer. "Why is there a demonic cultivator here?"

Ming Yue took a deep breath, drawing on reserves of composure that Slifer had to admire. "Elder Shan, please gather the other senior elders in the council chamber immediately. We have much to discuss."

"But Sect Master, the demonic—"

"Is my guest," Ming Yue said firmly. "And you will treat him with the respect due to someone who just saved my life and possibly our entire sect."

Elder Shan's mouth opened and closed several times before he finally bowed. "As you command, Sect Master." He disappeared back over the crater's edge.

Slifer felt a wave of relief wash over him. The Mind Liberation technique had worked. Ming Yue was free from Lady Chi's control, and more importantly, she was rational enough to help prevent their situation from spiraling into a larger conflict.

The System chimed softly in his mind.

> Mission Complete: Free Pure Soul Sect Master from mind control
> You have gained 5,000 Karmic Credits.

He dismissed the notification. They'd managed to complete this part without anyone dying, which was more than he'd hoped for when the battle started. Ming Yue's final attack had cost him several expensive Critical Block Cards, and the Temporal Stasis Field had been pricey, but overall, the credit expenditure had been manageable.

Now they just had to deal with explaining the situation to an entire sect full of cultivators who'd been mobilized for war and then somehow coordinate efforts to free the White Tiger Sect Master before Lady Chi realized what was happening.

Slifer looked at Ming Yue, who was staring at the ruined pavilion with an expression of deep sadness. She'd spent years building this sect into a place of peace and wisdom, only to have it corrupted into a weapon of war by someone else's malice.

"We'll fix this," he said quietly. "All of it. Lady Chi won't get away with what she's done."

Ming Yue nodded, her jaw setting with determination. "No. She won't."

Together, they climbed out of the crater to face whatever came next.

CHAPTER TWELVE

Mei Lin pressed herself against the corridor wall as another shock wave rolled through the building. Dust rained from the ceiling, and she could hear wood cracking somewhere above her. The spiritual pressure radiating from the Celestial Harmony Pavilion was so intense it made her teeth ache.

She'd been standing here for what felt like hours but was probably only minutes. After Slifer and his disciple had entered the sect, after they'd explained their purpose and she'd led them to the sect master's chambers, she'd retreated to what she thought was a safe distance. That safe distance had turned out to be not nearly far enough.

Another explosion. This one was different: bigger, brighter. White light flooded through every window and crack in the pavilion, so intense that Mei Lin had to shield her eyes. The entire building shook. She heard something massive collapse, the sound of stone and wood giving way under tremendous force.

Then silence.

The sudden absence of spiritual pressure was almost as shocking as its presence had been. Mei Lin's ears rang in the quiet. She lowered her hand from her eyes, blinking away afterimages, and stared at the pavilion. Smoke drifted from shattered windows. Half the roof had simply disappeared.

She'd felt powerful cultivators fight before. The sect had held sparring demonstrations, and she'd witnessed elders testing new techniques in controlled environments. But this had been something else entirely. The gap between her

Late Core Formation cultivation and what she'd just felt was so vast it made her feel like an insect watching gods clash in the heavens.

Sect Master Ming Yue was an Ascendant Realm cultivator, someone who could level mountains and part seas. Mei Lin had always known this intellectually, but experiencing it directly was different. Each technique the sect master had used carried enough power to kill Mei Lin a hundred times over. The casual way that power had been thrown around—walls erased, the building itself torn apart—made her realize how fragile her existence truly was.

And somehow, the demonic cultivator had withstood all of it.

Mei Lin hadn't sensed any offensive techniques from Slifer's side. No counterattacks, no overwhelming displays of superior cultivation. Just . . . survival. Defense after defense after defense. Which was somehow more terrifying than if he'd simply overpowered their sect master.

What kind of abilities did someone need to stand against an Ascendant's full assault without fighting back?

She stood frozen in the corridor, unsure what to do. Should she go check on the sect master? Run away and hide? The other elders had to have felt those explosions. Half the sect was probably converging on this location already.

But what if Slifer had lost? What if the sect master was injured? Or worse, what if the demonic cultivator had won and was now about to betra—

Footsteps.

Mei Lin tensed, and her hand moved instinctively to the small knife at her belt. Not that it would do any good against either of the cultivators who'd just fought, but the gesture made her feel slightly less helpless.

Two figures emerged from the damaged pavilion.

Sect Master Ming Yue walked with slow steps, her white robes torn and scorched. Blood stained the corner of her mouth. She looked exhausted, her usually perfect posture slightly hunched. But she was walking. She was alive.

And beside her, supporting her elbow with one hand, was Slifer.

Mei Lin's breath caught. The old cultivator looked exactly as he had when he'd entered: no visible injuries, his robes unmarred despite the destruction around them. He was speaking quietly to the sect master, and his face showed concern rather than triumph.

They looked less like victor and vanquished and more like . . . allies.

Sect Master Ming Yue's eyes found Mei Lin in the corridor. For a moment, their gazes locked, and Mei Lin saw something in her sect master's expression that she'd never seen before. Shame. Regret. And underneath it all, a bone-deep weariness that had nothing to do with physical exhaustion.

"Disciple Mei Lin," the sect master said, her voice hoarse. "Please, join us.

We need to find where Junior Caelum is currently engaged with the corrupted elders."

Corrupted elders. Not enemy elders. Not demonic infiltrators. Corrupted.

Mei Lin bowed quickly. She'd been right. The changes in their sect, the sudden shift toward violence and war—it hadn't been natural. Something had corrupted their leadership. And somehow, this demonic cultivator had freed their sect master from it.

He'd actually kept his word.

"The eastern training hall," Mei Lin said, falling into step beside them. "That's where the commotion was coming from earlier. Elder Yao and several others were heading there."

Slifer nodded. "Caelum should be fine. He's good at handling situations like this."

The casual confidence in his voice made Mei Lin glance at him again. This old man, with his white beard and grandfatherly appearance, had just survived a battle with an Ascendant cultivator without breaking a sweat. Now he was calmly walking through the Pure Soul Sect like he belonged here, discussing his disciple's combat abilities as if commenting on the weather.

Who were these people?

They walked through corridors that Mei Lin had known for her entire time at the sect. Past the meditation gardens where she'd spent countless hours in contemplation. Through the library halls where Elder Jinghua had taught her about the sect's peaceful philosophy. Every familiar sight now felt strange viewed through the lens of what she'd just learned.

How many of the decisions made in these halls had actually been made by her sect's leadership? How many orders given, missions assigned, disciples sent into danger, all based on corrupted judgment?

The sounds of combat reached them before they arrived at the eastern training hall—spiritual techniques clashing, the impact of bodies hitting walls, shouts of exertion and pain—but the sounds were growing fewer and farther between. The fight was winding down.

They rounded the final corner and stopped at the training hall's entrance.

Caelum stood in the center of the large room, surrounded by fallen elders. But he looked nothing like the composed young man Mei Lin had met earlier. His appearance had changed dramatically: his skin had taken on a metallic sheen with strange patterns etched across it like living runes, but upon closer inspection, Mei Lin realized they weren't runes at all. They were thorns. His demonic sword had somehow merged with his flesh and transformed him into something that was part human, part weapon.

Five elders lay scattered around him in various states of consciousness. Elder Yao was propped against the far wall, holding his ribs. Elder Fan had collapsed near the training dummies, breathing heavily. The others were in similar conditions: defeated but alive.

What struck Mei Lin most were the expressions on the fallen elders' faces. They weren't looking at Caelum with hatred or defiance. They looked confused. Lost. As if they'd woken from a nightmare and couldn't quite remember where they were.

Caelum turned toward the entrance as they arrived. His eyes, normally a warm brown, now glowed with an eerie red light. For a moment, Mei Lin thought he might attack. The power radiating from his transformed state was immense—easily Peak Origin Realm level, possibly higher.

Then he saw Slifer and immediately dropped to one knee, his head bowed. "Master."

The transformation reversed itself as he knelt. The metallic sheen faded from his skin. The thorn patterns retreated, flowing like liquid back into the sword at his hip. Within seconds, Caelum looked human again. Just a tired young man in slightly disheveled robes, kneeling respectfully before his teacher.

The sword at his hip gave one final pulse of red light before going dormant.

Mei Lin stared. She couldn't help it. The casual display of power, the effortless transformation, the complete control—it was all so far beyond anything she'd imagined from demonic cultivators. The stories always portrayed them as wild, uncontrolled, consumed by their dark practices. But Caelum had just merged with a demonic weapon, fought five elders simultaneously, and returned to normal with the calm precision of a well-practiced technique.

Two demonic cultivators had walked into the Pure Soul Sect, one of the three major righteous sects in the entire realm, and defeated their leadership. Not through overwhelming numbers or secret assault, but against superior numbers with their own power.

Just how strong was the Black Rose Sect, really? And how much had the righteous sects underestimated their enemies?

"Well done," Slifer said, moving past Caelum toward the fallen elders. "Any serious injuries?"

"Nothing life-threatening, Master. I made sure to incapacitate rather than harm." Caelum rose to his feet, though he maintained a respectful distance. "Four of them were corrupted. The fifth, Elder Zhou, was simply responding to what he thought was an intruder."

Slifer nodded and began moving among the fallen elders, placing his hand on each forehead in turn. Golden light flowed from his fingertips, and Mei

Lin watched as confused expressions gradually cleared. Elder Yao gasped as if surfacing from deep water. Elder Fan's eyes, which had held that same distant quality as the sect master's had earlier, suddenly focused with terrible clarity.

"What... what have I done?" Elder Fan whispered, staring at his hands.

"You were controlled," Slifer said gently. "None of your recent actions were truly your own."

By the time he finished with the fourth elder, Mei Lin understood the process. This old demonic cultivator, whom she'd feared, who'd appeared in her room like a nightmare given form, was healing people. Freeing them from some kind of spiritual corruption that had twisted their thoughts and actions.

The contradiction made her head spin. Demonic cultivators were supposed to be the enemy. They were supposed to corrupt and destroy, not heal and liberate. Everything she'd been taught, everything she'd believed about the division between righteous and demonic cultivation, felt suddenly uncertain.

Sect Master Ming Yue had moved to Elder Zhou, helping the unaffected elder to his feet. "Gather everyone in the main courtyard," she said, her voice carrying the authority of someone who'd regained control of herself. "All disciples, all elders, everyone who can walk. We have much to explain."

Elder Zhou bowed, though confusion still clouded his features. He hurried from the hall, likely relieved to have clear orders after the chaos of the evening.

"Are you sure about this?" Slifer asked, turning to face the sect master. "Once you tell them what happened, there's no taking it back."

Ming Yue straightened her torn robes, her exhaustion visible but her determination clear. "My sect deserves the truth. Or at least as much of it as they can handle without panicking." She looked at the newly freed elders, who were helping each other stand. "We were manipulated into war. Our disciples died because I was controlled like a puppet. They need to know why."

"They need to know we're better than this," Elder Fan added quietly. "That the Pure Soul Sect they believed in still exists."

Mei Lin followed as the group made their way toward the main courtyard. The other freed elders came as well, supporting each other, still processing what had been done to them. The corridor felt different now, not ominous like before, but somehow sad. Like walking through a home that had been burglarized: everything familiar but now tainted by violation.

The main courtyard of the Pure Soul Sect was massive, designed to hold gatherings of the entire sect when necessary. Stone tiles stretched across an area large enough to accommodate thousands, with raised platforms at the northern end where the leadership could address the disciples. Decorative gardens lined the edges, and the sect's banner hung from tall poles at each corner, white lotus flowers on a field of blue.

Tonight, the courtyard was filling rapidly. Disciples streamed in from every direction, their conversations a rising buzz of speculation and concern. The explosions had been impossible to miss. Everyone knew something significant had happened.

Mei Lin stood near the edge of the crowd watching as more and more people arrived. She could hear fragments of conversations around her.

"—heard the entire Celestial Harmony Pavilion collapsed—"

"—sect master was fighting someone—"

"—demonic infiltrators. Has to be—"

"—but why would Elder Yao and the others look so defeated—"

A young Outer Sect disciple nearby was explaining his theory to anyone who would listen. "I'm telling you, it was a tribulation! The sect master was breaking through to Half-Step Immortal Realm, and the heavens themselves attacked her! That's why there were so many explosions!"

"Don't be stupid," his companion replied. "Tribulations don't work like that. Besides, if the sect master were advancing, why would the elders look injured?"

"Maybe they were helping her resist the tribulation?"

"That's not how any of this works . . ."

The speculation continued, growing more outlandish by the minute. Mei Lin heard theories involving secret techniques gone wrong, attacking spirit beasts, spontaneous formation failures, and one particularly creative suggestion that the sect master had been testing a new ultimate technique that accidentally damaged the pavilion.

No one was close to the truth. How could they be? The reality was so much stranger than any of their theories.

The crowd quieted gradually as Sect Master Ming Yue stepped onto the raised platform. The two freed elders flanked her: Yao and Fan. All of them showed visible signs of their ordeals. Torn robes, bruises, exhaustion written across their features.

A murmur ran through the assembled disciples. Seeing their leadership in such a state was unprecedented. The Pure Soul Sect prided itself on composure and dignity. This kind of public display of weakness was unheard of.

"Disciples of the Pure Soul Sect," Ming Yue began, and the courtyard fell completely silent. Her voice carried clearly across the space, amplified by her cultivation technique. "I stand before you tonight to acknowledge a grave error in judgment."

The murmuring started again, louder this time. Mei Lin could feel the shock rippling through the crowd. Sect masters didn't admit errors. They were supposed to be infallible, wise beyond question.

"Over the past month, I have led this sect down a path that contradicts everything we stand for. I authorized attacks against other sects. I sent disciples into battles that served no purpose beyond escalation. I abandoned our core principles in favor of aggression and violence."

The crowd's reaction was growing more vocal. Disciples looked at each other, confusion and concern evident on their faces.

Elder Fan stepped forward, raising his hand for silence. The gesture worked; the courtyard quieted enough for Ming Yue to continue.

"I cannot undo the harm that has been done," the sect master said. "I cannot bring back those we lost or erase the pain we caused. But I can tell you that this path ends tonight. The Pure Soul Sect will no longer participate in this war. We will return to our founding principles: peace, understanding, and the preservation of life."

"But the demonic sects!" someone shouted from the crowd. "They're expanding, corrupting—"

"They are cultivators," Ming Yue interrupted firmly. "Different from us in practice but not inherently evil. Our conflict with them was based on false assumptions and flawed intelligence. Assumptions that I should have questioned more carefully."

She was being deliberately vague, Mei Lin realized. Not lying, but not explaining the mind control either. Probably wise; if the disciples learned their sect master had been a puppet for weeks, it would shatter any remaining trust in the leadership. Better to frame it as poor judgment that had been corrected.

"To demonstrate our commitment to this new path," Ming Yue continued, "I have invited a guest to join us tonight. Someone who helped me see the error of our recent actions. Someone who represents the possibility of cooperation between different cultivation paths." She gestured to the side of the platform. "I present Slifer, Supreme Elder and Sect Master of not one, but two demonic sects."

The reaction was explosive.

Gasps echoed across the courtyard. Several disciples actually stepped backward. Mei Lin heard someone behind her say, "Is she insane? Inviting a demon into our home?"

Slifer walked onto the platform, completely comfortable with being the center of attention. His white hair and beard gleamed in the moonlight. His black robes with their red trim stood in stark contrast to the sea of white and blue surrounding him.

He looked exactly like what he was: an ancient, powerful demonic cultivator standing before thousands of disciples who'd been taught to hate and fear everything he represented.

"That's him?" a voice near Mei Lin whispered. "He doesn't look that dangerous. Just some old man."

"Don't be fooled," someone else replied. "Demonic cultivators are masters of deception. He's probably suppressing his aura."

Slifer reached the center of the platform and tilted his head respectfully to the assembled crowd. The gesture was perfect: not too deep, not too shallow. Exactly the level of respect appropriate for greeting disciples of another sect.

"Disciples of the Pure Soul Sect," he said, his voice surprisingly warm and grandfatherly. "Your sect master has shown great courage tonight, both in battle and in her willingness to change course. I hope that our two sects can work together to build a future where differences in cultivation practice don't lead to bloodshed."

Ming Yue stepped forward to stand beside him. "Sect Master Slifer and I have resolved the misunderstandings between our sects. From this moment forward, the Pure Soul Sect and the Black Rose Sect are allies. Anyone who harms members of his sect will answer to me personally."

The declaration sent another wave of shock through the crowd. In the past, the Pure Soul Sect had remained neutral during conflicts. As for allying with a demonic sect, that was unthinkable. It went against centuries of tradition, against the very foundation of righteous cultivation.

Mei Lin found herself smiling despite the chaos around her. She'd been there. She'd seen Slifer keep his word, had watched him carefully free her sect master rather than harm her. If anyone in this courtyard understood that demonic cultivators weren't automatically evil, it was her.

Slifer was turning to return to his position at the platform's edge when movement caught Mei Lin's eye.

A disciple in the middle of the crowd suddenly launched himself forward. Peak Nascent Soul cultivation propelled him through the air like an arrow, his trajectory aimed directly at Slifer's unprotected back. Spiritual energy condensed around the disciple's fist—a technique meant not to disable or capture, but to kill.

Several things happened at once.

The assassin struck an invisible barrier one foot from Slifer's back. He bounced off like he'd hit solid stone, his momentum completely arrested by whatever protection the old cultivator had active.

Before the would-be assassin could recover his balance or launch a second attack, a figure appeared beside him faster than Mei Lin's eyes could track. Caelum grabbed the disciple by the throat with one hand and lifted him clear off the ground. The young cultivator's face was cold and emotionless, nothing like the respectful student who'd bowed to his master earlier.

Caelum looked to Slifer, still holding the struggling disciple aloft. The question was clear without words: What should I do with this one?

The courtyard had erupted into chaos. Disciples were shouting, some moving forward to attack the demonic cultivators, others trying to restore order. The elders were calling for calm, but the situation was seconds away from becoming a riot.

Slifer raised one hand, and somehow the gesture cut through the noise. People quieted, if only to see what the demonic sect master would do.

He walked calmly over to where Caelum held the assassin and placed his hand on the struggling disciple's forehead. Golden light flashed so briefly that Mei Lin almost missed it.

The assassin went limp. Not dead, she realized, but unconscious. The distant, controlled look in his eyes had faded, replaced by natural sleep, and two Pure Soul Sect members hurried forward to carry their fellow away.

The crowd remained tense, but the immediate crisis had passed. Mei Lin saw several disciples who'd been preparing to attack relax slightly, their postures shifting from aggressive to uncertain.

Sect Master Ming Yue stepped forward again. "What you just witnessed is exactly why we must change our approach. The true enemy isn't demonic cultivation or righteous cultivation. It's ignorance. It's allowing ourselves to be manipulated by fear and prejudice."

She began walking along the platform's edge, making eye contact with different sections of the crowd as she spoke. "The Pure Soul Sect was founded on principles of understanding and compassion. We were supposed to be the cultivators who saw the person beneath the label, who recognized that darkness can exist in any heart and light can be found in unexpected places." Her voice grew stronger, more passionate. "We lost sight of that. I lost sight of that. But tonight, we begin again. We return to what we were meant to be: Not warriors, but healers. Not destroyers, but protectors. Not judges of who deserves compassion, but practitioners of universal understanding."

Elder Yao stepped forward. "The sect master speaks truth. I spent weeks believing I was acting righteously while sending you into conflicts that served no righteous purpose. I am ashamed of what I did. But I am grateful that I've been brought out of that darkness."

Elder Fan nodded. "The demonic cultivators we've been taught to hate showed us more mercy tonight than we would have shown them. That should tell us something about the assumptions we've been making."

The crowd was quieting now, the initial shock wearing off into something more thoughtful. Mei Lin could see disciples exchanging glances, could hear whispered conversations that sounded less panicked and more contemplative.

"I'm not asking you to love demonic cultivation," Ming Yue said. "I'm not even asking you to like it. I'm asking you to recognize that the people who practice it are still people. They can be kind or cruel, wise or foolish, worthy of trust or deserving of suspicion, just like anyone else." She gestured to Slifer and Caelum. "These two entered our sect tonight. They could have killed me. They could have killed all the elders. Instead, they freed us from control we didn't even know we were under. They saved us, at great risk to themselves, because they believed it was the right thing to do."

Slifer looked vaguely embarrassed by the praise, which Mei Lin found oddly endearing.

"Go back to your quarters," Ming Yue told the disciples. "Think about what you've learned tonight. Tomorrow, we begin the work of rebuilding what was damaged. Both in our sect and in our understanding of the world."

The crowd began to disperse slowly. Mei Lin could still hear arguments and debates breaking out as people walked away, but the immediate danger had passed. The Pure Soul Sect wasn't going to tear itself apart. Not tonight, anyway.

Mei Lin stayed where she was, watching as disciples filed out of the courtyard in small groups. Some looked angry, others confused, many simply exhausted by the emotional upheaval of the evening. But none of them looked like they were preparing to attack the demonic cultivators, which felt like a victory of sorts.

Her eyes drifted back to the platform where Sect Master Ming Yue was speaking quietly with Slifer. The two sect masters stood side by side, discussing something, while Caelum waited nearby, ever the attentive student.

It was surreal. Wrong, according to everything she'd been taught. Demonic and righteous cultivators weren't supposed to cooperate. They were supposed to be eternal enemies, locked in philosophical combat until one side prevailed.

But watching them together, Mei Lin couldn't see any evil in Slifer's elderly face. She couldn't sense any malice in Caelum's respectful demeanor. They were just people. Cultivators who'd chosen a different path but who were still capable of kindness, of mercy, of keeping their word even when it would have been easier to break it.

A smile tugged at Mei Lin's lips.

Her sect was back. Not the warlike, aggressive organization it had become over the past month, but the real Pure Soul Sect. The one that valued understanding over judgment, peace over violence, wisdom over blind tradition.

And if someone had told her a week ago that it would be demonic cultivators who helped restore that vision, she would have thought them insane.

But here they were. Two members of the Black Rose Sect had walked into the Pure Soul Sect and defeated them utterly. Not through overwhelming force or brutal subjugation, but by freeing them from the corruption that had twisted them away from their true purpose.

Mei Lin looked up at the night sky, at the stars visible above the courtyard. Somewhere out there, the woman who did this was probably planning her next move, which meant there would be more conflicts ahead, more challenges to face.

But tonight, the Pure Soul Sect had taken its first step back toward the light. And they'd done it with the help of people they'd been taught to hate.

Maybe, Mei Lin thought, the world was more complicated than she'd been raised to believe. Maybe the labels of demonic and righteous were less important than the choices individuals made. Maybe there was hope for something better than endless conflict between different cultivation paths.

She turned and headed back toward her quarters, her heart lighter than it had been in weeks. Tomorrow would bring new challenges. But tonight, for the first time in a long time, she had hope.

And she'd learned an important lesson: never judge a cultivator by their sect's reputation.

Judge them by their actions.

CHAPTER THIRTEEN

As the excitement died down, Slifer stood in the courtyard of the Pure Soul Sect, looking at Ming Yue.

"Caelum and I need to move quickly," Slifer said, turning his attention back to the immediate problem. "If we want to free the White Tiger Sect Master from Lady Chi's control before she realizes what we're doing, we can't waste time."

Ming Yue straightened, her white robes still torn and scorched from their earlier confrontation. Despite her exhaustion, her eyes showed determination. "I should accompany you. The White Tiger Sect and Pure Soul Sect have maintained diplomatic relations for centuries. My presence might help avoid unnecessary conflicts."

Slifer opened his mouth to decline. Taking an Ascendant cultivator who had just been freed from mind control into another potentially dangerous situation seemed like asking for trouble. She needed time to recover, both physically and mentally. The weight of what Lady Chi had made her do was still visible in her expression, and throwing her into another fight so soon felt wrong.

But then he paused, reconsidering.

Ming Yue was a genuine Ascendant Realm cultivator. Her power was real, earned through centuries of cultivation rather than borrowed from System cards. If they encountered serious resistance at the White Tiger Sect, her abilities could make the difference between success and failure. More importantly, from a practical standpoint, having her there might save him a considerable number of Karmic Credits. His recent expenditure on Critical Block Cards and the Temporal Stasis Field had put a significant dent in his reserves.

"Actually," Slifer said slowly, "that would be helpful. Your knowledge of the other sects and their internal politics could prove valuable."

Ming Yue nodded, relief evident on her face. She wanted to help, needed to help after everything she'd been forced to do. The guilt of her actions under Lady Chi's influence wouldn't be washed away easily, but taking action against the woman responsible was a start.

Caelum had been standing quietly to the side, observing the exchange. His sword, Starforge, hung at his hip, the blade having returned to its dormant state after the earlier excitement. The young man's loyalty stat had been at one hundred percent for some time now, and it showed in how he waited patiently for his master's decisions without questioning or pushing.

"Gather what you need," Slifer told Ming Yue. "We leave in five minutes."

She bowed and hurried toward the remains of the pavilion, presumably to collect some belongings or inform her elders of the situation. Slifer watched her go, then turned his attention to his disciple.

"You ready for this?" Slifer asked.

Caelum's hand rested on Starforge's hilt. "Always, Master. Though, I have to admit, I'm curious about this White Tiger Sect. I've heard their cultivation methods focus heavily on physical transformation and beast integration."

"That's correct," Slifer replied, pulling up his System interface to check their current resources. "The White Tiger Sect practices a form of cultivation that merges them with tiger spirits. Their disciples are known for aggressive combat styles and transformation abilities. They're not subtle fighters."

His credit balance showed 90,570 Karmic Credits remaining. The earlier battle with Ming Yue had been expensive, burning through cards he'd hoped to save for emergencies. The Celestial Guardian Formation purchase for his own sect had cost fifty thousand alone. He needed to be more conservative with his spending, but he also couldn't afford to fail these missions.

The System had made it clear: convert or kill demonic cultivators to advance. The three major righteous sect masters being under Lady Chi's control complicated that mission significantly. If he could free them from her influence and potentially turn them into allies, it would open up new opportunities for fulfilling his objectives without bloodshed.

Ming Yue returned faster than expected, now wearing fresh robes and carrying what looked like a jade communication token. Her hair was tied back in a practical style rather than the elaborate arrangement from before. She looked ready for combat.

"My elders are securing the sect," she explained. "I've instructed them to be vigilant for any signs of Lady Chi's influence among our disciples. Elder Yao will lead in my absence."

Slifer nodded as he activated the Dimensional Slide technique. The spatial manipulation came more easily now after all his practice. Maybe it was the higher cultivation level, or maybe he was just getting used to tearing holes in reality. Neither option was particularly comforting when he stopped to think about it.

The portal opened with a quiet rushing sound. Through the swirling gateway, Slifer could see stone buildings and training grounds. He'd targeted the outer disciple area of the White Tiger Sect, hoping to avoid the heavily defended inner sections.

"Impressive," Ming Yue said, studying the portal. "I understand now how you managed to infiltrate my chambers so easily. Spatial techniques of this level are exceedingly rare."

"It has its uses," Slifer replied, stepping toward the opening. He didn't feel like explaining that he'd used the supernatural store that existed only in his head to copy the technique off his disciple. Some things were better left mysterious.

The transition through the portal was smoother than his earlier attempts. Slifer emerged on a stone pathway between two wooden buildings. Training dummies lined one wall, their straw stuffing spilling out from countless claw marks. The distinctive scent of tiger musk hung in the air.

Caelum followed a moment later, his hand instinctively moving to rest on Starforge's hilt. The young man had the good sense to look alert and ready. Ming Yue stepped through last, her spiritual senses already spreading out to map their surroundings.

Slifer glanced around, noting the empty pathways and quiet buildings. No disciples in sight. No one sleeping in the beds they'd accidentally portaled into. He'd take that as a win after the awkward situation with Mei Lin.

"I've been here many times for sect leader meetings," Ming Yue said, orienting herself. "The sect master's personal quarters are in the eastern section, near the main cultivation hall. If we take the north path and cut through the inner courtyard, we should be able to reach them without passing through the most heavily guarded areas."

"Lead the way," Slifer said. "But stay alert. If Lady Chi has the same control over this sect that she had over yours, we might run into problems."

They started down the path, moving with the enhanced speed of cultivators. The Outer Sect area remained eerily quiet. Most disciples were probably at the evening meal or in their quarters for personal cultivation. The timing had worked in their favor.

They were halfway across a large training courtyard when Slifer felt it. A massive spiritual pressure suddenly focused on their location, heavy and oppressive. The air itself seemed to thicken, and Slifer's instincts screamed danger.

All three of them looked up simultaneously.

An enormous white tiger's head materialized in the air above them, easily the size of a building. Its fur was pure white, almost glowing in the moonlight, with black stripes running across its face in elegant patterns. The eyes were intelligent and ancient. The creature hadn't fully manifested its body, just the head emerging from some spatial pocket or dimensional hiding place.

The tiger's mouth hung open lazily, revealing teeth the size of swords. It was looking directly at them with what could only be described as mild curiosity, the way a cat might observe a mouse it hadn't decided whether to eat.

"That's Baiyun," Ming Yue said, her voice tight. "The White Tiger Sect's guardian beast. Peak Ascendant Realm. I should have anticipated this."

Slifer felt his heart sink. Of course there would be a guardian beast. Major sects always had some kind of ultimate defense, whether it was a guardian spirit, a powerful formation, or in this case, a massive tiger that could probably eat him in one bite.

Caelum's hand had moved to Starforge's hilt. "Master, we're suppressing our auras completely. How did it detect us?"

"Smell, most likely," Ming Yue answered before Slifer could. "Baiyun's sensory abilities aren't based on detecting spiritual energy. The White Tiger bloodline grants enhanced physical senses, and Baiyun has cultivated those abilities for over a thousand years. He can smell foreign presences in his territory regardless of aura suppression."

The massive tiger's eyes narrowed slightly as he evaluated them. Then he opened his mouth wider.

The roar that emerged wasn't just sound. It was a physical force that slammed into them like a wall of compressed air, carrying enough spiritual pressure to make Slifer's bones ache. The shock wave spread outward from their position, and all across the sect, alarm formations activated. Bells began ringing. Lights flared to life in windows as disciples woke and scrambled to respond to the emergency.

Ming Yue turned to look at Slifer, her expression apologetic but expectant.

She was an Ascendant cultivator, but Baiyun was Peak Ascendant Realm, at least one sub-stage above her. More importantly, this was the guardian beast's territory. Fighting him here, where he held every advantage, would be suicide for her. She'd only just recovered from Lady Chi's mind control. She didn't have the strength for this kind of battle.

As for Slifer, he was the demonic sect master who'd survived an Ascendant's full assault without a scratch. The man who'd killed a Half-Step Immortal and sealed another in a cauldron. In her mind, a Peak Ascendant guardian beast was probably nothing to him.

Slifer sighed deeply, already calculating the absurd number of Karmic Credits this was going to cost him. Peak Ascendant Realm meant the beast was at least three full major realms above his Core Formation cultivation. Without System cards, he wouldn't last one second. With cards, this was going to drain his resources faster than water through a broken dam.

"Handle anyone who tries to interfere," Slifer said, looking at Caelum and Ming Yue. "And find out where Feng Lei is. I'll deal with our oversized friend here."

Ming Yue's eyes widened slightly, but she nodded. Caelum simply drew Starforge, the blade gleaming with starlight as it emerged from its sheath.

Slifer pushed off the ground, using a basic flight technique to rise into the air. He needed to draw the beast away from the others and give them room to work. As he ascended, the massive tiger's head tracked his movement, eyes glowing brighter.

When Slifer reached roughly the same altitude as Baiyun's floating head, he stopped and simply floated there, meeting the guardian beast's gaze. Up close, the creature was even more impressive. Each individual hair of his white fur was clearly visible, and the black stripes seemed to pulse with inner power. The teeth in that massive mouth could probably bite through a mountain.

"You are intruders," Baiyun rumbled, the voice deep and resonant like distant thunder. "Explain your presence in my territory or face the consequences."

At least he was willing to talk first. Some guardian beasts just attacked on sight.

"We're here on urgent business regarding your sect master," Slifer replied, keeping his tone respectful. "Feng Lei has been compromised by an external force. We're trying to help him."

Baiyun's eyes narrowed further. "The sect master shows no signs of compromise. He is strong, decisive, and is leading our sect toward proper glory. You speak lies to justify your invasion."

"Feng Lei's mind is being controlled by an Immortal Realm cultivator named Lady Chi," Slifer continued. "We've already freed the sect masters of both the Pure Soul Sect and Heavenly Light Sect from her influence. Ming Yue herself stands down there, freed from the same control."

The tiger's gaze shifted downward, focusing on Ming Yue for a long moment. She raised her hand in a simple wave, confirming her presence and presumably lending credibility to Slifer's words.

"The Pure Soul Sect Master appears genuine," Baiyun acknowledged. "But this changes nothing. I cannot allow unknown cultivators to approach our sect master based on unverified claims. If what you say is true, provide proof. If you cannot, leave our territory immediately."

Slifer had expected that response. Guardian beasts were notoriously stubborn about protecting their charges. It was literally their purpose for existing.

"I understand your position," Slifer said carefully. "But we don't have time for lengthy verification processes. Lady Chi will realize what we're doing soon, if she hasn't already. Every moment we delay gives her more time to prepare countermeasures or flee with Feng Lei."

"Then you have chosen consequences," Baiyun replied simply.

The massive head began to materialize more fully as the neck and shoulders emerged from the spatial pocket. The beast was enormous, dwarfing Slifer completely. His paws alone were the size of buildings, and claws like curved swords extended from each toe.

Slifer reached for his System interface, pulling up the Shop as fast as possible. He didn't have time for careful selection. He needed overwhelming power, and he needed it now.

Ten-Minute Ascendant Power Card	Cost: 15,000 Karmic Credits
Ascendant Strike Card	Cost: 8,000 Karmic Credits
Heavenly Judgment Card	Cost: 12,000 Karmic Credits
Critical Block Card x3	Cost: 2,700 Karmic Credits

He winced at the prices but started making purchases. The Ten-Minute Ascendant Power Card would temporarily raise his cultivation to Ascendant Realm. Three Critical Block Cards would keep him alive during the initial exchanges. An Ascendant Strike Card would give him offensive capability beyond his normal level.

Ding!
Purchase successful.
37,700 Karmic Credits deducted.
Current balance: 52,870 Karmic Credits

Nearly forty thousand credits gone in an instant. *This had better work.*

Slifer activated the Ten-Minute Ascendant Power Card first. Golden light erupted from his body as the transformation took hold, and his spiritual energy suddenly expanded to levels he'd rarely experienced before. His Core Formation cultivation remained, but a shell of Ascendant Realm power wrapped around it, giving him temporary access to abilities far beyond his actual stage.

Baiyun's eyes widened slightly, the first sign of genuine surprise the guardian beast had shown. "You conceal your true cultivation? Interesting. This explains your confidence."

Before Slifer could respond, the tiger struck.

Baiyun's paw swept through the air faster than something that size had any right to move. The attack carried enough force to pulverize stone, claws extended to rend through whatever they touched. The air itself screamed as the massive limb displaced it.

The first Critical Block Card activated automatically.

An invisible barrier materialized directly in the path of the attack. The paw struck the shield with a sound like thunder, and the impact sent shock waves rippling outward. Buildings below shook from the force. Windows shattered. But the barrier held, and Slifer remained completely unharmed.

Baiyun pulled back his paw and examined the claws as if checking for damage. "Fascinating. Your defensive techniques are formidable."

The tiger opened his mouth and roared again, but this time the sound carried visible distortions in the air. The roar became a weapon, compressed sound waves designed to shatter bones and rupture organs. The technique was called Heavenly Tiger's Verdict, and it had killed countless enemies over the centuries.

The second Critical Block Card triggered.

The sound wave struck the barrier and simply stopped, unable to penetrate the absolute defense. Slifer felt nothing, not even a vibration. The card's protection was complete.

"You're very durable," Baiyun observed, sounding more intrigued than frustrated. "But defense alone will not save you. Eventually, you will exhaust your techniques, and then I will end this."

The guardian beast was right, of course. Critical Block Cards were powerful but limited. He had one left, and then he'd be vulnerable. Time to test his offensive capabilities.

Slifer activated the Ascendant Strike Card.

His right hand blazed with golden light as the card's power channeled through his arm. He thrust his palm forward, and a beam of concentrated golden light erupted from his hand. The attack crossed the distance between him and Baiyun in an instant and struck the tiger directly in the chest. The explosion was massive, a sphere of golden fire that completely engulfed the guardian beast's upper body.

When the light faded, Baiyun was still there. The white fur was singed in places, and the beast had been pushed back over a dozen meters, but he was very much alive and conscious. The attack had hurt, but it hadn't been decisive.

"Impressive," Baiyun growled, and now there was genuine respect in his voice.

The tiger's body began to glow with white light, fur standing on end. This was the White Tiger's Divine Armor technique, a defensive ability that coated the user in layers of compressed spiritual energy. It would make the already durable beast even harder to damage.

Slifer grimaced. His expensive strike card had barely scratched the thing, and now the beast was activating defensive techniques. This was going exactly as he'd feared it would: a battle of attrition where Slifer burned through expensive cards while the guardian beast relied on his natural abilities.

He needed a different approach.

Baiyun lunged forward, closing the distance with frightening speed. One paw swung horizontally, claws extended, while the beast's mouth opened wide to reveal those sword-sized teeth. The attack came from two directions simultaneously, forcing Slifer to choose which threat to prioritize.

His last Critical Block Card activated as he chose to defend against the paw strike as the greater immediate danger. The invisible barrier appeared and caught the massive limb, but that left Slifer completely exposed to the bite attack.

Slifer activated his Phase Ability.

His body became intangible, and the massive jaws snapped shut on empty air. Teeth passed harmlessly through his incorporeal form, unable to make contact. The technique only lasted a few seconds, but it was enough. When he resolidified, he was already moving, dodging to the side to create distance.

Baiyun's eyes narrowed. "Spatial techniques and intangibility? Your abilities are diverse, intruder. But they will not be enough."

The guardian beast's form began to shift. His body grew even larger, muscles bulging beneath the white fur. Black stripes spread and multiplied, covering more surface area. The eyes blazed brighter, and a third eye opened in the center of his forehead, glowing with pure white light.

This was the True Guardian Form, a transformation that pushed Baiyun to the absolute peak of his power. In this state, the beast could battle even

Half-Step Immortal cultivators for extended periods. The spiritual pressure radiating from his body intensified dramatically.

Slifer felt the pressure like a physical weight pressing down on him. His temporary Ascendant Realm power helped, but the gap between Half-Step Immortal and Peak Ascendant was enormous. Without more cards, he was going to lose this fight.

He pulled up the System Shop again and searched frantically for something that could turn the tide. His credit balance had dropped significantly, but he still had enough for one more major purchase.

> Name: Binding of Eternal Servitude
> Description: Allows user to bind any target to complete obedience. Target must be weakened to 50% health first.
> Cost: 25,000 Karmic Credits

That wouldn't work. Baiyun was nowhere near weak enough, and burning that many credits on something that might fail seemed foolish.

> Name: Thundergod's Descent
> Description: Summons massive lightning tribulation to strike target area. Damage scales with target's cultivation level.
> Cost: 20,000 Karmic Credits

That was more promising. Lightning techniques were effective against beasts, especially ones focused on physical cultivation rather than spiritual defense.

Slifer made the purchase and immediately activated the card.

> *Ding!*
> Purchase successful.
> 20,000 Karmic Credits deducted.
> Current balance: 32,870 Karmic Credits

The sky above them split open.

Dark clouds materialized from nothing, swirling into a massive vortex directly overhead. Lightning began to arc between the clouds, growing brighter and more frequent with each passing second. The spiritual energy in the air became charged, crackling with barely contained power.

Baiyun looked up, and for the first time, the guardian beast's expression showed concern. "You summoned a tribulation? That is dangerous, even for you. The heavens do not discriminate in their targets."

"I know," Slifer replied grimly. His temporary Ascendant Realm power and Critical Block Cards should protect him from the worst of it, but this was definitely a gamble.

The lightning struck.

A massive bolt of pure white energy descended from the heavens and struck Baiyun directly. The light was blinding, forcing Slifer to look away. The sound was indescribable, a crack of thunder so loud it seemed to shake the foundations of reality itself.

When Slifer's vision cleared, Baiyun was falling.

The guardian beast's massive form dropped from the sky and crashed into the ground below with earth-shaking force. Disciples scattered in all directions as the impact created a crater easily thirty meters across. Dust and debris flew everywhere, obscuring the scene.

Slifer descended carefully, ready to retreat or attack as needed. The dust began to settle and revealed Baiyun's prone form in the center of the crater. The white fur was scorched black in places, and several of the guardian beast's legs were twisted at unnatural angles. The creature was breathing heavily but alive, his three eyes now closed.

He was unconscious.

Slifer landed gently on top of the beast's massive head, standing between his ears. The temporary Ascendant power would last for another few minutes or so, but the battle was effectively over. He'd burned through more than half his remaining Karmic Credits, but he'd successfully neutralized the White Tiger Sect's ultimate defense.

The disciples who'd been watching from a safe distance stared in shocked silence. Their supposedly invincible guardian beast, the Peak Ascendant Realm protector of their sect, had been defeated by a single intruder. The implications were terrifying.

Ming Yue and Caelum approached the crater's edge, and Slifer noticed they were both unharmed. Several White Tiger Sect elders lay unconscious on the ground behind them, along with a handful of disciples who'd apparently been foolish enough to engage them in combat.

"We interrogated the elders and disciples," Ming Yue reported. "The sect master was here until approximately ten minutes ago. According to witnesses, he suddenly flew away without explanation or destination. He simply left."

Slifer felt his frown deepen. Ten minutes. They'd missed Feng Lei by ten minutes. That couldn't be a coincidence. Lady Chi must have realized what they were doing and warned him to flee. Or perhaps she'd sensed something through her mind control connection and pulled him away preemptively.

Either way, they'd lost the element of surprise. She knew they were coming for her puppets now.

"Did any of the elders show signs of being under Lady Chi's control?" Slifer asked.

Caelum shook his head. "No detectable signs of mind manipulation, Master. We checked thoroughly using the detection method you taught us. Their spiritual signatures are clean."

That was puzzling. If Lady Chi only controlled the sect master, why was the White Tiger Sect so eager to go to war with the demonic sects?

Then Slifer remembered something about the White Tiger cultivation method. Their techniques emphasized physical transformation and beast-spirit integration, but they also had a secondary effect. The cultivation path gradually shifted practitioners' temperaments to match tiger behavior: territorial, aggressive, predatory. It wasn't mind control; it was just the natural result of their chosen path.

The White Tiger Sect didn't need to be controlled to want war with demonic cultivators. Their cultivation method made them aggressive by nature, and their history with demonic sects was filled with conflict. Lady Chi had simply found the easiest puppet to manipulate, someone whose natural inclinations aligned with her goals.

"They're just naturally confrontational," Slifer said, more to himself than to his companions. "Lady Chi picked the perfect target. She didn't need to change Feng Lei's personality, just nudge his existing aggressive tendencies in the direction she wanted."

Ming Yue nodded slowly. "That makes sense. The White Tiger Sect has always been more militant than the rest of us. It doesn't take much to declare war."

Slifer was about to respond when the System interface suddenly appeared before his eyes completely unbidden. A red alert box materialized, the text inside flashing urgently.

Ding!
Warning: Your disciple Hughie is in mortal danger.
Current status: Life-threatening injury. 87% probability of death within 60 minutes.
Immediate intervention required.

His blood ran cold.

CHAPTER FOURTEEN

Hughie shifted uncomfortably as the spiritual chains dug into his wrists. The chains were real, not just for show, and they were suppressing his cultivation down to practically nothing. Ace had insisted they make everything look authentic, which apparently meant actually restraining him like a proper prisoner.

"This is uncomfortable," Hughie muttered under his breath.

"Good," Li Fenghao's voice echoed in his mind from the ring on his finger. "If you looked comfortable, they'd know something was wrong. A captured disciple should look miserable."

"I am miserable. These chains hurt."

"They're supposed to hurt. That's how you know they're working."

Hughie resisted the urge to argue with the ancient immortal. Li Fenghao had been giving him commentary for the entire journey to the Heavenly Light Sect, offering observations about cultivation techniques and occasionally criticizing Hughie's posture. The old man meant well, probably, but his constant presence in Hughie's mind was exhausting.

Ahead of them, the gates of the Heavenly Light Sect rose into view. They were massive, easily fifteen meters tall, and made of some white stone that seemed to glow with a bright light. Golden script covered the surface, formations that Hughie couldn't begin to understand. The gates stood open, but the spiritual pressure emanating from them made it clear that entry was by permission only.

"Impressive architecture," Li Fenghao observed. "They've maintained the foundations properly. I remember when this sect was first established. The formations were crude back then, barely capable of stopping a determined Origin Realm cultivator. These, though... These could hold off an Ascendant for days."

Hughie didn't respond. He was too busy trying to look appropriately defeated and angry, which was harder than it sounded. Master Slifer had given him specific instructions about how to behave. Act scared but defiant. Show anger but not too much. Basically, behave like someone who'd been captured by their greatest enemy.

The problem was that Ace wasn't actually his enemy. The Heavenly Light Sect Master had been nothing but courteous during their journey, even apologizing for the chains being necessary. It was hard to maintain anger toward someone who kept asking if he needed water breaks.

Two guards stood at the gates, both wearing white robes trimmed with gold. They straightened as Ace approached, their expressions shifting from bored routine to shocked recognition.

"Sect Master!" The taller guard stepped forward, his eyes widening. "We heard that you were... that the Black Rose Sect had..."

"Had captured me?" Ace finished calmly. "The rumors were accurate. For a time."

The shorter guard's gaze shifted to Hughie, taking in the chains and the obvious suppression of his cultivation. "Is this...?"

"A prisoner from the Black Rose Sect," Ace confirmed. "One of Slifer's personal disciples. We have much to discuss, but first, I need to see Elder Lu Pan immediately. Where is he?"

The guards exchanged glances. Hughie noticed something pass between them, some unspoken communication that made his instincts prickle. Li Fenghao noticed it too because the old immortal's voice turned sharp in Hughie's mind.

"They're suspicious. Their spiritual signatures are fluctuating. Either they're very nervous, or they're preparing to attack."

"Send word to the council chamber," the taller guard said slowly. "All the elders will want to hear about this."

"I specifically asked for Elder Lu Pan," Ace repeated, his tone hardening slightly. "Not the full council. Just him."

"With respect, Sect Master, the council has been anxious about your fate. They'll want to verify your identity and hear your report directly." The guard's hand had moved closer to the sword at his waist, a subtle movement that probably wasn't meant to be threatening but absolutely was.

Hughie felt the spiritual pressure in the air shift. Ace's aura, which had been carefully suppressed during their approach, suddenly flexed outward. It wasn't an attack, just a demonstration of power. The two guards took an involuntary step backward.

"I am Ace, Sect Master of the Heavenly Light Sect," Ace said quietly. "I do not need to verify my identity to my own guards. Now, you will send for Elder Lu Pan, and you will do it immediately, or we will discuss why you felt the need to question your sect master's orders."

The taller guard's face went pale. "Of course, Sect Master. Forgiveness, please. I'll fetch Elder Lu Pan at once." He turned and practically ran into the sect grounds.

The shorter guard remained, looking distinctly uncomfortable. His eyes kept darting between Ace and Hughie, as if trying to reconcile what he was seeing with whatever information he'd received previously.

"How did you escape?" the guard asked, then immediately looked like he regretted speaking.

Ace's expression didn't change. "The Black Rose Sect made a mistake. They underestimated me, and I took advantage of that mistake. The details will be shared with the council in due time."

"And the prisoner?"

"Is leverage," Ace said simply. "Slifer values his disciples highly. This one, in particular, seems to hold special significance to him."

Hughie tried to look appropriately angry at being called leverage. He glared at Ace, putting as much genuine irritation as he could muster into the expression. The chains were still digging into his wrists, so that part wasn't difficult.

"You won't get away with this," Hughie said, trying to sound threatening despite his current state. "Master Slifer will come for me. He'll tear this whole sect apart to get me back."

"Let him try," Ace replied, playing his part perfectly. "I look forward to the confrontation."

"That was good," Li Fenghao commented in Hughie's mind. "You sounded genuinely angry. Keep that energy. These people need to believe you're a real prisoner, not a willing participant in whatever scheme your master has concocted."

Several minutes passed in uncomfortable silence. The remaining guard kept glancing at Hughie, probably trying to assess what level of threat a chained Nascent Soul cultivator could pose. Eventually, footsteps echoed from within the sect grounds.

Elder Lu Pan appeared, flanked by two other elders Hughie didn't recognize. Lu Pan was an older man with a long gray beard and sharp eyes that seemed to take in everything at once. He wore the traditional white and gold robes of the Heavenly Light Sect, but his were more elaborate, with additional embroidery that marked his senior status.

"Sect Master Ace," Lu Pan greeted. "We feared the worst when news reached us of your capture."

"The reports of my defeat were accurate," Ace replied. "The reports of my continued imprisonment were not."

Lu Pan's gaze shifted to Hughie, and Hughie felt a subtle probe of spiritual sense wash over him. The elder was checking his cultivation, his spiritual signature, probably trying to determine if he posed any threat. The chains made it difficult for anyone to get an accurate reading, which was probably intentional.

"This is one of Slifer's disciples?" Lu Pan asked.

"His name is Hughie," Ace confirmed. "He was present during my capture. When I escaped, I brought him with me."

One of the other elders, a woman with severe features and tightly bound hair, stepped forward. "How did you escape, Sect Master? We received intelligence that you were being held in the Black Rose Sect's highest security formation, guarded by multiple Origin Realm cultivators."

"Intelligence can be incomplete," Ace said. "Or deliberately misleading. The circumstances of my escape are complicated, and I would prefer to explain them to the full council rather than repeat the story multiple times."

"Of course," Lu Pan said smoothly. "But you understand our caution. The reports we received were quite specific about your capture and imprisonment. Some of us had begun discussing succession plans."

The air grew tense. Hughie didn't know much about sect politics, but even he could recognize the implications of that statement. Succession plans meant they'd been preparing to replace Ace as sect master. Either they'd genuinely believed he was lost forever, or someone had been actively working to push him out.

"I understand your caution," Ace said, his tone still calm but carrying an edge now. "What I don't understand is why you would discuss succession before confirming my death. The sect master's life token has not shattered, which means I remain alive. By sect law, any discussion of succession while I live is grounds for disciplinary action."

The severe-looking elder's expression tightened. "We meant no disrespect, Sect Master. We simply needed to prepare for all possibilities."

"Did you?" Ace said flatly. "Well, as you can see, that particular possibility has not come to pass. Now, I would like to secure this prisoner in our detention facilities and then convene with Elder Lu Pan. The rest of the council can be briefed at a more appropriate time."

"The council chamber would be more suitable," the severe elder insisted. "We can hold the prisoner there while we discuss matters of sect security."

"Elder Yulan," Lu Pan interrupted gently, "perhaps the sect master's suggestion has merit. He has just returned from captivity and likely needs time to gather his thoughts before a full council session."

Yulan's jaw clenched, but she bowed slightly. "As you say, First Elder."

Hughie noticed the way she said "First Elder" with just a hint of emphasis. There was tension here, factional disputes that went beyond the immediate situation. Li Fenghao noticed it too.

"The white-robed woman is under mental control." The immortal's voice came sharp and certain in Hughie's mind. "Her spiritual signature has the same distortion pattern that your master described. From what I can sense, the others appear clean, but she's definitely compromised."

Hughie tried not to react to that information. He kept his expression angry and defeated, which was getting easier the longer he stood there in chains. His wrists were starting to go numb.

"Take the prisoner to detention cell three," Ace ordered, addressing the guards. "Standard restraints. No visitors without my direct authorization."

"Sect Master," Yulan interjected, "surely such a valuable prisoner should be held in the high security cells? If Slifer truly values this disciple, he may attempt a rescue."

"If Slifer attempts anything, the entire sect will know about it long before he reaches the detention facilities," Ace replied. "Cell three will suffice."

The guards moved to either side of Hughie, taking hold of his arms. Their grip was professional but not cruel, which he appreciated. As they led him away, he caught Li Fenghao's voice one more time.

"Watch for an opportunity to break those chains. I can help, but I need you conscious and relatively uninjured for my assistance to be effective."

That was less reassuring than Hughie would have liked.

The detention facilities turned out to be underground, accessed through a series of descending staircases that took them deep beneath the sect's main buildings. The air grew cooler as they descended, and Hughie could feel layers of formations pressing down from above. These weren't just physical barriers; they were spiritual locks designed to suppress cultivation and prevent escape.

Cell three was actually fairly comfortable, as prison cells went. It had a simple bed, a small table, and a bucket in the corner that Hughie tried not to think too hard about. The walls were smooth stone and covered in formation script that glowed faintly in the dim light. The guards removed his chains once they'd pushed him inside, which was a relief until he realized his cultivation was still being suppressed by the cell's formations.

"Food will be brought at regular intervals," one of the guards said through the barred door. "Don't try anything stupid."

Then they were gone, their footsteps echoing up the stairwell until silence settled over the underground chamber.

Hughie sat on the bed and immediately started examining the ring on his finger. It looked like a simple black band, the kind of thing a commoner might wear, but he could feel the vast spiritual presence contained within. Li Fenghao's consciousness resided in that ring, a Greater Immortal reduced to a fraction of his former power by some ancient curse or binding.

"How long do you think we'll be here?" Hughie asked mentally, knowing the Immortal could hear him even when he wasn't speaking aloud.

"Hours, probably. Your Sect Master Ace needs time to identify which elders are compromised and which aren't. He'll need to be thorough."

"And then what?"

"Then he'll call a meeting, probably claiming it's to discuss your fate. He'll have prepared formations to break the mind control, which is actually quite clever. Gathering all the compromised individuals in one place allows him to free them simultaneously, preventing any from alerting this Lady Chi person."

"You think it will work?"

"I think your master wouldn't have sent you here if he didn't believe there was a reasonable chance of success. Though, I note with some concern that 'reasonable' and 'guaranteed' are very different things."

Hughie leaned back against the wall. The stone was cold, and the cell's formations made him feel disconnected from his own spiritual energy, like trying to move a limb that had fallen asleep. It was deeply uncomfortable.

"Can you still help me if something goes wrong?" he asked. "With the formations suppressing everything?"

"The formations are designed to suppress mortal realm cultivation," Li Fenghao replied. "I am a Greater Immortal, trapped though I may be. If the situation becomes truly desperate, I can manifest through you briefly. The cost will be significant, possibly damaging to your spiritual channels, but it's possible."

"How damaging are we talking?"

"Probably not permanent, assuming you survive whatever necessitates my intervention."

"That's not very reassuring."

"I'm not here to reassure you. I'm here to teach you proper cultivation techniques and occasionally save your life when you make poor decisions."

Hughie wanted to argue that coming to the Heavenly Light Sect wasn't his decision, it was Master Slifer's, but he decided against it. Li Fenghao had been teaching him genuine techniques during their time together, including the Dimensional Slide technique that had saved his life more than once. The old Immortal was prickly and demanding, but he'd proven useful.

Time passed slowly in the cell. Hughie tried to meditate, but the suppression formations made it nearly impossible to sense his own spiritual energy clearly. Instead, he found himself thinking about Oliviare, wondering what she was doing back at the sect. She'd been terrified when he left with Master Slifer, convinced she'd never see him again.

He'd promised to return. He intended to keep that promise.

Eventually, footsteps echoed down the stairwell. Multiple sets moving with purpose. Hughie stood up from the bed as the guards appeared along with Ace and Elder Lu Pan.

"Time to determine your fate, prisoner," Ace announced formally. "The council has agreed to convene."

Hughie was fitted with new chains, lighter than the ones before but still effective at suppressing his cultivation. The guards led him back up the stairs and through the sect's corridors. Hughie tried to memorize the path, noting exits and gathering points where disciples congregated, but there were too many twists and turns to keep straight.

The council chamber was impressive. It was circular, with a domed ceiling covered in formation script that created the illusion of a starry sky. Twelve seats were arranged in a semicircle, each occupied by an elder in white and gold robes. Ace sat in a larger throne-like chair at the center, elevated slightly above the others.

Hughie was positioned in the middle of the room, chains attached to a metal ring embedded in the floor. He couldn't move more than a meter in any direction. The elders all studied him with varying expressions of curiosity, suspicion, and, in Elder Yulan's case, barely concealed hostility.

"This is the disciple Hughie, of the Black Rose Sect," Ace announced to the assembled council. "He was present during my capture and has knowledge of Slifer's operations, defensive formations, and strategic capabilities."

"Has he been interrogated?" one of the elders asked.

"Not yet. I wanted the council's input on how to proceed. The Black Rose Sect is known for training their disciples in resistance to mental techniques. Standard interrogation methods may prove ineffective."

"We have other methods," Elder Yulan said, her voice cold. "Methods that don't rely on the prisoner's cooperation."

"Such methods are forbidden by sect law," Lu Pan countered immediately. "We are not demonic cultivators. We do not torture prisoners for information."

"Even when that prisoner serves a demonic sect master who captured our leader?"

"Even then."

The debate continued, with various elders offering opinions about interrogation techniques, prisoner treatment, and the larger strategic implications of holding one of Slifer's disciples. Hughie tried to look appropriately nervous, which wasn't difficult, since he was standing chained in the middle of a room full of people discussing his fate.

"Something is wrong," Li Fenghao's voice suddenly cut through his thoughts. "The formations beneath your feet. They're not standard binding formations. There's something else woven into them, a secondary array that's recently been activated."

Hughie's heart rate picked up. "What kind of array?"

"Suppression. Very powerful suppression. It's targeting your Sect Master Ace specifically, designed to weaken him. Someone prepared this in advance."

Before Hughie could figure out how to warn Ace, the trap sprang.

The formations beneath the floor blazed to life, but instead of the white light of purification that Ace had presumably prepared, they glowed sickly red. Ace's eyes widened in shock as the spiritual pressure in the room suddenly inverted and pressed down on him specifically while leaving the elders untouched.

It didn't take long for the sect master to realize who was the cause of this.

"Lu Pan," Ace gasped, his voice strained. "What have you done?"

The First Elder's expression was apologetic but firm. "I'm sorry, old friend. But it was necessary. You've been compromised by that demonic sect master. Lady Chi has shown us the truth of what happened to you."

Hughie felt his stomach drop. Lu Pan was controlled too. He'd seemed clean—his spiritual signature had been normal—but somehow Lady Chi had gotten to him anyway.

"Elder Lu Pan's spiritual signature is different now," Li Fenghao observed. "It must have changed within the last few seconds. This Lady Chi can activate her control remotely, without being physically present. That's . . . concerning."

The other elders were rising from their seats, their expressions ranging from confused to determined. Some clearly knew this was coming. Others were just now realizing something was wrong.

Ace tried to stand, but the red formations pulled him back down. Spiritual chains erupted from the floor and wrapped around his arms and legs. These weren't physical restraints like the ones holding Hughie. These were pure spiritual energy, designed specifically to bind Ascendant-level cultivators.

"The Mind Liberation technique will not work if I cannot maintain concentration," Ace gritted out. "Lu Pan, fight this. You know this isn't right."

"On the contrary," Lu Pan replied, his voice taking on that distant quality Hughie had heard in other controlled individuals. "This is perfectly right. You've been corrupted by Slifer. Lady Chi opened our eyes to the truth. The demonic sects have developed techniques to turn even the strongest cultivators into their puppets."

Hughie pulled against his chains, but they held firm. The suppression formations beneath his feet made his cultivation feel like trying to run through deep mud. He could barely generate enough spiritual energy to reinforce his body, let alone break free.

"Young man," Li Fenghao said urgently, "I need you to listen carefully. In your storage ring, you have the teleportation talisman that Slifer gave you. If you can activate it, we can escape this situation."

Hughie's storage ring. Right. He'd almost forgotten about it. The problem was that storage rings required at least minimal spiritual energy to access, and the formations were suppressing him nearly completely.

"Try," Li Fenghao insisted. "Focus everything you have on opening that ring. I'll help guide your energy."

Hughie closed his eyes and concentrated. His spiritual energy felt sluggish and distant, but with Li Fenghao's guidance, he managed to form a thin thread of qi. It reached toward the ring on his left hand, seeking the dimensional space where his possessions were stored.

The storage ring opened. Hughie felt the teleportation talisman materialize in his palm, a small jade disc covered in transportation formation script.

"Now activate it," Li Fenghao urged. "Push your qi into the center point."

Hughie tried. He pushed every bit of spiritual energy he could muster into the talisman, but nothing happened. The jade remained cool and inert in his palm.

"The suppression formations," Li Fenghao realized. "They're blocking spatial techniques. Clever. This was well planned."

Elder Yulan stepped forward. "Did you really think we wouldn't prepare for the possibility of escape? Lady Chi thought of everything."

The temperature in the room began to drop. Not the natural cold of winter, but the supernatural chill of death qi. Hughie's breath formed clouds in the suddenly frigid air, and frost began to spread across the floor.

"Something is coming," Li Fenghao said, his voice tense. "Something powerful. The spatial formations are bending to allow it entry. This was all a trap, and you walked right into it."

The wall behind the council seats simply dissolved. Stone and formation script crumbled to dust as reality itself seemed to part like curtains. Through the opening stepped a woman who made every instinct Hughie possessed scream "danger."

Lady Chi.

She was beautiful in the way a venomous flower was beautiful: striking and deadly in equal measure. Long black hair flowed down her back, and her red eyes seemed to glow. Her robes shifted between black and deep green, like leaves in shadow. But what caught Hughie's attention was the aura of wrongness that surrounded her.

This was the person who'd been manipulating sect masters. This was who Master Slifer had warned them about.

"Well done, my dear puppets," Lady Chi said, her voice carrying easily through the council chamber. "You've delivered both prizes directly to me."

Ace tried to speak, but red vines erupted from the floor and wrapped around his throat, cutting off his words. The vines looked organic, like plant matter, but they pulsed with dark spiritual energy that made Hughie's skin crawl.

"Don't bother," Lady Chi continued, walking casually toward Ace. "Those formations are specifically designed to counter your particular cultivation methods. The more you struggle, the tighter they bind."

She turned her attention to Hughie, and he felt her spiritual sense wash over him like cold water. Those red eyes studied him as if he were a specimen to be catalogued rather than a person.

"And this must be young Hughie," she mused. "One of Slifer's precious disciples. I must admit, I'm curious what makes you special. Your cultivation is unremarkable. Your appearance is common. Yet he sent you on this mission with his strongest ally." She stepped closer, her presence making it hard to breathe. "What aren't you showing me?"

"Nothing," Hughie managed to say. "I'm nobody special."

"Liar." The word was soft but carried the weight of absolute certainty. "Everyone is special in their own way. You simply haven't revealed yours yet."

Blood-red vines erupted from the floor around Hughie. They moved faster than he could track and wrapped around his chest, his arms, his legs. The thorns on the vines bit into his skin, and Hughie gasped as pain shot through his body.

"Stop talking to her," Li Fenghao advised. "Any information you give her is information she can use. Just endure."

The vines lifted Hughie off the ground and pulled him toward Lady Chi. She examined him like a piece of artwork, tilting her head as she studied his face.

"Your spiritual signature is unusual," she observed. "There's something... layered about it. As if you're not entirely alone in that body of yours."

Hughie's heart hammered. Could she detect Li Fenghao?

"The ring," she said suddenly, her eyes focusing on his hand. "There's something in that ring. A soul, perhaps? Or a remnant spirit?" She reached toward his hand, and Hughie tried to pull away, but the vines held him immobile.

"Don't let her touch it," Li Fenghao said urgently. "If she realizes what I am, she'll either destroy the ring or try to claim me for herself. Neither option ends well for you."

Before Lady Chi's fingers could close around the ring, Ace made his move.

The Heavenly Light Sect Master had been gathering his spiritual energy while Lady Chi was distracted, building it up despite the suppression formations weighing him down. Now he released it all at once in a burst of golden light that shattered the red vines around his throat.

"HUGHIE!" Ace roared. "THE TALISMAN!"

But Hughie had already tried that. The talisman didn't work.

Lady Chi turned toward Ace with an expression of mild annoyance. "Really? Must you be difficult?"

She gestured casually, and the vines around Ace tightened, wrapping around him completely until only his head remained visible. More vines sprouted from the walls and ceiling to create a cage of thorned plant matter that completely enclosed him.

"You should be grateful," Lady Chi told Ace. "I could simply kill you, but you're more useful alive. A sect master under my control is valuable. A dead sect master is merely tragic." She turned back to Hughie. "Now, where were we?"

Her hand closed around the ring on Hughie's finger. He felt Li Fenghao's presence pulse within it, like a heartbeat of ancient power. Lady Chi's eyes widened slightly.

"Oh," she breathed. "Oh, this is interesting. There's someone quite powerful bound in here. How delightful."

She tried to remove the ring, but it wouldn't budge. No matter how hard she pulled, the band remained fixed on Hughie's finger. It was as if the ring had fused with his very flesh.

Lady Chi frowned. "A binding oath? Or perhaps the ring itself has chosen its bearer." She released his hand and stepped back. "No matter. I have other ways of extracting information."

The vines around Hughie's chest tightened, and thorns pushed deeper into his skin. He couldn't help the cry of pain that escaped. Blood began to soak through his robes where the thorns had penetrated.

"Stop!" Ace shouted from his vine prison. "He's just a boy!"

"He's a tool," Lady Chi corrected. "And I'm determining how useful that tool might be." She tilted her head, studying Hughie's face as he struggled against the pain. "I could kill you. That would hurt Slifer, which would satisfy me. But perhaps you're worth more alive. I could use you to lure him out of that sect of his."

She raised one hand, and Hughie felt spiritual energy gather in the air around him. The energy was wrong, tainted with the same deathly corruption that surrounded Lady Chi herself. It pressed against his consciousness, seeking entry into his mind.

"Let's see what secrets you're hiding," she murmured.

The mental invasion hit him like a hammer. Hughie felt Lady Chi's consciousness slam into his own, probing and searching through his thoughts and memories. It was violating in a way physical pain could never be. She was inside his head, rifling through everything he was.

But then her presence encountered something unexpected.

The jade medallion around Hughie's neck, hidden beneath his robes. The Mind Fortress Talisman that Master Slifer had given him.

Lady Chi's mental probe struck the talisman's defense and simply stopped. Her red eyes widened in surprise and then narrowed in anger.

"Of course," she hissed. "Slifer would protect his precious disciples. A Mind Fortress Talisman. Expensive and rare. He must value you highly."

The vines shifted, and one thin tendril snaked up Hughie's neck to the chain holding the medallion. Lady Chi's expression was coldly determined now, all pretense of idle curiosity gone.

"Let's remove that troublesome protection, shall we?"

"Don't let her," Li Fenghao said urgently. "The moment that talisman comes off, you'll be completely vulnerable to her mental techniques. She'll turn you into a puppet."

But Hughie couldn't do anything. The vines held him completely immobile. He could only watch as the tendril wrapped around the chain and pulled. The medallion came free with a soft click, the chain snapping easily under the vine's pressure.

Lady Chi caught the falling talisman and examined it briefly before tossing it aside. "Now, then, let's try this again."

The mental invasion returned, but this time there was no protection. Lady Chi's consciousness poured into Hughie's mind like poison. He tried to resist, tried to push her out, but she was too strong. Her will crushed his attempts at defense, sweeping aside his mental barriers like they were made of paper.

"Stop fighting," she whispered, her voice echoing in his thoughts. "It will hurt less if you simply submit."

But Hughie couldn't submit. He thought of Master Slifer, who'd given him a purpose. He thought of his fellow disciples, who'd become like siblings to him. He thought of Oliviare waiting for him to return home.

He thought of all these things, and he fought.

The pain in his head grew excruciating. It felt like his skull was splitting apart, like his thoughts were being shredded and reformed according to Lady Chi's desires. He could feel his resistance weakening, his sense of self beginning to blur.

"That's better," Lady Chi's voice was almost soothing now. "Just let go. Let me in. It will all be over soon."

Hughie felt something fundamental begin to shift inside him. His thoughts became sluggish, distant. Lady Chi's presence filled more and more of his consciousness, pushing out everything that made him who he was.

And then, suddenly, he felt nothing at all.

His mind went blank, thoughts ceasing their frantic spinning. The pain vanished. Everything vanished. He existed in a state of perfect empty calm.

Lady Chi smiled as she watched the young man's eyes go glassy and unfocused. His struggles ceased. His body went limp in the vines' grip. Another successful conversion. Another puppet for her collection.

"Much better," she said, satisfied. "Now, let's see what you know about Slifer's—"

She stopped mid-sentence.

Something was wrong.

The spiritual energy emanating from Hughie's body suddenly surged. Not the normal fluctuation of a cultivator accessing their power, but an explosion of force that made the air itself tremble. The energy signature shifted as it transformed from nothing to Core Formation to Nascent Soul to Origin Realm and climbed still higher.

Lady Chi released the vines and took a quick step backward, her expression shifting from satisfaction to alarm.

The thorny vines around Hughie's body began to wither and die. The wounds they'd inflicted closed in seconds as flesh knitted itself back together with a speed that should have been impossible. The blood staining his robes evaporated, leaving the fabric clean.

The spiritual energy kept building. Half-Step Immortal. For a moment, it seemed like it would continue to Immortal Realm, but then it stabilized, settling at a level of power that made the council chamber's formations groan under the pressure.

Hughie's head lifted slowly. When his eyes opened, they were different: still his eyes, still his face, but the consciousness looking out through them was ancient beyond measure.

Li Fenghao smiled with Hughie's mouth.

"Thank you, Lady Chi," the Greater Immortal said, his voice carrying harmonics that mortal vocal cords shouldn't be able to produce. "I've been trying to find a way out of that ring for quite some time. You forcing the boy into a mentally blank state created just enough of an opening for me to take temporary control."

Lady Chi's face went pale. "What . . . what are you?"

"Someone who has existed far longer than you, child." Li Fenghao flexed Hughie's fingers. "These mortal bodies are so limiting. But it will suffice for what needs to be done."

He looked down at his hands, now glowing with spiritual energy that made the air ripple with heat distortion. Then he raised his gaze to meet Lady Chi's, and his smile widened into something that wasn't friendly at all.

"Now, then," Li Fenghao said pleasantly, "shall we discuss how you nearly killed a boy under my protection?"

CHAPTER FIFTEEN

Lady Chi took three steps backward, her red eyes fixed on the transformed young man floating before her. The spiritual energy radiating from Hughie's body had shifted completely. The raw, unrefined power of a Nascent Soul cultivator was gone and had been replaced by something ancient and refined. The kind of presence that only came from hundreds of thousands of years of cultivation.

Li Fenghao smiled with Hughie's mouth, though the expression carried none of the boy's usual awkwardness.

"You are from the Immortal Realm," Lady Chi said. Her voice had lost its cruel edge, replaced by something more cautious. "I can sense it in your spiritual signature. The density, the quality. You are no mortal cultivator wearing a disguise."

"Observant," Li Fenghao replied. The words came easily through Hughie's vocal cords, though he adjusted the tone to sound less like a frightened boy and more like what he was. "Your own aura carries the same markers. Tell me, which sect claims your allegiance in the higher realms?"

Lady Chi's posture relaxed slightly. She lowered her hands, the red vines that had been coiling around the council chamber beginning to withdraw. "The Crimson Lotus Pavilion. We are one of the three great nature cultivation sects that govern the Eastern Territories. Perhaps you have heard of us?"

Li Fenghao kept his expression neutral. Oh, he had heard of them. The Crimson Lotus Pavilion was notorious among the higher realms for their methods. They specialized in mental manipulation and corruption techniques, turning gardens into torture chambers and flowers into weapons. Their disciples were taught that lesser cultivators existed only to serve as resources. Stepping stones. Disposable tools to be used and discarded.

"The name is familiar," he said carefully. "I have spent considerable time in the mortal realms. My knowledge of current Immortal Realm politics may be somewhat outdated."

"Then you understand my position." Lady Chi gestured around the destroyed council chamber. "I have descended to these lower realms seeking justice. A man named Slifer killed my beloved Darius. I am merely honoring his memory by ensuring appropriate consequences."

"By controlling the minds of sect masters and starting wars?" Li Fenghao's tone remained conversational, but he was already mapping potential attack vectors. The woman stood six meters away, well within range for most techniques. Ace remained bound in vines against the far wall, conscious but helpless.

"These mortals live such brief lives," Lady Chi said. "What does it matter if I accelerate their schedules by a few decades? They die regardless. At least this way, their deaths serve a greater purpose."

There it was. The casual dismissal of mortal life that marked every Crimson Lotus disciple Li Fenghao had ever encountered. They viewed the lower realms the way farmers viewed livestock: useful when needed, but otherwise beneath consideration.

"I see we have different philosophies," Li Fenghao said. "It seems we were destined to battle."

Lady Chi studied him carefully. "You are using that boy as a vessel. A soul possession technique, judging by the seamless integration. Such methods are frowned upon by most righteous sects, but the Crimson Lotus Pavilion understands practical necessity." She took a small step forward. "Perhaps we could reach an arrangement. You allow me to complete my work here, and I promise not to interfere with your possession of that young cultivator. We are both from the higher realms, after all. Why should we fight over mortals?"

Li Fenghao let the smile fade from Hughie's face. "You tortured this boy nearly to death. You invaded his mind and attempted to turn him into a puppet. You did this while he was under my protection."

"I did not know he carried a Greater Immortal in his ring," Lady Chi said quickly. "Had I been aware—"

"You would have killed him more carefully?" Li Fenghao's spiritual pressure expanded outward, pressing against the walls of the council chamber. Stone cracked. The remaining intact windows shattered outward. "Or perhaps you would have tried to capture me as well? Add a Greater Immortal's power to your collection?"

Lady Chi's expression hardened. The red glow in her eyes intensified. "I was extending courtesy to a fellow Immortal. Do not mistake that for weakness."

"And I was explaining why that courtesy is undeserved," Li Fenghao replied. "Your sect's methods are abhorrent. Your treatment of mortals is disgusting. And your presence in this realm has caused enough suffering." He raised Hughie's right hand, and spiritual energy began to coalesce around the fingers. "Leave now, or I will ensure you never return to the Immortal Realm at all."

For a moment, Lady Chi seemed to consider retreat. Her eyes darted toward the hole in the wall where she had entered. Then her lips pulled back in a snarl. "You dare threaten a Core Disciple of the Crimson Lotus Pavilion? My master is an Immortal Emperor! When word reaches him of this disrespect—"

"Your master is eight realms away and trapped behind a dimensional barrier," Li Fenghao interrupted. "Here, in this council chamber, you face me alone." He settled into a combat stance, adjusting for Hughie's shorter frame and different center of gravity. "Show me if your sect's reputation is deserved, or if you are merely another spoiled disciple coasting on your master's name."

Lady Chi's face twisted with rage. Red spiritual energy exploded from her body. The force of it blasted apart the remaining furniture in the council chamber. The elders who had been frozen in place during her earlier display now scrambled for the exits, desperate to escape the battle between two Half-Step Immortals.

She moved first.

Vines erupted from the floor. Not the wild, grasping tendrils from earlier, but precise spears of corrupted plant matter moving faster than most Ascendant cultivators could track. Each vine carried enough force to punch through steel, their thorns dripping with spiritual poison.

Li Fenghao twisted Hughie's body sideways, the movement flowing like water despite the boy's usual clumsiness. Three vines passed through the space where he had been standing. He caught the fourth with his left hand, spiritual energy coating the palm to prevent the thorns from penetrating. With a sharp pull, he ripped the vine from the floor and swung it like a whip at Lady Chi.

She dissolved into red mist and reformed three meters to the left. Her hands came together in a complex seal, and the air around Li Fenghao suddenly became thick with paralytic pollen. Each grain carried a fragment of her consciousness that attempted to invade through any opening in his spiritual defenses.

Li Fenghao exhaled sharply and expelled pure spiritual pressure from every pore. The pollen burned away before it could settle, leaving only ash that drifted to the destroyed floor. He pressed forward, closing the distance with a burst of speed that cracked the stone beneath Hughie's feet.

Lady Chi summoned a wall of thorned roses between them. Each flower bloomed the size of a shield, their petals sharp as razors. Li Fenghao's fist punched through the first rose, spiritual energy shattering it into fragments. The second rose tried to wrap around his arm. He ignited his qi and burned away the petals before they could constrict.

"You fight like a street brawler," Lady Chi sneered. She gestured, and the walls themselves came alive with creeping vines. They reached for Li Fenghao from every direction, countless grasping tendrils seeking to bind and crush. "Where is your technique? Your refinement?"

"Refinement is for tea ceremonies," Li Fenghao replied. He activated a cultivation technique he had not used in five thousand years. Spatial qi rippled outward from his body in concentric rings. Every vine within three meters of him simply ceased to exist, cut from reality by precisely controlled dimensional tears. "I prefer methods that work."

He was across the chamber before Lady Chi could react. His fist shot at her sternum with enough force to shatter ribs. She twisted at the last moment, and his punch grazed her shoulder instead of landing squarely. Even that glancing impact sent her spinning backward, feet sliding across the floor as she fought to maintain balance.

Blood dripped from where his strike had connected. Not much, but enough to prove she could be hurt.

Lady Chi's eyes widened in genuine alarm. She must have assumed they were evenly matched, two Immortals whose true power was suppressed to Half-Step Immortal by the realm's limitations. But Li Fenghao had been fighting for eons before she had even existed. Experience counted for more than raw cultivation when both parties were restricted to the same level.

"Crimson Lotus: Bleeding World," she shouted.

Red light burst from her body like a nova. The technique transformed the entire council chamber into her domain. The walls turned red. The floor became soft and yielding, like standing on muscle tissue. Thorned vines burst from every surface, hundreds of them, all moving with coordinated intelligence.

Li Fenghao stood at the center of the crimson domain, noting how the technique tried to drain his spiritual energy through contact with the changed floor. Clever. Lady Chi was attempting to turn this into a battle of attrition in a bet that her techniques were more efficient than his.

She would lose that bet.

He clapped Hughie's hands together once. The sound echoed like thunder through the chamber. Then he pulled them apart slowly, a sphere of pure white light forming between the palms. No fancy technique names. No elaborate hand seals. Just raw spiritual energy condensed to a point where it bent the laws of physics.

Li Fenghao released the sphere.

It expanded outward in a perfect circle as it burned away Lady Chi's domain. The red walls returned to gray stone. The soft floor became hard tile once more. Every vine within fifteen meters withered to ash. The technique was simple, almost crude by Immortal Realm standards, but against an opponent at the same cultivation level, simple and effective beat complex and flashy every time.

Lady Chi stumbled as her domain collapsed. Creating and maintaining such a large-scale technique required enormous concentration. Having it forcibly dispelled caused spiritual backlash, the kind that felt like someone had kicked you in the chest from the inside.

Li Fenghao did not give her time to recover. He was on her in three steps, Hughie's hands moving in patterns too fast for mortal eyes to follow. Each strike targeted a vital point on her body. Left shoulder, right hip, center of the chest, both knees. She blocked two strikes out of five. The other three connected with solid impacts that sent cracks spreading through her spiritual defense.

"You are skilled," Li Fenghao admitted, pressing his advantage. "Your techniques show creativity. Your sect has trained you well in theory." He caught her wrist as she tried to retreat, holding firm despite her attempts to dissolve into mist. "But you have never fought someone who genuinely wanted to kill you, have you? Not really. Not beyond staged duels and controlled tournaments."

Lady Chi's other hand came up, and her fingers transformed into wooden claws. She raked them across Li Fenghao's face, drawing blood from Hughie's cheek. Li Fenghao ignored the pain as he twisted her captured wrist until bones ground against each other. She gasped, the sound turning into a shriek as he forced her to her knees.

"I have fought in realm wars," Li Fenghao said quietly. "I have battled demons that could devour worlds. I have stood against Immortal Emperors who thought their power made them gods." He released her wrist and stepped back, spiritual energy still coiling around Hughie's body like armor. "You are a talented disciple with good training and bad habits. Nothing more."

Lady Chi surged to her feet, her face twisted with humiliation and rage. "You dare—"

Li Fenghao's backhand caught her across the jaw, the impact spinning her completely around. She crashed into the wall hard enough to leave cracks in the stone. When she peeled herself away, blood leaked from the corner of her mouth.

"I dare," Li Fenghao confirmed. "Because you tortured a boy I have sworn to protect. Because you control the minds of innocents for your petty revenge. Because you embody everything I despise about the Crimson Lotus Pavilion." He walked toward her slowly. "Your sect takes promising young cultivators and twists them into monsters. They teach you that power gives you the right to harm others. They are wrong."

Lady Chi spat blood onto the floor. Her red eyes blazed with hatred, but beneath that, Li Fenghao saw something else. Fear. The realization that she might actually die here, in this mortal realm, killed by some ancient fossil inhabiting a boy's body.

She raised both hands, and thorns erupted from her palms to create a shield of twisted wood. "This is not over," she hissed. "When my master learns of this—"

"He will do nothing," Li Fenghao interrupted. "Because you are not going to tell him." He raised Hughie's right hand, gathering spiritual energy for a finishing strike. "You are going to leave this realm, return to whatever hole you crawled from, and never mention this encounter to anyone. Because if the Crimson Lotus Pavilion learns that one of their Core Disciples was defeated by a mortal demonic sect master, well . . ." He smiled without humor. "That would be embarrassing, would it not?"

Lady Chi's face went pale. The shield of thorns trembled, then collapsed into splinters. She understood the threat perfectly. Face was everything in the Immortal Realm. A story like that could ruin her standing within the sect. She would be mocked, demoted, possibly even cast out as worthless.

"I will remember this," she said through clenched teeth. Spatial qi began gathering around her body, preparing for escape. "I will remember you. What is your n—"

"No names," Li Fenghao said sharply. "You do not get to know my sect, my lineage, or anything else about me. You get to live. Take that gift and be grateful."

Lady Chi's form began to fade, her escape technique finally activating. Before she fully vanished, she locked eyes with Li Fenghao one final time. "Slifer will still die," she promised. "My oath is binding. I cannot leave until he falls."

Then she was gone, the spatial distortion marking her departure fading within seconds.

Li Fenghao stood in the destroyed council chamber, breathing carefully through Hughie's lungs. The boy's body was tough for his age, but channeling Half-Step Immortal techniques through a Nascent Soul cultivation base was taking its toll. Small cracks had formed in the meridians—nothing permanent, but painful regardless.

Had it been up to him, he would have killed the demonic mistress, but the lifesaving treasures she had would have likely taken out this body with her, and sacrificing Hughie was not something Li Fenghao felt comfortable doing.

Behind him, the red vines binding Ace suddenly withered and fell away. The Heavenly Light Sect Master remained pressed against the wall for a moment, then slowly pushed himself upright. His eyes never left Hughie's body as he watched the way Li Fenghao held himself, the subtle differences in posture and expression.

"The boy," Ace said carefully. "Is he . . . alive?"

Li Fenghao turned to face him, aware of how this must look: a young disciple's body inhabited by an ancient presence, blood dripping from wounds that should have been fatal, speaking with authority that belonged to someone else entirely.

"He sleeps," Li Fenghao said. His tone was gentle, the way you might speak to someone who had just survived a traumatic experience. "The mental attack forced his consciousness into a dormant state. I have taken temporary control to ensure his body remains functional until he recovers."

Ace's hand had moved toward his sword hilt, though he had not drawn the weapon. "And you are?"

"A spirit bound to the ring on his finger," Li Fenghao replied honestly. "I have been teaching him cultivation techniques. When Lady Chi nearly destroyed his mind, I intervened." He gestured at the destruction around them. "The situation required direct action."

"You inhabit his body without permission." Ace's tone carried accusation, though his posture remained cautious rather than hostile.

"Would you prefer I had let Lady Chi complete her mind control?" Li Fenghao asked. "The boy would have become her puppet. She would have used him against his master, his friends, everyone he cares about. I prevented that." He met Ace's gaze steadily. "When he wakes, Hughie will remember everything. He can decide then whether my actions were justified."

Ace studied him for a long moment. Finally, he nodded slowly. "How long until he recovers?"

"Hours, perhaps a day at most. The human mind is resilient, especially at his age." Li Fenghao rolled Hughie's shoulders again, checking for damage. "I will maintain control until he is ready to resume. It would not do to have his body collapse from injuries while his consciousness is elsewhere."

"And I am supposed to keep this secret?" Ace asked.

"That would be preferable," Li Fenghao admitted. "Possession techniques, even temporary and consensual ones, carry negative associations. If others learn that Hughie shares his body with an ancient spirit, it could cause . . . complications."

Ace opened his mouth to respond but stopped as spatial qi suddenly rippled through the council chamber. A dimensional tear opened in the center of the room, its edges crackling with precisely controlled energy. Li Fenghao recognized the technique immediately: Dimensional Slide.

An old man stepped through the portal first. His hair was white, his robes elegant but practical.

Behind him came a younger man with a sword strapped to his back. The blade radiated righteous qi. His eyes immediately scanned the destroyed chamber, cataloging threats and exit routes.

Li Fenghao's ancient instincts screamed warning. The old man was dangerous. Not because of raw power, but because of something harder to define. Despite being a Greater Immortal, Li Fenghao still had yet to determine this old monster's true power level. All he knew was that the sick man had a tendency to act like a wolf in sheep's clothing.

"Hughie!" The younger cultivator's face lit up with relief when he saw Hughie's body. He rushed forward, his spiritual sense already probing for injuries. "Are you alright? Master said you were dying and needed help."

Li Fenghao forced Hughie's face into a tired smile. The expression felt awkward, but he managed something approximating the boy's usual sheepish grin. "I am fine, Senior Brother Caelum. Just . . . very tired."

Caelum gripped Hughie's shoulder, checking for broken bones or internal damage. "You are covered in blood. Your spiritual channels show signs of severe stress. What happened here?"

"Lady Chi happened," Li Fenghao said, keeping his voice pitched to match Hughie's usual tone. "She tried to control my mind like she did Sect Master Ace. I . . . managed to resist. Barely."

Ace remained silent, his expression unreadable. Li Fenghao could see the conflict playing out behind the man's eyes. The Heavenly Light Sect Master knew the truth, but was he honorable enough to keep the secret? Or would he expose Li Fenghao immediately to protect his newfound allies?

The old man had not moved from his position near the portal. His eyes swept across the destroyed council chamber, taking in every detail. The withered vines. The blood splattered on the walls. The cracks in the floor showing where powerful techniques had been exchanged. His gaze settled on Ace for a moment, reading something in the other cultivator's expression, then returned to Hughie's body.

He stared.

Not the casual glance of someone checking on a disciple's wellbeing. This was intense scrutiny, the kind that peeled away layers of deception like removing the skin from an onion. It seemed that the old monster had realized that something was different.

Li Fenghao kept the smile fixed in place, though he could feel sweat beginning to form on Hughie's forehead.

The old man's eyes narrowed slightly. Then he spoke.

"Hughie," the old man said slowly. "Or should I say . . . old grandpa in the ring?"

He had been exposed.

Li Fenghao felt cold sweat break out across Hughie's entire body.

CHAPTER SIXTEEN

Li Fenghao stood perfectly still in Hughie's body. The old man with white hair and elegant robes had just spoken those words, and now everything hung in balance. Every instinct the ancient Immortal possessed screamed at him that this situation was dangerous beyond measure.

"Senior," Li Fenghao said carefully, keeping his voice measured and respectful. He made no sudden movements. When dealing with beings of unknown power, one wrong gesture could mean annihilation. "This one greets the esteemed elder. Your insight is truly profound."

The old man studied him with those sharp eyes. The younger cultivator standing beside him, the one with the sword at his back, tensed slightly. His hand moved toward his weapon but stopped, apparently having received some unspoken command.

"I asked you a question," the old man said. His tone wasn't angry. That somehow made it worse. Anger could be predicted, negotiated with, redirected. This calm certainty was the mark of someone who never doubted their ability to enforce their will.

Li Fenghao bowed deeply, which looked awkward in Hughie's shorter frame. "This humble one is indeed Li Fenghao, formerly of the Heavenly Cloud Sect. I have been bound to this ring for many years and have been teaching young Hughie cultivation techniques in exchange for the chance to observe the mortal realm once more."

"Teaching," the old man repeated. "Is that what you call taking over my disciple's body?"

DEMONIC SECT ELDER AND THE GREAT WAR

The words hung in the air like a blade waiting to fall. Li Fenghao felt Hughie's heart hammering in his chest. The boy's body was still recovering from Lady Chi's mental assault, and the stress wasn't helping matters.

"Senior, if I may explain—"

"I made it clear during our first meeting," the old man interrupted, his voice growing colder. "When I discovered your presence in that ring, I specifically warned you against attempting to possess this boy. Did you think I wouldn't notice? Or did you simply decide my warning didn't apply to you?"

Li Fenghao raised Hughie's hands in a placating gesture. "Senior, please allow this one to explain the circumstances. The boy was subjected to a mental attack by an Immortal Realm cultivator. Lady Chi, the woman who was here moments ago, she invaded his consciousness and attempted to enslave his mind. The attack was devastating. It forced young Hughie's awareness into a completely dormant state to protect itself from being destroyed."

The old man's expression didn't change, but he didn't interrupt either. Li Fenghao took that as permission to continue.

"When Lady Chi performed her mind-control technique, she believed she had succeeded. Hughie's consciousness had retreated so deeply that he appeared blank. Empty. It was in that moment of total mental vacancy that I was able to break free from my normal constraints within the ring. The void in his mind allowed me to manifest temporarily."

"Temporarily," the old man said, and there was something dangerous in how he emphasized that word.

"Yes, Senior. Absolutely temporary." Li Fenghao spoke quickly now, aware that his continued existence likely depended on this explanation being believed. "I had no intention of keeping this body. How could I? You are watching. Even if you weren't, this boy has been kind to me. He wears my ring willingly, seeks my guidance, treats me with respect. I am a teacher, not a thief."

The younger cultivator spoke for the first time. "Master, his spiritual signature is still partially merged with Hughie's. If he's not trying to possess him, why hasn't he fully separated?"

Smart question. Li Fenghao had worried someone would notice that detail.

"The boy's consciousness is healing, but it's not yet stable," Li Fenghao explained, looking at the younger man before returning his attention to the old man who clearly held authority here. "If I were to withdraw completely right now, there would be nothing anchoring his mind to his body. Lady Chi's attack created severe spiritual trauma. I am essentially holding the door open, maintaining a connection between his awareness and his physical form while his mind repairs itself."

"How long?" the old man asked.

"Hours at most, Senior. Perhaps a day if the damage is more extensive than I initially assessed. But I swear upon my true name and my former station as Sect Leader of the Heavenly Cloud Sect, I have no designs on permanently claiming this vessel. Once young Hughie has recovered sufficiently, I will return to my ring of my own accord."

The council chamber fell silent except for the occasional drip of water from broken pipes in the destroyed walls. Then the old man finally nodded slowly. "If what you say is true, then there's no reason for Hughie to remain unconscious any longer."

Li Fenghao felt Hughie's body stiffen involuntarily. "Senior, with respect, the boy's mind needs time to—"

"I'll wake him now."

Those four words carried absolute finality. Li Fenghao wanted to protest, to explain that rushing the process could cause further damage, that the boy's consciousness was still too fragile. But he looked into those eyes and knew better than to argue. This wasn't a request. It wasn't even a command. It was simply a statement of what would happen next.

The old man walked forward while Li Fenghao remained perfectly still in Hughie's body, watching as this mysterious monster approached. Up close, the pressure was even more intense. It wasn't the crushing weight of superior cultivation that some Immortals used to intimidate lesser beings. This was subtler. More dangerous. It was the certainty of someone who had survived impossible odds and emerged stronger for it.

"Senior," Li Fenghao tried one more time. "Please, the process requires delicacy. If we force his consciousness to return before it's ready—"

"I know what I'm doing."

The old man raised his hand and pressed it against Hughie's forehead. Li Fenghao felt the contact, and his first instinct was to resist, to protect the boy's fragile mind from whatever technique this being was about to employ. But he suppressed that instinct. Interfering would be seen as hostile. Hostility would be fatal.

A flash of golden light erupted from the old man's palm. It wasn't the harsh, blinding glare of an attack. The light was warm. Gentle. It spread through Hughie's body like morning sunlight breaking through storm clouds. Li Fenghao observed with growing amazement as the energy worked its way through the boy's meridians, seeking out and carefully soothing the spiritual damage Lady Chi's assault had caused.

The technique was elegant. Masterful. Each thread of golden qi moved with precision that suggested either vast experience or instinctive understanding of healing arts. The energy found the places where Hughie's consciousness had been battered and torn, and it carefully knitted them back together. Not forcing. Not rushing. Just providing support, creating stability, allowing natural healing to proceed at an accelerated pace.

Li Fenghao felt Hughie's awareness stirring. The boy's mind, which had retreated into protective dormancy, began to expand again, cautiously at first, like someone emerging from a dark cave into daylight, then with growing confidence as he realized the danger had passed and his thoughts were once again his own.

"Wha . . ." Hughie's consciousness brushed against Li Fenghao's presence. "Old man? What happened? Why do I feel like I got trampled by a herd of Origin Realm spirit beasts?"

Li Fenghao couldn't help the small smile that crossed Hughie's face. The boy's personality was intact. His memories seemed functional. The mental trauma had been severe, but this mysterious old man's healing technique had done the impossible and restored stability in mere moments when Li Fenghao had estimated days of careful recovery.

"Young Hughie," Li Fenghao said internally, his voice resonating directly into the boy's consciousness. "Welcome back. You've been unconscious for several minutes after a rather unpleasant encounter."

"Unconscious? But I remember . . ." Hughie's thoughts grew sharper as his mind fully awakened. "Lady Chi. She was in my head. She was crushing my thoughts, trying to make me obey her. I couldn't fight back. It hurt so much that I just . . . stopped. Everything went dark."

"Yes. Her mental techniques were formidable. You survived by essentially shutting down before she could completely dominate your will. It was a near thing, young one."

"How did I get away? Did Master Slifer arrive?"

"Not quite. I'll explain shortly, but first, your master wishes to speak with you."

Li Fenghao carefully withdrew his consciousness back toward the ring and allowed Hughie's awareness to fully reclaim control of his body and senses. The transition was smooth. Natural. Exactly as it should be when a spirit returned to a vessel it had temporarily vacated, not when one soul tried to permanently displace another.

Hughie's eyes refocused, and he blinked several times as his vision adjusted. He was looking directly at his master's face, which was far too close for comfort.

He tried to step back but couldn't, still held in place as he was by spiritual restraints Li Fenghao had been too occupied to notice.

"M-Master Slifer?"

The old man removed his hand from Hughie's forehead and stepped back. "How do you feel?"

Hughie flexed his fingers experimentally. "Like someone scrambled my brain and then put it back together. Everything's working, I think? But there's this weird echo in my head." He paused. "Wait, where am I?"

"Heavenly Light Sect," the younger cultivator offered. "You were brought here as a prisoner, but things got complicated."

Hughie's eyes widened as memory returned. "The council chamber! Sect Master Ace, the trap, Lady Chi—" He struggled against the invisible restraints holding him in place. "Master, Lady Chi was here! She tried to take over my mind. She—"

"I'm aware," Slifer said calmly. "She left before we arrived."

Only then did Hughie seem to notice Caelum standing nearby, looking relieved but exhausted. The vines holding Ace had withered away at some point, and the Heavenly Light Sect Master sat against the wall, conscious but drained.

"How did you find me so fast?" Hughie asked. "A technique?"

"Something like that." Slifer made a small gesture, and whatever was holding Hughie in place released. The boy stumbled, caught himself, and then straightened. "More importantly, are you actually in control right now? The old ghost hasn't decided to make your body his permanent residence?"

Hughie glanced down at the black ring on his finger. "You know about Li Fenghao?"

"I've known since you first returned with that ring," Slifer said. "A Greater Immortal soul doesn't exactly hide well from someone who knows what to look for."

"Then why didn't you—"

"Why didn't I force him out immediately?" Slifer shrugged. "Because he was teaching you useful techniques, and I determined he wasn't an immediate threat to your wellbeing. I simply made it clear to him that attempting to steal your body would result in consequences. Permanent consequences."

Hughie felt Li Fenghao's presence shrink back in the ring at those words. The ancient immortal was clearly taking Slifer's warning very seriously.

"I remember now. He saved me," Hughie said quietly. "If Lady Chi had broken my mind, I would have become her puppet. Li Fenghao broke free from the ring and fought her off. He nearly died doing it."

Slifer's expression softened slightly. "I know. I witnessed the aftermath.

That's the only reason we're having this conversation instead of me destroying that ring immediately."

Hughie felt Li Fenghao release a breath.

"Master," Hughie said, and his voice cracked slightly. "I'm sorry. The mission went so wrong. Sect Master Ace was supposed to have freed the elders easily, but it was all a trap. Lady Chi must have sensed what we were planning. She manipulated the elders into setting up formations specifically targeting Sect Master Ace, and when I tried to help—"

"Stop." Slifer held up one hand. "You're not responsible for Lady Chi's schemes. She's an Immortal Realm cultivator with centuries of experience in manipulation and strategy. Expecting you to outmaneuver her was unrealistic."

"But I failed—"

"You survived. That's what matters." Slifer's tone became gentler, which somehow made Hughie feel worse. His master rarely showed open emotion. "I sent you on this mission knowing it would be dangerous. I didn't anticipate an ambush of this scale, but I should have prepared better contingencies. The fault lies with me, not you."

Hughie wanted to argue, to insist that he should have been more careful, should have detected the trap somehow. But looking at his master's face, he realized the old man was genuinely concerned. Not angry. Not disappointed. Just relieved that his disciple had survived.

"I understand if you want to punish me for failing," Hughie said quietly.

"Punish you?" Slifer actually looked surprised. "For what? You infiltrated an enemy sect, maintained your cover as a prisoner despite extreme pressure, and survived a mental assault from an Immortal cultivator. Those are accomplishments, not failures."

"Really?"

"Really." Slifer's expression became stern again. "Though, I am reassigning you for the immediate future. The war against Lady Chi and her controlled sect masters is escalating, and I can't risk her targeting you again. She knows your face now, knows you're my disciple. If she captures you again, she'll use you as leverage."

Hughie felt a spike of anxiety. Being reassigned usually meant being sent somewhere even more dangerous. "Where are you sending me, Master?"

"Nowhere. You're going back to the Black Rose Sect."

Hughie blinked. "Back to . . . the sect? But the war—"

"You'll sit it out," Slifer said firmly. "Take time to recover from your mental trauma. Train your techniques. Spend time with your friends. Cultivate. Do normal disciple things instead of risking your life every other week."

Was this real? Was his master actually giving him permission to avoid the dangerous missions? Hughie opened his mouth to express his gratitude, then closed it, then opened it again. "I . . . Thank you, Master. Truly. I was actually going to ask if I could return to the sect for a while, but I didn't expect you to agree so easily."

Slifer's lips twitched in what might have been amusement. "Don't sound so shocked. I'm not completely heartless. Besides, you've earned some rest. Between the tournament, the Sealed Realm, and now this disaster, you've been through more in the past few months than most cultivators experience in a lifetime."

"Thank you," Hughie said again, meaning it deeply. He had been preparing arguments, ready to beg if necessary. The idea of spending time at the sect, away from Lady Chi and mind control and near-death experiences, sounded like paradise. And if he was at the sect, he could see Oliviare. His chest tightened at the thought of seeing her again.

"Don't thank me yet," Slifer said dryly. "You'll still be expected to maintain your cultivation progress. I won't have you slacking off completely. But the active combat missions are suspended for now."

"I understand, Master." Hughie could barely keep the relief from his voice.

While Hughie had been talking with Slifer, he hadn't noticed Sect Master Ace approaching. The Heavenly Light Sect leader looked terrible, his white robes torn and stained, dark circles under his eyes. But he was standing upright and seemed alert.

"Slifer," Ace said, and there was weight in his voice. "We need to discuss our next move. Lady Chi won't wait long before attempting to regain control."

Slifer nodded. "Agreed. But not here. This sect is compromised. We need neutral ground to plan."

Hughie tuned out their conversation as it shifted to tactical discussion about sect defenses and communication networks. His attention had turned inward, where Li Fenghao's presence was waiting patiently in the ring.

"Old man," Hughie said internally. "Thank you. For everything. I know I already said it before, but I mean it. You didn't have to break free and fight Lady Chi. You could have stayed hidden in the ring and let her take over my body. Nobody would have blamed you."

Li Fenghao's voice resonated with quiet dignity in Hughie's mind. "Young one, I am many things, but I am not a coward who abandons his students to torture. You have treated me with respect, sought my counsel, and trusted my teachings. The least I could do was ensure you retained your own consciousness."

"Still. You took a huge risk. If my master had decided you were trying to steal my body . . ."

"I am aware of the danger I was in. Your master is not someone to be trifled with. I sensed that the moment his spiritual pressure touched my awareness." Li Fenghao paused. "He is far more than he appears, young Hughie. I cannot determine his true cultivation, which means it exceeds my ability to measure. Be grateful you have such a teacher."

"I am," Hughie said quietly. "Even if he's terrifying sometimes."

"The best teachers often are."

Hughie smiled slightly at that. His attention drifted back to the conversation happening in front of him.

A portal had appeared between Slifer and Caelum, its edges crackling with spatial energy. The swirling gateway revealed glimpses of stone corridors and black and red robes on the other side—the Black Rose Sect, if he had to guess.

Slifer glanced at Caelum and nodded once. The younger cultivator adjusted his sword and stepped toward the portal without hesitation. Slifer followed, his expression unreadable as always.

It was then that Hughie realized they were leaving without him.

"Wait!" He lunged forward, trying to reach the portal before it closed.

He was three steps too slow.

The portal snapped shut with a faint *pop*, leaving only empty air where Slifer and Caelum had been standing. Hughie's hand grasped at nothing.

He sighed. Of course. Master was always doing this, disappearing without warning and leaving others to catch up on their own.

"Why are you disappointed?" Li Fenghao's voice held amusement. "Use the technique yourself."

Hughie groaned. "I was hoping to save the energy. That technique takes a lot of qi."

"You're a dual cultivator now," Li Fenghao pointed out. "Your reserves are deeper than you realize. And more importantly, do you really want to spend days flying back to the sect when you could be there in seconds?"

He had a point.

Hughie took a deep breath and began gathering his qi. The Dimensional Slide technique was still relatively new to him, but Li Fenghao had drilled him thoroughly in its use. The key was visualizing the destination clearly, then tearing a hole through the space between here and there.

Simple in theory. Exhausting in practice.

He pictured the Black Rose Sect in his mind. Not the main halls or training grounds, but the small courtyard near the Outer Sect where Oliviare had been staying. The cherry blossom tree that grew near her window. The stone bench where they'd shared their first kiss.

His qi surged outward as it converted from standard spiritual energy into the strange spatial variant required for the technique. The air in front of him began to ripple and distort. Purple light bled through reality's fabric as he carved an opening between dimensions.

The portal stabilized after a few seconds of concentration. Through it, Hughie could see the familiar sight of the Black Rose Sect's outer grounds. Evening light painted everything in warm orange tones.

He glanced at Ace, who watched the portal with obvious interest. "Thank you for trying to help, Sect Master. I appreciate it."

Ace inclined his head. "I should be the one thanking you. You went out of your way to help my people. I hope to invite you to the sect one day, and this time *not* as a prisoner."

"That would be more fun, I imagine." Hughie laughed and stepped through the portal.

The sensation of dimensional travel was still strange, like being pulled through a too-small space while simultaneously being stretched in all directions. It only lasted a heartbeat, but that heartbeat felt like it took hours.

Then his foot touched solid ground, and the portal collapsed behind him.

Hughie stood in the courtyard near Oliviare's quarters. The cherry blossom tree swayed in a gentle breeze, pink petals drifting across the stone pathway. The evening air was cool and smelled faintly of jasmine from the nearby gardens.

He'd made it.

For a moment, Hughie just stood there letting the familiar peaceful atmosphere wash over him. This place was safe. No enemies, no mind control, no ancient Immortals possessing his body. Just home.

"Hughie?"

He turned toward the voice. Oliviare stood in the doorway of her quarters, one hand gripping the frame like she couldn't quite believe what she was seeing. Her long black hair was pulled back in a simple braid, and she wore the plain robes of an Outer Sect disciple.

She looked beautiful.

"I'm back," Hughie said, suddenly aware of how terrible he must look. His robes were torn and stained with blood. His face probably had cuts and bruises. He smelled like a battlefield.

Oliviare didn't seem to care about any of that.

She ran across the courtyard and threw her arms around him, holding him so tightly that his ribs protested. Hughie wrapped his arms around her in return, burying his face in her hair.

"I was so worried," she said, her voice muffled against his chest. "You left so suddenly, and then there were all these rumors about battles and righteous sects attacking, and I didn't know if you were hurt or—"

"I'm fine," Hughie interrupted gently. "I'm here. I'm safe."

She pulled back slightly to look at his face, her eyes scanning for injuries. "You're covered in blood."

"Most of it's not mine," he said, which was technically true. The blood on his robes belonged to various people who had tried to kill him over the past few hours. His own blood had been cleaned up when Li Fenghao healed his wounds during the possession.

Oliviare's expression suggested she didn't find that particularly reassuring.

"I convinced Master to give me some time off," Hughie said quickly, changing the subject. "A few days at least. Maybe a week. I thought we could . . . I don't know, spend time together? Without worrying about sect business or cultivation missions or any of that?"

Her worry transformed into a radiant smile. "Really? You can stay?"

"For a little while, yeah."

She hugged him again, and Hughie felt the tension finally drain from his body. This was what he'd been fighting for. Not abstract concepts like sect honor or cultivation advancement. This. This feeling of coming home to someone who genuinely cared whether he lived or died.

"Come inside," Oliviare said, pulling him toward her quarters. "You need to clean up and eat something. You look exhausted."

"I am exhausted," Hughie admitted. "Today was . . . complicated."

That was an understatement. He'd been captured, tortured, nearly had his mind controlled, been possessed by an ancient Immortal, and had watched that Immortal battle an Immortal Realm cultivator. Complicated didn't begin to cover it.

But all of that felt distant now, like something that had happened to someone else. Here, in this quiet courtyard with Oliviare's hand in his, the war and the chaos seemed impossibly far away.

"You can tell me about it later," she said, reading his expression. "Right now, just rest."

Hughie nodded. Inside the ring, he felt Li Fenghao's consciousness settle into a comfortable silence. The ancient Immortal seemed content to observe without commentary, giving Hughie privacy for this reunion.

They walked into Oliviare's quarters together. The small room was exactly as Hughie remembered it: simple furnishings, a few personal belongings, the scent of incense burning in the corner. It felt more like home than his own chambers ever had.

Oliviare made him sit while she heated water for tea. They talked about small things. How her cultivation was progressing with the new technique Slifer had given her. The gossip among the Outer Sect disciples. The new instructor who had arrived last week and was apparently terrible at teaching.

Normal things. Mundane things.

Hughie let the normalcy wash over him like a healing balm. This was what he'd been missing during all those dangerous missions. The simple pleasure of sitting with someone he cared about and talking about nothing important.

Eventually, after the tea was finished and the sky had darkened fully, Oliviare made him promise to stay the night. Not for anything inappropriate: she just didn't want him wandering around the sect in his condition. He was welcome to sleep on the floor if he preferred.

Hughie agreed immediately. He didn't have the energy to walk back to his own quarters anyway.

As he settled onto the mat she'd laid out for him, Hughie felt genuine contentment for the first time in months. The war would still be there tomorrow. Lady Chi would still be hunting them. The righteous sects would still see them as enemies.

But tonight, he was home. He was safe. He was with someone who loved him for who he was rather than what he could do for their sect's political machinations.

And that was enough.

"Thank you," Hughie thought to Li Fenghao as his eyes drifted closed. "For saving my life today."

"You're welcome, young man," the ancient Immortal replied. "Now get some rest. Tomorrow's troubles can wait until tomorrow."

For once, Hughie didn't dream of battles or cultivation breakthroughs. He didn't have nightmares about Lady Chi's red eyes or the sensation of thorns piercing his flesh.

He dreamed of cherry blossoms falling in spring, of peaceful courtyards, and of simple happiness that didn't require risking his life to achieve.

It was the best dream he'd had in months.

CHAPTER SEVENTEEN

Lady Chi materialized in a cave system three hundred thousand kilometers from the Heavenly Light Sect. The spatial jump had drained more energy than she wanted to admit, but distance mattered more than efficiency right now. She needed somewhere the old ghost could not track her. Somewhere she could tend to her wounds without interruption.

The cave was one of several hideouts she had prepared after first arriving in the mortal realm. Nothing fancy. Just a dry space with basic formations to hide her presence and prevent spiritual detection. She had stockpiled supplies here weeks ago. Healing pills, spare robes, emergency talismans. The kind of resources someone needed when operating in hostile territory.

She collapsed against the cave wall, finally allowing herself to feel the full extent of her injuries. Her left shoulder throbbed where the old man's strike had connected. The bone was cracked, not completely broken, but the damage went deeper than flesh. His spiritual energy had invaded her meridians, leaving traces that burned like acid through her channels.

Her ribs ached. Three were fractured from when he had thrown her into the wall. Lady Chi pressed a hand against her side and felt the unnatural give where bone should have been solid. Each breath sent sharp pains through her chest.

The humiliation hurt worse than the physical damage.

She had been defeated. Soundly, completely, humiliatingly defeated. Not by some legendary hero or powerful sect master, but by an old ghost inhabiting a boy's body. The spirit had toyed with her. He could have killed her at any point during their fight. Instead, he had chosen to wound her pride, to make her feel weak and helpless.

Lady Chi reached into her storage ring with trembling fingers. The emergency healing pill was there, wrapped in protective silk. She swallowed it dry and felt the medicinal energy spread through her body. Not enough to fully heal her injuries, but sufficient to stop the bleeding and stabilize the broken bones.

She sat there for several minutes just breathing. The cave was silent except for the occasional drip of water from somewhere deeper in the system. Lady Chi closed her eyes and focused on circulating her qi, directing the pill's energy toward the worst injuries first.

Her master had always warned her about arrogance. Elder Crimson Petal said disciples who relied too heavily on their sect's reputation often found themselves unprepared for genuine threats. Lady Chi had dismissed those warnings as the paranoid rambling of someone who had grown cautious with age.

She would not make that mistake again.

But even through the pain and humiliation, a small smile crossed her face. Because the spirit had made a critical error. He had revealed himself. He must be Li Fenghao—the Greater Immortal who had vanished from the higher realms ten thousand years ago. Who knew that he would be here, in the mortal realm, trapped in a ring worn by some insignificant boy.

That information was valuable. Extraordinarily valuable.

Lady Chi pulled herself to her feet, wincing as her ribs protested the movement. She moved deeper into the cave, past the main chamber where she had collapsed, into a smaller alcove that held her most important supplies. The communication talisman sat in a jade box, wrapped in preservation formations to keep it from degrading.

She lifted the talisman carefully. It was an heirloom from her sect, one of only three in her possession. Each use consumed a portion of the talisman's spiritual essence. After five activations, it would crumble to dust. She had only used it once to report her arrival in the mortal realm.

This would be the second time.

The connection process was not simple. The Immortal Realm existed in a higher dimensional space, separated from the mortal realm by barriers that prevented easy communication. Forcing a message through required tremendous energy. Energy she would have to provide personally through blood sacrifice.

Lady Chi retrieved a ceremonial knife from her storage ring. The blade was made of spirit silver etched with formations designed to channel blood qi efficiently. She had used this knife many times during her cultivation journey. Blood sacrifice was a standard technique in the Crimson Lotus Pavilion. They taught their disciples early that power required cost.

She rolled up her left sleeve, exposing the pale flesh of her forearm. Scars from previous sacrifices crisscrossed the skin in thin white lines. Dozens of them. Maybe hundreds. Each one represented a technique that demanded blood, a formation that required life force, or a cultivation breakthrough that consumed vitality.

The knife bit into her flesh. Blood welled up immediately, far more than should have come from such a shallow cut. But this was not normal blood. This was blood qi, the condensed essence of her life force drawn forth through specialized technique. It flowed thick and dark, almost black in color, and carried fragments of her spiritual energy with every drop.

Lady Chi held her arm over the communication talisman and let the blood qi drip onto its surface. Each drop was absorbed instantly, and the talisman glowed a brighter red as it fed on her sacrifice. She needed at least thirty drops to establish a stable connection. Each drop represented a day off her lifespan. A small price for information this important.

One drop. Five drops. Ten drops. The talisman began to pulse with inner light.

Lady Chi gritted her teeth as the blood continued to flow. This part always hurt. The technique literally pulled life force from her body, converting years into energy. She could feel herself growing weaker with each passing second. Her vision blurred slightly. Her hands began to shake.

Fifteen drops. Twenty drops. The talisman was singing now, a high-pitched whine that set her teeth on edge.

Twenty-five drops. Twenty-eight drops. Almost there.

On the thirtieth drop, the talisman erupted with crimson light that filled the entire alcove. Lady Chi quickly pressed her thumb against the cut on her forearm and used qi to seal the wound before she bled out completely. The blood qi stopped flowing immediately, though she had lost enough that her head swam with dizziness.

The light from the talisman coalesced into a projection. Not a full-body image like some advanced communication techniques could create, but a face floating in the air before her. The features were indistinct, blurred by the dimensional separation, but Lady Chi recognized the presence immediately.

Elder Crimson Petal. Her master. One of the seven core elders who governed the Crimson Lotus Pavilion. She wasn't an Immortal Emperor like she had bragged to Li Fenghao, but that didn't mean she was weak. She was a genuine Greater Immortal.

"Disciple Chi." The voice was distant, echoing as if coming from the bottom of a well. "Your report comes earlier than expected. Has your mission been completed? Some of my rivals are already asking about your whereabouts."

Lady Chi bowed her head respectfully, ignoring the way the movement made her broken ribs grind together. "Master, I report with urgent intelligence. I have located Li Fenghao of the Heavenly Cloud Sect."

The projection flickered. For a moment, Lady Chi thought the connection had failed. Then Elder Crimson Petal's blurred features sharpened slightly as the elder on the other side poured more energy into maintaining clarity.

"Repeat that," the elder commanded.

"Li Fenghao," Lady Chi said clearly. "The Greater Immortal who vanished ten thousand years ago. He is here, in the mortal realm. I engaged him in combat less than an hour past."

Silence from the other side. Lady Chi waited, hands clasped in proper disciple posture despite the pain radiating through her entire body. She knew what her master was thinking.

Li Fenghao had been one of the most powerful cultivators in the Immortal Realm before his disappearance. Not an Immortal Emperor, but close. A Greater Immortal who had achieved the ninth stage, standing at the very threshold of Emperor Realm. His sect, the Heavenly Cloud Sect, had controlled territories spanning three continents. Their influence reached into every major city, every trading hub, every cultivation-resource-rich location across the Eastern Territories.

Then one day, Li Fenghao vanished. No warning. No explanation. He simply ceased to exist, leaving his sect leaderless and vulnerable. Within a century, the Heavenly Cloud Sect had collapsed. Their territories were absorbed by rivals. Their disciples scattered. Their legacy reduced to cautionary tales about the dangers of closed-door cultivation.

Many assumed Li Fenghao had died attempting breakthrough to Immortal Emperor. Some whispered he had been assassinated by enemies. A few conspiracy theorists suggested he had fled to avoid debts or political entanglements.

Nobody suspected he was severely injured and hiding in the mortal realm.

"Explain the circumstances of this encounter," Elder Crimson Petal said. Her voice had taken on the sharp edge it carried during interrogations. "Where did you find him? What was his condition? Did he recognize you?"

Lady Chi organized her thoughts carefully. The communication talisman would only maintain connection for a few minutes at most. She needed to convey the essential information quickly and clearly.

"He is imprisoned in a soul-bearing ring," she said. "A young cultivator named

Hughie wears the ring on his finger. I was interrogating the boy when Li Fenghao manifested and took temporary control of the body. We fought. He was limited to Half-Step Immortal cultivation due to realm restrictions, same as myself."

"And the outcome?" The question carried no judgment, but Lady Chi felt shame burn through her anyway.

"I was defeated, Master. Li Fenghao's combat experience proved superior to my own. He allowed me to escape rather than kill me." She kept her voice level, reporting facts without emotion. "However, he revealed his identity during our confrontation. He is definitely Li Fenghao of the Heavenly Cloud Sect. His techniques, his spiritual signature, his manner of speech. All match the historical records."

More silence. Lady Chi could picture her master's expression: the calculating look Elder Crimson Petal wore when processing valuable intelligence and determining how best to exploit it.

"This information changes everything," the elder finally said. "Li Fenghao made many enemies during his reign. The Black Sky Consortium lost three trade routes to his sect's expansion. The Thousand Blade Alliance suffered humiliating defeats in territorial disputes. The Golden Lotus Sect . . ." She paused meaningfully. "The Golden Lotus Sect particularly has reason to want Li Fenghao found."

Lady Chi understood immediately. The Golden Lotus Sect was the Crimson Lotus Pavilion's bitter rival. They competed for the same territories, the same resources, the same prestigious disciples. Any intelligence that gave her sect advantage over Golden Lotus was worth its weight in immortal stones.

But there were other buyers too. The organizations Elder Crimson Petal had mentioned would pay fortunes for confirmed information about Li Fenghao's location. Especially if that information came with proof he was weakened, trapped, vulnerable.

"How big of a bounty could this intelligence command, Master?" Lady Chi asked carefully.

"Conservative estimate? Nine hundred thousand high-grade immortal stones." The projection flickered again as Elder Crimson Petal spoke. "Possibly more if we include bidding war factors. The Azure Sky Consortium alone would pay four hundred thousand just to confirm Li Fenghao cannot interfere with their operations anymore."

Lady Chi felt her heart race despite her injuries. Nine hundred thousand immortal stones. That was enough wealth to purchase territory, establish new sect branches, hire mercenary cultivators by the hundreds. It was enough wealth to elevate her status within the Crimson Lotus Pavilion dramatically.

"However," Elder Crimson Petal continued, "this intelligence is only valuable if we can verify it. You need proof. Something concrete that confirms Li Fenghao's presence and location."

"What kind of proof, Master?"

"Ideally? The ring itself, with Li Fenghao's soul still trapped inside. Failing that, a detailed description of his current circumstances, witnesses who can testify to his identity, and perhaps a recording talisman capturing his spiritual signature." The projection's features sharpened as the elder leaned closer on the other side. "Can you acquire such proof?"

Lady Chi thought about Hughie. The boy was under the protection of that demonic sect master Slifer. The same Slifer who had killed Darius. The same Slifer she had sworn a binding oath to destroy.

An idea began to form.

"I believe I can, Master," she said slowly. "But it will require time and careful planning. Li Fenghao's host body is protected by powerful allies. Direct assault proved ineffective. I will need to be more subtle."

"Subtle is acceptable. Dead is not." Elder Crimson Petal's voice carried a clear warning. "If Li Fenghao escapes or is destroyed before we can verify his identity, this opportunity vanishes. Proceed carefully. Take whatever time necessary. The bounty will wait."

"I understand, Master."

"One more thing." The projection began to fade as the talisman's energy depleted. "Say nothing of this discovery to anyone else in the pavilion. Not until we have proof. If word spreads prematurely, rival sects may attempt their own operations. The Golden Lotus Sect in particular has spies everywhere. Do you understand?"

"Complete secrecy until verification," Lady Chi confirmed. "I will report only to you directly."

"Good." The projection was barely visible now as the elder's features dissolved into red mist. "You have done well, my disciple. Very well indeed. When this intelligence proves accurate, your rewards will be substantial. Position as inner elder. Personal territory. Perhaps even—"

The connection severed. The talisman crumbled to dust in Lady Chi's palm, its spiritual essence completely exhausted. She had three communication talismans remaining. She would need to use them wisely.

Lady Chi remained kneeling in the alcove for several minutes after the projection disappeared. Her injuries still hurt. Her pride still burned from the defeat. But now she had purpose beyond simple revenge.

Li Fenghao was worth nine hundred thousand immortal stones. Maybe more. That kind of wealth could change everything. It could elevate her from talented disciple to genuine power within the sect. She would have resources to pursue her own cultivation without restriction. She would have authority to command others rather than following orders.

All she needed was proof.

And to get proof, she needed to capture Hughie alive. Needed to take the ring without destroying the soul trapped inside. That meant dealing with Slifer first. The demonic sect master who protected the boy. The same sect master she was already sworn to kill.

Two birds with one stone, as the mortals said.

Lady Chi pulled herself to her feet again, this time with purpose rather than desperation. The pain was still there, but it felt different now. Not the agony of defeat, but the temporary discomfort of someone who had suffered a setback on the path to greater victory.

She would heal. She would plan. She would wait for the perfect opportunity.

And when that opportunity came, she would take everything. Li Fenghao's ring. Slifer's life. Her rightful place among the Crimson Lotus Pavilion's elite.

The cave suddenly felt less like a hiding place and more like a tactical position. Lady Chi began organizing her remaining supplies, taking inventory of what resources she still possessed. She had healing pills. Combat talismans. Surveillance formations. Escape treasures.

Enough to work with. Enough to turn defeat into eventual triumph.

Outside the cave, dawn was breaking across the mortal realm. Lady Chi could sense the shift through the formations protecting her hideout. A new day beginning. New opportunities emerging.

She smiled despite the pain in her ribs.

Let Slifer and his disciples celebrate their victory. Let Li Fenghao think he had frightened her away. Let them all believe she was beaten, broken, running scared.

They would learn the truth soon enough.

CHAPTER EIGHTEEN

Slifer sat in his private quarters. He should have been exhausted; the past few hours had been a blur of portals, battles, and mind-controlled sect masters. Instead, he felt oddly energized, the kind of restless energy that came from accomplishing something genuinely difficult.

The Pure Soul Sect was freed. Ming Yue had regained control of her consciousness and immediately allied with the Black Rose Sect. The shock on the righteous cultivators' faces when their own sect master announced an alliance with demonic cultivators had been something to witness.

The Heavenly Light Sect was similarly liberated. Ace had managed to identify and free the compromised elders once Lady Chi fled. That sect's alliance was more tentative—centuries of animosity between righteous and demonic paths didn't vanish overnight—but it was holding.

Two major righteous sects now stood with him against Lady Chi.

Slifer reached into his robes and pulled out a letter that had arrived just an hour ago. The paper was expensive, the kind with threads of gold woven into the fibers. The White Tiger Sect's official seal was pressed into red wax at the bottom. He unfolded it to read it again.

To the Esteemed Leaders of the Demonic Sects,

The White Tiger Sect, in recognition of recent developments, and after careful consideration of the greater good of all cultivation communities, has determined that continued military operations against your sect serves no beneficial purpose at this time.

> *Our sect has always prided itself on strategic wisdom and the ability to recognize when circumstances have evolved beyond initial assessments. Recent events have demonstrated that the current conflict arose from misunderstandings and external manipulations that do not reflect the true interests of our noble sect.*
>
> *Therefore, the White Tiger Sect hereby announces a cessation of all hostile activities. We look forward to the restoration of peaceful relations among all sects and the pursuit of cultivation advancement that benefits our entire community.*
>
> *Respectfully, The Council of Elders, White Tiger Sect*

Slifer couldn't help the small smile that crossed his face. The letter was a masterpiece of political doublespeak. It said absolutely nothing about their guardian beast being defeated, their elders being subdued, or their sect master fleeing. Instead, it painted their withdrawal as a magnanimous decision made for the cultivation world's benefit.

He had to respect it. They'd been thoroughly beaten. He, Caelum, and Ming Yue had handled their strongest defenses without breaking a sweat, but they'd managed to phrase their surrender in a way that preserved face. That took skill.

The important thing was that the war was over. Officially, completely over. No more raids on supply lines. No more disciples dying in pointless skirmishes. The Black Rose Sect could return to normal operations, and he could stop worrying about managing three different crisis situations simultaneously.

Well, almost over. There was still Lady Chi.

Slifer folded the letter and set it on the small table beside him. His smile faded as he considered the problem that remained. She was still out there somewhere, nursing her wounded pride and plotting revenge. An Immortal Realm cultivator with a personal grudge, bound by oath to remain in the mortal realm until he was dead.

In the web novels he used to read, this was exactly the kind of situation that led to escalating revenge cycles. The hero would spare the villain, who would then come back stronger. The villain would spare the hero out of arrogance, allowing them time to power up. Back and forth, each encounter raising the stakes until something catastrophic happened.

Slifer had no intention of playing that game.

When he found Lady Chi, and he would find her eventually, he was going to kill her. Not capture, not seal, not banish. Kill. Permanently. No chances for dramatic returns or surprise resurrections.

He knew that decision made him sound ruthless, maybe even villainous from certain perspectives. But he'd seen what happened when you left dangerous enemies alive in this kind of world. They came back, usually at the worst possible moment, and caused exponentially more damage than if you'd just finished them the first time.

Lady Chi had demonstrated she was willing to control the minds of sect masters, start wars, and torture his disciples. She'd sworn a binding oath to kill him. There was no redemption arc coming for someone like that. The smart play, the survival play, was permanent removal.

As for her connections in the Immortal Realm—the Crimson Lotus Pavilion and whoever else might care about her death—he'd deal with that when the time came. Worrying about Immortal Realm politics while still stuck in the mortal realm was premature. First survive the immediate threat, then worry about the long-term consequences.

Slifer stood and walked to the window, pushing aside the paper screen. The view looked out over one of the sect's main training grounds. Even in the fading light, he could see disciples going through their forms, practicing spiritual techniques and cultivation exercises. Their movements were relaxed, casual. No urgency. No fear.

They'd already returned to their normal routines. The war was yesterday's news. They were back to worrying about breakthrough attempts and learning new techniques and gossiping about whoever was dating whom.

Slifer felt something in his chest ease at the sight. This was what he'd been fighting for, really. Not grand political alliances or defeating powerful enemies. Just this. Normal people living normal lives without the constant threat of violence hanging over their heads.

He let himself enjoy the moment, watching the sun sink lower and paint the training grounds in deepening shadows. Then he sensed it.

The air behind him changed. Not dramatically. No explosive burst of energy or reality-tearing roar. Just a subtle shift in pressure that made every instinct he'd developed scream "danger."

Slifer turned.

A white portal hung in the center of his quarters, its edges perfectly smooth and stable. No rough tears or crackling energy. This was controlled. Professional. Someone who'd opened dimensional gateways so many times they could do it in their sleep.

Slifer sighed deeply. "What now?"

He barely got the words out before a figure exploded through the portal.

Too fast. Way too fast. Slifer's eyes couldn't track the movement properly.

One moment the portal was empty, the next a hand was reaching for his throat, fingers spread to grab.

Slifer felt the Critical Block Card activate automatically.

The hand struck an invisible barrier and stopped. The figure's momentum caused them to recoil back a half step before they caught themselves.

That brief pause gave Slifer his first good look at his attacker.

Male, probably early thirties, though cultivation made age estimates unreliable. Long black hair pulled back in a high ponytail that fell to his shoulders. Sharp eyes, the kind you saw in people accustomed to getting their way through force. Noble features: high cheekbones, strong jaw, the kind of face that probably made women swoon. He wore white robes that were almost luminous in their cleanliness and embroidered with silver patterns that suggested wealth and status.

But what made Slifer's blood run cold was the aura.

Half-Step Immortal. The absolute peak of what the mortal realm could contain without triggering heavenly intervention. The kind of power that should have been unique, or at least rare enough that Slifer would have heard about it.

Slifer's mind raced. He'd thought Ace was the strongest cultivator in the mortal realm. That's what all the intelligence suggested: Heavenly Light Sect Master, the pillar of righteous cultivation, unmatched in power. But this person radiated the same level of strength, maybe even more refined.

Was this some hidden master? Someone who'd been in seclusion for centuries and just emerged? That happened in cultivation stories all the time.

"Who are you?" Slifer kept his voice level despite his hammering heart. "What do you want?"

The young man looked at his hand, turning it over as if checking for damage. Then he looked at Slifer, and his expression shifted to something between annoyance and interest.

"Interesting," the man said. His voice was smooth, cultured. "That barrier. It's not a normal defensive technique."

Slifer didn't respond. His mind was already pulling up the System interface and mentally scrolling through available cards. If this person attacked again, he needed to be ready.

The man seemed to be offended by Slifer's silence because he scoffed, then he vanished.

Slifer's eyes widened. He spun, but it was useless. The man was already behind him, moving faster than Slifer's cultivated senses could track. He felt the presence behind him, felt the hand reaching for the back of his neck.

Another Critical Block activated.

The invisible barrier appeared between Slifer's neck and the reaching hand. The man's fingers stopped against nothing, and Slifer heard a small sound of frustration.

Slifer didn't waste the opportunity. He was already making purchases.

Thundergod's Descent Card	Cost: 20,000 Karmic Credits
Ascendant Strike Card x3	Cost: 24,000 Karmic Credits
Ten-Minute Ascendant Power Card	Cost: 15,000 Karmic Credits

The numbers flashed past. His credit balance plummeted. But dying was more expensive than any purchase.

He activated the Ten-Minute Ascendant Power Card immediately.

Golden light erupted from Slifer's body as temporary power flooded his cultivation base. His Core Formation stage remained, but a shell of Ascendant Realm strength wrapped around it, granting him access to techniques and speed far beyond his normal capabilities.

The young man's eyes widened slightly. "Oh? You were hiding your cultivation?"

Slifer didn't answer. He pushed off the ground, putting distance between them, and activated the first Ascendant Strike Card. His right hand blazed with golden light, and he thrust his palm forward. A beam of concentrated energy shot across the room.

The man crossed his arms, and the beam struck him directly. The explosion was massive, filling the small quarters with light and force. The paper screens disintegrated. The wooden furniture shattered. The floor cracked under the pressure.

When the light faded, the man was still standing. His white robes were singed but intact. His arms showed faint burns, but nothing serious. He was smiling.

"Now this is more like it," the man said.

He moved again, a blur of motion that crossed the ten-foot gap in a heartbeat. His fist came at Slifer's face with enough force to shatter bone.

Slifer ducked, the movement enhanced by his temporary Ascendant power, and the fist passed over his head close enough to ruffle his hair. He countered with a palm strike to the man's midsection as he channeled spiritual energy through the blow.

The strike connected. The man grunted and slid backward a meter, his boots leaving marks on the floor. But he recovered instantly and swept his leg around in a kick aimed at Slifer's head.

Slifer blocked with his forearm. The impact sent shock waves through his arm, and he felt something crack despite his enhanced durability. He gritted his teeth against the pain and grabbed the man's ankle, trying to throw him off balance.

The man twisted in midair with impossible flexibility, breaking Slifer's grip and landing in a crouch. He swept his arm out, and spiritual energy burst from his palm like a blade. The invisible attack carved through the remaining furniture, cutting wooden tables and chairs in half, before reaching Slifer.

A Critical Block activated and stopped the blade of energy in its tracks.

"How many times can you use that technique?" the man asked, genuine curiosity in his voice.

"Enough," Slifer replied. He activated another Ascendant Strike Card and fired it point-blank.

The golden beam caught the man in the chest as he tried to dodge. The explosion threw him backward through the wall, his body smashing through wood and paper and creating a man-sized hole that opened to the evening air.

Slifer heard shouts from outside. Disciples responding to the noise, no doubt. He needed to end this fast before someone got caught in the crossfire.

The man floated back through the hole he'd created, completely unharmed despite the direct hit. "You're stronger than the intelligence suggested," he said conversationally, brushing dust from his robes. "The reports said you were a lucky Ascendant at best. But these techniques . . ." He gestured at the destruction around them. "These are powerful. Someone has been badly underestimating you."

Slifer just stared directly at him. "Are you going to tell me what you want, or do we just keep destroying my quarters?"

"I want—" the man started to say, but then he stopped. His expression shifted from casual amusement to something sharper. His eyes narrowed, and he began gathering spiritual energy. Real energy, not the casual exchanges they'd been having. The air pressure in the room tripled. The remaining walls began to crack under the strain.

Slifer felt his stomach drop. This person had been playing. Barely trying. And now he was about to get serious.

He activated the Thundergod's Descent Card.

Dark clouds materialized over the sect. Thunder rumbled. Lightning began arcing between roiling masses of storm energy that shouldn't exist in the clear evening sky.

The young man looked up, his eyes widening for the first time. "You're summoning a tribulation? Here? Are you insane?"

"Desperate," Slifer corrected.

The lightning struck.

A massive bolt of pure white energy descended from the clouds, targeting the area around Slifer's quarters. The man's eyes went wide, and he moved, his body blurring with speed as he tried to escape the strike zone.

He was too slow.

The lightning caught him mid-dodge, and the sound of the impact was deafening. Light filled everything. Slifer felt the shock wave pass through his body, rattling his bones and making his teeth ache despite his Critical Block protection.

When his vision cleared, the young man was on the ground. His white robes were scorched black in places, his hair singed. Blood trickled from his nose and ears. He pushed himself up on one elbow, looking genuinely surprised for the first time.

"That actually hurt," he said, touching his bleeding nose. "You're full of surprises."

Before Slifer could activate another card, a voice rang out across the devastated quarters.

"Jian Wei! That's enough!"

A second figure stepped through the white portal, which had remained stable throughout the entire fight. This was an old man, probably late sixties by appearance, with long white hair and a scholarly face marked by laugh lines. He wore robes of the same white material but cut in a simpler style. His expression carried the tired patience of someone who'd had this exact conversation many times before.

And his aura—Slifer felt it wash over him like a wave—was also Half-Step Immortal.

Two of them. Two cultivators at the peak of mortal realm power emerging from a portal in his quarters. This couldn't be coincidence. Their manner, their techniques, their casual power . . . They couldn't both be hidden masters, could they?

Unless . . .

They weren't Half-Step Immortals at all.

They were genuine Immortals suppressing their cultivation to fit within the mortal realm's limits.

The old man walked calmly across the destroyed floor, glass and splinters crunching under his boots. He looked around at the devastation—the shattered walls, the scattered furniture fragments, the scorched marks from lightning—and his expression became pained.

"My sincere apologies," he said, bowing to Slifer. "My junior brother has a . . . particular way of doing things. I had instructed him to approach you peacefully and request a conversation. Instead, he . . ." The old man gestured helplessly at the destruction. "Well. This."

Jian Wei picked himself up, dusting off his robes with only moderate concern for the burns covering his body. "You told me to retrieve him quickly. I was being quick."

"I said to speak with him, not attack him on sight!"

"Same result," Jian Wei muttered, though he had the grace to look slightly embarrassed.

Slifer kept his defensive stance, not trusting this sudden civility. His temporary Ascendant power was still active and would give him a chance if this was some kind of trick. "Who are you? What do you want?"

The old man's expression became more serious. He straightened from his bow and met Slifer's eyes directly. "My name is Han Shu, and this hot-headed fool is my junior brother, Jian Wei. We are from the Immortal Realm, specifically from an organization tasked with monitoring and managing . . . problems that arise when Immortals interfere in lower realms."

That confirmed Slifer's suspicion. These weren't local cultivators. They were from above, literally and figuratively.

"Problems," Slifer repeated carefully. "You mean Lady Chi."

Han Shu's expression brightened slightly. "So, you are aware of her. That simplifies matters considerably. Yes, Lady Chi is our primary concern. An Immortal Realm cultivator who has descended to the mortal realm and is causing significant disruption through mind control and manipulation. Our organization received reports of her activities and sent us to investigate and, if necessary, intervene."

Slifer processed this. An organization from the Immortal Realm that policed rogue Immortals. That made sense, actually. You couldn't have powerful cultivators just descending whenever they wanted and wreaking havoc. There had to be some kind of enforcement mechanism.

But something didn't add up. "If you're here about Lady Chi, why are you wasting time in my quarters?"

Jian Wei opened his mouth to respond, but Han Shu held up a hand, cutting him off. The old man sighed deeply, the sound of someone who was dealing with a persistent headache.

"The original instruction was to locate you and ask questions about Lady Chi's activities, whereabouts, and capabilities. However, Jian Wei has certain . . . philosophical differences with how we conduct our investigations." Han Shu looked pointedly at his junior brother. "He believes that observing someone's combat capabilities provides more useful information than simple conversation. Therefore, he took it upon himself to 'test' you instead of speaking with you like a civilized person."

"I learned plenty," Jian Wei said defensively. "He has multiple high-tier defensive techniques, at least three different attack formations, and access to lightning tribulation summoning. Plus, his real cultivation is hidden. That's valuable intelligence."

"Intelligence we could have obtained by asking!" Han Shu's patience was clearly wearing thin. He turned back to Slifer, his expression apologetic again. "I cannot express how sorry I am for this entire situation. The damage to your quarters, the disruption to your sect, the completely unnecessary combat—all of it could have been avoided if someone had simply followed instructions."

Slifer looked around at the destruction. His quarters were effectively gone. Three walls had holes in them. The floor was cracked and scorched. Every piece of furniture was shattered. The ceiling had a massive hole where the lightning had struck, and he could see the evening sky through it.

Han Shu followed his gaze, and the old man's expression became deeply embarrassed. "I will, of course, ensure appropriate compensation for the damage. And a formal apology to your sect master. Though, I understand that's you as well, which makes this even more awkward."

The absurdity of the situation was starting to sink in. Slifer had just fought an Immortal Realm cultivator, admittedly one who was suppressing their power and apparently not trying very hard, and now that same person's senior brother was apologizing for property damage like a parent whose child had broken a neighbor's window.

Slifer heard footsteps approaching from outside. Multiple sets running fast. The disciples had definitely noticed the lightning tribulation and the destruction. They'd be here in seconds.

Han Shu heard them too. His eyes flicked toward the approaching sounds, then to the white portal that still hung stable in the air. "Perhaps we could continue this conversation somewhere more private? I would prefer not to have dozens of witnesses to an Immortal Realm presence in your sect. It tends to cause . . . complications."

Slifer looked at the portal. His instincts screamed caution. These people had just attacked him. Following them through a dimensional gateway to an unknown location was exactly the kind of stupid decision that got people killed in every cultivation story ever written.

But.

They could have killed him already if they wanted to. Jian Wei had held back considerably during their fight; Slifer could tell that now, looking back.

The man had been testing him, playing with him really, not actually trying to end his life.

More importantly, this was contact with the Immortal Realm. A chance to gather real information about the higher levels of cultivation, organizations that operated above mortal politics, and enforcement mechanisms he'd only theorized about. The System had given him knowledge about cultivation, but it was limited. Talking to actual Immortals could fill in massive gaps in his understanding.

And if they were here about Lady Chi, that meant potential allies. Or at least people with a shared interest in removing her from the mortal realm permanently.

The footsteps were getting closer. Slifer could hear voices now, disciples calling out to each other, organizing a response to the perceived threat.

Slifer made his decision.

"Fine," he said. "But if this is a trap, I have techniques that will ensure we all die together."

That was a complete bluff. He had no such techniques. But it sounded good.

Han Shu smiled, apparently seeing through the bluff but appreciating it anyway. "No traps, young friend. Just conversation. You have my word as an enforcer of the Celestial Court."

The Celestial Court. Slifer filed that name away for later consideration. It sounded official and intimidating, which probably meant it was both.

He walked toward the portal, his temporary Ascendant power still active just in case. The white gateway swirled with gentle energy, its interior showing nothing but blank whiteness. No glimpse of what lay beyond. That was either sophisticated craftsmanship or deliberate obfuscation.

Slifer took a breath and stepped through.

The transition was smooth, professional. No disorientation, no sensation of being pulled or stretched. One moment he was in his destroyed quarters, the next he was somewhere else entirely.

The first person to reach the scene that Slifer had left behind was a young Outer Sect disciple named Lin, who took one look at the devastation and froze. The entire structure was barely standing. Scorch marks covered the floor. Three walls had gaping holes. The ceiling was partially collapsed. It looked like a battlefield.

"What in the heavens . . . ?" Lin whispered.

More disciples arrived, their expressions ranging from shock to alarm to confusion. They spread out around the perimeter of the destroyed quarters, staring at the damage and trying to make sense of what had happened.

"Was it an attack?" one disciple asked.

"Did someone target the sect master?" another asked.

"Where is he? Is he hurt?"

The speculation built quickly, and voices rose as more people arrived and saw the destruction. Some disciples were already preparing to sound general alarm formations. Others were checking for bodies or signs of their sect master's fate.

Then Morvran arrived.

The right-hand man of Sect Master Slifer pushed through the crowd of disciples with the authority of someone who didn't need to ask permission. His expression was thunderous as he surveyed the damage, his eyes tracking the scorch marks and shattered furniture with practiced assessment.

"Everyone back!" Morvran's voice cut through the rising panic. "Form a perimeter. Nobody enters the area until I've completed my investigation."

The disciples obeyed immediately, some of them looking relieved to have someone take charge of the situation. They backed away from the destroyed quarters and formed a loose circle around the devastation.

Morvran walked carefully through the debris, his spiritual sense extended to its maximum range. He was looking for traces of the sect master's aura, signs of what kind of technique had been used—anything that might indicate what had happened.

He found the lightning marks first. Tribulation lightning, judging by the pattern. Someone had summoned a storm directly over these quarters. That took power and precision. The sect master had definitely been here, and he'd been fighting something serious.

But there was no blood. No body. No sign of the sect master being injured or killed. Instead, Morvran found traces of two foreign spiritual signatures. Both of them were refined beyond anything he'd encountered in the mortal realm. Immortal level, or close enough that the difference didn't matter.

The sect master had been fighting Immortals. Plural.

Morvran felt his stomach clench. He'd served Sect Master Slifer long enough to know the man was far more capable than he appeared. The way he'd handled Lady Chi and the ease with which he'd defeated multiple Ascendant cultivators suggested hidden depths of power. But fighting multiple Immortals?

A young disciple approached cautiously. Morvran recognized him: it was his own personal disciple, Dusty. The boy looked nervous, his round face showing obvious concern, but that could be because there were no snacks in sight.

"Master," Dusty said hesitantly. "What should we do?"

Morvran looked around at the destruction one more time. The evening light was fading, casting long shadows across the shattered quarters. The sect master was gone. The other spiritual signatures had vanished as well. No portal remained, no trail to follow.

He could mobilize the sect. Sound the alarms. Prepare for war or rescue or whatever the situation demanded. But something in his gut told him that wasn't the right move. The sect master had left willingly. There was no sign of forced capture or defeat. He'd gone somewhere, probably through one of those spatial portals he was so fond of using.

"Clean this up," Morvran said finally, gesturing at the destroyed quarters. "Salvage what you can. Dispose of what's beyond repair. I want this area completely cleared and documented within the hour."

Dusty blinked. "Clean it up? But shouldn't we—"

"The sect master is handling whatever needs to be handled," Morvran interrupted firmly. "Our job is to ensure everything is in order when he returns. Understood?"

Dusty nodded quickly. "Yes, Master. I'll organize the cleanup immediately."

The young disciple hurried off, already calling out to other disciples to help with the effort. Morvran watched him go, then looked back at the destroyed quarters one more time.

Sect Master Slifer had a talent for walking into impossibly dangerous situations and emerging not just alive but somehow better off than before. First the tournament, then the Sealed Realm, then the war with Lady Chi. Each time, Morvran had been certain disaster was imminent. Each time, the sect master had surprised everyone.

But Immortals were different. They operated on a level so far beyond mortal cultivation that the gap was almost incomprehensible. Even if the sect master could fight them—and the evidence suggested he could, somehow—there was no guarantee he could survive whatever they wanted from him.

Morvran closed his eyes and sent a silent prayer to whatever ancestors or heavenly powers might be listening. He wasn't particularly religious, but this seemed like an appropriate time to start.

Keep him safe, Morvran thought. *Whatever he's dealing with, wherever he's gone, just keep him safe and bring him back to the sect.*

He opened his eyes and looked out over the sect grounds. Disciples were going about their evening routines, most of them unaware of the drama that had just unfolded. The war was over. Peace had returned. Life was getting back to normal.

Morvran hoped desperately that this new development wouldn't shatter that peace.

But knowing the sect master, it probably would.

CHAPTER NINETEEN

The white void resolved into something that looked like a traditional tea house. Slifer blinked as his surroundings came into focus. Wooden floors polished to a mirror shine, paper screens decorated with painted mountains, and low tables arranged in neat rows. Through the open walls, he could see nothing but white mist stretching in all directions.

Not exactly the sinister dimensional trap he'd been half expecting.

Han Shu walked calmly toward one of the tables and sat down. His white robes settled around him as he gestured for Slifer to join him. Jian Wei followed, still brushing scorch marks from his clothes and looking considerably less composed than his senior brother.

"Please, sit," Han Shu said. His voice carried the patient tone of someone who dealt with complicated situations regularly. "I understand this has been an unusual introduction, but I assure you we mean no harm. This space is neutral territory maintained by the Celestial Court specifically for situations like this."

Slifer studied the space more carefully as he approached the table. The tea house felt real enough. The wood beneath his feet had weight and texture. The air smelled faintly of incense. But something about it all seemed just slightly off, like reality had been painted on rather than grown naturally.

He sat across from Han Shu, keeping his posture relaxed despite every instinct screaming to stay alert. Jian Wei took a position to Han Shu's right, sitting with the rigid formality of someone who'd been lectured about proper behavior very recently.

"So," Slifer said, deciding direct questions were better than dancing around the topic, "what exactly is the Celestial Court?"

Han Shu's expression brightened slightly, as if pleased by the straightforward question. "Ah, of course. You were brought up in the mortal realm; you don't know much about Immortal politics and how they have changed in the past thousands of years."

Thousands of years. Right. Because that was a normal timeframe to discuss politics. Slifer kept his face neutral and waited for Han Shu to continue.

"The Celestial Court was established approximately fifty thousand years ago," Han Shu explained as he poured tea from a pot that had appeared on the table. Slifer hadn't seen anyone bring it. "Before that, the Immortal Realm was . . . chaotic. Powerful cultivators descended to lower realms whenever they pleased, either to harvest resources, establish puppet kingdoms, or simply to amuse themselves at mortal expense."

He poured three cups, then slid one across to Slifer and another to Jian Wei.

"Many of us found this distasteful," Han Shu continued. "The strong preying on the weak is natural in cultivation, but there should be limits. Balance. When Greater Immortals began competing over mortal realms like children fighting over toys, the consequences became catastrophic. Entire continents were rendered uninhabitable. Bloodlines were corrupted beyond repair. Dimensional barriers were weakened to the point of collapse."

Slifer picked up the teacup, mostly to have something to do with his hands. The liquid inside was pale green and smelled like flowers he couldn't identify. He took a careful sip. It tasted like spring rain, if spring rain could be a flavor.

"So, a group of concerned Immortals formed the Celestial Court," Han Shu said. "We established rules for interaction between realms, created enforcement mechanisms, offered mediation services for disputes that might otherwise escalate to realm-destroying conflicts. It's been . . . mostly successful."

"Mostly," Slifer repeated.

Han Shu smiled slightly. "Perfect systems don't exist. We do our best with what we have."

Jian Wei leaned forward, apparently recovered enough from his earlier embarrassment to contribute. "The court operates through regional branches, each overseen by a panel of Greater Immortals. We're from the Eastern Territories branch, which handles everything from the Crimson Sea to the Jade Mountains."

Slifer had absolutely no idea where those places were, but he nodded as if the geography made perfect sense.

"Our specific role," Jian Wei continued, warming to the topic, "is enforcement. When we receive reports of Immortal Realm cultivators causing problems in lower realms, we investigate and intervene if necessary. Usually, it's something simple: Someone getting drunk and accidentally destroying a sect or two. A romantic dispute spilling over into mortal politics leading to the destruction of a kingdom. Junior disciples testing new techniques without proper supervision resulting in the destruction of a continent."

That's what they classify as simple?

"Sometimes," Han Shu added quietly, "it's more serious. Like Lady Chi."

The name hung in the air between them. Slifer set down his teacup.

"Tell me about her," he said.

Han Shu and Jian Wei exchanged a look. Some kind of silent communication passed between them, the way it did with people who'd worked together for a very long time. Finally, Han Shu nodded slightly.

"Her full name," Han Shu said, "is Chi Xifeng. She's a Core Disciple of the Crimson Lotus Pavilion, one of the three great cultivation sects in the Eastern Territories. Extremely talented. Achieved Lesser Immortal Realm at age two hundred, which is considered prodigious by any standard."

Lesser Immortal. So that's what they called the cultivation stage above Half-Step Immortal. Good to know.

"She also," Han Shu continued, his tone becoming more somber, "has a history of instability. The Crimson Lotus Pavilion specializes in corruption techniques. They teach their disciples to twist natural growth into weapons—flowers that bloom with poison, trees that drink blood, gardens that consume intruders. It's effective cultivation, but it tends to . . . affect the practitioner's mind."

"Makes them crazy," Jian Wei translated bluntly.

Han Shu shot him a look that suggested this wasn't the diplomatic phrasing he would have chosen, but he didn't contradict it.

"Chi Xifeng has demonstrated concerning behavior for decades," Han Shu said. "Nothing that rose to the level of court intervention, but enough that our master requested we keep an eye on her. Then, approximately one hundred years ago by mortal realm time, she entered into a relationship with a man named Darius."

The name triggered something in Slifer's memory. The letter he'd found in Grand Elder Darius's belongings. The love poems. The desperate declarations of eternal devotion.

"Darius was . . ." Han Shu paused, choosing his words carefully. "Not a good match for her. He was a mortal cultivator from your sect, known primarily for his skill at flattery and manipulation. He courted Chi Xifeng with the kind of intensity that suggested ulterior motives."

"He wanted access to the Crimson Lotus Pavilion's techniques," Jian Wei said. "Everyone knew it except her. She was completely obsessed with him. Wrote poetry about him. Commissioned paintings. Started wearing his favorite colors. It was honestly painful to watch."

"When Darius died," Han Shu continued, "Chi Xifeng's reaction was . . . extreme. She blamed everyone around her: her sect elders for not protecting him adequately, her fellow disciples for not mourning properly—in short, she blamed the entire cultivation world for allowing such a tragedy to occur."

"And then she found out he'd been killed by a demonic cultivator in the mortal realm," Jian Wei said. "That's when things got really bad."

"She descended to get revenge," Slifer finished.

"Worse," Han Shu added. "She descended without permission or proper documentation and violated at least seven major regulations about realm crossing. And instead of simply hunting the person responsible for Darius's death, she began manipulating mortal sect politics to orchestrate a war."

Slifer knew better. Lady Chi had walked up to the Black Rose Sect and tried to kill him immediately. It was only when she failed that she began building a powerbase.

"We received multiple reports about unusual activity in this region," Han Shu continued. "Sect masters acting against their nature. Conflicts escalating beyond rational boundaries. Mind control signatures consistent with Crimson Lotus techniques. When we investigated, we confirmed Chi Xifeng had been here for a few months systematically corrupting the region's leadership."

"And now you want to capture her," Slifer said.

"Ideally," Han Shu said, "we'd bring her back to the Immortal Realm and let the court deal with her rehabilitation, then restore normal order to this region and seal any dimensional damage she might have caused."

"And if capture isn't possible?" Slifer asked.

Jian Wei's expression became harder. "Then we kill her. The court authorizes lethal force when an Immortal's actions threaten fundamental realm stability. Starting a continental war through mind control definitely qualifies."

Slifer considered this. On one hand, having powerful allies against Lady Chi seemed like exactly what he needed. On the other hand, working with Immortal Realm enforcers meant increased scrutiny of his own activities. They were already suspicious about his capabilities. How long before they started asking uncomfortable questions about how a mortal had broken through the Immortal Realm despite the restrictions in this world?

As if reading his thoughts, Han Shu spoke again. "We understand this puts you in an awkward position. You clearly have your own methods, your own approach to handling problems. We're not here to interfere with your work in the mortal realm or question your techniques. Our only goal is containing Chi Xifeng."

"You mean the woman who's sworn an oath to kill me," Slifer said dryly.

"Yes, well." Han Shu had the grace to look slightly embarrassed. "That does complicate matters. But it also gives us a point of agreement. You want her gone for personal survival. We want her gone for realm stability. Our goals align."

Slifer picked up his tea again, taking another sip while he thought. The liquid was still somehow the perfect temperature despite sitting for several minutes. Immortal Realm tea houses apparently had some very sophisticated temperature control.

"What would this partnership look like, practically speaking?" he asked.

Han Shu seemed to relax slightly, as if he'd been worried Slifer would refuse outright. "Information sharing, primarily. Chi Xifeng knows we're here now. She'll adapt her strategies, become more cautious. But she's also obsessed with killing you, which means she'll make mistakes trying to get to you. We coordinate efforts, share intelligence about her movements, and strike when an opportunity presents itself."

"I have resources you don't," Slifer said, thinking of his System cards and the various tools he'd accumulated. "Defensive techniques that can counter her attacks. Ways to track spiritual signatures. I'm assuming you have similar capabilities from your side."

"We have authority," Jian Wei said. "Official backing from the Celestial Court. Access to techniques specifically designed for capturing rogue Immortals. And we can operate openly in ways you might not want to, given your"—he gestured vaguely—"unique situation."

Unique situation. That was one way to describe being a transmigrator with a mysterious System pretending to be a powerful Immortal.

"There's another consideration," Han Shu added. "Chi Xifeng isn't working alone. She's been in this realm for a few months now. That's enough time to establish a network, recruit mortal agents, set up contingencies. When we move against her, we need to be thorough. We need to capture or kill her but also dismantle whatever organization she's built."

That made sense. Slifer had already seen evidence of her influence across multiple sects. The mind-controlled sect masters were just the most obvious pieces. How many other cultivators had she corrupted? How many plans were still in motion, waiting to spring?

"I'll work with you," Slifer said finally. "But I have conditions."

Han Shu nodded, clearly expecting this. "Name them."

"First, no interference in my sect's operations. I'm reforming the Black Rose Sect away from demonic cultivation. I don't need Immortal Realm oversight questioning my methods or timeline."

"Agreed," Han Shu said immediately. "The court has no interest in micromanaging mortal sect politics."

"Second, if we capture Chi Xifeng alive, I want assurances she'll be properly contained. No chance of escape. No possibility of her sending agents after me once she's back in the Immortal Realm."

"She'll be placed in the court's secure facilities," Han Shu said, "with specialized formations designed to suppress her specific techniques. And if she violates her confinement terms, the court will execute her. You have my word that if we capture her, she won't be a threat to you again."

"Third," Slifer said. "No questions about my background or cultivation methods. I know you're curious. I know it doesn't make sense to you how I'm doing what I'm doing. But that's not your concern. We're working together against Chi Xifeng, not becoming best friends who share all our secrets."

There was a longer pause this time. Jian Wei looked like he wanted to argue, but Han Shu held up a hand.

"That's . . . fair," Han Shu said slowly. "Though, I will say, purely for your own benefit, that operating in Immortal Realm spaces without proper backing can be dangerous. If you ever want assistance or protection beyond this specific mission, the court offers membership to qualified cultivators. We don't pry into past histories. We just require that members uphold our core principles about realm interaction."

It was a recruitment pitch, Slifer realized. And not a bad one. Having official backing from an Immortal Realm organization could solve a lot of future problems. But it would also mean more oversight, more expectations, more chances for someone to discover his true nature.

"I'll keep that in mind," Slifer said, which was a polite way of saying no without burning bridges. If he later needed their backing, he would consider it.

Han Shu seemed to understand. He smiled slightly and inclined his head. "Then we have an agreement. We share information about Chi Xifeng, coordinate our efforts, and work together to resolve this situation. After which, you return to your sect and we return to the Immortal Realm, our paths diverging naturally."

"One more thing," Slifer added. "I have disciples in the mortal realm. Some of them are talented enough that they might attract attention. If they do, I want your word that they won't be harassed by other Immortals looking for easy resources."

"Done," Han Shu said without hesitation. "I'll flag their spiritual signatures as protected by court authority. Any Immortal who bothers them will answer to us."

That was actually better than Slifer had hoped for. Having his disciples protected by official decree would save him a lot of future headaches. Now, all that was left was to find out more about the Immortal Realm.

"If I'm going to be dealing with an Immortal Realm cultivator and working with Celestial Court enforcers, I need to understand the context better," Slifer began. "What's the Immortal Realm actually like? How does it relate to the mortal realm? What are the cultivation levels above Ascendant? Basic information that might help me understand what I'm facing."

"Curious, aren't you?" Jian laughed. "Most mortals are too intimidated to ask direct questions about the higher realms."

"Most mortals haven't been forced into a situation where an Immortal is trying to kill them," Slifer countered.

Han Shu chuckled. "Fair point. Very well. I'll provide you with a basic education. Consider it part of our arrangement."

The old Immortal refilled their teacups. The gesture seemed almost meditative, like he was organizing his thoughts about how to explain something vast and complex to someone with limited context.

"The cultivation realms," Han Shu began, "progress from Qi Refining through Foundation Establishment, Core Formation, Nascent Soul, Origin Realm, and, finally, Ascendant Realm. These are considered the mortal cultivation stages. A cultivator can theoretically achieve all of them without ever leaving the mortal realm."

Slifer nodded. He knew all this, but hearing it explained by an actual Immortal was different. More real.

"Ascendant Realm is divided into four sub-stages," Han Shu continued. "Early, Mid, Late, and Peak. Once someone reaches Peak Ascendant and has thoroughly consolidated their cultivation, they can attempt the Immortal Ascension. This is the breakthrough to immortality proper."

"What does that involve?" Slifer asked.

"Many things," Han Shu said. "Physical tribulation, soul refinement, comprehension trials, and surviving your own Heavenly Tribulation designed specifically to test whether you're worthy of immortality. The failure rate is over ninety percent. Most Ascendant cultivators who attempt the breakthrough die in the process."

That was sobering. Slifer had barely survived the Core Formation tribulation. He couldn't imagine something ten times worse.

"Those who succeed become Immortals," Han Shu went on. "The first stage is called Lesser Immortal. Your body becomes truly immortal, immune to normal aging and most diseases. Your cultivation no longer requires external spiritual energy; you generate your own. Your techniques reach a level of refinement that allows you to affect space, time, and fundamental forces."

Jian Wei jumped in. "Lesser Immortals can live for ten thousand years without any issue. Their power exceeds Ascendant Realm by several magnitudes. A single Lesser Immortal could probably destroy your entire mortal realm if they weren't restricted by the Celestial Court's laws."

Slifer's hand tightened on his teacup. One Lesser Immortal could destroy the entire realm. Lady Chi was beyond even that level. The scale of power he was dealing with was almost incomprehensible.

"But I'm sure you already knew all of this." Han Shu gave Slifer a knowing look, clearly assuming him to be a mortal cultivator who had somehow found a way to break through to the Lesser Immortal Realm. "You likely want to know what comes next."

Slifer didn't respond. It was probably better that they saw him as their equal rather than the truth: that he was merely a Core Formation cultivator playing dress up.

"After Lesser Immortal comes Greater Immortal," Han Shu continued. "The breakthrough from Lesser to Greater requires another tribulation, though it's not as severe as the Immortal Ascension. Greater Immortals have complete mastery over space, can traverse between realms freely, and possess spiritual senses that can detect events across vast distances. Their techniques can affect reality itself, not just manipulate qi."

"And above Greater Immortal?" Slifer asked.

"Immortal Lord," Han Shu replied. "They can create their own pocket dimensions, establish sects that span multiple realms, and their cultivation approaches the very limits of what's possible under Heaven's laws. There are perhaps a few hundred Immortal Lords across all of existence."

"And beyond that?" Slifer pressed.

Han Shu smiled. "Immortal Emperor. But we're entering the realm of legends now. Immortal Emperors are beings who have transcended normal cultivation entirely. They can reshape continents with a thought, create or destroy entire species, and their lifespans are essentially infinite. There are fewer than ten Immortal Emperors in all the realms combined."

The numbers were staggering. Slifer had barely reached Core Formation. The gap between his cultivation and an Immortal Emperor's power was so vast, it couldn't even be properly measured. He might as well be comparing an ant to a planet.

"Lady Chi is a Lesser Immortal," Slifer said. "Like you two."

"Correct," Han Shu confirmed. "Which is why she's so dangerous when suppressed to the mortal realm. Even at Half-Step Immortal power, she retains all her technique knowledge, her combat experience, and her refined cultivation methods. She's essentially fighting you with one hand tied behind her back, but that free hand is still far stronger than anything you've encountered."

"Why does the realm's power limit affect her?" Slifer asked. "If she's genuinely Lesser Immortal level, why can't she just manifest that power here?"

"The mortal realm has a cultivation ceiling," Jian Wei explained. "Think of it like a building with weight limits on each floor. Your realm can support up to Ascendant-level cultivation naturally. Go beyond that, and the realm's fundamental structure starts to crack. If Chi Xifeng released her full Lesser Immortal power here, she'd trigger massive spatial fractures, possibly tearing holes between your realm and others."

"The Heavenly Dao enforces this limit," Han Shu added. "If someone exceeds the realm's natural ceiling, Heaven itself intervenes. Tribulation lightning strikes them down. The punishment for violating realm limits is severe and usually fatal."

So, Lady Chi couldn't just release her full power, because Heaven would kill her for it. That was both reassuring and terrifying. It meant she had limits here, but it also meant there were cosmic forces watching and ready to execute anyone who broke certain rules.

"What about the Immortal Realm itself?" Slifer asked. "What's it like?"

Han Shu considered the question. "Vast. The Immortal Realm is thousands of times larger than your mortal realm. It consists of multiple continents, each the size of several mortal realms combined. The spiritual energy density is so high that mortal cultivators would suffocate if they tried to breathe it. The plant life, the animals, even the insects are all spirit beasts with cultivation."

"Sects in the Immortal Realm operate on a completely different scale," Jian Wei said. "A small sect might have ten thousand disciples. A major sect could have millions. The competition is fierce, the politics are Byzantine, and the strong truly dominate the weak without any pretense otherwise."

That painted a grim picture. Slifer had seen how brutal the mortal realm's cultivation world could be. The Immortal Realm sounded worse.

"The Celestial Court exists above all of that," Han Shu continued. "We don't belong to any sect. We serve Heaven's mandate directly. Our job is to enforce the fundamental laws that prevent complete chaos. Realm restrictions. Cultivation prohibitions. Treaties between major powers. When someone like Lady Chi violates those laws, we're the ones sent to handle it."

"You're cosmic police," Slifer said.

"Essentially, yes," Han Shu agreed. "Though we prefer the term 'enforcers.' We have jurisdiction across all realms, authority to arrest or execute violators, and we answer only to the Heavenly Dao itself. It's not a glamorous job, but someone has to do it."

Slifer sipped his tea, processing all this information. The cultivation world was so much larger than he'd understood. The mortal realm was just one small piece of a vast cosmic hierarchy. Above him were Immortals. Above them were Immortal Lords. Above them were Immortal Emperors. And presumably above them was Heaven itself, whatever that actually meant.

He was so far down the power ladder that he couldn't even see the top.

"You seem troubled," Han Shu observed.

"I'm realizing how insignificant I am in the grand scheme of things," Slifer admitted.

"Everyone starts at the bottom," Jian Wei said. "Even Immortal Emperors were once in Qi Refining, struggling to sense spiritual energy for the first time. The difference between you and them is time, resources, and determination. You have potential. You're already punching above your weight class. Keep cultivating, keep advancing, and eventually, you'll reach heights you can't imagine right now."

It was surprisingly encouraging coming from someone who'd attacked him less than an hour ago. Maybe Jian Wei wasn't as bad as his first impression suggested.

"Thanks," Slifer said. "Now, what do you know about Chi Xifeng's current location and plans?"

Jian Wei leaned forward eagerly, apparently glad to finally be talking tactics instead of politics. "We tracked her spiritual signature to a location in the northern mountain range, about three hundred thousand kilometers from your sect. She's established a base there, probably using it as a staging ground for operations."

He waved his hand and a shimmering map appeared in the air above the table. Slifer recognized the general geography of the region, though the map showed considerably more detail than any mortal cartographer could achieve.

"Here." Jian Wei pointed to a red mark in the mountains. "We detected significant corruption energy emanating from this valley. The kind of signature that suggests she's used her full cultivation abilities once or twice despite suppression. That level of power usage should have triggered realm defenses, but somehow, she's avoiding detection."

"She's using a masking technique," Han Shu said. "Something her sect provided, probably without realizing what she intended to do with it. The Crimson Lotus Pavilion has always been . . . loosely supervised. They tend to prioritize individual achievement over collective responsibility."

"So, we know where she is," Slifer said. "Why haven't you moved against her already?"

"Because we can't be certain it's actually her," Han Shu admitted. "The signature matches, but Chi Xifeng is clever. She might have left a decoy, something that radiates her energy while she operates elsewhere. We need confirmation before committing to a full assault."

"And that's where I come in," Slifer guessed.

Han Shu nodded. "She's obsessed with you. If we can use that obsession to draw her out, confirm her location, we can strike with overwhelming force. But we need her to reveal herself first."

Slifer didn't love the idea of being bait. Then again, he was already Chi Xifeng's target. At least this way he'd have backup.

"What kind of overwhelming force are we talking about?" he asked.

Jian Wei grinned, the expression making him look younger despite his Immortal cultivation. "Me and my senior brother, obviously. Plus three additional court enforcers we have on standby in the Immortal Realm. All of us are at least Lesser Immortal stage. We hit her with coordinated attacks, suppress her cultivation, seal her in a dimensional prison, and transport her back for trial."

"And if she resists?"

"Then we kill her," Jian Wei said simply. "Honestly, I'm hoping she resists. The woman controls the minds of innocent people and starts wars for fun. The world's better off without her."

Han Shu shot his junior brother another look but didn't contradict him this time. Apparently, even the diplomatic senior brother had limits to his patience with Chi Xifeng's behavior.

"There's something else you should know," Han Shu said, his tone becoming more serious. "Chi Xifeng has a particular cultivation method that makes her extremely dangerous in direct combat. She doesn't just corrupt plant life. She can corrupt spiritual connections, emotional bonds, even memories if she gets deep enough into someone's mind."

Slifer thought about the mind-controlled sect masters. Ming Yue's distant expression. Ace's complete lack of memory about the manipulation. Feng Lei's flight from his own sect.

"How do we protect against that?" he asked.

"Primarily? Don't let her touch you," Jian Wei said. "Her corruption techniques require physical contact to work at full strength. Spiritual pressure alone isn't enough unless she catches someone with very weak mental defenses."

"I have a Void Being Aura technique," Slifer said, deciding that sharing some information was necessary for proper coordination. "It provides reduction against mental intrusions."

Both Immortals looked interested at that.

"Fascinating," Han Shu said. "Void Being abilities are extremely rare. How did you acquire such a skill?"

"You said no questions about my methods," Slifer reminded him gently.

Han Shu smiled and raised his hands in surrender. "Fair point. Well, that Void Being Aura should provide significant protection. Combine that with our suppression formations, and she shouldn't be able to corrupt you even if she tries."

The map floating above the table shifted and zoomed in on various locations around the northern mountain range. Small marks appeared indicating different points of interest.

"These are confirmed locations where Chi Xifeng has been active," Han Shu explained. "She moves frequently, never staying in one place for more than a few days. But the pattern suggests she's circling back to that valley regularly. It's her anchor point, the place she feels safest."

"Or the place she wants us to think is her anchor point," Slifer said.

"Also possible," Han Shu agreed. "Which is why we need proper confirmation before committing resources. False trails waste time, and time is something we're running short on."

"Why?" Slifer asked. "What's the timeline here?"

Jian Wei pointed to several other marks on the map, these ones in blue. "These are dimensional weak points. Places where the barrier between this realm and the Immortal Realm has been damaged. Normally this kind of damage heals on its own over years or decades. But Chi Xifeng has been deliberately widening them."

"Why would she do that?" Slifer asked, though he had a sinking feeling he already knew.

"Because she's not planning to leave," Han Shu said quietly. "She's preparing to bring more Crimson Lotus disciples down here and turn this entire region into an extension of her sect's territory. She genuinely believes she can reshape the mortal realm into whatever twisted vision she's imagined."

That was significantly worse than just a revenge quest. Chi Xifeng wasn't just trying to kill him. She was trying to conquer the entire region, remake it according to her own corrupted ideals.

"How long until she can bring reinforcements through?" Slifer asked.

"Two weeks, maybe three," Jian Wei said. "The dimensional damage needs to reach critical mass before stable portals can form. Once that happens, we're dealing with a full invasion scenario instead of a single rogue Immortal."

Two to three weeks. That was his timeline. Stop Chi Xifeng before she could call in backup, or face an entire sect of corruption specialists trying to reshape reality.

"Then we don't have time to waste," Slifer said. "What's the plan?"

Han Shu's expression became more focused, the casual tea house atmosphere shifting into something more tactical. "First, we need to draw her out. You're already her primary target, so we use that. You make yourself visible, act as bait, and get her to commit to an attack."

"I do that every day just by existing," Slifer pointed out.

"True, but this time you'll have support nearby. We'll set up observation positions around your sect. When Chi Xifeng makes her move, we track her back to her base, confirm her location, then we strike with everything we have."

"What about my sect?" Slifer asked. "She's already attacked once. I can't leave them vulnerable while we're setting up this trap."

"We'll establish protective formations," Han Shu said. "Nothing too obvious, but enough to slow her down if she tries another direct assault. That should give us time to mobilize."

Slifer considered the plan. It wasn't perfect, but it was workable. Use himself as bait, track Chi Xifeng back to her base, hit her with overwhelming force. Simple enough in theory.

The problems would come in execution. Chi Xifeng was clever and motivated. She'd survived this long in a hostile realm by being cautious. Making her commit to a direct attack would require something that pushed her beyond caution.

"I have an idea," Slifer said slowly. "Something that might make her angry enough to attack directly."

Both Immortals looked at him with interest.

"Revoke Darius's status as elder," Slifer continued. "Whenever a sect member becomes an elder, their name is added to the Wall of Elders. Despite the unfortunate situation between me and Darius resulting in his death, his name is still on the wall and will be there forever."

"You want to publicly remove it?" Jian Wei cut in. "I like it. Wound her pride, make it even more personal. She'll come at you with everything she has."

"Which is exactly what we want," Han Shu agreed. "Though, we'll need to be prepared for her to bring significant force. An enraged Lesser Immortal is extremely dangerous, even when suppressed."

"I have defensive techniques," Slifer said. "And my disciples are strong enough to hold their own against most threats. As long as you're in position when she arrives, we can handle it."

Han Shu nodded slowly, his expression thoughtful. "This could work. Make the announcement tomorrow. Give her time to hear about it and plan her response. We'll spend tonight setting up observation posts and preparing our strike force. When she attacks, we'll end this."

"And if she doesn't attack?" Slifer asked.

"Then we know she's more patient than we thought," Han Shu said. "But I don't think that's likely. Chi Xifeng has demonstrated repeatedly that she acts on emotion rather than strategy. Attacking her lover's character and achievements will infuriate her beyond reason."

Slifer hoped they were right. He was getting tired of looking over his shoulder, wondering when the next attack would come. Better to force the confrontation on his terms than wait for her to strike at the worst possible moment.

"There's one more thing," Slifer said. "When we capture or kill Chi Xifeng, what happens to the people she's been controlling? The sect masters, the disciples, anyone else she's corrupted?"

"The corruption should fade naturally once she's removed," Han Shu said. "Mind-control techniques require ongoing connection to the practitioner. Break that connection and the victims gradually recover. There may be some lingering effects, emotional trauma from the experience, but no permanent damage."

That was a relief. Slifer had been worried he'd have to find some way to manually free everyone Chi Xifeng had touched.

"How long will recovery take?" he asked.

"Days to weeks, depending on how deep the control went," Jian Wei said. "The sect masters you freed probably experienced it faster because you used an active liberation technique. The others will heal more slowly, but they will heal."

Good enough. Slifer could work with that timeline.

"Then we have a deal," Slifer said, setting down his teacup with finality. "You provide support and coordinate the strike force. I'll draw Chi Xifeng out and help confirm her location. Together we remove the threat and restore stability to this region."

Han Shu smiled and raised his own cup in a small toast. "To successful cooperation and swift resolution."

Jian Wei followed suit, though his grin suggested he was mostly excited about the upcoming fight.

Slifer raised his cup as well, though privately he was already thinking about which System cards to purchase, which disciples to brief, and how exactly to phrase his public announcement to maximize Chi Xifeng's rage while minimizing panic among the general population.

"One last question," Slifer said as they lowered their cups. "This neutral space we're in. How do I leave?"

"Simple," Han Shu said. He made a gesture and a door appeared in one of the paper walls. Through the opening, Slifer could see his quarters back in the Black Rose Sect. "Just walk through. The spatial anchor will transport you back to your point of origin."

Slifer stood, noting that his legs felt steady despite the strange nature of this dimensional space. "Then I should get back. I have preparations to make."

"We'll be in contact," Han Shu said. "You won't see us, but we'll be watching. When Chi Xifeng makes her move, we'll be ready."

Slifer nodded and walked toward the door. Just before stepping through, he paused and looked back.

"Thank you," he said. "For the tea and the conversation. And for not just trying to kill me for being in your way."

While Jian Wei's face reddened slightly in embarrassment at the latter part of the comment, Han Shu's expression softened slightly. "Some of us still believe that the strong have a responsibility to the weak. Not all Immortals are tyrants or madmen. Remember that."

Slifer stepped through the door and back into his familiar quarters, which, thanks to Morvran, had been restored to their normal state.

CHAPTER TWENTY

Slifer stood in his private quarters. Not his sect master chamber, but the sect elder chamber that had once been destroyed. He was staring at the wall where a portrait of the original Slifer hung. Looking at that face always made him uncomfortable, a reminder that he was living someone else's life, but he felt that it was weirdly appropriate considering what he was about to do today.

The plan was simple but brutal in theory: publicly humiliate Lady Chi's dead lover to provoke her into attacking. The execution, however, required careful preparation.

He walked to his desk and pulled out a jade slip. Inside was a copy of every communication talisman frequency for the major sects in the region.

"Master?" Morvran's voice came from beyond the door. "The preparations are complete."

"Come in."

His servant entered holding a wooden box. Morvran set it on the desk and opened it, revealing a dozen high-grade communication talismans. Each one would broadcast Slifer's announcement to a different major sect simultaneously.

"These will reach the Heavenly Light Sect, Pure Soul Sect, White Tiger Sect, Jade Mountain Sect, Crimson Phoenix Sect, and six others," Morvran explained. "Elder Tarnyx's old trading contacts helped secure the proper frequencies."

Slifer picked up one of the talismans. The jade was cool against his palm and inscribed with formation script he barely understood. The System's Insight ability identified it as a Profound Message Relay Talisman, capable of projecting voice and image across hundreds of thousands of kilometers.

"Good work." Slifer set the talisman down. "What about the defensive formations?"

"Master Hong completed the final adjustments yesterday. The Celestial Guardian Formation is operating at full capacity." Morvran hesitated. "Master, if this woman truly is a Lesser Immortal suppressing her cultivation, even our strongest defenses may only slow her down."

"I know." Slifer had run the calculations a dozen times. Lady Chi could probably tear through the sect's defenses if she committed to it. The key was controlling when and where she attacked. "But if she uses her full power, the Heavenly Dao will strike her down. That's what we're counting on."

Morvran didn't look convinced, but he nodded. "The disciples are gathering at the Wall of Elders as you requested. They're confused about the sudden assembly."

"Let them be confused for now." Slifer walked to his wardrobe and pulled out his formal sect master robes. Black with red trim, embroidered with silver formations. He'd never worn them before, preferring simpler clothing. But today required ceremony.

As he dressed, his mind wandered to the disciples.

Hughie, Amelia, Caelum, Fenlock, and Val. Slifer had gathered them all here deliberately. Not just for appearances, but for a very specific reason that he hadn't shared with anyone.

Their combined luck stat.

Hughie alone had a luck rating of eight, which was protagonist-level fortune. Caelum, Amelia, and Fenlock all had respectable luck scores as well. Having them all present would theoretically increase the odds that this ridiculous plan actually worked without getting everyone killed.

Slifer wasn't sure if luck actually worked that way, but he'd seen enough improbable things happen around Hughie to believe there might be something to it.

Slifer needed every advantage he could get.

He finished adjusting his robes and turned to Morvran. "I'm ready. Let's go."

They walked through the sect's corridors in silence. Disciples pressed themselves against walls as Slifer passed, bowing respectfully. He'd gotten used to the deference over the past year, though it still felt odd. In his previous life, nobody had respected him. He'd been an overweight nobody who'd choked to death during a pie-eating contest.

The irony wasn't lost on him.

They emerged into the main courtyard. The Wall of Elders stood at the far end, a massive stone monument carved with thousands of names. Every elder who'd ever served the Black Rose Sect was recorded there, their names glowing faintly with preserved spiritual energy. It was tradition. When someone achieved elder status, their name was added. When they died, the name dimmed but never disappeared.

Grand Elder Darius's name was near the top of the current generation's section, glowing as brightly as the others.

Not for much longer.

The courtyard was packed. Easily a thousand disciples had assembled, from Outer Sect members in simple black robes to Core Disciples in more elaborate attire. Grand elders stood on a raised platform to the left, their expressions ranging from curious to concerned. Slifer spotted Lydia, Wyatt, and several others he'd come to rely on during his time as sect master.

His personal disciples waited near the front. Caelum stood with perfect posture, his hand resting on Starforge's hilt. The sword had transformed after receiving its bloodline blessing in the Sealed Realm, becoming something beyond a simple demonic weapon. It gave him the power to fight and defeat multiple Origin Realm cultivators. Amelia shifted her weight from foot to foot, clearly impatient. Her Spectral Lotus Bloodline had changed her in subtle ways, adding a faint luminescence to her skin that she absolutely hated.

Fenlock stood beside Lenvari, the girlfriend he'd been so nervous to introduce. The two had made significant progress on their dual cultivation technique, though Slifer tried not to think too hard about what that entailed.

Val, in her small dragon form, perched on Amelia's shoulder. The baby dragon had grown slightly larger after feeding on that Void Being, and she'd developed a concerning habit of demanding tribute from visiting elders.

Zack stood apart from the others, leaning against a pillar with his arms crossed. His avatar body was younger and more conventionally attractive than Slifer's elderly form, which sometimes created awkward situations. Right now, Zack's expression was carefully neutral, but Slifer could feel the connection between them. The avatar knew this plan was risky.

Slifer walked to the center of the courtyard. Morvran handed him the box of communication talismans, then stepped back. The crowd's murmuring died down as everyone noticed their sect master's formal attire.

"Thank you all for gathering on such short notice," Slifer began. His voice carried across the courtyard without need for amplification. One benefit of Core Formation cultivation was enhanced lung capacity. "I have an important announcement to make, and I wanted the entire sect to witness it."

He could see the confusion rippling through the crowd. Important announcements usually involved breakthrough achievements, mission assignments, or policy changes. This felt different.

Slifer turned to face the Wall of Elders. He pulled a chisel from his storage ring, a tool specially prepared for altering the stone monument. The chisel glowed faintly with formation script designed to etch spiritual stone without damaging the underlying structure.

"Darius served this sect for many years," Slifer continued. "He held the position of grand elder, commanded respect, and trained numerous disciples."

More confusion. Some disciples nodded, remembering Darius fondly. Others frowned, recalling the man's less savory reputation.

"However, after extensive investigation into Grand Elder Darius's activities, I have discovered serious violations of sect law." Slifer kept his voice level, matter-of-fact. "Grand Elder Darius maintained a secret correspondence with an Immortal Realm cultivator. He shared sect intelligence, provided information about our defensive formations, and deliberately sabotaged internal operations to impress his lover."

Gasps rippled through the crowd. Grand Elder Wyatt stepped forward, his expression shocked. "Sect Master, these are grave accusations. What evidence supports this claim?"

Slifer had prepared for this question. He pulled a jade slip from his storage ring and held it up. "This contains copies of correspondence recovered from Grand Elder Darius's private quarters. Love letters detailing his relationship with someone named Chi Xifeng, a Core Disciple of the Crimson Lotus Pavilion in the Immortal Realm. He promised her information and assistance in exchange for cultivation resources and techniques. Grand Elder Darius's actions directly contributed to multiple security breaches. His betrayal cannot be tolerated, even in death. Therefore, I am officially revoking his elder status and removing his name from the Wall of Elders."

Silence. Complete, absolute silence.

Then the murmuring started. Disciples turned to each other, whispering frantically. Some looked angry. Others seemed vindicated, as if suspicions they'd held for years were finally being acknowledged.

"This is unprecedented," Grand Elder Lydia said. "Sect Master, revoking a deceased elder's status is extremely rare. It dishonors not just the individual, but their entire lineage."

"I'm aware." Slifer walked to the Wall of Elders and raised the chisel. "But this sect will not honor traitors, regardless of their current state. Grand Elder Darius made his choices. Now he faces the consequences."

DEMONIC SECT ELDER AND THE GREAT WAR   183

He pressed the chisel against the stone, directly over Darius's name. The formation script activated, and the tool began scraping away the carved letters. Stone dust drifted down as the name slowly disappeared.

The murmuring grew louder. Disciples debated among themselves. Some argued this was justified. Others claimed it was a petty attack on a man who couldn't defend himself. One voice rose above the others.

"Sect Master, Grand Elder Darius was my teacher!" A young woman pushed forward through the crowd. "He trained me personally, helped me break through to Core Formation. This is wrong!"

Slifer paused his work and turned to face her. He recognized her vaguely: one of Darius's former students, talented but loyal to a fault.

"Your teacher's actions endangered this entire sect," Slifer said quietly. "I understand your loyalty, but the evidence is clear. He chose personal gain over his duty. That cannot be forgiven."

"Then show us the evidence!" someone else shouted. "Let us read these letters ourselves!"

Slifer considered that. It would be easy enough to pass around the jade slip and let everyone verify the accusations. But that would take time, create more debate, and potentially derail the entire plan.

"The evidence will be made available for review," Slifer said. "Grand Elder Wyatt will coordinate access for anyone who wishes to verify my claims. But the decision stands. Grand Elder Darius's name is being removed."

He turned back to the wall and continued scraping. The name was half gone now, the spiritual energy that had kept it glowing fading with each stroke.

Morvran stepped up beside him, holding the box of communication talismans. "Master, are you ready?"

Slifer nodded. He activated the first talisman, channeling his spiritual energy into the jade. A formation array appeared in the air above the courtyard, which projected his image outward. Similar projections would be appearing at major sects across the region to broadcast his announcement to thousands of cultivators.

"I am Slifer, Sect Master of the Black Rose Sect." His amplified voice echoed across the courtyard and beyond. "I am making this announcement to inform all cultivators of the following matter. Grand Elder Darius of the Black Rose Sect has been found guilty of treason and conspiracy. His crimes include consorting with Immortal Realm infiltrators, sharing sect secrets, and deliberately compromising our security."

He paused, letting that sink in. Then he continued.

"As of this moment, Darius's status is revoked. His name is being removed from our Wall of Elders. His teachings are declared tainted by foreign influence. Any disciples who studied under him are encouraged to seek reeducation from untainted sources."

More gasps from the crowd. Declaring someone's teachings tainted was even more serious than removing their name. It suggested that everything Darius had taught might contain hidden corruption.

"Furthermore," Slifer pressed on, "I am formally declaring Darius a traitor to all demonic cultivation sects. His actions were motivated by his relationship with Chi Xifeng of the Crimson Lotus Pavilion. This woman has been manipulating events in our realm and using Darius as her tool. I call upon all sects to remain vigilant against her influence."

He let the communication talismans remain active for a few more seconds, then released them. The formation arrays faded, and the projections disappeared.

Slifer turned back to the Wall of Elders. Darius's name was almost completely gone—just a few letters remained. He scraped away the last traces, leaving only smooth stone where the name had once glowed.

"It is done," Slifer announced. "Darius is no longer recognized by this sect. His legacy is erased. His memory is declared unwelcome within these walls."

The courtyard remained silent for a long moment. Then, slowly, some disciples began nodding. Others looked uncomfortable but didn't protest. A few were clearly upset, but none spoke up against the decision.

Grand Elder Wyatt stepped forward. "Sect Master, this was an extreme action. I hope you understand the implications."

"I do." Slifer lowered the chisel. "And I accept responsibility for them."

He scanned the crowd, looking at each of his disciples in turn. Caelum's expression was thoughtful—clearly, he was working through the political ramifications. Amelia looked vaguely bored, probably wondering when she could leave. Fenlock seemed nervous, as usual. Val yawned, showing tiny dragon fangs.

Zack met Slifer's gaze and gave a barely perceptible nod. The avatar understood what they were really doing here.

"You are all dismissed," Slifer said. "Return to your duties. Grand Elder Wyatt will make the evidence available for review tomorrow."

The crowd began dispersing slowly. Disciples filed out of the courtyard in small groups, their conversations animated. Some headed directly for the training grounds, probably wanting to process their confusion through physical activity. Others moved toward the dining halls or dormitories.

Slifer stood alone in the center of the courtyard, still holding the chisel.

DEMONIC SECT ELDER AND THE GREAT WAR

He'd done it. The announcement had been made, broadcast to every major sect within a thousand kilometers. If Lady Chi had any informants left, and she almost certainly did, she would hear about this within the hour.

Now came the waiting.

Minutes passed. Then an hour. The courtyard slowly emptied as disciples returned to their normal routines. Slifer remained standing there watching the Wall of Elders. The blank space where Darius's name had been seemed to mock him.

"Master, perhaps you should return to your chambers," Morvran suggested quietly. "If she's going to respond, it may take time."

"No." Slifer shook his head. "She'll respond quickly. Anger makes people impulsive."

But another hour passed and nothing happened. The sun continued its slow arc across the sky. Clouds drifted past peacefully. Birds chirped in nearby trees.

Slifer felt frustration building in his chest. Had the plan failed? Maybe Lady Chi had more self-control than he'd anticipated. Maybe publicly dishonoring her dead lover wasn't enough to provoke her into revealing herself.

He sighed deeply, lowering the chisel. "Perhaps you're right, Morvran. We should—"

The sky darkened.

It wasn't a gradual change like clouds gathering before a storm. One moment the sun was shining, and the next moment shadows covered everything. Slifer looked up and saw the sky itself had turned gray, as if someone had drawn a curtain across the world.

Then he felt it.

Power. Overwhelming crushing power that made his knees want to buckle. This wasn't the spiritual pressure of an Ascendant cultivator. This wasn't even the aura of someone at Half-Step Immortal Realm.

This was a Lesser Immortal releasing their true cultivation.

The pressure originated from the west, beyond the sect's outer walls. Slifer could feel it pressing against the Celestial Guardian Formation, testing the defensive array's limits. The formation was powerful, designed by a formation master and upgraded with Immortal-grade materials. It should be able to resist attacks from Ascendant cultivators indefinitely.

But this wasn't an Ascendant cultivator.

Alarms began blaring throughout the sect. Disciples ran from buildings, looking around wildly for the source of danger. Grand elders appeared on rooftops, their expressions grave as they sensed the incoming threat.

"Master!" Morvran grabbed Slifer's arm. "The formation is straining. Whatever's attacking us—"

Thunder cracked across the sky. Not natural thunder. This was the sound of the Heavenly Dao responding to a violation of its laws. The mortal realm had a cultivation ceiling for a reason. Anyone who exceeded Half-Step Immortal would trigger tribulation lightning. It was Heaven's way of enforcing the boundaries between realms.

Slifer watched as massive storm clouds materialized directly above the western section of the sect. Lightning arced between them, building toward a devastating strike. The Heavenly Dao was preparing to eliminate the cultivator who'd broken its laws.

But then the aura vanished.

One moment it was there, crushing and overwhelming. The next moment, nothing. Whoever had been releasing their power had pulled it back below the threshold and just barely avoided Heaven's retaliation.

The storm clouds began dissipating, and the lightning faded. The Heavenly Dao's attention moved elsewhere, satisfied that the violation had ended.

But it was too late.

There was a sound like breaking glass. Slifer felt the Celestial Guardian Formation shatter, its complex arrays unraveling all at once. The defensive barrier that had protected the sect for months simply ceased to exist.

Someone had used their full Lesser Immortal power, just for an instant, to breach the formation. Then they'd suppressed their cultivation again before the Heavenly Dao could finish gathering its response.

It was clever. Ruthlessly, dangerously clever.

"She's here," Slifer whispered.

Footsteps echoed from the western gate. Slow, deliberate footsteps that somehow carried across the entire sect despite the distance. Every disciple froze, then turned to look in that direction.

A female figure appeared at the gate, wearing robes that shifted between black and deep green like leaves in shadow. Long black hair cascaded down her back, moving in a wind that didn't exist. Her eyes glowed red, brightly enough to be visible from across the courtyard.

Lady Chi had arrived.

She walked forward slowly, her presence radiating malice. The ground beneath her feet withered, grass turning brown and flowers wilting instantly. She carried no visible weapons, but Slifer could see thorny vines writhing beneath her robes.

Disciples scrambled to get out of her path. Some were too slow. Lady Chi gestured casually, and red vines erupted from the ground and wrapped around their legs, then lifted them into the air. The disciples screamed as thorns bit into their flesh.

"Slifer!" Her voice echoed across the courtyard, amplified by spiritual energy. It carried rage, grief, and an edge of madness that made Slifer's blood run cold. "Show yourself, you coward! You dare dishonor Darius's memory? You dare erase his name while hiding behind your sect's walls?"

She threw the captured disciples aside like trash. They hit the ground hard, groaning in pain but alive. For now.

Slifer took a deep breath. This was it. The moment everything had been building toward. He stepped forward, moving to the center of the courtyard where Lady Chi could see him clearly.

"I'm here," he called out. "And I'm not hiding."

Lady Chi's red eyes locked onto him. For a moment, neither moved. The entire sect held its breath, watching as two powerful cultivators faced each other across empty stone.

Then Lady Chi smiled. It was the most terrifying expression Slifer had ever seen.

"Good," she said softly. "Because I'm going to tear you apart."

CHAPTER TWENTY-ONE

Lady Chi's spiritual pressure intensified. The air around her rippled visibly, distorting like heat waves rising from scorched earth. Red qi coalesced around her hands and formed into thorny vines that writhed with their own life. Each vine dripped with something dark and viscous. Poison, probably, or maybe corrupted spiritual energy.

Slifer stood his ground. His disciples had scattered to the edges of the courtyard, exactly as planned. Morvran had moved to the rear, staying close to the grand elders. Everyone was in position, though they didn't know it yet.

"You think erasing his name makes you powerful?" Lady Chi's voice trembled with barely contained rage. "You think your petty gestures matter? Darius was worth a thousand of you, a million of you insects crawling in the dirt!"

The vines around her hands expanded, growing thicker and longer. Thorns the size of daggers protruded from their surface. The ground beneath her feet cracked and split as more vines burst upward, spreading across the courtyard in a web of corrupted plant matter.

"He was a traitor," Slifer said simply. "And you're the one who made him that way."

Lady Chi screamed. It wasn't a human sound. It was raw fury given voice, echoing across the sect and beyond. Birds fled from nearby trees. Windows shattered in the surrounding buildings. Several disciples collapsed, clutching their ears against the assault of pure spiritual pressure.

She raised both hands, and the vines launched forward—dozens of them, moving faster than arrows, each one aimed directly at Slifer's heart. The attack carried enough force to puncture through Ascendant Realm armor like it was paper.

Slifer didn't move a muscle—

A figure materialized directly in front of Lady Chi.

The man wore white robes and had long black hair pulled back in a high ponytail with one hand extended in a stopping gesture. The vines hit an invisible barrier and simply stopped, frozen in midair as if they'd struck an immovable wall.

"Now, now," the man said cheerfully. "Is that any way to greet someone? You didn't even introduce yourself properly."

Lady Chi's eyes widened in recognition and shock. "Jian Wei." She spat the name like a curse. "The Celestial Court's attack dog. What are you doing here?"

"My job." Jian Wei smiled, but there was no warmth in the expression. "You violated quite a few laws descending to this realm, Chi Xifeng. Breaking cultivation limits, initiating unauthorized realm interference, binding yourself with an oath to remain indefinitely. My superiors take a very dim view of such behavior."

Lady Chi pulled her vines back, but more sprouted from the ground around her. She circled slowly, keeping Jian Wei in her line of sight. "One enforcer. They sent one enforcer to stop me? How insulting."

"Oh, I'm not alone."

A second figure appeared from Lady Chi's left flank. This one was older, with white hair and a scholarly face marked by laugh lines. He wore the same white robes as Jian Wei, but his demeanor was completely different: calm, almost apologetic.

"Chi Xifeng," Han Shu greeted with a slight bow. "I had hoped we could resolve this peacefully. Your sect has already been notified of your unauthorized departure from the Immortal Realm. If you surrender now, the penalties will be relatively light. Perhaps a few centuries of disciplinary confinement."

Lady Chi's laugh was bitter. "Surrender? To you? I swore an oath, old man. I cannot leave this realm until Slifer is dead. Heaven itself binds me to that promise."

"An oath you made rashly," Han Shu countered. "The Celestial Court can petition Heaven for special dispensation under certain circumstances. Your case qualifies. But only if you cooperate."

"Cooperate?" Lady Chi's red eyes blazed brighter. "They killed Darius! They erased his name! They dishonored everything he was! And you expect me to cooperate with these animals?"

A third figure descended from above and dropped silently to land behind Lady Chi. This one was female, with silver hair braided down her back and a scar across her left cheek. Her white robes bore additional markings: enforcement badges that identified her rank within the Celestial Court hierarchy.

"Three enforcers," the woman said coldly. "That's what it takes for someone of your cultivation level, Chi Xifeng. You should feel honored. We don't usually deploy in teams for simple retrieval missions."

Lady Chi spun, vines whipping around, to face all three opponents simultaneously. "Honored? You think I care about your protocols?" She laughed again, the sound edging toward hysteria. "I'll kill all three of you. Then I'll kill that dog Slifer. Then I'll burn this entire sect to ash and salt the earth so nothing grows here for a thousand years!"

Slifer watched the confrontation unfold with growing satisfaction. The trap had worked perfectly. He'd known Lady Chi's emotional state would override her tactical sense. Publicly dishonoring Darius had been designed to make her furious enough to attack immediately, without scouting or preparation.

What she didn't know was that he'd been coordinating with the Celestial Court.

Slifer made a subtle hand gesture. Spiritual energy flowed from his fingertips into the ground and activated formation script that had been carved into the courtyard stones the night before. A transparent barrier snapped into existence around the edges of the courtyard, enclosing all the disciples and sect members in a protective dome.

The Aegis of Ten Thousand Shields. One of Master Hong's masterworks, powered by a High Heaven Rank spirit stone Slifer had purchased from the System. The formation could withstand attacks from Ascendant Realm cultivators indefinitely, and even Half-Step Immortals would need sustained effort to break through.

His disciples and elders were safe. They could watch the battle without risk.

Several disciples noticed the barrier immediately. Caelum's hand went to his sword hilt, then relaxed as he realized the formation was protecting rather than trapping them. Amelia tilted her head and studied the barrier's structure with interest. Val chirped excitedly as she recognized the type of defensive array.

"Master planned this," Fenlock whispered to Lenvari. "He knew she was coming."

"Obviously," Lenvari whispered back. "Why else would he gather everyone in one place?"

Grand Elder Wyatt's face had gone pale. "Those are Celestial Court enforcers. Immortal Realm cultivators suppressing their power to fit within our realm's limits. This is . . . this is unprecedented."

"The sect master allied with the Celestial Court?" Grand Elder Lydia looked stunned. "How did he even make contact with them?"

Slifer kept his expression neutral, but internally he was pleased. The plan was working exactly as intended. Let his sect see him cooperating with Immortal Realm authorities. Let them understand he had connections that extended beyond the mortal realm.

It would cement his position and discourage future challenges.

Lady Chi's vines erupted outward in all directions. Thousands of them, far more than should have been possible. The courtyard disappeared beneath a sea of writhing thorny plant matter. Each vine moved independently as they sought targets with predatory intelligence.

Jian Wei moved first. His form blurred as he moved too fast for mortal eyes to track properly. He appeared behind Lady Chi and struck at her spine with a palm reinforced by white spiritual energy. The attack should have shattered her vertebrae.

Lady Chi twisted impossibly, her body bending at angles that defied human anatomy. The palm strike passed through empty space as she flowed around it like water. A vine whipped up from below and wrapped around Jian Wei's ankle.

He cut it with a blade of compressed qi before it could tighten, but three more vines replaced it instantly. They wrapped around his arms and torso, thorns biting into flesh.

Han Shu gestured, and golden chains materialized from the air. They wrapped around the vines binding Jian Wei and pulled them away. The chains moved like living things as they coiled and struck at Lady Chi's body.

She summoned a wall of thorns to intercept them. The chains punched through, but more vines grew to replace those destroyed. The courtyard had become a battlefield of spiritual techniques clashing against each other.

The silver-haired enforcer—Slifer still didn't know her name—attacked from above. She wielded twin daggers that glowed with formation script, each blade capable of cutting through spiritual energy itself. She descended in a spinning strike, aiming for Lady Chi's neck.

Lady Chi raised both arms. Vines exploded upward and created a dome of thorny protection. The daggers cut through the first layer, then the second, then the third. But there were dozens more layers, and each one slowed the attack fractionally.

By the time the enforcer penetrated the defense, Lady Chi had already moved. She was three meters to the left, hands weaving complex formations in the air. Red light gathered between her palms and condensed into a sphere of concentrated death qi.

"Withering Blossom," she intoned.

The sphere exploded outward. Red petals made of pure spiritual energy scattered across the battlefield, each one carrying enough corrupted qi to age an Origin Soul cultivator to death in seconds.

Jian Wei's eyes narrowed. He clapped his hands together, and white light erupted from his body. "Purification Aura!"

The red petals hit the white light and simply ceased to exist, annihilated by the opposing energy. But the technique required immense concentration to maintain. Jian Wei stood motionless as he focused entirely on keeping the purification field active.

Han Shu took advantage of Lady Chi's distraction. He appeared directly behind her, moving through space with the ease of someone who'd mastered dimensional techniques. His hand pressed against her back, and formation script blazed to life.

"Sealing Array of Thousand Locks."

Golden light spread across Lady Chi's body and formed into hundreds of tiny glowing chains. Each chain attempted to bind a different part of her spiritual energy, restricting her ability to channel qi through specific meridians.

Lady Chi screamed again. The vines around her went berserk, thrashing wildly. Several struck Han Shu, sending him flying backward. He crashed into a stone pillar hard enough to crack it but rolled to his feet immediately.

"She's stronger than the reports indicated." Han Shu coughed, wiping blood from his lip. "The emotional state is amplifying her power."

"No kidding," Jian Wei replied. He dropped the purification field and attacked directly, closing the distance in a single step. His fist, wreathed in white flames, struck Lady Chi's sternum.

The impact created a shock wave that shattered nearby windows and cracked the courtyard stones. Lady Chi stumbled backward, but vines caught her before she could fall. They lifted her up and supported her weight while she regained her balance.

She retaliated with a technique Slifer had never seen before. Her hands moved in circular patterns as she drew symbols in the air with trails of red light. The symbols combined into a formation circle that hung suspended between them.

"Garden of Eternal Torment."

DEMONIC SECT ELDER AND THE GREAT WAR

The formation activated. Reality within the circle shifted. The ground became soft and yielding like flesh. Thorny plants sprouted from every surface, growing at impossible speeds. The plants weren't normal vegetation; they were composed of condensed spiritual energy, each leaf and petal a weapon that could tear through protective qi.

The three enforcers found themselves surrounded. Vines erupted from below, above, and all sides simultaneously. Each vine carried multiple attack vectors: physical force from the thorns, spiritual poison from the corrupted qi, and mental attacks from the death energy woven into their structure.

The silver-haired enforcer's daggers flashed. She cut through dozens of vines in rapid succession, her movements economical and precise. But for every vine she destroyed, two more grew in its place. The Garden of Eternal Torment was a self-sustaining technique that fed on the spiritual energy of those trapped within it.

"This is troublesome," Han Shu observed. He raised both hands, and his own spiritual pressure expanded outward. "Celestial Court Authority, Fourth Rank. By the mandate of Heaven, I invoke suppression protocols."

White light radiated from his body, filling the entire garden formation. The light didn't attack directly; instead, it simply asserted dominance over the space itself. This was the authority granted to high-ranking Celestial Court enforcers: the right to override other cultivators' techniques through sheer bureaucratic power.

Lady Chi's garden began to wither. The vines slowed their growth. The corrupted qi dissipated. Within seconds, the entire technique had collapsed, leaving only a normal stone courtyard behind.

"You and your rules," Lady Chi snarled. "Always hiding behind authority instead of real power."

"Authority is power," Han Shu replied calmly. "You should have learned that before descending."

Jian Wei used the opening to press his attack. He moved in close, too close for the vines to intercept effectively. His hands struck in rapid succession, hitting pressure points, meridian nodes, and spiritual centers. Each strike disrupted Lady Chi's qi flow, making it harder for her to channel techniques.

She blocked three strikes and dodged two more, but the sixth connected with her solar plexus. Spiritual energy exploded into her body, disrupting her internal cultivation.

Lady Chi coughed blood. Real blood, not spiritual manifestation. The technique had damaged her physically, not just spiritually.

But she was far from defeated.

Her body transformed. The human shape dissolved and was replaced by something that was more plant than person. Her limbs became thorny branches. Her hair spread into a canopy of poisonous leaves. Her torso thickened into a trunk covered in blood-red bark.

This was her true form, or something close to it. The result of centuries spent cultivating the Crimson Lotus Pavilion's corruption techniques until the boundary between cultivator and plant had blurred beyond recognition.

"You want to see power?" Her voice emerged from somewhere within the plant-thing's structure, distorted and inhuman. "I'll show you power!"

Roots exploded from beneath the courtyard stones, each one as thick as a man's torso. They moved with terrifying speed, seeking to impale the three enforcers. The silver-haired woman leaped straight up, avoiding the roots. Jian Wei phased through them, his body becoming temporarily intangible. Han Shu erected a barrier of golden light that the roots couldn't penetrate.

But Lady Chi wasn't targeting them anymore.

The roots changed direction mid-strike to aim instead at the protective dome surrounding Slifer's disciples. The Aegis of Ten Thousand Shields had been designed to resist attacks from outside, but these roots were coming from below, tunneling through the earth.

Several disciples screamed as roots burst upward directly beneath their feet. The barrier held, barely, but cracks appeared in its structure. Master Hong's formation was powerful, but it had limits.

Slifer had cards that could reinforce the barrier, strengthen its foundation, repair the damage. But using them would drain a lot of Karmic Credits, and he wasn't sure if the Immortals would be able to deal with Lady Chi or if he would need to get involved in the battle himself.

Before he could decide, Jian Wei appeared directly in front of the attacking roots. His body blazed with white fire—not spiritual flames, but something purer. This was the manifestation of his Immortal Realm cultivation. It was compressed down to fit within mortal realm limits but still carried a fraction of its original power.

"Burning Judgment."

The fire spread along the roots and consumed them instantly. The technique was so precise that it didn't damage the surrounding ground or the protective barrier. It simply erased the roots from existence, turning corrupted plant matter into ash.

Jian Wei turned to face Lady Chi's transformed body. His expression had lost all trace of humor. "Attacking protected civilians. That's another violation. You're making this very easy for us to justify lethal force."

"Let them all die!" Lady Chi shrieked. "Let this entire sect burn! None of it matters if Darius is gone!"

She attacked again, this time with everything she had. The plant-form expanded, growing larger and more monstrous. Thorny branches whipped through the air fast enough to create sonic booms. Poisonous pollen spread in clouds that dissolved stone on contact. Roots tore through the earth, destroying the careful architecture of the courtyard.

The three enforcers met her assault head-on.

Han Shu moved to the left as he drew Lady Chi's attention with chains of golden light. Each chain attempted to bind her branches and restrict her movement. She broke them, but they kept reforming, infinite and patient.

The silver-haired enforcer attacked from the right, her daggers finding gaps in Lady Chi's wooden armor. Each strike removed a branch or severed a root. The damage was minimal individually, but it accumulated. Lady Chi was being cut apart piece by piece.

Jian Wei went for the center. He dove through the mass of thorny branches, weaving between attacks with inhuman precision. His goal was the trunk: the core where Lady Chi's consciousness resided. If he could strike there, he could end the battle.

Lady Chi realized his intention. All her remaining vines converged on Jian Wei simultaneously and created a cage of thorns that closed around him from every direction. He tried to phase through them, but Lady Chi had anticipated that. The vines were infused with formation script specifically designed to disrupt intangibility techniques. Jian Wei's body solidified mid-dodge, and dozens of thorns pierced through his torso.

Blood sprayed across the courtyard. Real blood from real wounds. Jian Wei's face contorted in pain, but he didn't scream. Instead, he grabbed the vines impaling him and yanked hard to pull himself deeper into the thorn cage.

Toward Lady Chi's core.

"Junior brother, no!" Han Shu's voice carried genuine alarm.

But Jian Wei was already moving. Even impaled on thorns, even bleeding from a dozen wounds, he refused to stop. His hands reached Lady Chi's trunk and pressed flat against the blood-red bark.

"Heavenly Purification."

White light exploded from his palms. It poured into Lady Chi's core, burning away the corruption from the inside. This wasn't a normal technique; this was something only Celestial Court enforcers could use, a method specifically designed to cleanse corrupted cultivation.

Lady Chi screamed. Her entire plant-form convulsed, branches thrashing wildly. The trunk began to crack, splitting apart as the purification energy spread through her spiritual channels.

But the technique was taking too much from Jian Wei. His face had gone pale, and blood continued flowing from his wounds. Maintaining the purification while impaled was draining his life force at an unsustainable rate.

Han Shu appeared beside him. The older enforcer grabbed Jian Wei's shoulder and added his own spiritual energy to the technique. The white light intensified, becoming almost blinding.

The silver-haired enforcer joined them moments later. She placed both hands on the trunk beside Jian Wei's and channeled her own energy into the purification. Three Immortal Realm cultivators working in concert, all their power focused on breaking Lady Chi's corruption from within.

Lady Chi's plant-form began collapsing. The branches withered. The roots retracted. The trunk shrank as it reverted toward something resembling a human shape. She tried to resist, tried to maintain the transformation, but the combined assault was too much.

The purification reached critical mass. Lady Chi's form exploded outward in a shower of dead leaves and broken branches. When the debris settled, she stood in the center of the devastation, returned to her original human appearance.

But she wasn't defeated yet.

Her hands moved in desperate patterns as she formed a final technique. Red light gathered around her fists, darker and more concentrated than before. This was death qi in its purest form, compressed to the point where it could kill with a touch.

She lunged at Jian Wei, aiming for his heart. The enforcers had been weakened by channeling so much power into the purification. Their defenses were down, their spiritual reserves depleted. If this attack connected, Jian Wei would die.

Han Shu tried to intercept, but he was too slow. The silver-haired enforcer's daggers swung up, but they wouldn't reach in time.

Lady Chi's fist, wreathed in death qi, drove toward Jian Wei's chest.

Then she stopped.

Not voluntarily. She simply froze mid-strike, her entire body locked in place. Red light flared around her wrists and ankles; formation cuffs materialized from nowhere, inscribed with countless layers of binding script.

The cuffs yanked her backward with irresistible force. She crashed to the ground, arms pulled behind her back by invisible chains. More formations appeared around her neck, waist, and legs. Within seconds, she was completely immobilized.

Han Shu straightened, his hands still glowing with residual spiritual

DEMONIC SECT ELDER AND THE GREAT WAR

energy. "Binding Array of Celestial Judgment. I've been preparing that formation since we arrived. You gave me plenty of time to complete the setup while you were focused on attacking."

Lady Chi thrashed against the bindings, but the cuffs didn't budge. Forged in the Celestial Court's highest-security facilities, they were specifically designed to restrain Immortal Realm cultivators. No amount of struggling would break them.

"No," she gasped. "No, I swore an oath! I have to kill him! I have to avenge Darius!"

"Your oath is now in conflict with Celestial Court custody regulations," Han Shu said wearily. "We'll petition Heaven for special dispensation to override it. Until then, you'll remain in our secure facilities."

Jian Wei collapsed, the thorns finally sliding free from his body. The silver-haired enforcer caught him before he hit the ground. She pulled healing pills from her storage ring and forced them down his throat.

"You're an idiot," she told him flatly. "Sacrificing yourself like that. What would I tell your master?"

"Worked . . . didn't it?" Jian Wei coughed blood but managed a weak smile. "We got her."

The three enforcers stood over Lady Chi's bound form. She continued struggling, screaming incoherent threats about Slifer and revenge and burning the world. But the formation cuffs held firm, draining her spiritual energy with each passing second.

Eventually, her struggles weakened. The screaming faded to hoarse whispers. She slumped forward, held upright only by the chains binding her wrists.

Defeated. Captured. Completely neutralized.

Slifer watched from his position at the edge of the courtyard. The protective barrier around his disciples had held perfectly, and not a single person was injured, despite the devastating battle that had raged just meters away. The plan had worked exactly as intended.

Lady Chi, the woman who'd been manipulating sect masters and orchestrating wars, was on her knees in chains.

And Slifer smiled.

The smile wasn't triumphant or cruel. It was simply . . . satisfied. The kind of expression someone wore when a long, difficult project finally reached completion. It had been months of constant war and manipulation, and he'd spent hours coordinating with the Celestial Court, preparing the trap, gathering everyone in position. He'd publicly dishonored Darius to provoke Lady Chi's attack at the exact right moment.

And now it was over.

Around him, his disciples were reacting to what they'd just witnessed. Caelum looked stunned, his hand still resting on Starforge's hilt. Amelia was grinning, clearly impressed by the violence. Fenlock held Lenvari close, both of them trembling slightly from the residual spiritual pressure. Val chirped excitedly, wanting to join the battle herself.

The grand elders wore expressions of awe and fear in equal measure. They'd just watched three Immortal Realm cultivators battle someone from the same level, all of them suppressing their power to fit within mortal realm limits. It was the kind of conflict that shouldn't be possible in their world.

"Did you see that technique?" one disciple whispered.

"The garden formation," another replied. "I've never seen anything like it."

"The enforcers were amazing," a third added. "They worked together perfectly."

"But the sect master knew," Caelum said quietly. Everyone near him turned to listen. "He planned this entire thing. The announcement, gathering everyone here, the protective formation. He coordinated with the Celestial Court beforehand."

Grand Elder Wyatt nodded slowly. "The sect master's connections extend further than any of us realized. To have the authority to summon Immortal Realm enforcers . . ." He trailed off, leaving the implications unstated.

Slifer's smile widened slightly as he listened to the comments come in.

CHAPTER TWENTY-TWO

Slifer stared at the woman kneeling before him.

Lady Chi looked nothing like the terrifying Immortal Realm cultivator who had controlled the minds of sect masters and started wars. The chains binding her wrists glowed with golden script, the same formations that had restrained her during the battle. Her long black hair fell forward, obscuring most of her face. The robes that had shifted between black and green now just looked like expensive fabric, no supernatural qualities visible.

She was dangerous. Slifer knew that. He'd spent months dealing with the consequences of her actions. The wars, the manipulation, the disciples who'd died because she wanted revenge for her lover Darius. But right now, chained and kneeling in his quarters with three Celestial Court Enforcers watching her every breath, she just looked tired.

Han Shu stood to Lady Chi's right, his white robes pristine despite the battle. The old man's expression was unreadable. Jian Wei was on her left, still looking slightly pale from the battle. The silver-haired female enforcer whose name Slifer still didn't know stood directly behind the prisoner, one hand resting on her dagger hilt.

"So," Slifer said, breaking the silence. "Here we are."

Lady Chi's head lifted slightly. Her red eyes fixed on him, and for a moment Slifer saw the hatred burning there. It was personal. Deep. The kind of rage that came from genuine loss rather than political grudges or territorial disputes.

"You killed him," she said quietly. Her voice was steady despite everything. "You killed Darius, and you erased his name. You dishonored his memory."

"I did," Slifer confirmed. "He attacked me first. And he was a traitor to the sect. He shared intelligence with someone from the Immortal Realm. That someone was you."

"He loved me." Lady Chi's voice cracked on the word. "He would have done anything for me. And you killed him for it."

Slifer wanted to point out that betraying your sect for a lover was exactly the kind of thing that got people killed in the cultivation world. That Darius had made his choice and faced the consequences. But looking at Lady Chi's expression, he realized she wouldn't hear any of that. Love made people do stupid things. He'd seen enough web novels where characters threw away everything for romance. Usually those were the protagonists, though, not the villains.

"You started wars over him," Slifer said instead. "You controlled the minds of sect masters. Manipulated disciples. Got hundreds of people killed in conflicts they wanted no part of. All for revenge."

"They were mortals." Lady Chi said the word like it meant nothing. "Brief sparks that flicker and die within a century. What does it matter if they die slightly sooner? Darius was special. He could have achieved true cultivation. He could have joined me in the Immortal Realm."

There it was. The casual dismissal of mortal life that marked so many higher realm cultivators. Slifer had dealt with this attitude before, back when he'd first started understanding the System and the broader cultivation world. The strong viewed the weak as resources. Tools. Stepping stones on the path to greater power.

It was one of the things that had always bothered him about cultivation stories. The way mortals were treated as expendable by anyone with sufficient power. Sure, sometimes there were righteous cultivators who protected the innocent, but even they tended to value other cultivators' lives more highly than ordinary people.

"He couldn't have," Slifer said flatly. "His talent was mediocre at best. He reached Ascendant Realm through political maneuvering and serving the right people, not cultivation skill. You were fooling yourself if you thought he'd ever reach the Immortal Realm."

Lady Chi's chains rattled as her hands clenched into fists. "You know nothing about him! Nothing about what we shared!"

"I know he betrayed his sect for you. I know he fed you information about our defenses, our techniques, our weaknesses. I know he was planning to help sacrifice the Black Rose Sect for his cultivation before I stopped him." Slifer paused. "And I know he wasn't worth starting a war over."

The red glow in Lady Chi's eyes intensified. Slifer felt his Void Being Aura activate automatically to provide protection against her mental influence. The chains binding her flared brighter as Han Shu channeled more spiritual energy into them.

"Careful," the old enforcer warned. "The bindings will drain your cultivation if you try to break free. You're already weakened from the battle. Don't make this worse for yourself."

Lady Chi's gaze shifted to Han Shu. "You dare lecture me? You, who have served the Celestial Court for thousands of years like a loyal dog? I am a Core Disciple of the Crimson Lotus Pavilion. My master is an Immortal Emperor. When he learns of this treatment—"

"Your master already knows," Han Shu interrupted gently. "We sent word the moment we confirmed your identity and actions. He has chosen not to intervene."

That seemed to hit Lady Chi harder than anything else. Her expression crumpled, the rage giving way to something that looked like devastation. "He . . . he abandoned me?"

"You violated multiple Celestial Court regulations," Jian Wei said. His tone was less sympathetic than Han Shu's. "You descended without permission, manipulated mortal realm politics, started wars, and bound yourself with an oath to remain until your revenge was complete. Your master may be powerful, but even Immortal Emperors don't interfere with court jurisdiction lightly."

The silver-haired enforcer spoke for the first time. "Your sect has paid the required fines for your misconduct. They've also agreed to accept whatever punishment the court decides. That should tell you everything about how they view your actions."

Lady Chi's shoulders sagged. The fight seemed to drain out of her completely. She looked at Slifer again, and this time there was no hatred. Just emptiness. "I swore an oath. I cannot leave until you're dead. The Heavenly Dao will force me to remain here, bound to this realm, until I fulfill my vow or die trying."

"Like I mentioned before, the court can petition Heaven for special dispensation," Han Shu said. "It's a complicated process, but for cases like yours where the oath was made rashly during emotional distress, there's precedent. You'll serve your sentence in our secure facilities, and when you're released, the oath will be nullified. You'll be able to return to the Immortal Realm."

"How long?" Lady Chi asked. Her voice was barely a whisper.

"For your crimes? Five thousand years. Minimum."

Five thousand years. Slifer tried to imagine spending thousands of years in prison. For an Immortal, it probably wasn't as long as it sounded to his mortal sensibilities, but it was still a huge chunk of time. Lady Chi would emerge to a completely different Immortal Realm. Everyone she knew might have advanced to higher realms or died in tribulations. Her entire life would be gone.

"You could have just talked to me," Slifer said. He didn't know why he was bothering, but the words came out anyway. "When you first arrived. You could have explained about Darius, asked for his body back, maybe negotiated some kind of compensation for his death. Instead, you went straight to attacking me, and when that failed, you declared war."

Lady Chi laughed. It was a broken sound. "Talk? To a demonic cultivator who killed my beloved? You expect me to believe you would have shown mercy?"

"No," Slifer admitted. "But I would have tried to avoid all of this." He gestured around the room, encompassing not just his quarters, but the entire sect, the region, and all the chaos that had resulted from her quest for revenge. "Wars cost resources. They waste time. They create problems that take years to clean up. I'm trying to reform the demonic sects, to make them less . . . demonic. Your interference set that work back by months."

"Reform." Lady Chi's tone made it clear what she thought of that idea. "Demonic cultivation cannot be reformed. It's built on suffering and death. On consuming others to strengthen yourself. You cannot change our fundamental nature."

"Maybe not completely," Slifer said. "But you can direct it. Channel it toward targets that actually deserve it instead of innocent villagers and rival sects. Create rules, establish consequences for excessive cruelty, reward disciples who show restraint." He'd been thinking about this a lot lately. "Demonic cultivation gets a bad reputation because most demonic cultivators are psychopaths who torture people for fun. But the cultivation methods themselves are just tools. It's how you use them that matters."

Han Shu nodded thoughtfully. "An interesting philosophy. Most would say you're trying to fit a square peg in a round hole, but I've seen stranger reformations succeed over the millennia."

"It won't work," Lady Chi insisted. "You're fooling yourself. The demonic path corrupts everyone who walks it. Eventually, you'll become just like the rest, like me. Cruel, sadistic, willing to sacrifice anything for more power."

Slifer thought about the original Slifer, the man whose body he'd inhabited.

That person had absolutely been cruel and sadistic. He'd been exactly what Lady Chi was describing.

But Slifer wasn't that person. He had the original's memories, his face, and his cultivation, but he wasn't cruel by nature. He'd made mistakes, sure. Used questionable methods sometimes. The world had forced him into situations where violence was the only option. But he'd tried to be better than the original. To treat his disciples with respect, to minimize unnecessary deaths, to build something sustainable rather than just accumulating power for its own sake.

"Maybe," Slifer said. "Or maybe I'll prove that that path doesn't have to lead where everyone thinks it does." He turned to Han Shu. "What happens now?"

The old enforcer pulled a small jade token from his robes. "We take her back to the Celestial Court's detention facilities. She'll be held there while her case is processed. The trial will take approximately three years, after which she'll be sentenced and moved to long-term confinement."

"Three years?" Slifer asked. "What takes years?"

"Bureaucracy," Jian Wei said with a grimace. "The court handles hundreds of thousands of cases across multiple realms. Each one requires proper documentation, witness testimony, evidence verification, appeals processing. It's incredibly tedious."

"Incredibly necessary," Han Shu corrected. "Without proper procedures, the court would devolve into arbitrary enforcement based on individual enforcers' preferences. The bureaucracy ensures fairness."

Slifer had never thought about the logistics of policing Immortal Realm cultivators across multiple realms. It made sense that you'd need a huge organization to manage it, but three years just for processing seemed excessive. Then again, when you dealt with beings who lived for tens of thousands of years, maybe three years wasn't considered long.

"So, she's definitely going away?" Slifer asked. "Not coming back to cause more problems?"

"She'll be in the most secure facility the court maintains," Han Shu assured him. "Specifically designed to hold Immortal Realm cultivators who've violated realm-crossing regulations. The formations there can suppress even Greater Immortals. She won't escape."

Lady Chi said nothing. She was staring at the floor now, completely defeated. Slifer almost felt sorry for her. Almost. Then he remembered all the disciples who'd died in the wars she'd started, the families torn apart, the infrastructure destroyed. His sympathy evaporated quickly.

"I still think you should just kill her," Slifer said bluntly.

The three enforcers looked at him with various expressions of surprise. Even Lady Chi's head snapped up.

"That's not how the Celestial Court operates," Han Shu said carefully.

"I know. You've explained that." Slifer crossed his arms. "But from a practical standpoint, execution makes more sense than five thousand years of imprisonment."

"How so?" Han Shu asked. He seemed genuinely curious rather than offended.

Slifer organized his thoughts. "First, there's the resource problem. You're going to spend five thousand years guarding her, feeding her, maintaining the formations that keep her contained. That's five thousand years of resources that could be used elsewhere. On actually productive things instead of just keeping one person locked up."

"The court has vast resources," the silver-haired enforcer said. "Maintaining prisoners isn't a significant burden."

"Maybe not for you," Slifer countered. "But it's still wasteful. Second, there's the escape risk. You say your facilities are secure, but she's an Immortal Realm cultivator. She's got hundreds of years to study the formations, look for weaknesses, and plan an escape. Maybe she never finds one, but maybe she does. And if she gets out after you've spent all that time and effort imprisoning her, all those resources are wasted and she's back causing problems."

Jian Wei frowned. "Our security has never been breached."

"Never?" Slifer asked skeptically.

"Well . . . there have been a few incidents over the millennia," Jian Wei admitted. "But they were all recaptured eventually."

"Eventually. After causing how much damage during their freedom?" Slifer shook his head. "Third, and this is the big one, there's the revenge factor. You imprison her for five thousand years, then she comes out with five thousand years of anger built up. She's had all that time to plot, to plan, to figure out exactly how she wants to make everyone who wronged her suffer. And I'm at the top of that list."

"Your concern is noted," Han Shu said diplomatically. "But the court's mission is rehabilitation as well as punishment. Five millennia gives her time to reflect on her actions, to mature beyond her current emotional state, and to hopefully emerge as a better person."

"Does that actually work?" Slifer asked. "In your experience, do Immortals who've been imprisoned for centuries actually come out rehabilitated?"

Han Shu hesitated. That hesitation told Slifer everything he needed to know.

"Some do," the old enforcer finally said. "Others . . . remain unchanged. It varies by individual."

"So, you're gambling that she'll be one of the reformed ones," Slifer said. "And if she's not, she comes after me again in five thousand years, except now with millennia of planning and prison-hardened determination."

"You'll likely have ascended to the Greater Immortal Realm yourself by then," Jian Wei pointed out, "given your current trajectory and apparent talent. You could defend yourself."

That was a fair point, except Slifer had no idea if he'd actually reach the Lesser Immortal Realm. The System had gotten him this far, but who knew if it would continue working at higher cultivation stages?

"I'm not saying this to be cruel," Slifer continued. "I'm saying it because execution is cleaner. It solves the problem permanently. No resource drain, no escape risk, no future revenge plots. One quick technique and it's done."

"The court doesn't execute prisoners except in extreme circumstances," Han Shu said firmly. "Mass genocide, realm destruction, or violations that threaten the fundamental order of Heaven itself. Lady Chi's crimes, while serious, don't rise to that level."

"She started multiple wars and controlled the minds of sect masters," Slifer said. "How many people died because of her actions? Hundreds? Thousands?"

"Mortal casualties aren't counted the same way as Immortal casualties," the silver-haired enforcer said matter-of-factly. "It's unfortunate, but that's reality. The court exists primarily to regulate Immortal conduct, not to protect mortals."

And there it was. The truth Slifer had been dancing around since the enforcers first arrived. The Celestial Court didn't actually care about all the damage Lady Chi had caused in the mortal realm. They cared that she'd broken their rules: Descended without permission. Violated realm-crossing protocols. Bound herself with an unauthorized oath.

The wars, the deaths, the destruction, all of that was just background noise to them. Unfortunate side effects of rule-breaking rather than the actual crimes. Lady Chi was being punished because she'd disrespected the court's authority, not because she'd hurt people.

Slifer's opinion of the Celestial Court dropped several notches.

"So, Immortals get centuries of rehabilitation," Slifer said slowly, "but mortals get nothing. If I'd killed hundreds of people, you'd execute me without hesitation. But she kills hundreds and gets prison with eventual release."

"You're not an Immortal," Jian Wei said, as if that explained everything. And maybe it did, from their perspective.

Han Shu looked uncomfortable. "The system isn't perfect. I'll acknowledge that. But it's what we have. The court was established to prevent catastrophic conflicts between Immortal powers. Mortal realm collateral damage, while regrettable, isn't our primary concern."

"Then why did you help me?" Slifer asked. "If you don't care about mortal casualties, why coordinate with me to stop her?"

"Because her actions were escalating," Han Shu explained. "The mind control, the wars, the oath binding her to this realm, all of it suggested she was losing control. If left unchecked, she might have eventually caused enough damage to destabilize this entire realm's dimensional structure. That would have required much more extensive court intervention. It was more efficient to stop her now."

More efficient. Not more moral, not to save lives, just more efficient. Slifer was really starting to dislike the Celestial Court's approach to justice.

But he couldn't do anything about it. These were Immortal Realm enforcers who could kill him without breaking a sweat if they wanted to. And they'd helped him defeat Lady Chi, which he appreciated, even if their motives weren't as altruistic as he'd hoped.

"Fine," Slifer said. "Take her away. But I want your word that if she escapes or if the rehabilitation fails, you'll tell me immediately. I deserve a warning if she's coming after me again."

"That's reasonable," Han Shu agreed. "I'll arrange for a communication talisman to be sent to you. If Lady Chi's status changes in any way that might threaten you, we'll inform you."

Slifer nodded. It wasn't ideal, but it was better than nothing. He looked at Lady Chi one more time. She was still staring at the floor, completely broken. The woman who'd terrified sect masters and started wars looked small now, defeated.

"One last thing," Slifer said. "When you're released in five thousand years, stay out of the mortal realm. Go back to your sect, continue your cultivation, live your life. But leave me and mine alone. I didn't want this conflict. You forced it on me. Don't make the same mistake twice."

Lady Chi's head lifted. For a moment, her red eyes met his. Then she looked away without responding.

"We should go," Jian Wei said. "The portal window is optimal for the next hour. After that, we'll need to wait six more hours for the dimensional convergence."

Han Shu nodded. He made a gesture, and Lady Chi's chains began glowing brighter. She rose to her feet, moving stiffly. The three enforcers positioned themselves around her, forming a triangle with the prisoner at the center.

"Thank you for your cooperation," Han Shu said to Slifer. "The court appreciates your assistance in this matter. As discussed, we'll provide protection for your disciples if any other Immortals cause problems. Simply activate the talisman we gave you."

"I will," Slifer said. "Safe travels."

Han Shu smiled slightly. "We'll be traveling through dimensional space using court portals. It's as safe as travel gets." He raised his right hand, and the air in front of him began to shimmer. A portal formed, its edges stabilizing into a perfect oval. Through it, Slifer could see white stone corridors lit by some kind of spiritual illumination.

"The Celestial Court's administrative complex," Jian Wei explained, noticing Slifer's interest. "Where we process new arrivals before transferring them to appropriate facilities."

The silver-haired enforcer went through first, followed by Lady Chi. The prisoner didn't look back. She walked through the portal with her head down, chains clinking softly. Jian Wei went next, and finally Han Shu paused at the portal's edge.

"One more thing," the old enforcer said. "To survive against Lady Chi for this long, you are clearly talented. If you ever decide you want backing from the Immortal Realm, the court is always looking for talented individuals. We don't pry into past histories or question cultivation methods. We just require that members uphold our core principles about realm interaction."

It was the recruitment pitch again. Slifer had turned it down before, but Han Shu was giving him another chance. The offer was tempting in some ways. Official Immortal Realm backing would solve a lot of problems. But it would also mean oversight, expectations, and potentially getting dragged into conflicts he wanted no part of.

"I'll think about it," Slifer said noncommittally.

Han Shu nodded, unsurprised by the non-answer. "The offer stands. Farewell, Slifer. May your cultivation advance smoothly."

"You too," Slifer replied.

The old enforcer stepped through the portal. The opening hung in the air for another moment, showing the white corridors beyond, then collapsed in on itself and disappeared. The only evidence it had ever existed was a faint shimmer in the air that faded after a few seconds.

Slifer was alone in his quarters.

He walked to his bed and sat down heavily. The tension he'd been carrying since Lady Chi's arrival drained out of him all at once, leaving him feeling exhausted. It was over. The sect masters were freed. The wars had ended. Lady

Chi was gone, imprisoned in an Immortal Realm facility for the next five thousand years.

It was done.

Slifer lay back on the bed, staring at the ceiling. His body was tired, but his mind was still racing. Too much had happened too quickly. The tournament, the Sealed Realm opening, the Black Death Sect invasion, discovering Lady Chi's manipulation, fighting her multiple times, allying with the Celestial Court. It felt like years of events compressed into months.

He should feel relieved. The major threat was gone. His sect was safe. His disciples had survived. The System would give him credits for resolving the situation. Everything had worked out.

So why did he feel uneasy?

Slifer sat up, frowning. Something about the whole situation bothered him. It nagged at the back of his mind, a persistent itch he couldn't scratch. He tried to identify what exactly was wrong.

The battle against Lady Chi had been intense, sure, but the Celestial Court enforcers had handled most of it. Still, the whole thing felt . . . easy? Wrong word. Not easy, exactly. Lady Chi was genuinely dangerous. But it had all resolved so cleanly. Bad guy defeated, imprisoned, taken away. No complications, no unexpected twists, no last-minute reversals.

Slifer had read enough web novels to know that problems rarely resolved that cleanly. There was usually another layer. A hidden scheme, a backup plan, a final surprise before the arc actually ended. The protagonist would think they'd won, then something would go wrong, and they'd have to deal with one more crisis.

But this wasn't a web novel. This was his actual life. And sometimes in real life, problems did just get solved. The right people showed up and took the bad guy away, and that was that. It didn't have to be more complicated.

Except Slifer's instincts were screaming that it was more complicated.

He stood and paced around his quarters. What was he missing? Lady Chi was imprisoned. The Celestial Court had confirmed they'd keep her locked up for five thousand years. Han Shu had seemed genuine in his assurances. The man was an Immortal Realm enforcer; lying to a mortal cultivator would gain him nothing.

Unless the lie wasn't from Han Shu. What if someone else was involved? Someone Han Shu didn't know about?

Lady Chi had mentioned her master was an Immortal Emperor. The Crimson Lotus Pavilion's leader. What if that person decided five thousand years was too long and arranged for his disciple's early release? Or escape?

But Han Shu had said the master already knew about Lady Chi's situation and had chosen not to intervene. The sect had even paid fines. That suggested they'd accepted the court's jurisdiction.

What if there were other Crimson Lotus disciples who didn't accept it? Friends or allies of Lady Chi who might want revenge on Slifer for getting her imprisoned?

Slifer's frown deepened. That was a possibility. If Lady Chi had friends in the Immortal Realm, they might come after him. But Han Shu had offered protection for Slifer's disciples if other Immortals caused problems. Presumably that would include revenge-seeking Crimson Lotus members.

So, what was bothering him?

Maybe it was the System's silence. Usually, when Slifer completed a major mission or defeated a significant enemy, the System would chime in with credit rewards or new missions. But it had been quiet since Lady Chi's defeat. No completion notification, no congratulations, nothing.

That was odd. The System was usually very prompt about giving rewards. Had it not registered Lady Chi's imprisonment as completing the mission? Or was there something else that needed to happen first?

Slifer pulled up his System interface mentally. The mission log showed the same tasks as before. Reform demonic sects, elevate disciples, accumulate credits. Nothing about Lady Chi specifically, which made sense since she'd been an unexpected complication rather than a planned objective.

But there were no new notifications. No updates. Just the same ongoing missions he'd been working on for months.

Maybe that was normal. Not every event triggered a System response. Lady Chi had been a personal threat rather than a System-assigned challenge. The System probably didn't care about his personal enemies as long as they didn't interfere with his main missions.

Slifer dismissed the interface and continued pacing. His logical mind said everything was fine. Lady Chi was imprisoned, the threat was over, and he could return to normal sect operations. But his gut said something was wrong. That things had resolved too neatly, too completely.

He'd learned to trust his instincts over the past year. They'd kept him alive through multiple close calls. When something felt wrong, it usually was wrong.

But what could he do about a vague feeling? He couldn't investigate a threat that didn't have a clear shape or direction. He couldn't prepare defenses against an enemy he couldn't identify.

Maybe he was just being paranoid. After months of constant crisis, maybe his brain was having trouble accepting that the crisis was actually over. Maybe he'd gotten so used to looking over his shoulder that he couldn't stop even when the danger was gone.

That made sense. Post-crisis anxiety or something like that. Perfectly normal reaction.

Slifer walked to the window and looked out at the Black Rose Sect grounds. Disciples moved between buildings, going about their daily training and duties. The sun was setting, painting the sky in shades of orange and red. Everything looked peaceful. Normal.

He should rest. He'd been pushing himself hard lately. The Core Formation breakthrough, the body cultivation advancement, the constant battles and political maneuvering. His body and mind needed time to recover.

But the uneasy feeling persisted. A knot in his stomach that wouldn't go away no matter how much he tried to rationalize it.

Fine. He'd stay alert. Keep his guard up. Watch for anything unusual. If something was coming, he'd be ready for it.

And if nothing was coming? If this was just paranoia?

Then he'd look like an idiot, but at least he'd be a cautious idiot. Better than being a confident dead idiot.

Slifer turned away from the window and headed for the door. He couldn't just sit here stewing in his own anxiety. He'd check on his disciples, make sure the sect defenses were properly maintained, and maybe visit Elder Feng and work on some alchemy to take his mind off things.

Staying busy would help. It always did.

As he reached for the door handle, Slifer paused. One last look around his quarters. Everything seemed normal. No hidden threats, no lurking danger, just a comfortable room in a well-protected sect.

He really hoped he was being paranoid for no reason.

The door opened under his hand, and Slifer stepped out into the corridor. Whatever came next, he'd deal with it. That was what sect masters did.

Even if they had a bad feeling in their gut that wouldn't go away.

CHAPTER TWENTY-THREE

The underground chamber smelled of copper and incense. Stone walls carved with formation script that pulsed with a sickly red light pressed in from all sides. The air was thick enough to choke on, heavy with spiritual energy that had been twisted into something wrong.

Lady Chi's hideout sat deep beneath an abandoned temple compound, accessible only through a series of collapsed passages that looked like natural cave-ins. Anyone investigating would find rubble and dead ends. They wouldn't notice the spatial distortions that opened when specific formations were activated from the inside.

In the center of the chamber, a massive circular array covered the floor. Blood channels formed intricate patterns that connected seven positions marked by obsidian bowls. Each bowl contained offerings: fresh organs that still glistened wetly, spirit stones that had been soaked in death qi, and talismans inscribed with characters that hurt to look at directly.

Six of the seven bowls were complete. The seventh sat empty, its preparations only half finished. A jar of prepared blood sat beside it, still sealed. Ritual implements lay scattered nearby: a ceremonial knife with a jade handle, strips of paper covered in dense script, and a small golden bell that would normally be rung at specific intervals during the summoning.

Lady Chi had been in the middle of the ritual when Slifer's announcement reached her. The communication talisman had exploded, carrying news that made her blood boil. Darius's name had been stripped from the Wall of Elders.

His legacy declared tainted. Everything they had shared together dismissed as manipulation and betrayal.

She'd left immediately, abandoning days of preparation for a moment of rage. The ritual chamber sat frozen in time, waiting for completion.

Footsteps echoed down the stone corridor.

Nomed emerged from the shadows. He looked exactly as he had when he'd infiltrated the Black Rose Sect: young, unassuming, with carefully average features that helped him blend into crowds. His robes were simple gray, the kind worn by traveling cultivators who couldn't afford sect colors.

But his eyes were different now, no longer hiding behind a facade of earnest youth. They were cold, calculating, and filled with the kind of patience that came from centuries of planning.

He surveyed the chamber, taking in the incomplete ritual with a single glance. His expression remained neutral, but something flickered across his face. Satisfaction, perhaps. Or vindication.

Nomed walked to the seventh bowl and knelt beside it. He picked up the jar of prepared blood, broke the seal with his thumb, and poured it carefully into the obsidian container. The liquid was darker than normal blood, almost black in the dim light. It had been treated with herbs and spiritual essences that prevented coagulation while enhancing its connection to the living donor.

"Always so impulsive," Nomed murmured to himself. His voice carried none of the nervous energy he'd displayed at the Black Rose Sect. This was his true voice: calm, precise, utterly emotionless. "Months of preparation abandoned for a moment of anger. Typical of her generation."

He placed the talismans around the seventh bowl in specific positions, checking each one against a diagram he pulled from his storage ring. The golden bell went last, positioned directly in front of the bowl where it could be easily reached.

Nomed stood and walked to the edge of the formation. His hands moved through a series of complex gestures, activating the array one layer at a time. The blood channels began to glow, starting from the outermost ring and spiraling inward. Red light filled the chamber, casting dancing shadows on the walls.

The seven bowls resonated in harmony. The organs withered and crumbled to ash. The spirit stones cracked and released their stored death qi in controlled bursts. The talismans ignited with colorless flames that consumed the paper but left the script floating in the air like ghostly afterimages.

Nomed picked up the golden bell and rang it once. The sound was pure and clear, seeming to come from every direction at once. It echoed through dimensions, a signal that pierced the barriers between realms.

He rang it again. And again. Seven times in total, each chime precisely spaced.

The formation array blazed with power. The red light intensified until it was painful to look at directly. The air in the center of the chamber began to ripple like heat distortion over a desert road, except this distortion moved in ways that hurt the eyes to follow.

A crack appeared in reality itself. Not a physical crack, but something deeper. A tear in the fundamental fabric that separated one realm from another. Through the opening, something vast and ancient stirred.

Spiritual pressure began leaking through the crack. Not the overwhelming but ultimately limited pressure of an Ascendant cultivator. Not even the terrifying weight of a Half-Step Immortal like Vowron had been. Not even the almost divine energy of a Lesser Immortal.

This was different. This pressure carried the weight of genuine immortality, of cultivation that had transcended mortal limitations entirely. It pressed down on the chamber with such force that the stone walls groaned. Cracks appeared in the ceiling. Dust rained down from above.

A figure became visible through the tear, obscured by the dimensional boundary but slowly growing clearer. It was humanoid, but the details remained frustratingly vague. The aura radiating from the figure made it clear that this was no Lesser Immortal who had recently achieved their breakthrough.

This was a Greater Immortal. Someone who had spent thousands of years consolidating their cultivation, refining their techniques, and pushing toward even higher realms. The difference between a Lesser Immortal and a Greater Immortal was like comparing a candle to the sun.

The figure moved toward the opening, attempting to pass through into the mortal realm.

The world itself resisted.

Reality buckled and warped around the tear. The dimensional barrier, which had been carefully weakened by the blood ritual, suddenly reinforced itself with desperate strength. This wasn't conscious opposition. This was automatic defense, the mortal realm's intrinsic protection against beings that exceeded its capacity.

The figure pushed harder. Spiritual pressure flooded through the opening in waves, each one stronger than the last. The formation array on the floor began to crack under the strain. Blood channels shattered. Two of the obsidian bowls exploded into fragments.

Nomed stumbled backward, raising his hands to shield his face from the overwhelming aura. He felt like an ant standing before a mountain. The gap between his main body's cultivation and a Greater Immortal was vast beyond measure.

The world pushed back harder. Reality itself seemed to scream in protest.

The figure stopped advancing. For a long moment, nothing happened. The tension in the chamber built to unbearable levels, as if the very air might tear apart from the conflicting forces.

Then, slowly, the figure's power began to decrease.

It wasn't willing suppression, like an Ascendant cultivator deliberately restraining their aura. This was forced reduction as the figure's spiritual energy was compressed and sealed by external forces beyond even their control.

The pressure in the chamber lessened incrementally. From the crushing weight of a Greater Immortal down to something more manageable. Still immensely powerful, still far beyond anything a mortal cultivator could achieve naturally, but no longer exceeding the realm's absolute limits.

The aura stabilized at Half-Step Immortal Realm—the peak of what the mortal realm could tolerate without triggering catastrophic backlash from the Heavenly Dao.

The dimensional barrier finally relented. The tear widened just enough to permit passage.

The figure stepped through.

An old man emerged from the tear in reality. He appeared ancient, perhaps in his late seventies or early eighties in mortal years, though true Immortals could look however they chose. His face was weathered but dignified, with deep lines around his eyes and mouth that suggested someone accustomed to both smiling and scowling. A long white beard reached his chest, meticulously groomed and tied with a jade clasp.

He wore robes that immediately caught Nomed's attention. Pure white fabric embroidered with silver clouds that seemed to drift across the material as he moved. The style was formal and traditional, the kind worn by sect masters during official ceremonies. On his left breast, a symbol had been stitched in silver thread: a stylized cloud with nine layers, each one representing a stage of cultivation mastery.

The robes of the White Cloud Sect.

The old man's first action was to look down at the shattered ritual array beneath his feet. His nose wrinkled in disgust. His mouth pulled into a frown that showed exactly what he thought of blood sacrifices and dimensional manipulation through death qi.

"Barbaric," he said quietly. His voice was cultured, refined, with the precise diction of someone who chose their words carefully. "Absolutely barbaric.

Using death and suffering as a key to force open dimensional barriers. This is exactly the kind of technique the Immortal Realm banned three hundred thousand years ago."

He knelt and touched one of the blood channels with a single finger. The moment he made contact, his expression shifted from disgust to grim understanding.

"But necessary," he continued, withdrawing his hand. "Without preparation at this level, even an avatar technique wouldn't have been able to cross the dimensional barrier. The mortal realm's defenses have grown stronger since I last visited." He looked at his own hands, flexing his fingers slowly. "And being reduced to Half-Step Immortal Realm is . . . unpleasant. Like trying to move while wearing lead weights."

The old man stood and finally turned his attention to Nomed. His eyes were sharp, the kind of gaze that had evaluated thousands of disciples over countless years. He studied Nomed the way a scholar might examine an interesting insect: with curiosity but no real concern.

"Who are you?" The question was direct, neither hostile nor friendly.

Nomed bowed respectfully, recognizing someone far above his current station. "This one is called Nomed, though that name is merely a convenient identity. My true designation is Avatar Seven of the Moon God King, created to operate independently in hostile environments."

The old man's eyebrows rose slightly. "An avatar. That explains the unusual spiritual signature." He walked in a slow circle around Nomed, examining him from all angles. "Sophisticated construction. The connection to your main body is well hidden. If I weren't specifically looking for it, I might have missed it entirely. Your creator possessed considerable skill for a lesser being."

"The Moon God King ruled the Northern Region of the Sealed Realm for over two thousand years," Nomed said. There was no pride in his voice, just a statement of fact. "His expertise in avatar creation was renowned throughout multiple regions."

"Was?" The old man caught the past tense immediately.

Nomed's expression hardened. "The Black Rose Sect destroyed my main body during their invasion of the Sealed Realm. A cultivator named Slifer and his disciples interrupted a crucial ritual, killed our forces, and shattered the demonic tree that housed the Moon God King's consciousness. I am the last remaining fragment of his existence."

"I see." The old man didn't sound particularly sympathetic. He returned to examining the ritual chamber, studying the formation script on the walls with interest. "And Lady Chi? I assume she's the one who prepared this summoning ritual?"

"Correct. Lady Chi of the Crimson Lotus Pavilion has been operating in this mortal realm for several months. She descended from the Immortal Realm seeking revenge against the Black Rose Sect for killing her lover, a man named Darius. I have been . . . assisting her efforts."

The old man made a small sound that might have been amusement. "Assisting. What a diplomatic way to phrase it. You've been using her resources and connections while pursuing your own agenda, haven't you?"

Nomed didn't deny it. "Our goals aligned sufficiently to make cooperation beneficial. Lady Chi wanted to destroy the Black Rose Sect and kill Slifer personally. I wanted to get revenge for my main body's death. To put it simply, we both want Slifer's death."

"And now?" The old man turned to face Nomed directly. "Why did Lady Chi arrange for you to summon me if something happened to her?"

"Because she understood her own limitations," Nomed replied. "Lady Chi is powerful, a Core Disciple of the Crimson Lotus Pavilion with extensive training in corruption techniques and mind control. But she's also impulsive, driven by emotion rather than strategy. She knew there was a chance she might be captured or killed before achieving her goals." Nomed gestured at the ritual chamber. "She prepared this contingency months ago. If she failed to check in with me at designated intervals, I was to complete the summoning and contact whoever came through. She didn't know who would answer the call, only that the ritual was designed to reach specific individuals in the Immortal Realm who might have reasons to visit the mortal realm."

The old man nodded slowly. "Clever, in a crude way. Cast a wide net and see what swims into it." He walked to the edge of the chamber and examined the formation script more closely. "The targeting parameters in this ritual are quite specific, actually. It would only connect to Greater Immortals who have existing ties to this particular mortal realm and who possess certain . . ." He paused, searching for the right word. "Aggressive tendencies toward specific targets currently present here." His gaze shifted back to Nomed. "Now, it is time I have a proper introduction. My name is Yan Shenhua. I am the current Sect Master of the White Cloud Sect, one of the three great righteous sects that govern the Western Territories of the Immortal Realm. I have held this position for forty-seven thousand years, ever since my predecessor ascended to the Immortal Emperor Realm."

Forty-seven thousand years. The number hung in the air like a weight. Nomed's avatar was perhaps a few hundred years old at most. Some Ascendant

Realm cultivators lived a few thousand years. This being had ruled a major sect for longer than some civilizations had existed.

Yan Shenhua continued speaking. "The White Cloud Sect has existed for nearly three hundred thousand years. We were founded by disciples of the Celestial Court who believed that righteousness should be enforced through strength rather than bureaucracy. We specialize in purification techniques, light-based cultivation, and the systematic elimination of demonic corruption." He gestured at his robes. "These colors represent our core philosophy: pure white for righteousness, silver clouds for adaptability. We flow like clouds, finding the path of least resistance when possible, but we are also capable of gathering into storms when necessary."

The old man's expression shifted subtly. "The Heavenly Cloud Sect was founded by cultivators who split from the White Cloud Sect approximately two hundred thousand years ago. They disagreed with our methods, believing we had become too aggressive, too willing to compromise our principles for political advantage. The split was . . . unpleasant. Wars were fought. Territories were lost. Eventually, both sects agreed to a ceasefire and established neutral zones between our territories."

"A philosophical split," Nomed observed. "Not uncommon among long-lived sects."

"No, not uncommon," Yan Shenhua agreed. "But the rift between our sects runs deeper than simple disagreement. It became personal." His voice took on a harder edge. "Particularly between myself and the former Sect Master of the Heavenly Cloud Sect."

The old man walked to the wall and traced his fingers over the formation script, not really seeing it. His mind was clearly somewhere else, sometime else.

"His name was Li Fenghao. We were born as twin brothers in a small village on the outskirts of the Western Territories. Our parents were mortal farmers who had no understanding of cultivation. When we were five years old, a traveling Immortal passed through our village and sensed our spiritual potential. Both of us had Heaven-grade talent—rare enough individually but almost unheard of in twins."

Yan Shenhua's expression softened slightly with the memory. "The Immortal offered to take us as disciples, but his sect could only accommodate one new student that year. Our parents couldn't bear to separate us, so they refused. Instead, they saved for years to purchase basic cultivation manuals and spirit stones, hoping to give us enough foundation that we could enter sects together when we were older. We trained together. Pushed each other. Competed but never with malice. We were brothers in the truest sense, not just by blood but by shared purpose. When we were eighteen, we took the entrance exams for the great sects. I was accepted into the White Cloud Sect. He was accepted into the Heavenly Cloud Sect."

"Different sects but still close," Nomed said, following the story.

"Exactly. For decades, we maintained our bond. We would meet during inter-sect tournaments and share cultivation insights, even collaborate on research into advanced techniques. The sectarian rivalry meant nothing to us. We were brothers first, disciples second."

Yan Shenhua's hand clenched into a fist against the wall. "Then we met her. Bai Lianhua, a peerless beauty from the Moonlit Lotus Pavilion. Both of us fell in love with her. Both of us courted her with everything we had." The old man's voice became bitter. "She chose Li Fenghao. I should have accepted it gracefully. I should have been happy for my brother. But I wasn't. The rejection festered. The jealousy grew. What had been friendly competition became bitter rivalry. Every interaction became charged with unspoken hostility. The gap between us widened until we could barely stand to be in the same room.

"The sects noticed, of course. They encouraged the rivalry, using it to fuel inter-sect competition. When I made breakthroughs, the White Cloud Sect would boast about my success to humiliate the Heavenly Cloud Sect. When Li Fenghao achieved his own victories, the process reversed. We became symbols of our sects' conflict, prisoners of our own pride."

Yan Shenhua turned back to face Nomed. His eyes were hard, filled with old anger that had never truly faded. "Centuries passed. We both advanced rapidly, climbing through the cultivation realms faster than anyone in our generation. We both achieved Lesser Immortal Realm within two hundred years. We both broke through to Greater Immortal Realm within a thousand years. Always competing, always pushing each other, always separated by that gulf of resentment."

"And Bai Lianhua?" Nomed asked.

"She left," Yan Shenhua said flatly. "Grew tired of the conflict she'd inadvertently caused. Last I heard, she achieved Immortal Lord Realm and departed for territories beyond the Celestial Court's jurisdiction. Both of us lost her, but the rivalry remained."

The old man's spiritual pressure flared briefly, making the air in the chamber feel thick. "Li Fenghao was attempting to break through from Greater Immortal Realm to Immortal Lord Realm. A difficult advancement, requiring years of preparation and perfect conditions. He found an ancient cultivation site with natural formations that would support his breakthrough. He meditated there for three years, gathering power, refining his understanding of the

Dao." Yan Shenhua's smile was cold. "I ambushed him on the final day of his breakthrough. I waited until he was fully committed to the advancement, his defenses lowered, his cultivation in a vulnerable transitional state. Then I struck with everything I had, techniques I'd spent centuries preparing specifically for that moment."

"You tried to kill him," Nomed said. Not a question.

"I tried to kill him," Yan Shenhua confirmed without shame. "The attack should have been fatal. I hit him with enough force to shatter a small continent, with techniques designed to unravel a Greater Immortal's spiritual core from the inside out. But Li Fenghao was always resilient, always managed to survive impossible situations through sheer stubborn will." The old man's expression darkened. "He escaped. Badly wounded, his cultivation severely damaged, but alive. He triggered some kind of emergency spatial technique and vanished before I could finish him. I searched for years but found no trace. The Heavenly Cloud Sect claimed ignorance. My own investigations led nowhere. It was as if he'd been erased from existence entirely."

"Until recently," Nomed suggested.

"Until recently," Yan Shenhua agreed. "A few days ago, I received intelligence from my sect's information network. Someone matching Li Fenghao's spiritual signature had been detected in a mortal realm. The signature was faint, concealed, but distinct enough to catch my attention. I began researching dimensional access points, searching for ways to descend without triggering the Celestial Court's attention." The old man gestured at the chamber around them. "Lady Chi's ritual provided the perfect opportunity. Her summoning was designed to reach powerful beings with aggressive intent toward targets in this realm. The ritual's parameters aligned perfectly with my situation: a Greater Immortal seeking entry to a mortal realm to eliminate a specific individual who had fled here."

"And that's why you're here now," Nomed said. "To kill Li Fenghao."

"To finish what I started two thousand years ago," Yan Shenhua corrected. "The wound I inflicted should have killed him within days, but somehow, he survived long enough to reach this realm. I imagine his cultivation is severely reduced, possibly even sealed or dormant. Otherwise, the Celestial Court would have detected his presence years ago." The old man's eyes gleamed with anticipation. "He's here. Hiding in this mortal realm like a rat in a hole. And this time, there will be no escape. No emergency techniques to whisk him away. No Heavenly Cloud Sect to provide sanctuary. Just him and me, finishing the confrontation we should have concluded millennia ago."

Nomed considered this information carefully. "Lady Chi has been captured by Celestial Court enforcers. They arrived in this realm specifically to retrieve her for violating multiple interdimensional regulations. You should know that they're still present and actively monitoring for other violations."

"Enforcers," Yan Shenhua said dismissively. "Lesser Immortals playing at being cosmic police. They have no jurisdiction over Greater Immortals, particularly not Greater Immortals using proper avatar techniques to enter lower realms."

He raised his hand, palm up. A small sphere of white light materialized above it, rotating slowly. The sphere was made of condensed spiritual energy so pure it was painful to look at directly.

"This body is an avatar," Yan Shenhua explained. "A projection created using techniques specifically approved by the Celestial Court for emergency interventions in lower realms. My true body remains in the Immortal Realm, safely within proper jurisdictional boundaries. The enforcers have no grounds to interfere with an authorized avatar deployment."

"Even if that deployment is for personal revenge rather than an emergency intervention?" Nomed asked.

Yan Shenhua smiled. "The Celestial Court's regulations have many loopholes. As long as I don't directly threaten the stability of the mortal realm or violate fundamental cosmic laws, they can't force me to withdraw. Eliminating a single Greater Immortal fugitive falls well within acceptable parameters." The sphere of light dissipated. "What about you, Avatar Seven? You mentioned that this Slifer and his disciples destroyed your main body. That suggests you have your own grievances to settle. I don't particularly care about your grudge against Slifer. My only goal is eliminating Li Fenghao. However, I'm willing to form a temporary alliance if it benefits both of us."

"What kind of alliance?" Nomed asked cautiously.

"Information sharing and mutual support," Yan Shenhua said. "You help me locate Li Fenghao. In exchange, I'll assist you with eliminating Slifer and his disciples after my primary objective is complete. A Greater Immortal avatar, even one suppressed to Half-Step Immortal Realm, possesses capabilities far beyond what any native cultivator can match. With my help, your revenge becomes achievable."

Nomed considered this. "Why would you help me at all? You said yourself that you don't care about my grievances."

"Because cooperation is more efficient than working at cross-purposes," Yan Shenhua replied. "You know this realm, its political dynamics, the locations of various sects and cultivators. I don't. You've been operating here for months, building networks and gathering intelligence. That information has value to me." The old man gestured at the ruined ritual chamber. "Furthermore, my avatar needs time to adapt to this realm's reduced spiritual energy. The forced suppression from Greater Immortal to Half-Step Immortal Realm created internal instabilities that require careful adjustment. If I attempt to engage in serious combat before my avatar stabilizes, there's a risk of catastrophic failure that could destroy this projection entirely."

As if to emphasize his point, Yan Shenhua suddenly coughed. His hand came away from his mouth flecked with blood. His expression remained calm, but the blood was undeniable evidence of his current weakness.

"Internal damage from the dimensional crossing," he explained, pulling a silk handkerchief from his robes to wipe his hand. "The mortal realm's rejection of my power level caused spiritual backlash through the avatar's connection to my true body. Nothing permanent, but it will take time to fully heal." He coughed again, and more blood stained the white fabric. "Several months, likely. Perhaps three or four at minimum. During that time, I need to remain relatively inactive and allow the avatar to acclimate to this realm's conditions. Operating at full combat capacity while improperly stabilized would be . . . unwise."

Yan Shenhua looked at Nomed with calculating eyes. "During my recovery period, you can gather more intelligence about Slifer, his disciples, and their current activities. Find out where they're operating, what resources they have access to, who their allies are. Most importantly, determine if any of them have connections to Li Fenghao."

"Connections to Li Fenghao?" Nomed repeated. "Why would Slifer's disciples know anything about an ancient Immortal?"

"Because Li Fenghao didn't descend to this realm alone," Yan Shenhua said. "When he fled from my ambush, he was wounded severely enough that he couldn't survive in the Immortal Realm without medical intervention. But seeking help from his sect would have alerted me to his location. So, he would likely do the only thing he could: seal himself into a spiritual artifact and get help descending to the mortal realm to hide." The old man's eyes narrowed. "It's a ring, most likely. Li Fenghao specialized in soul techniques and artifact refinement. Creating a soul-bearing ring capable of sustaining a Greater Immortal's consciousness would have been within his capabilities, even while severely wounded. He could have hidden his presence inside such a ring to wait for either his injuries to heal or for an opportunity to possess a new body."

"You think someone in the mortal realm has this ring," Nomed said, understanding dawning.

"I know someone does," Yan Shenhua confirmed. "The spiritual signature

I detected was faint but distinct. It came from this realm, from a location that corresponds roughly to where we are now. Li Fenghao is here, contained within an artifact likely attached to a mortal cultivator who has no idea what they're carrying." The old man smiled coldly. "Find that cultivator for me. Find whoever is wearing Li Fenghao's ring. Once my avatar has stabilized, once I've adapted to this realm's limitations, I will kill my brother once and for all. And then," he added almost as an afterthought, "I'll help you destroy Slifer and everyone he cares about."

Nomed bowed slightly, acknowledging the agreement. "I accept your terms. I'll begin gathering intelligence immediately. The Black Rose Sect has several key disciples: Hughie, Caelum, Amelia, Fenlock, and others. I'll investigate each one to determine if any of them possess unusual spiritual artifacts."

The old immortal nodded then walked toward the exit. The blood on his handkerchief had started to glow faintly, indicating that the wound was spiritual rather than physical in nature.

"I'll need a secure location to complete my recovery," Yan Shenhua said. "Somewhere isolated with natural formations that can help stabilize spiritual energy. Do you have such a place?"

"Lady Chi maintained several hideouts throughout the region," Nomed replied. "One of them is an abandoned monastery in the mountains, which is surrounded by natural qi-gathering formations. It should serve your purposes adequately."

"Excellent. Take me there."

They left the ritual chamber together, two beings united by convenience rather than trust, each pursuing their own goals while temporarily sharing resources. Behind them, the broken formation array continued to glow faintly, the residual energy slowly dissipating into the stone floor.

Yan Shenhua coughed again as they climbed the stairs toward the surface. More blood, more evidence of the damage his avatar had sustained during the forced dimensional crossing. He wiped it away mechanically, already planning his recovery schedule.

"Four months," he murmured to himself. "Four months to stabilize, four months to adapt, four months to prepare. And then I'll find you, Li Fenghao. I'll find your host, tear your ring from his finger, and finally finish what I started two thousand years ago."

His smile was terrible to see, filled with anticipation and ancient hate. "You've run far enough, brother. It's time to stop running."

CHAPTER TWENTY-FOUR

Slifer stood at the edge of the main training grounds, hands clasped behind his back as he watched two outer disciples spar. The morning sun cast long shadows across the courtyard, and the air carried the familiar scent of spiritual herbs from the nearby Medicine Hall.

A month had passed since Lady Chi had been captured and sent back to the Immortal Realm. A month of reforms, restructuring, and countless headaches.

The two disciples below moved through their forms with surprising discipline. No demonic qi, no soul-devouring techniques, just straightforward martial cultivation. One of them stumbled, and his opponent immediately paused to help him correct his stance rather than exploiting the opening.

Slifer felt something in his chest ease slightly. Progress. Actual progress.

"Sect Master!" A young woman in black robes hurried up the path, then bowed deeply. "The weekly assembly is ready for your inspection."

Slifer nodded and gestured for her to lead the way. He'd implemented weekly assemblies as part of the reforms, mostly to keep track of everyone and ensure they weren't secretly practicing forbidden techniques in their spare time. It was usually one of the elders who oversaw it, but Slifer thought it would be a good idea to see the progress they had made over the month.

As they walked through the sect, Slifer took in the changes with a critical eye. The blood-red banners that had once decorated every building were gone, replaced with simple black ones bearing a silver rose emblem. The original

Black Rose Sect aesthetic had been aggressively demonic, all skulls and threatening imagery. Slifer had ordered most of it removed within the first week.

"The aesthetic alone was probably recruiting demonic cultivators," he'd told Morvran at the time. "We need to look like a normal sect, not a villain's lair."

The courtyards they passed through were cleaner now too. No more bloodstains on the training platforms, no more bone decorations hanging from doorways. It looked like an actual cultivation sect instead of a horror movie set.

They reached the main assembly plaza where several hundred disciples had gathered in neat rows. Slifer ascended the central platform while the young woman returned to her position among the inner disciples.

"Good morning," Slifer called out.

"Good morning, Sect Master!" The response came in unison, though Slifer noticed varying levels of enthusiasm. Some disciples shouted eagerly, others mumbled the words, and a few looked like they'd rather be anywhere else.

Fair enough. He'd upended their entire way of life in four weeks.

"I'll keep this brief," Slifer continued. "Grand Elder Wyatt will be reviewing the new merit system today in the eastern hall. Those of you who've earned points through righteous deeds can exchange them for resources. Master Hong has also finished upgrading the defensive formations, so we'll be testing them this afternoon. Try not to die."

A ripple of nervous laughter went through the crowd. The formations had been destroyed by Lady Chi's Immortal Realm aura, and they were supposedly Ascendant proof now, but testing them meant subjecting volunteers to increasingly powerful attacks until something broke. Either the formation or the volunteer.

"Additionally," Slifer went on, "I want to remind everyone that the Medicine Hall is now open to all disciples regardless of rank. If you're injured during training, get yourself healed. We're not a demonic sect anymore. Stop treating wounds as badges of honor and just go see Grand Elder Lydia."

More murmuring. This had been one of the harder changes to implement. The demonic cultivation mindset treated pain and suffering as necessary parts of growth. Slifer had been systematically dismantling that attitude, but old habits died hard.

"That's all. Dismissed."

The disciples dispersed in organized groups rather than the chaotic scramble that used to happen. Another small victory. Slifer waited until most had left before descending from the platform.

"That went well," Morvran said, appearing at his elbow. The man had a talent for materializing out of nowhere. "No one challenged your authority or attempted assassination."

"The bar for success has gotten depressingly low," Slifer muttered.

Morvran's expression remained perfectly neutral. "Master, I believe you're being too modest. A year ago, disciples tried to poison each other's breakfast. Today, no one even attempted violence. That's significant improvement."

They walked together toward the administrative building, passing through gardens that had once been filled with carnivorous plants. Slifer had ordered those replaced with normal flowers. The gardening disciples had looked at him like he'd grown a second head, but they'd complied.

"How are the new recruits settling in?" Slifer asked.

Last week, the sect had opened itself up for new disciples.

"Surprisingly well, Master. The influx of neutral cultivators has been steady. Many are attracted by our new policies and the reputation you've built."

Slifer grimaced. "What reputation?"

"That you're a Half-Step Immortal who has ties to the Immortal Realm; you reformed an entire demonic sect and closed a portal to the Nether Realm." Morvran ticked off the points on his fingers. "Oh, and that you have a Nascent Soul Realm dragon."

"Val is not part of my reputation."

"Val is fifty percent of your reputation, Master."

They entered the administrative building where Grand Elder Wyatt was already waiting with a stack of reports. The man bowed respectfully. His attitude toward Slifer had changed completely after finding out about his connection with the Immortals.

"Sect Master, the quarterly resource allocation needs your approval." Wyatt spread several jade slips across the table. "I've also prepared the financial report on our new trade agreements with the Pure Soul Sect."

Slifer picked up one of the slips and pretended to study it carefully. In reality, he was using his Insight skill to scan for any hidden problems or sabotage. Trust but verify. Especially with a man who'd tried to undermine him multiple times.

The numbers looked legitimate. Income from spirit stone mining, herb cultivation, and artifact sales. Expenditures for disciple stipends, building maintenance, and formation upgrades. Everything balanced properly.

"This looks acceptable," Slifer said, pressing his spiritual seal onto the approval document. "What about the Disciplinary Hall reforms?"

Wyatt's expression soured slightly. "Elder Amelia has been . . . enthusiastic in her new role."

"Explain."

"She's caught seventeen disciples breaking the no-bullying policy in the past week alone." Wyatt shuffled through his papers. "Her methods of punishment remain controversial."

"Is she torturing them?"

"No, Master. She's making them do community service."

Slifer blinked. "Community service."

"Yes. Cleaning the latrines, helping in the kitchens, maintaining the training grounds. Several disciples have complained that it's more humiliating than physical punishment would be."

A laugh escaped before Slifer could stop it. A while ago, he'd assigned Amelia to the Disciplinary Hall specifically because she needed to learn restraint and empathy. Making bullies clean toilets was definitely better than her previous approach of removing their souls.

"Tell her to keep up the good work," Slifer said. "But remind her that mercy and rehabilitation are the goals, not humiliation for its own sake."

"As you command, Sect Master."

After finishing with Wyatt, Slifer excused himself and resumed his tour of the sect. He wanted to see how the changes were actually working in practice, not just on paper.

The training grounds were his next stop. Here, disciples of various cultivation levels practiced their techniques under the supervision of inner disciples and elders. Slifer stood at the edge and observed.

A group of Qi Refining disciples worked on basic forms, their movements synchronized. Not far from them, Foundation Establishment cultivators sparred with spiritual arts, focusing on technique rather than raw power. Further away, Core Formation disciples meditated in a circle, their spiritual energy flowing in controlled patterns.

It all looked very . . . normal. Like an actual cultivation sect from the web novels he used to read.

Near the edge of the open area, Slifer found a Core Formation instructor calling out corrections to rows of Foundation Establishment disciples moving through synchronized sword forms. Their movements weren't perfect, but they had the fundamentals down.

Slifer recognized the technique as Flowing Water Blade Style, one of the less popular methods in the sect. It emphasized fluid transitions and defensive positioning over raw power.

"No, no, no!" The instructor, a middle-aged woman with her hair pulled back in a severe bun, stopped the formation. "Zhang Wei, your stance is too narrow. You'll lose balance the moment someone applies real pressure."

Zhang Wei, a lanky teenager who looked like he'd grown fifteen centimeters in the last month and hadn't figured out what to do with his new height, tried to adjust his footing. His sword wobbled as he overcorrected.

The instructor sighed. "Everyone, take five minutes. Zhang Wei, with me."

As the other disciples relaxed and began chatting, Slifer noticed the instructor pulling Zhang Wei aside for one-on-one instruction. She demonstrated the proper stance several times, her movements economical and precise. Zhang Wei watched intently, his brow furrowed in concentration.

This was one of those xianxia tropes Slifer had read about a thousand times. The struggling young disciple who couldn't quite get the basics right. In novels, this kid would either (a) turn out to have some hidden talent that would only manifest later, (b) get a fortuitous encounter that would rocket him to success, or (c) just keep struggling and eventually wash out of cultivation entirely.

Slifer found himself hoping it was option A or B. The kid was clearly trying hard. He deserved a break.

Then Slifer noticed something that made him pause. Two disciples were arguing loudly near the weapon racks. The older one, probably Inner Sect, was berating a younger outer disciple who'd apparently used a training sword incorrectly.

Slifer watched to see how it would play out. This was the kind of low-level conflict that used to escalate into violence constantly in the old demonic sect culture.

The inner disciple raised his hand as if to strike, and Slifer tensed, ready to intervene. But then another inner disciple stepped between them.

"Brother Han, please calm yourself," the mediator said. "Junior Brother Wang made an honest mistake. There's no need for punishment."

Han's face reddened with anger, but he lowered his hand. "He broke the sword! That comes out of our hall's budget!"

"Then we'll report it properly and replace it. But hitting him won't fix the sword."

Han glared at both of them but ultimately stalked away. The mediator helped the younger disciple return the broken weapon to storage, explaining the proper technique as they went.

Slifer let out a breath he hadn't realized he was holding. No violence. No abuse of authority. Just disciples handling a minor conflict like reasonable people. Progress.

He continued walking and passed the alchemy workshops where Elder Feng presided over a group of students. The old man was in fine form, berating someone for improper temperature control while simultaneously praising another for their qi circulation technique. Through the open door, Slifer could see the Jade Skyfire Cauldron gleaming on its pedestal. Elder Feng had basically adopted it as his child.

Near the residential quarters, Slifer encountered Fenlock and Lenvari walking together. The young couple bowed respectfully when they noticed him.

"Master Slifer," Fenlock said. "We were just heading to the library."

"Still working on your dual cultivation technique?" Slifer asked awkwardly, not knowing what else to talk to the two about.

Lenvari nodded enthusiastically. "We're making excellent progress! The resonance between our spiritual roots has increased by twenty percent this week."

Slifer had no idea what that actually meant. Dual cultivation had a reputation for being sexual in nature, so he didn't want to inquire too much and make them uncomfortable.

"Good . . ." Slifer paused, then added, "And Fenlock, your music cultivation is developing well. I heard your performance last week. You're finding the balance between power and control."

Fenlock's face lit up with pride. "Thank you, Master! I've been practicing the harmonic resonance techniques you suggested."

They parted ways, and Slifer continued his rounds. He passed the beast stables where Val was supposedly resting but was probably terrorizing the handlers. The small dragon had grown slightly, and her appetite had increased proportionally.

The Medicine Hall was next. Slifer pushed open the doors to find a surprisingly busy scene. Disciples of various ranks waited on benches while healers moved between them, treating injuries and dispensing pills. Grand Elder Lydia oversaw everything.

"Sect Master," she greeted with a bow. "To what do we owe this visit?"

"Just checking in. How's the new open-door policy working?"

Lydia's expression softened. "Better than expected. We've treated twice as many disciples this month compared to last year's average. Minor injuries that would have been ignored are now being properly cared for." She gestured to a young outer disciple getting his arm bandaged. "Young Chen here broke his wrist three days ago during training. In the old sect, he would have tried to tough it out and likely developed permanent damage. But he came to us immediately."

Slifer nodded approvingly. "And the healers have enough resources?"

"More than enough, thanks to your increased budget allocation. We've even begun stockpiling for emergencies."

They discussed the Medicine Hall's operations for a few more minutes before Slifer excused himself. The tour was taking longer than expected, but he needed to see everything firsthand.

The cafeteria was serving lunch when he arrived. Disciples sat at long tables, eating simple but nutritious meals. No more fights over food, no more stronger disciples stealing from weaker ones. Just people eating and talking.

Slifer grabbed a tray and got in line like everyone else. Several disciples stared at him in shock, but he ignored them. The cook, a plump woman who'd been with the sect for decades, nearly dropped her ladle when he reached the serving station.

"S-Sect Master! You don't need to wait in line! I can prepare something special—"

"This is fine," Slifer interrupted, accepting a bowl of rice and vegetables. "I eat what the disciples eat."

He found an empty seat and began eating. The food was decent, properly seasoned and cooked. Nothing fancy, but nobody was being poisoned or served suspicious meat, which counted as a win.

A brave Foundation Establishment disciple approached his table. "Sect Master, may I ask a question?"

"Go ahead."

"Why did you change the sect? I mean . . ." The young man struggled for words. "We were a demonic sect. Everyone knew what that meant. Now we're supposed to be neutral, but what does that even mean?"

Slifer set down his chopsticks. This was a conversation he'd been having variations of for the past month, but it was important. "What's your name?"

"Zhen, Sect Master."

"Alright, Zhen. Let me ask you something. What did being a demonic cultivator actually get you?"

Zhen looked confused. "Power? The freedom to pursue any technique without moral restrictions?"

"And how many techniques did you actually learn?" Slifer asked. "How much did you actually advance compared to the resources you consumed? How many of your fellow disciples died from forbidden technique backlash or infighting?"

The young man's face went through several expressions before settling on uncomfortable realization.

"Demonic cultivation isn't inherently evil," Slifer continued. "But the culture it fostered here was self-destructive. You were all so busy fighting each other and pursuing reckless power that nobody actually advanced properly. The sect was eating itself alive."

"But now we're neutral," Zhen said slowly. "Which means . . ."

"Which means you focus on your own advancement without constantly watching your back. You help your fellow disciples instead of seeing them as rivals or resources. You build something sustainable instead of burning bright and dying young." Slifer picked up his chopsticks again. "Also, significantly fewer people will be trying to kill you, which I'm sure you'll come to appreciate."

That got a laugh from several disciples who'd been eavesdropping. Zhen bowed deeply. "Thank you for the wisdom, Sect Master."

After lunch, Slifer made his way to the formation testing grounds where Master Hong was preparing the afternoon demonstration. The eccentric formation master had erected a series of barriers and arrays around a central platform.

"Ah, Sect Master!" Hong waved enthusiastically. "Perfect timing! We're about to test the new defensive layers!"

A group of disciples stood nearby—the volunteers who'd be attacking the formation. They looked various degrees of nervous and excited.

"Is this going to explode?" Slifer asked bluntly.

"Almost certainly not!" Hong replied with disturbing cheer. "I've accounted for most variables. The only concerns are minor spatial fluctuations and potential temporal displacement, but those should be within acceptable parameters."

"Define acceptable parameters."

"Nobody gets permanently stuck in a time loop."

Slifer pinched the bridge of his nose. "Start the test."

The first volunteer, a Peak Foundation Establishment disciple, stepped onto the platform and began attacking the barrier with increasing force. Spiritual energy flashed as his techniques struck the translucent wall, but nothing penetrated. After several minutes, he stepped back, sweating but impressed.

"The barrier absorbed everything," he reported. "I felt like I was hitting a mountain."

Subsequent tests with stronger disciples produced similar results. Even when a Core Formation elder unleashed her full power, the formation held steady. Hong made notes on a jade slip after each attempt, muttering calculations under his breath.

Finally, Grand Elder Wyatt himself stepped up. As a Peak Origin cultivator, his attacks would truly test the formation's limits.

"Are you sure about this?" Wyatt asked as spiritual pressure built around him.

"Absolutely!" Hong's eyes gleamed with scientific fervor. "Hit it with everything!"

Wyatt shrugged and unleashed a devastating palm strike. The air itself seemed to crack as Origin Realm–level energy slammed into the barrier. The formation flared brilliant white, and everyone held their breath.

The barrier held. Barely. Wyatt hit it three more times with increasing force, and each time the formation adapted, redirecting the energy into the ground rather than reflecting it back.

"Magnificent!" Hong ran up to the barrier with his detection tools. "The resonance patterns are perfect! The energy dispersion is within point-three percent of my calculations!"

Slifer had to admit, he was impressed. This formation could protect the sect from almost any threat short of a genuine Ascendant cultivator going all out. And even then, it would buy time for evacuation or reinforcement.

"Good work, Master Hong," Slifer said. "How many of these can we deploy?"

"I have materials for three more of this quality," Hong replied, still examining his readings. "Smaller versions can be produced in greater quantity. I estimate full sect coverage within two months."

"Make it happen."

As the sun began setting, Slifer returned to his quarters. The day had been long but productive. His sect was actually functioning like a proper organization rather than a violent gang. Disciples were cultivating steadily, injuries were being treated, and nobody had tried to assassinate anyone.

That alone was worth celebrating.

He settled into his meditation chamber, intending to review his own cultivation progress. The Demonic Devourer Dragon Bloodline required regular feeding, and he'd been supplementing his needs by having disciples bring him small amounts of demonic qi from sealed artifacts in the treasury.

Slifer closed his eyes and turned his attention inward, examining his Core Formation Realm cultivation. The Chaos Core spun slowly in his dantian; its universal energy compatibility made qi absorption significantly easier than it should be while his body cultivation was at Peak Core Formation.

Everything was stable. Everything was progressing well. The sect reforms were working, his disciples were loyal, and the immediate threats had been neutralized.

So why did he feel uneasy?

Something was wrong. He couldn't put his finger on it, but after a year in this world, Slifer had learned to trust his instincts. When something felt off, it usually meant trouble was coming.

He was still pondering this when light flashed in his vision, and the System interface appeared.

> *Ding!*
> Mission Complete: Defeat Lady Chi
> You have gained 1,000,000 Karmic Credits.
> Additional Reward:
> Name: The Unmovable
> Description: This Title reduces spiritual attacks against you by an additional 25%.

Slifer stared at the notification as his unease solidified into active concern. One million credits. A full million for defeating an enemy who'd escaped.

The System had never been this generous. Ever. Even killing a Half-Step Immortal Realm cultivator had only given him a few thousand credits. Lady Chi was just a Lesser Immortal, so why was the reward so massive?

Unless she wasn't actually defeated. Unless she was still out there planning her next move, and the System was giving him this enormous sum because he'd need it to survive.

Or worse, the System was rewarding him so heavily because the next threat would make Lady Chi look like a minor inconvenience.

Slifer pulled up his status screen to confirm the credits had indeed been added to his balance. He now had over 1,200,000 Karmic Credits total. Enough to buy almost anything from the Shop. Enough to purchase multiple Ascendant-level techniques or artifacts.

Too much. Way too much.

"This is a setup," he muttered. "The System's setting me up for something horrible."

He was still staring at his credit balance when another notification appeared.

> Urgent mission detected.
> New Mission: Eliminate the traitor
> Your former disciple Nomed has been detected making preparations to attack the Black Rose Sect. He remains an active threat to your life and the lives of your disciples. Capture or Kill Nomed.
> Reward: 5,000,000 Karmic Credits
> Failure: Death by Soul Extraction
> Time Limit: None

Slifer's blood ran cold. Nomed. He'd assumed the traitor had died in the Sealed Realm along with the Moon God King. But apparently not. The System would have marked him as deceased in the Disciple Management Panel if he'd truly died.

Which meant Nomed had survived somehow. And now he was actively planning an attack.

Slifer opened the Disciple Management interface and scrolled to Nomed's entry. The status still showed "Active" with his loyalty at zero percent. The location tracker was grayed out, meaning Nomed was either too far away to detect or using some technique to mask his presence.

"Of course he survived," Slifer said bitterly. "He's an avatar of some ancient god. They always survive."

He thought back to what he knew about Nomed. The disciple had shown exceptional talent and luck stats. He'd performed adequately in training without standing out too much. He'd maintained a friendly relationship with Dusty and other outer disciples. Nothing overtly suspicious until the betrayal in the Sealed Realm.

But what was Nomed exactly? An avatar of the Moon God King, clearly. If the Moon God King had died, what had happened to his avatar? Had it gained independence? Transferred to a new master?

Too many unknowns. Slifer needed more information, but first he needed to secure the sect.

He stood and headed for the door. Morvran would be in the administrative building at this hour, coordinating the evening patrols.

The corridors were quiet as Slifer walked, his footsteps echoing on stone floors. Disciples he passed bowed respectfully and moved aside. The evening meal had just ended, so most would be in their quarters or at the training grounds.

He found Morvran exactly where expected: reviewing reports with two junior administrators.

"Master," Morvran greeted, immediately dismissing the others. "What's wrong?"

Slifer waited until they were alone before speaking. "We have a traitor. Nomed is alive and planning to attack the sect."

Morvran's expression didn't change, but his hand moved to the sword at his hip. "The Moon God King's avatar? I thought he died in the Sealed Realm."

"So did I. Apparently, we were wrong." Slifer moved to the map of the sect displayed on the wall. "I need you to send word to all elders immediately. Nomed is to be killed on sight. No capture, no questioning. Just kill him."

"Understood. Should we alert the disciples as well?"

"Yes, but carefully. Tell them Nomed has been revealed as an enemy agent working with the Moon God King. Anyone who sees him should report to an elder immediately and not engage unless absolutely necessary."

Morvran began writing on several jade slips, his spiritual energy infusing them with the messages. Each would be sent directly to specific elders throughout the sect.

"What about external security?" Morvran asked. "If he attacks, he'll likely bring reinforcements."

"Have Master Hong activate the defensive formations. Tell Wyatt to organize patrol schedules for all Nascent Soul and above cultivators. And get Val; tell her someone's threatening her hoard. That'll motivate her."

A slight smile crossed Morvran's face. "Indeed, Master. What about you?"

Slifer was silent for a moment. The mission's reward was five million credits. For a reward that high, whatever Nomed was planning was more dangerous than anything Lady Chi had been able to do. But more importantly, the System had labeled this as urgent with a death penalty for failure.

Which meant the threat was immediate. And Slifer wasn't strong enough to handle it at his current level.

"I'm going into closed-door cultivation," Slifer said. "It's time I advanced."

"Master, if I may . . . What exactly are you breaking through to?"

Slifer looked at his servant. Morvran had been unfailingly loyal since they'd properly established their relationship. The man had organized the entire sect, managed resources, handled endless administrative details. He deserved some honesty.

But not too much honesty.

"I'm pursuing higher realms of cultivation," Slifer said vaguely. "The specifics are complex and not relevant to anyone else."

Morvran's eyes widened slightly. "You're truly transcending the mortal realm, then. I had suspected as much. Your power has always seemed . . . beyond what our world should contain."

Well, that was one interpretation. It was completely wrong, but Slifer wasn't about to correct it.

"How long do you anticipate the seclusion lasting?"

"No idea. Days, maybe weeks. Breakthroughs are unpredictable." Slifer headed for the door. "Send someone to bring me pills and spirit stones from the treasury. Everything I might need."

As Slifer walked back to his quarters, he considered the situation. With exposure to real immortals, Slifer needed to actually get stronger. No more relying entirely on System cards and defensive techniques. He needed real cultivation advancement. Nascent Soul Realm was the next step. According to the cultivation texts he'd studied, the breakthrough required several things.

First, he needed a completely stable and refined core. His Chaos Core was already top-quality, so that box was checked. Second, he needed sufficient spiritual energy to fuel the transformation. He'd need to consume spirit stones and pills to push his cultivation to the absolute peak of Core Formation before attempting the breakthrough. Third, he needed to gain comprehension of his spiritual nature. This was the tricky part. Nascent Soul cultivation involved manifesting a miniature soul above one's head, a spiritual representation of the cultivator's true self. It required deep introspection and understanding. And fourth, he needed to survive the tribulation. Because of course there was a tribulation. Heaven apparently wanted to kill anyone who tried to advance beyond mortal realms.

Back in his private chambers, Slifer found that Morvran had already sent supplies: pills in jade bottles, spirit stones in storage boxes, formation flags to protect the room during cultivation, and even some prepared food in preservation arrays.

Efficient as always.

Slifer began setting up the space. He arranged the formation flags in specific patterns around his meditation cushion, creating barriers against external disturbances. The room's existing formations would help, but extra protection never hurt.

Next, he reviewed the pills. Foundation Perfection Pills to stabilize his base. Spirit Accumulation Pills to increase qi density. Breakthrough Pills that were supposed to smooth the transition between realms. And several emergency healing pills in case something went wrong.

The System Shop beckoned, but Slifer resisted the urge to browse. He had plenty of credits now, but he'd save them for actual emergencies. The breakthrough should be survivable with what he had.

Probably.

He sat on the cushion and began cycling his qi, feeling the Chaos Core spin in his dantian. The energy within was dense and pure, ready to undergo transformation. His body cultivation at Peak Foundation Establishment would help stabilize the process—dual cultivation had advantages.

Slifer took a deep breath and reached for the first Foundation Perfection Pill. Time to begin.

But first, he had one more thing to do.

"System," he said quietly. "Question."

A text box appeared in his vision.

> Yes?

"Why are you being so generous with credits lately? First a million for Lady Chi, then five million for Nomed. What's the catch?"

> Rewards are proportional to threat level and successful mission completion.

"That's not an answer. What are you preparing me for?"

> Unable to provide information on future events.

"Of course not." Slifer dismissed the screen. The System never gave straight answers about anything important.

He closed his eyes and began the breakthrough attempt, feeling his spiritual energy respond to his will. The Chaos Core pulsed as it drew in qi from his meridians, from the spirit stones placed around him, and from the ambient spiritual energy in the room.

This was going to take a while.

The first stage of Nascent Soul breakthrough was expanding the core to its absolute limit. Slifer focused on this as he carefully fed more and more energy into the rotating sphere at his center. The Chaos Core drank it in greedily, growing denser and more powerful with each cycle.

Hours passed. Or maybe minutes. Time became fluid during deep cultivation.

When the core reached critical mass, Slifer began the next phase: fragmenting it. This was the dangerous part. He had to carefully break apart the core's structure while maintaining control of the released energy. Too fast and it would explode, killing him instantly. Too slow and the energy would dissipate, wasting months of cultivation.

He thought of his understanding of spiritual cultivation. The Chaos Core represented universal potential, the ability to adapt and absorb any form of energy. His Nascent Soul should embody that concept: flexibility, adaptation, and strength through diversity rather than specialization.

The core began to crack. Spiritual energy leaked out in controlled streams, and Slifer guided it upward through his meridians. The energy rose through his body, flooding his spiritual channels before finally reaching his head.

This was it. The moment of transformation.

Slifer felt something shift inside him. The fragmented core's energy coalesced above his head and formed into a miniature figure. His Nascent Soul. The spiritual representation of his true self.

DEMONIC SECT ELDER AND THE GREAT WAR

Thunder rumbled outside.

Of course there was a tribulation. There was always a tribulation.

Slifer opened his eyes and looked up. Through the ceiling, through the roof, through the clouds, he could sense it. Heaven's attention was focused on him like a spotlight. The universe itself was examining whether he deserved to advance.

As he stood slowly, he could feel the Nascent Soul hovering above his head. It was strange, like having a second body made of pure energy. He could sense its presence, feel it as an extension of himself.

The formations he'd set up activated automatically and created protective barriers. The room's spiritual energy density spiked as defensive arrays came online.

The first lightning strike would come soon. Slifer needed to be ready.

He had bought dozens of Critical Block Cards in preparation. His Phase Ability was available if things got too dangerous. The Qi Armor Manifestation Card could provide additional protection.

Thunder cracked again, closer this time.

Slifer took a deep breath. This was it. The beginning of his Nascent Soul tribulation.

The real question was what grade it would be.

CHAPTER TWENTY-FIVE

Slifer pulled up what he remembered from the cultivation manuals he'd studied. Nascent Soul tribulations followed a similar ranking system to the Core Formation ones, but the power scale was completely different. More dangerous. More deadly. And the rewards for surviving higher grades were proportionally better.

The lowest was Grade 1, called the Silver Awakening. A straightforward test where three lightning bolts descended one after another. Nothing fancy. Most cultivators who broke through to Nascent Soul faced this grade. It tested whether your spiritual foundation could handle the strain of manifesting your soul outside your body. Survive it, and your Nascent Soul would be stable but unremarkable.

Grade 2 was the Emerald Ascension. Five lightning bolts struck simultaneously, forcing the cultivator to defend on multiple fronts at once. This grade appeared when someone had cultivated with above-average dedication and their breakthrough momentum was strong. The reward was a Nascent Soul with enhanced durability and slightly improved cultivation speed.

Grade 3 earned the name Sapphire Monarch. It consisted of nine lightning strikes arranged in three waves of three, each wave stronger than the last. Only cultivators with exceptional foundations and high-quality cultivation methods triggered this grade. Those who survived gained Nascent Souls capable of manifesting unique abilities tied to their cultivation path.

Grade 4 was legendary territory. The Diamond Sovereign. Thirteen consecutive lightning strikes that escalated from Nascent Soul level power all the way up to Origin Realm intensity by the final bolt. Triggering this grade required perfect cultivation, a Heaven Rank method, and usually some kind of special constitution or bloodline. The survivors developed Nascent Souls that could partially manifest in the physical world, which granted tremendous combat advantages.

And then there was Grade 5. The Celestial Apex. Nobody really knew the exact details because so few people had ever experienced it and lived to tell about it. The ancient texts just said it involved "tribulation beyond mortal comprehension" and "transformation that touches the divine." The descriptions were vague and poetic in that annoying way cultivation manuals tended to be when discussing the highest levels.

Slifer rubbed his temples. He had a Chaos Core, which was supposed to be legendary. He'd survived a Grade 4 Core Formation tribulation and gained a mysterious locked bloodline. His luck stat had been messed with by Heaven itself because he'd antagonized a Son of Heaven. And he'd been using Heaven Rank techniques and treasures regularly.

All of that pointed toward triggering at least a Grade 3, probably a Grade 4 tribulation. Maybe higher.

"System," he said quietly. "Any chance you want to tell me what grade tribulation I'm about to face?"

No response. Of course not. The System only chimed in when it had missions or wanted to sell him something. Asking for free information was apparently too much to expect.

The tribulation was close.

Slifer stood up and stretched. His joints popped, and he felt the cultivation energy shifting restlessly inside him. He couldn't delay any longer. His body was giving him clear signals that if he didn't break through soon, all that pent-up energy would start causing internal damage.

But he definitely wasn't doing this here. Not in his quarters. Not in the sect at all.

The last tribulation had completely destroyed his courtyard. The formations, the buildings, everything. It had taken hours and a fortune in spirit stones to repair. And that was just his personal space. When Malachar had gone berserk, entire sections of the sect grounds had been devastated.

Slifer walked to the window and looked out over the Black Rose Sect. Disciples were going through their evening routines: training on the grounds, heading to the dining halls, gathering in small groups to discuss cultivation techniques. It all looked peaceful. Normal.

He was not about to ruin that by bringing a Nascent Soul tribulation down on top of them.

Slifer visualized a location he'd scouted months ago during one of his flights on the Divine Azerion Ark. A massive canyon in the Desolate Waste, hundreds of thousands of kilometers from any civilization. The canyon stretched for kilometers in every direction, with sheer rock walls and a barren floor. No plants, no animals, no people. Just empty wasteland perfect for getting hit by lightning without collateral damage.

The space qi conversion felt easier now than when he'd first learned the technique. His Core Formation cultivation made manipulating spatial energy more intuitive. Slifer gathered his qi, compressed it into the specific pattern the technique required, and tore a hole in reality.

The familiar white void of the dimensional space opened before him. He'd gotten better at navigating this place too. Instead of the terrifying emptiness he'd experienced the first time, he now saw it as just another tool. A shortcut between two points in space.

He stepped through.

The transition was disorienting. One moment he stood in his quarters. The next moment he was at the bottom of a massive canyon, surrounded by red-brown rock walls that stretched nearly a hundred meters into the air on all sides.

The temperature was scorching. This region of the Desolate Waste was known for its extreme heat during the day and freezing cold at night. Right now, with the sun still visible between the canyon walls, the air shimmered with heat waves.

Slifer ignored the temperature. His Core Formation body cultivation made environmental discomfort mostly irrelevant. He walked to the center of the widest part of the canyon floor and looked up.

The clear sky had transformed. Dark clouds materialized from nothing and swirled into a massive formation directly above the canyon. Lightning arced between the clouds in brilliant white-blue flashes.

The tribulation had arrived.

Slifer kept his awareness split between his body and his Nascent Soul. The little spiritual duplicate floated with him, maintaining its position above his head. Controlling it felt instinctive, like moving a limb he'd always had but never noticed before.

The clouds churned faster. The lightning increased in frequency. And then the color started changing.

At first the clouds were just dark gray—normal storm clouds. But as Slifer watched, they began shifting. Silver light mixed with the gray and spread through the formation like ink in water.

Grade 1. Silver Awakening.

Then emerald-green energy threaded through the silver and transformed the entire cloud formation into a swirling mass of gray, silver, and green.

Grade 2. Emerald Ascension.

Sapphire blue joined the mix, overwhelming the previous colors and making the entire sky glow with blue-tinged light.

Grade 3. Sapphire Monarch.

Slifer felt his stomach sink. Of course it wouldn't be easy. Of course his tribulation would escalate.

But the transformation didn't stop. Diamond-white light erupted from the center of the formation and spread outward until the entire sky glittered like a massive gem.

Grade 4. Diamond Sovereign.

"Oh, come on," Slifer muttered. He reached for his storage ring, ready to pull out defensive cards. A Grade 4 tribulation would require everything he had.

And then the sky exploded into rainbow light.

Every color imaginable burst through the diamond-white clouds. Red, orange, yellow, green, blue, indigo, violet, and colors that didn't have names. The formation expanded, growing larger than any tribulation Slifer had seen before. It stretched from one end of the canyon to the other, nearly a hundred meters in diameter, and pulsed with power that made the air itself vibrate.

Grade 5. Celestial Apex.

Slifer stared up at the impossible display. The highest possible grade of Nascent Soul tribulation. The one the manuals said touched the divine. The one almost nobody survived.

"Well," he said, his voice surprisingly calm given the circumstances, "this seems excessive."

The rainbow clouds began to condense. All that scattered light compressed toward a single point at the center of the formation. The pressure in the air increased exponentially. Slifer's Nascent Soul trembled above his head as it instinctively tried to retreat back into his body.

He held it in place through sheer willpower. Running now wouldn't help. The tribulation would follow him anywhere. The only way out was through.

The condensed light at the center of the formation started taking shape. A face emerged from the swirling energy. Not a human face, but something close. Strong features carved from pure light and power. A massive beard flowing down into the clouds. Eyes that crackled with contained lightning.

And then the rest of the body appeared.

Slifer had seen this face during his Core Formation tribulation. A Zeus-like figure made of lightning: the representation of Heaven's Will testing his worthiness. But back then, only the face and one hand had manifested before the tribulation was cut short.

This time, the entire upper body emerged from the clouds. Shoulders broader than mountains. Arms thick as ancient tree trunks. A torso rippling with muscles made of condensed storm energy. The figure sat on some kind of throne that remained hidden in the clouds, but everything from the waist up was fully visible.

The Zeus-like lightning figure opened its eyes. They glowed with such intense light that Slifer had to look away. When he forced himself to look back, the figure was staring directly at him.

It raised one massive hand and pointed at Slifer.

Thunder cracked so loud that Slifer felt it in his bones. The canyon walls trembled. Rocks broke free and tumbled down to the floor, sending up clouds of dust.

The lightning-Zeus opened its mouth. Sound emerged, but not words. It was something deeper than language: a vibration that resonated with reality itself. Slifer's Nascent Soul responded involuntarily and burned brighter as if answering some cosmic call.

The figure lowered its pointing hand and formed a fist. Lightning gathered around that fist and compressed into a sphere of pure destructive energy. The sphere grew larger and larger, expanding until it matched the size of the figure's head.

Then the lightning-Zeus threw it.

The sphere descended like a meteor. It moved fast, too fast for a normal Nascent Soul cultivator to react. But Slifer had spent the last year training his reflexes and buying the best defensive tools the System offered.

A Critical Block Card activated.

An invisible barrier materialized above him. The lightning sphere struck it and detonated. The explosion filled the entire canyon with light and sound. The shock wave blasted outward, pulverizing the rock walls and sending debris flying in every direction.

When the light faded, Slifer still stood in the same position. His Critical Block had absorbed the impact completely. His hair whipped around from the residual wind, but he was unharmed.

The lightning-Zeus frowned. It raised both hands this time, and two more spheres formed. These ones were larger and crackled with more concentrated energy. The figure hurled them simultaneously.

Slifer activated another Critical Block. The two spheres detonated against the barrier, creating an even more massive explosion. The canyon floor cracked beneath his feet. The walls collapsed in several places, tons of rock sliding down into the center.

He remained standing, protected by the invisible shield.

The lightning-Zeus's frown deepened into something that looked almost angry. It raised both hands above its head and began gathering energy between them. Lightning arced from the clouds into a glowing ball of destruction. This one kept expanding, growing larger than the figure's entire torso.

Slifer watched the preparation with growing concern. The previous attacks had each triggered one Critical Block Card. Those cards weren't infinite. He had thirty-five of them in total, purchased specifically for this tribulation. But if each attack cost him one or two cards, and this tribulation was just getting started . . .

The mathematics were not in his favor.

The lightning-Zeus finished charging its attack. The massive sphere pulsed with enough energy to level a small mountain. The figure looked down at Slifer with eyes that contained both a test and judgment.

Then it threw the attack with both hands.

The sphere descended like the end of the world. It moved slower than the previous attacks, but only because of its tremendous size. Slifer could feel the power radiating from it even before impact.

He activated two Critical Blocks simultaneously, layering the defenses. The sphere struck the first barrier and punched through it. The second barrier held for a moment before also shattering. The remnants of the attack continued downward, still dangerous despite being weakened.

Slifer dove to the side, using his enhanced body-cultivation speed. The weakened sphere struck the canyon floor where he'd been standing and exploded. The impact created a crater ten meters wide and sent a shock wave that threw Slifer tumbling across the ground.

He rolled to his feet, spitting out dust. His robes were torn and dirt covered his face, but he was alive. His Nascent Soul still floated above his head, protected by its connection to his body.

The lightning-Zeus observed the result with what might have been satisfaction. Then it raised all four arms.

Wait. Four arms?

Slifer looked up in horror. The figure had sprouted two additional arms from its sides. All four limbs began gathering energy simultaneously, forming four separate lightning spheres.

"You have got to be kidding me," Slifer said.

The attacks launched in perfect synchronization. Four meteors of destructive lightning descended on him from different angles, making dodging impossible.

Slifer activated four Critical Blocks at once. The cards materialized as invisible barriers around him, forming a protective box. The four spheres struck from all sides simultaneously.

The explosion was cataclysmic. The entire canyon floor shattered. Massive fissures opened up, running over a hundred meters in every direction. The walls collapsed completely, sending avalanches of rock pouring inward. The shock wave propagated outward for kilometers and was strong enough that distant cultivators would feel the tremor and wonder what had happened.

When the dust cleared, Slifer stood at the center of the destruction, completely untouched. The Critical Blocks had held.

But he'd just used four more cards. That was seven total, leaving him with twenty-eight. And the tribulation showed no signs of slowing down.

The lightning-Zeus grew larger. The figure's torso expanded, the shoulders broadened, and the arms lengthened. More arms sprouted from its sides until it had six total. Each arm began forming a lightning sphere.

Slifer reached into his storage ring and pulled out a jade slip. This particular slip contained an advanced defensive technique he'd learned from Master Hong. The Celestial Shield Formation, capable of blocking attacks up to Origin Realm level.

He crushed the jade slip and released the formation. Golden light erupted around him and wove into an intricate pattern of interconnected barriers. The formation settled into place just as the six lightning spheres launched.

The attacks struck the Celestial Shield Formation from all sides. The golden barriers flared brilliantly as they absorbed the impacts. Cracks appeared in the formation after the third sphere. The fourth sphere shattered part of the structure. The fifth sphere broke through completely.

Slifer activated two more Critical Blocks to stop the remaining attacks. The sixth sphere dissipated harmlessly against the invisible barriers.

Nine cards used. Twenty-six remaining.

The lightning-Zeus grew even larger. Eight arms now. Eight spheres forming.

This was getting ridiculous. Slifer activated his Phase Ability, the power he'd gained from Val devouring that phantom being. His body shifted slightly out of sync with normal reality and became semi-intangible.

The eight spheres launched and passed harmlessly through him. Lightning and destruction tore through the space where his physical form would normally exist, but his Phase Ability kept him safe.

The effect lasted for thirty seconds. When it ended, Slifer immediately activated it again, using one of his precious charges. He only had a limited number of times he could phase per day before the ability needed to recharge.

The lightning-Zeus paused in its assault. The massive figure stared down at Slifer with an expression that might have been confusion. Testing someone's worthiness was harder when that someone kept cheating the test.

But Heaven adapted. Of course it did.

The figure's eight arms merged back into two. Instead of forming more lightning spheres, the Zeus-like face opened its mouth. Light gathered in its throat and built into something far more concentrated than the previous attacks.

Slifer felt his Phase Ability deactivate as the thirty seconds expired. He was solid again, vulnerable, and the lightning-Zeus was charging something new.

A beam of pure energy erupted from the figure's mouth. Not a sphere that could be blocked or dodged, but a continuous stream of destructive force that spanned the entire width of the canyon.

Slifer activated three Critical Blocks simultaneously. The beam struck the first barrier and burned through it in seconds. The second barrier held for maybe five seconds. The third barrier was already cracking.

He ran. Not away from the beam—that would be pointless. Instead, he ran perpendicular to it as he tried to get out of its path before the final Critical Block failed.

The third barrier shattered. The beam continued its sweep across the canyon. Slifer dove behind a massive boulder that had fallen from the wall earlier. The beam struck the boulder and disintegrated it, then continued on to carve through the canyon wall behind it.

He rolled away as rock and energy rained down around him. The beam finally stopped, leaving a perfectly straight line of destruction carved through the landscape.

Twelve Critical Blocks used. Twenty-three remaining.

Slifer pushed himself to his feet and looked up. The lightning-Zeus was gathering energy again, preparing for another beam attack.

This wasn't sustainable. At this rate he'd burn through all his defensive cards before the tribulation ended and would need to buy more cards. He needed a different approach.

The Demonic Devourer Dragon Bloodline stirred inside him. His body cultivation had reached Peak Core Formation, and the bloodline wanted to be used. It hungered for energy, and the tribulation represented an enormous source of power.

Slifer made a decision that was either brilliant or suicidal. Possibly both.

Instead of defending against the next beam attack, he charged toward it.

The lightning-Zeus unleashed its energy. The beam swept down toward Slifer, promising annihilation to anything it touched.

Slifer activated his Purification Aura, the bloodline ability that converted demonic energy into cultivation resources. But he modified it on the fly using his understanding of the Chaos Core to make it work on any form of energy, not just demonic qi.

The beam struck him directly.

Pain. Incredible, overwhelming pain as tribulation energy poured into his body. Every cell felt like it was burning. His meridians stretched to the breaking point as they tried to contain the influx of power.

But the Purification Aura worked. The destructive lightning was being converted, filtered, transformed into something his Chaos Core could absorb. It wasn't perfect. Most of the energy still threatened to tear him apart. But a portion of it was being captured and turned into cultivation resources.

Slifer screamed—not from fear, but from the sheer intensity of the experience. His Nascent Soul above his head blazed brighter than ever, fed by the converted energy. His Core Formation cultivation began advancing, pressing toward Nascent Soul Realm from a different direction than the traditional method.

The beam cut off. Slifer collapsed to his knees, smoke rising from his body. His robes were completely destroyed. Burns covered his skin. But he was alive.

And more importantly, his cultivation had advanced. The absorbed energy had pushed him right to the threshold of Nascent Soul Realm. His external soul wasn't just a miniature spiritual duplicate anymore. It had substance. Weight. Presence.

The lightning-Zeus stared down at him with what looked like surprise. Then the massive figure began to smile.

Apparently, Heaven was pleased that someone had tried to eat its tribulation instead of just blocking it.

The rainbow clouds started to disperse. The Zeus figure's form became less solid, the details fading as the tribulation energy dissipated. The massive arms, the powerful torso, the stern face, all of it started dissolving back into scattered light.

But something was wrong.

Slifer tried to stand but found his body wouldn't respond properly. His

DEMONIC SECT ELDER AND THE GREAT WAR 247

qi flow was disrupted. His Nascent Soul flickered above his head, its form becoming unstable.

The human tribulation. He'd forgotten about that part.

Last time, it had been Sect Master Malachar. This time would be different. But who could it be?

Slifer's vision blurred. He felt something pulling at his consciousness, trying to draw him inward. His Nascent Soul trembled and then suddenly dove back into his body, retreating from whatever new threat was manifesting.

The world tilted. Slifer found himself standing in a formless white void, which was empty except for two figures.

Himself. And someone else.

No. Not someone else.

The other figure was also Slifer. But different. Younger, maybe. The face had fewer wrinkles. The beard was shorter. The eyes burned with a hunger and cruelty that Zack had never possessed.

This was the original Slifer. The demonic cultivator who had died when Zack transmigrated into his body. The man whose memories had merged with Zack's, creating the confused mess that became the current Slifer.

The original Slifer smiled. It wasn't a friendly expression. It was the smile of a predator who'd finally cornered his prey.

"Hello," the original Slifer said. His voice was Slifer's voice but wrong. Twisted. Full of malice that Zack had never put there. "Did you really think I was gone?"

Slifer tried to speak but found his voice wasn't working in this space.

The original stepped closer. "You've been living in my body. Using my cultivation. Wearing my face. But you're not me. You're just a pretender. A weak, pathetic soul from another world who got lucky."

The original raised a hand, and spiritual energy gathered around it. Demonic qi, pure and unfiltered by any righteous techniques or System modifications. The kind of power the original Slifer had spent centuries cultivating.

"This is my Nascent Soul Realm we're standing in," the original continued. "My spiritual space. My territory. Here, I'm the one in control."

Slifer finally found his voice. "You're dead. You died a year ago when I took over this body."

"Did I?" The original smiled wider. "Or did I just retreat deep enough that you couldn't sense me? Waiting. Growing stronger as you advanced my cultivation. Every breakthrough you achieved, every realm you reached was helping me recover."

The original's hand shot forward and grabbed Slifer by the throat. The grip was iron strong despite being made of spiritual energy.

"Now that you've reached Nascent Soul Realm, I'm strong enough to take back what's mine. This body. This cultivation. This life. All of it belongs to me."

Slifer struggled against the grip but couldn't break free. The original's spiritual presence pressed down on him like a mountain. In this internal space, cultivation level didn't matter. This was a battle of souls, of will, of fundamental identity.

And the original Slifer had been a demonic cultivator for hundreds of years. He'd murdered, stolen, betrayed, and sacrificed countless people to advance his power. That kind of ruthless determination was hard to overcome.

"Thank you," the original said mockingly. "Thank you for repairing my cultivation. Thank you for defeating all my enemies. Thank you for reforming the sect and making alliances. You've done wonderful work preparing everything for my return."

The grip on Slifer's throat tightened. The original's face leaned in close, until they were almost nose to nose.

"Now die, and let me have my body back."

CHAPTER TWENTY-SIX

The original Slifer's grip burned like acid against Zack's throat. Not physical pain, because they had no physical bodies here. This was worse. Spiritual agony that struck at the core of his existence.

"You're not even fighting back," the original said, his voice dripping with contempt. "What kind of cultivator are you? Oh, that's right. You're not a cultivator at all. You're just some fat loser who choked to death on pie."

Zack tried to pull the hand away, but his fingers passed through it like smoke. The original's spiritual form was more solid than his, more real in this space. That made sense. This was the original's Nascent Soul. His territory. His domain.

"I saw your memories when we merged," the original continued. "Sitting in your basement. Reading web novels. No friends. No job. No life. And you died the most pathetic death imaginable. During a pie-eating contest."

The white void around them flickered. Images appeared, pulled from Zack's memories. His old apartment. The computer screen. The empty food containers. His reflection in the bathroom mirror, overweight and exhausted.

Zack closed his eyes, but the images remained. They weren't being projected externally. The original was pulling them directly from his mind.

"You were nothing," the original said. "You are nothing. A temporary ghost inhabiting my body. And now it's time for you to fade away."

The grip tightened. Zack felt his consciousness starting to compress, to shrink under the pressure. Parts of himself were being pushed aside, squeezed out of existence by the original's overwhelming presence.

But something in the original's words triggered a response. Not anger, exactly. More like . . . clarity.

"You're right," Zack said, his voice strained but steady. "I was pathetic. I wasted my entire life on Earth. No accomplishments. No relationships. Nothing worth remembering."

The original paused, surprised by the admission.

"But that's exactly why I'm still here," Zack continued. "I got a second chance. The System chose me. Not you. Me. There had to be a reason for that."

"The System chose my body," the original corrected. "You just happened to be compatible enough to survive the transfer. Pure luck. Nothing more."

"Maybe." Zack managed to grab the original's wrist. His hand didn't pass through this time. He was starting to solidify in this space. "But I'm the one who's been living this life for the past year. I'm the one who reformed the sect. Who took disciples. Who made alliances. Who survived tribulations and fought demons and dealt with all the insane situations this world kept throwing at me."

The original's eyes narrowed. "Using my cultivation. My reputation. My resources. You built on my foundation."

"A foundation you destroyed." Zack pushed back against the grip on his throat. The pressure eased slightly. "You were dying when I arrived. Your disciples hated you. Your cultivation was shattered. Your sect was falling apart. Everything you'd built for hundreds of years was collapsing because you'd made yourself into a monster."

"I was powerful!" The original's voice rose, echoing through the void. "I achieved Half-Step Origin Realm through my own efforts. I commanded respect through strength. That's how cultivation works. The strong dominate the weak."

"And where did that get you?" Zack asked. "Killed by your own disciple. Betrayed by everyone around you because you'd spent decades treating people like disposable tools."

The original's face twisted with rage. He released Zack's throat and struck at his chest instead. The blow landed like a hammer, sending spiritual energy tearing through Zack's form. Cracks appeared in his spiritual body, lines of darkness spreading from the impact point.

"I died because I was betrayed by worthless disciples!" the original shouted. "I should have killed them all when I had the chance. That was my only mistake: showing too much mercy!"

Zack stumbled back, trying to hold his fragmenting form together. The cracks spread further, and he could feel pieces of himself starting to dissolve.

DEMONIC SECT ELDER AND THE GREAT WAR

His memories of Earth became hazier. His sense of identity blurred at the edges.

The original pressed his advantage. He struck again and again, and each blow shattered more of Zack's spiritual structure. The void around them darkened and filled with red light that pulsed in rhythm with the original's fury.

"You pretended to be me," the original said, his voice becoming a snarl. "You used my name. My face. My life. But you were never strong enough to truly be Slifer. You're just a weak soul playing dress-up."

Zack fell to his knees. More cracks appeared. His arms started to fade, becoming transparent. The original loomed over him, solid and substantial and radiating decades of accumulated spiritual power.

"I'll consume you now," the original said. "Your memories, your experiences, everything you learned in this past year will all become mine. And then I'll take my body back and continue what I started."

"What you started?" Zack looked up despite the pain. "You mean more murder? More betrayal? More turning everyone around you into enemies?"

"I mean true power." The original reached down and grabbed Zack by the head. Spiritual energy flowed from the touch, invasive and consuming. "I'll reach Ascendant Realm. Then Half-Step Immortal. Then genuine Immortal Realm. I'll climb to the peak of cultivation by walking over the corpses of everyone who stands in my way. That's the demonic path. That's what you never understood."

Zack felt his thoughts being pulled apart. The original was literally digging through his mind, extracting memories and knowledge. The past year flashed before him in reverse. His disciples. His battles. His struggles. All of it was being stripped away.

But as the original rifled through those memories, Zack saw something. The original was focused entirely on the power Zack had accumulated: the techniques learned, the treasures gained, the cultivation advanced. He wasn't looking at the other parts. The connections made. The relationships built. The moments where Zack had chosen differently than the original would have.

"You don't get it," Zack said, his voice barely a whisper. "This isn't about power."

"Everything is about power!" The original's grip tightened. "Power is all that matters in cultivation. Without it, you're nothing but prey."

"Then why did you die?" The question stopped the original's extraction process. Zack forced himself to keep talking despite the agony. "If power is everything, why did Tyrus manage to kill you? He was weaker than you. But he still won."

"He cheated! He used poison and—"

"He used strategy. Preparation. And most importantly, he had help from others you'd wronged." Zack's form stabilized slightly as he spoke. The cracks stopped spreading. "You were strong. But you were alone. And that's why you lost."

The original pulled his hand back as if burned. The red light in the void flickered uncertainly.

"I have disciples now," Zack continued. "Real disciples who actually care about me. Hughie brought me his girlfriend because he trusted me to help her. Caelum reached one hundred percent loyalty because I saved his mother. Amelia is learning empathy. Fenlock found confidence. Even Val chose to bond with me as a soul companion."

"Weakness," the original spat. "Caring about disciples is weakness. They'll betray you the moment it's convenient."

"Some of them might. Probably will, honestly." Zack managed to stand, though his legs were barely solid. "But that's the risk you take when you actually connect with people. And it's worth it. Because having allies who genuinely support you is stronger than being alone with power."

The original laughed. It was a harsh, bitter sound. "Naive. Foolish. You sound like a righteous cultivator."

"Maybe I do." Zack steadied himself, and his form became more defined. "The System did force me to practice righteous cultivation methods. At first, I hated that. Resented the credit penalties for using demonic techniques. But now I think it was teaching me something important."

"That righteousness is superior?" The original's voice dripped with sarcasm. "That demonic cultivation is inherently evil? Please. That's propaganda from the righteous sects. They fear us because we pursue true power without their artificial restraints."

"No." Zack shook his head. "It was teaching me that the labels don't matter. Righteous and demonic are just words. What matters is how you treat people. Whether you see them as resources to exploit or as individuals with their own value."

The original struck at him again, but this time Zack was ready. He raised his hand and caught the blow. Their spiritual energies clashed, red against white, and for the first time neither one dominated.

"You've been hiding in my Nascent Soul," Zack said. "Feeding off my advancement. Growing stronger as I broke through each realm. But you've been isolated. Cut off from reality. You didn't experience anything that happened this past year. You just watched from the shadows."

"I saw everything you did," the original countered. "Every weakness you showed. Every mistake you made."

"Then you saw me survive." Zack pushed back, and the original actually stepped backward. "You saw me face Ascendant Realm cultivators and live. Survive Half-Step Immortal attacks. Make alliances with the most powerful people in the realm. Build something that wasn't just about personal power."

The white void began to change. The red light from the original's rage started mixing with golden light that came from . . . somewhere. Zack wasn't sure where it originated, but it felt like his own energy responding.

"I'm not you," Zack said. "I never claimed to be. But I'm also not the pathetic person I was on Earth. This past year changed me. I learned. I grew. I became someone who could handle this world and its challenges."

The original gathered energy for another attack, but his form was less solid now. The centuries of accumulated spiritual power were still there, but something about his presence had weakened.

"You're trying to take philosophical victory because you know you can't win with strength," the original said. "It won't work. This is my Nascent Soul. My spiritual space. I control everything here."

"Do you?" Zack looked around the void. The golden light was spreading, pushing back the red. "Because I've been living in this body. I've been feeding this cultivation. I've been making the choices and fighting the battles. At what point does it stop being yours and start being mine?"

The original lunged forward, abandoning subtlety for raw aggression. His spiritual form blazed with demonic qi as he tried to overwhelm Zack through sheer force.

But Zack didn't retreat. He met the charge head-on.

Their forms collided. Their spiritual energies mixed, red and white and gold all swirling together in chaotic patterns. The void shattered around them and fractured into countless reflections. In each reflection, a different moment from the past year played out.

Zack saw himself sitting with Hughie and offering advice about his transformation. Helping Caelum with sword techniques. Teaching Amelia restraint. Supporting Fenlock's confidence. Bonding with Val. Negotiating with Ace. Reforming the Black Rose Sect. Defeating enemies. Saving disciples.

The original saw it too. And Zack felt his confusion through their merged energies.

"These aren't the memories of a demonic cultivator," the original said. "Where's the ruthlessness? The exploitation? The sacrifice of others for personal gain?"

"I did what I had to do," Zack replied. "But I tried to minimize the harm. Tried to find better solutions than just killing everyone who got in my way."

"That's not strength. That's hesitation."

"Maybe. Or maybe it's a different kind of strength."

Their spiritual forms began to merge more deeply. Zack could feel the original's memories flooding into him. Hundreds of years of demonic cultivation. Decades of betrayal and violence and single-minded pursuit of power. The original had been born into a weak clan. His talent had been mediocre. He'd clawed his way up through ruthless determination, stepping on anyone who could have been a rival.

And the original felt Zack's memories in return. A life on Earth filled with missed opportunities and wasted potential. But also moments of kindness. Small acts of decency that never led anywhere because Zack had been too afraid to commit to anything.

"We're both broken people," Zack said quietly. "You were so obsessed with strength that you destroyed everything else. I was so afraid of failure that I never tried anything. We're both incomplete."

The original's resistance weakened further. His spiritual form was dissolving into the merged energy, losing definition.

"But together," Zack continued, "we might be something better. I have your knowledge of cultivation. Your understanding of this world. Your centuries of experience. And you have my perspective. My different way of thinking. My ability to see options you never considered."

"You're trying to consume me," the original realized. "Turn me into just another memory."

"Yes," Zack admitted. "Because I can't let you take control. The things you'd do with this power would destroy everything I've built. You'd go back to the old ways. Treat disciples as disposable. Make enemies of everyone. Eventually die alone again, betrayed by someone you wronged. But you're also right that I've been using your foundation," he added. "Your body. Your cultivation base. Your sect. I couldn't have survived without all of that. So, I'm not going to pretend you don't matter. I'm going to integrate you. Keep the knowledge and experience while leaving behind the cruelty."

The original tried to pull away, to separate their merged forms, but he couldn't. The golden light had spread through their combined spiritual energy and bound them together.

"No," the original said. "No, this is my body. My life. You can't just—"

"I already did." Zack felt the truth of it. The original's spiritual presence was fading and becoming part of the larger whole rather than a separate entity.

"This past year, every choice I made, every advancement I achieved made this body more mine than yours. You've been a passenger. A memory waiting to wake up. But the Nascent Soul that's forming isn't yours anymore."

The original made one last desperate attempt to assert dominance. He pulled every scrap of power he had left, every fragment of his former self, and tried to overwhelm Zack's consciousness.

For a moment, it almost worked. Zack felt himself being pushed back, compressed, squeezed into a smaller and smaller space. The original's centuries of willpower pressed down like a mountain: all that accumulated determination, all that ruthless drive to survive and advance was focused on reclaiming control.

Zack's consciousness flickered. His sense of self became fuzzy. He couldn't remember if he was Zack or Slifer or some confused mixture of both. The boundaries blurred. The identities merged. He was drowning in centuries of demonic cultivation and dark memories.

And then he remembered something simple.

His disciples' faces.

Hughie grinning after a successful technique. Caelum's serious expression when learning sword forms. Amelia's slow transformation from sociopath to someone capable of empathy. Fenlock's joy when gaining confidence. Val chirping happily while curled up in his arms.

These weren't the original's memories. They were Zack's. His experiences. His connections. His life.

The golden light blazed brighter. Zack pushed back against the original's assault with renewed strength. Not from demonic cultivation or ruthless determination, but from something simpler: the basic truth that he'd been living this life, making these connections, and earning his place in this world.

"I'm not going away," Zack said. His voice was steady now. Certain. "This is my second chance. My opportunity to be something more than I was. And I'm not giving that up."

The original's form shattered. His spiritual presence fractured into countless pieces, each one containing a fragment of his knowledge and experience. The pieces dissolved into the golden light and became part of the merged consciousness rather than separate entities.

Zack felt the memories and knowledge flowing into him not as an invasive force, but as information being naturally integrated. Hundreds of years of cultivation experience. Techniques the original had mastered. Understanding of sect politics and demonic cultivation. Combat instincts honed through decades of survival.

All of it became his. It didn't replace what he already knew but added to it. Expanded his understanding. Made him more complete.

The original's voice echoed one last time through the dissolving void. "You better be strong enough to survive with my memories. The enemies I made won't care that you're different. They'll still come for you."

"I know," Zack replied. "And when they do, I'll handle them. My way."

The red light disappeared completely. The golden glow filled the entire space, warm and bright. The white void reformed into something new: a spiritual space that belonged entirely to Zack. His Nascent Soul Realm. His domain.

In the center of that space, a small figure floated, eight centimeters tall and glowing with golden-white light. The Nascent Soul had fully formed, and it looked exactly like Slifer. Old face, long beard, slightly hunched posture from all those years of cultivation. But the eyes were different. They held awareness and intelligence that belonged to Zack, not the original.

The spiritual space began to fade. Zack felt himself being pulled outward, back toward his physical body. The human tribulation was complete. He'd passed the test by integrating with his predecessor rather than being consumed by him.

The transition was smooth this time. The spiritual space dissolved, and Zack's consciousness snapped back into his physical form.

His eyes opened.

The canyon looked like a war zone. The floor was shattered into countless pieces, with cracks and fissures running in every direction. The walls had collapsed in most places, creating massive piles of debris. Scorch marks covered every surface from the tribulation lightning.

And the sky above was clear. Not a cloud in sight. The tribulation had ended.

Zack took a breath. His lungs filled with hot desert air. His body felt different, stronger. The Nascent Soul was connected to him now, floating invisibly above his head but still part of his existence. He could feel it there, like a second presence that was also himself.

Power coursed through his meridians. The breakthrough to Nascent Soul Realm had been completed successfully. His cultivation base had transformed, becoming denser and more refined. His spiritual senses extended outward, covering the entire canyon and stretching beyond to detect anything within several kilometers.

He stood up, and his body responded perfectly. The burns from the tribulation beam had healed. His torn robes regenerated themselves, mended by spiritual energy. Even the dirt and dust vanished, leaving him clean and presentable.

DEMONIC SECT ELDER AND THE GREAT WAR

The System interface appeared in his vision. Multiple notifications stacked on top of each other, waiting to be reviewed.

> *Ding!*
> Congratulations!
> You have broken through to Nascent Soul Realm.
> Breakthrough Difficulty: Celestial Apex (Grade 5)
> Human Tribulation Status: Resolved. Original soul integrated.
> Cultivation advancement confirmed.
> You have gained 100,000 Karmic Credits.

Zack blinked. One hundred thousand credits. Not bad.

More notifications appeared.

> Tribulation rewards calculating . . .
> Grade 5 Celestial Apex completion detected.
> Special Rewards:
> Nascent Soul Quality: Immaculate (Highest Possible)
> Spiritual Sense Range: 10x standard
> Qi Capacity: 5x standard
> Cultivation Speed: 3x standard
> Technique Comprehension: Enhanced
> Hidden reward unlocked.
> Name: Primordial Awareness
> Description: Passive ability to detect threats and opportunities within spiritual sense range. Danger level automatically assessed.
> Hidden bloodline partially unlocked.
> Demonic Devourer Dragon Bloodline (Stage 2): New abilities available.
> Bloodline evolution path revealed.

More text scrolled past. Zack tried to focus on it all, but there was too much information at once.

> Soul integration bonus detected.
> Original Slifer's knowledge and experience successfully merged.
> You have gained an additional 20,000 Karmic Credits.
> Warning: Memories from merged soul may cause temporal disorientation. Allow 24 hours for full integration.

Zack sat down heavily. He'd survived. The Grade 5 tribulation that nobody was supposed to survive. The human tribulation that had threatened to erase his existence. All of it overcome.

He was now a genuine Nascent Soul cultivator. As for his body cultivation, it was lagging behind now. He'd need to work on that eventually. But for the moment, he had the pure power of an elder of a major sect. All of that without counting the cards available to him.

The System had mentioned that the Demonic Devourer Dragon Bloodline had leveled up. New abilities were available, though the System wasn't showing details without him specifically requesting them.

It was time to have a look at that.

CHAPTER TWENTY-SEVEN

Slifer pulled up the bloodline interface in his System menu. The text appeared in his vision, floating against the backdrop of the destroyed canyon.

> Demonic Devourer Dragon Bloodline (Stage 2)
> Previous Abilities:
> Demonic Qi Assimilation
> Purification Aura
> Infernal Empowerment
> New Abilities Unlocked:
> Draconic Transformation (Partial)
> Qi Dominance
> Essence Extraction

He focused on the first new ability, and more details expanded across his vision.

> Draconic Transformation (Partial): Manifest draconic features for enhanced combat capability. Current stage allows transformation of limbs, scales, and minor physical enhancement. Full transformation locked until Stage 3.
> Duration: 10 minutes
> Cooldown: 6 hours

> Effects: +300% physical strength, +200% defense, draconic claws capable of rending spiritual energy, limited flight capability through wing manifestation.

Slifer stared at the description. He could turn into a dragon. Well, partially. That was both amazing and deeply concerning. The original Slifer's memories contained information about bloodlines, but draconic ones were supposed to be incredibly rare. Most cultivators with beast bloodlines could only manifest minor features or temporary enhancements. Full transformations were the stuff of legends.

Then again, he'd just survived a Grade 5 tribulation. Maybe legends were becoming his new normal.

He moved to the second ability.

> Qi Dominance: Assert control over ambient spiritual energy within your domain. Effectiveness of foreign qi techniques is suppressed by 40%. Your own techniques receive 25% power increase when in your domain.
> Domain range: 100 meters. Can be expanded with cultivation advancement.

That was useful. Very useful. It meant anyone fighting him within a hundred meters would be at a significant disadvantage. Their attacks would be weaker, and his would be stronger. It wasn't quite the overwhelming advantage of a true domain that Origin cultivators possessed, but it was close enough to matter in combat.

The third ability expanded when he focused on it.

> Essence Extraction: Directly absorb the spiritual essence of defeated enemies to fuel cultivation advancement. Warning: Only compatible essences can be absorbed safely. Incompatible essences may cause cultivation deviation.
> Current compatible essences: demonic qi, draconic energy, chaos energy
> Absorption efficiency: 15% of target's total cultivation

Slifer felt his stomach turn slightly. This ability sounded dangerously close to demonic cultivation at its worst. The kind of technique that required killing other cultivators to advance. He'd spent the past year trying to move away from that mentality.

But the description did say "defeated enemies." Not innocents. Not random cultivators. Just people who'd already tried to kill him and lost. That was different, wasn't it? Self-defense leading to cultivation advancement?

He pushed those thoughts aside for the moment. There would be time to worry about the moral implications later. Right now, he needed to understand what his new bloodline stage meant for practical survival.

The addiction requirement had changed too. He pulled up that section.

> Demonic Devourer Dragon Bloodline
> Maintenance Requirements:
> Stage 1: 100 units demonic qi per day
> Stage 2: 250 units demonic qi per day, or 100 units draconic energy per day
> Alternative fuel sources unlocked. Bloodline can now subsist on draconic energy as well as demonic qi.
> Note: Higher quality energy sources provide better cultivation benefits.

So, he needed more than twice as much demonic qi now, or he could feed the bloodline with draconic energy instead. That second option was interesting. Val was a dragon. Her energy signature was draconic by nature. He'd have to check if their soul bond allowed for some kind of energy sharing arrangement. Otherwise, he'd be hunting down demonic cultivators on a regular basis just to keep himself functional. That thought didn't thrill him.

Slifer sat cross-legged on the shattered canyon floor and closed his eyes. Time to test the new abilities in a controlled way before something tried to kill him and he had to use them under pressure.

He focused on the Draconic Transformation first. The bloodline responded immediately to his intent, eager to manifest after being unlocked. Energy coursed through his right arm, and he felt his flesh shifting.

The sensation was deeply uncomfortable. Not painful exactly, but wrong. His bones lengthened, his muscles thickened, and his skin hardened into scales. He opened his eyes and looked down at his transformed limb.

His arm had turned into something that belonged on a dragon. Dark red scales covered it from shoulder to fingertips, each scale overlapping the next like natural armor. His hand had become a massive claw with four talons that looked sharp enough to tear through stone. The entire limb was easily twice the size of his normal arm.

Slifer flexed the clawed hand experimentally. The talons moved smoothly, and he could feel the raw power contained in the transformed limb. He reached out and raked the claws across a nearby boulder. The stone split cleanly, deep gouges marking where the talons had passed through.

He released the transformation and watched as his arm returned to normal. The scales retracted, the claws shortened, and within seconds, he had his regular elderly cultivator's hand back. The whole process took maybe five seconds in each direction.

Not bad. He could transform specific body parts quickly when needed. That meant he wouldn't have to walk around looking like a monster unless he chose to.

Next, he tested the Qi Dominance ability. This one required more concentration. He had to project his Nascent Soul's presence outward to establish a sphere of influence around himself. The golden-white glow of his Nascent Soul spread from his position and created an invisible field that extended exactly one hundred meters in all directions.

Within that field, Slifer could feel everything. Every rock, every grain of sand, every slight movement of air. It was like having an extra sense that perceived spiritual energy rather than physical matter. If someone in range had been using a cultivation technique, he would have felt that too.

He experimented with suppressing different types of energy. He pulled a small flame talisman from his storage ring and activated it outside his domain range. The talisman produced a fist-sized fireball that hovered in the air, burning normally.

Then Slifer expanded his domain to include the fireball's position. The flames immediately dimmed, shrinking to about half their original size. The talisman was still functioning, but his domain was suppressing its effectiveness. When he pulled the domain back, the flames returned to full strength.

Forty percent suppression, as advertised. Against an enemy cultivator, that would make a massive difference in combat. Their techniques would be noticeably weaker, giving him a significant edge.

The Essence Extraction ability was harder to test without an actual target. Slifer wasn't about to go murder someone just to see if it worked. He'd have to trust the System's description on that one and hope it functioned as intended when the situation arose.

He stood up and brushed dust from his robes. The canyon was thoroughly destroyed from his tribulation, but that couldn't be helped. At least it was far from any civilization. Nobody had been hurt by the devastation.

Time to head back to the sect. He'd been gone long enough, and there was probably a mountain of administrative work waiting for him. Plus, his disciples would be wondering where he'd disappeared to.

Slifer gathered his qi and prepared to use the Dimensional Slide technique. The space manipulation felt easier now that he'd reached Nascent Soul Realm. His spiritual energy was denser and more refined, which made the qi conversion process smoother.

He visualized his quarters in the Black Rose Sect and focused on the specific spatial coordinates. The technique required extreme precision. You couldn't just think "home" and expect it to work. You needed an exact mental image of your destination, complete with spatial awareness of where that location existed relative to your current position.

Slifer compressed his qi into the proper pattern and tore open a rift in space. The familiar white void appeared before him, and he stepped through without hesitation.

The transition was instantaneous.

One moment he stood in the canyon, the next moment he was in his quarters.

Slifer looked around his quarters and immediately noticed something was off. There was dust everywhere. Not a thin layer from a day or two of absence, but thick accumulation that suggested weeks of neglect. His desk was buried under it. His meditation cushion looked like it hadn't been touched in a long time.

He walked to the window and looked out at the sect grounds. The sun was high in the sky—it was probably midday, based on the shadows. Disciples were going about their normal routines below. Everything seemed peaceful and orderly.

But something felt wrong about the timing. His breakthrough felt like it had taken maybe a few hours from start to finish. The tribulation, the human tribulation, the integration with the original Slifer's soul, all of it had seemed relatively quick.

Apparently, he was wrong about that.

Slifer left his quarters and headed toward the administrative building. He needed to find Morvran and get a status report on what had been happening during his absence.

The corridors were busier than usual. Disciples hurried past on various errands, and he noticed several new faces among them. New recruits, probably. The sect had been accepting applicants regularly since the reforms.

One of the older inner disciples spotted him and froze mid-step. The young man's eyes went wide, and he immediately dropped to one knee.

"Sect Master! You've returned!"

The disciple's shout carried down the corridor, and suddenly everyone in earshot was turning to look. More disciples dropped to their knees in respect. Some looked relieved, others shocked, and a few seemed uncertain whether he was real or some kind of illusion.

"How long have I been gone?" Slifer asked the kneeling disciple, worried by their reaction that he had been missing for years.

"Three weeks, Sect Master. We feared . . . that is, Grand Elder Wyatt said you were in closed-door cultivation and shouldn't be disturbed, but after the first week, some disciples worried that something had gone wrong with your breakthrough."

Three weeks. He'd been in that tribulation for three weeks while it had only felt like hours to him. That explained the dust in his quarters and the sense of wrongness he'd felt. But at least it wasn't as bad as he'd feared.

"I'm fine," Slifer said. "The breakthrough was successful. Where is Morvran?"

"The, um, Vice Sect Master is in the administrative building, Sect Master. He's been managing sect affairs during your absence."

Vice Sect Master? When had Morvran gotten that title? Slifer made a mental note to ask about it later.

He continued walking, and disciples parted to make way for him. The reactions were interesting. Some showed pure relief, clearly genuinely happy he'd returned safely. Others looked nervous, probably worrying that his return meant changes or assignments. A few seemed calculating, no doubt wondering what his successful breakthrough meant for the sect's power structure.

The administrative building was busy when he entered. Several elders were gathered in the main hall, reviewing documents and discussing sect business. They all turned when he walked in, and the conversations died immediately.

Grand Elder Wyatt recovered first. He stood and bowed deeply. "Sect Master, welcome back. Your breakthrough was successful, I take it?"

"It was." Slifer looked around at the assembled elders. Grand Elder Lydia was there, along with Master Hong and several others he recognized. "I apologize for the extended absence. Time moves differently during high-level tribulations."

"We understand completely," Wyatt said quickly. "In fact, we're relieved you returned so soon. High-level breakthroughs can take months or even years to complete. Three weeks is remarkably fast."

That was news to Slifer. He'd thought his breakthrough was taking too long, not that it was unusually quick. Maybe the Grade 5 tribulation had compressed the timeframe somehow. Or maybe his Chaos Core processed the advancement faster than normal cultivation methods. Either way, three weeks was apparently impressive rather than concerning.

"Where is Morvran?" Slifer asked.

"In your private office, Sect Master. He's been coordinating the defense preparations." Wyatt hesitated. "There have been some developments during your absence that require your attention."

That didn't sound good. Slifer headed for his private office, leaving the elders to resume their discussions. He could hear them starting to talk the moment he left, probably speculating about his new cultivation level and what it meant for the sect.

The private office was exactly as he'd left it except cleaner and more organized. Morvran had clearly been using the space regularly. His servant was bent over the desk, writing something on a jade slip with focused concentration.

"Master!" Morvran looked up and immediately set down his writing brush. The man's normally composed expression cracked into genuine relief. "You've returned. We weren't certain when to expect you. The tribulation's aftermath could be felt even here, and when you didn't emerge after the first week, some feared the worst."

"I'm fine." Slifer settled into his chair behind the desk. "Wyatt mentioned that I've been gone three weeks. It felt much shorter from my perspective."

"Yes, Master. Three weeks and two days to be precise." Morvran remained standing, his hands clasped behind his back in his usual formal posture. "The sect has functioned smoothly in your absence. No major incidents, though there have been several developments requiring your attention."

"Wyatt mentioned defense preparations. What's going on?"

Morvran's expression grew serious. He pulled out a different jade slip and handed it across the desk. "We've received reports of increased demonic sect activity in the Eastern Region. Several smaller sects have been attacked or absorbed by larger demonic organizations. The pattern suggests coordinated movement rather than random aggression."

Slifer took the jade slip and scanned through it. The reports detailed multiple incidents over the past two weeks. Villages raided, cultivators killed or captured, resources stolen. It was the kind of activity that indicated someone was building up power for something bigger.

"Do we have any intelligence on who's behind it?" he asked.

"Nothing concrete. The attackers have been careful to avoid leaving evidence. However . . ." Morvran hesitated. "There's something else. Something more urgent. We've received reports that Tyrus has been spotted in the Western Continent."

Slifer's hand tightened on the jade slip. Tyrus. His former disciple who'd murdered the original Slifer and left him for dead. The betrayal that had set everything in motion for Zack's soul to transmigrate into this body.

"How reliable are these reports?" His voice came out calmer than he felt.

"Very reliable, Master. The information comes from a merchant caravan that does regular trade routes through the Western Continent. One of their scouts recognized Tyrus from the description we've been circulating. The scout was a former Black Rose Sect member who knew Tyrus personally before defecting to mercantile work." Morvran pulled out another jade slip with more details. "According to the report, Tyrus has reached Peak Origin Realm and is currently operating in the Crimson Wastes region. He's been seen with a group of demonic cultivators, possibly recruiting or building his own organization."

Peak Origin Realm. That meant Tyrus had advanced significantly since their last encounter: he had been at Peak Nascent Soul Realm when he killed the original Slifer, which meant the disciple must have broken through during the past year.

Slifer set down the jade slip and leaned back in his chair. Tyrus represented unfinished business. Not just for revenge, though that was part of it. The System had given him that urgent mission about eliminating the traitor Nomed, but Tyrus was also technically a traitor to the sect.

More importantly, Tyrus knew things. The original Slifer's memories contained gaps, places where information was fuzzy or missing entirely. Tyrus might know details about the original's past that could be useful. Techniques the original had learned, enemies he'd made, secrets he'd hidden.

"Has he made any moves toward our territory?" Slifer asked.

"Not that we're aware of. The Western Continent is extremely far from here, hundreds of thousands of kilometers. It's unlikely he even knows about the changes to the Black Rose Sect. The last he would have heard, you were dead and the sect was in chaos."

That was true. Tyrus had fled immediately after killing the original Slifer, probably expecting to be hunted down like a dog for killing an elder and betraying the sect. He wouldn't know that Zack had taken over the body or that the sect had been reformed and strengthened.

Which meant Tyrus would be completely unprepared for a confrontation with the current Slifer.

"I'm going to the Western Continent," Slifer said. The decision felt right the moment he made it. "If Tyrus is building power out there, he needs to be dealt with before he becomes a real threat."

Morvran nodded, unsurprised by the decision. "Will you be taking disciples with you, Master?"

"No. This is something I need to handle personally." Slifer stood up. "I'll be using the Dimensional Slide technique. I can be there in seconds."

That made Morvran pause. "Master, are you certain? Space manipulation over such vast distances is extremely dangerous. If your coordinates are even slightly off, you could emerge inside solid rock or hundreds of meters in the air."

"I have memories of the Western Continent." Slifer tapped his head, referring to the original's time spent there. "I traveled there multiple times early in my life. I know the landmarks, the spatial coordinates, the major cities. I can reach the Crimson Wastes safely."

Morvran looked like he wanted to argue further but ultimately bowed his acceptance. "As you command, Master. Should I alert the elders of your departure?"

"Tell them I'll return within a few days. If I'm not back within a week, assume something went wrong and send Caelum to investigate." Slifer walked toward the door, then paused. "Actually, where are my disciples? I should let them know I'm leaving again."

"Most are training or on assigned missions. Caelum is instructing sword students at the training grounds. Amelia is at the Disciplinary Hall, handling her duties there. Hughie and Oliviare are in the Outer Sect quarters together, though I'm not certain what they're doing. Fenlock and Lenvari are in the library researching their dual cultivation technique. And Val . . ." Morvran smiled slightly. "Val is in the beast stables demanding tribute from the handlers. She's eaten approximately fourteen spirit beast eggs this morning."

Slifer sighed. Of course, Val was extorting the sect for food. That dragon had expensive tastes.

"I'll speak with them when I return. Right now, Tyrus takes priority." He headed for the door. "Maintain normal operations while I'm gone. If there are any emergencies, use the communication talisman to reach me."

"Understood, Master. Safe travels."

Slifer left the administrative building and headed toward the sect's outer walls. The walk gave him time to think about what he was about to do. Confronting Tyrus wasn't just about revenge or justice. It was about closure. The original Slifer's memories included the moment of his death, the betrayal by someone he'd trained and trusted. That anger and hurt still existed somewhere in Slifer's merged consciousness.

But more than that, it was about establishing that the past was truly past. Tyrus represented everything wrong with the old Black Rose Sect. The backstabbing, the casual cruelty, the constant power struggles. By dealing with Tyrus, Slifer would be making a clear statement that those days were over.

He reached the outer wall and found a quiet section where no disciples were training. The sky above was clear, and the late morning sun cast sharp shadows across the stone.

Slifer closed his eyes and reached into the original Slifer's memories. The Western Continent was vast, covering nearly as much territory as the eastern landmass where the Black Rose Sect resided. The Crimson Wastes were in the southern section, a region of red sand deserts and ancient ruins.

The original Slifer had visited a city called Bloodstone Keep fifty years ago. It was the largest settlement in the Crimson Wastes, built around an ancient fortress. That would be his destination. From there, he could gather information about Tyrus's current location.

He visualized the city clearly. Red sandstone buildings clustered around a massive keep built from dark red stone that gave the city its name. The streets were wide to accommodate the desert heat, and the walls were high to defend against sandstorms and beast attacks.

The spatial coordinates crystallized in his mind. Thousands of kilometers to the west and south, across mountains and seas and countless smaller territories. The distance was enormous, but space manipulation didn't care about distance. It cared about precision and power. Slifer had both now. His Nascent Soul cultivation provided the power, and the original's memories provided the precision.

He gathered his qi and began the technique. His qi reserves drained steadily as he compressed the energy into the proper pattern.

The air in front of him began to shimmer. Reality bent, twisted, and finally tore open. The white void of dimensional space appeared, but this time it looked different. Instead of the usual empty whiteness, he could see fragments of the landscape he'd be passing through. Mountains, forests, rivers, all flickering past in rapid succession.

Slifer stepped through the portal.

The transition felt longer this time. He could sense the enormous distance being crossed, the countless kilometers being bypassed. His Nascent Soul stabilized the spatial tunnel, preventing it from collapsing prematurely.

Then he emerged on the other side.

The first thing that hit him was the heat. Bloodstone Keep was in the middle of a desert, and the afternoon sun beat down mercilessly. The second thing was the smell: sand, dust, and the dry scent of a place where water was precious.

Slifer stood facing a wide street between sandstone buildings. Cultivators and mortals alike moved about their business, most wearing light-colored robes and head coverings to protect against the sun. Nobody seemed to notice his sudden appearance; he'd emerged in an alley between two buildings rather than in the middle of the street.

He stepped out into the main thoroughfare and looked around. Bloodstone Keep looked exactly as the original Slifer's memories suggested. The massive keep dominated the skyline, its dark red stone walls rising nearly a hundred meters into the air. The city sprawled around it in roughly concentric circles, with the wealthiest areas closest to the keep and the poorer districts farther out.

The cultivation level here was interesting. Slifer's Nascent Soul level spiritual sense detected dozens of Foundation Establishment cultivators, several Core Formation, and a handful of Nascent Soul. Nobody at Origin Realm, though. That made sense: Origin cultivators were rare enough that they typically served as sect masters or clan patriarchs.

Which meant if Tyrus was here, he'd be the most powerful cultivator in the immediate area. That thought made Slifer frown. A Peak Origin cultivator building power in this region could cause serious problems. The smaller sects and clans wouldn't be able to resist if Tyrus decided to conquer or absorb them.

Slifer needed information. He walked toward what looked like a tavern, a large building with open windows and the sound of conversation drifting out. Taverns were always good places to gather intelligence. Cultivators and mortals alike gathered to drink and gossip, and useful information flowed freely when alcohol was involved.

The interior was dim compared to the bright sunlight outside. His eyes adjusted quickly, and he scanned the room. Dozens of tables were occupied by various groups. Most were cultivators based on their dress and bearing, ranging from Qi Refining to Core Formation.

Slifer approached the bar where a stocky man was cleaning glasses with a dirty cloth. The bartender looked up and sized him up with experienced eyes.

"Welcome, traveler. What can I get you?"

"Information first, then perhaps some wine." Slifer placed a spirit stone on the bar. It was only a low-grade stone, but in a place like this it represented significant wealth. "I'm looking for someone. A man named Tyrus. Black hair, probably late twenties in appearance. He would have arrived within the past few months. Origin Realm cultivation."

The bartender's expression shifted immediately. He glanced at the spirit stone, then at Slifer, clearly weighing his options.

"Origin Realm, you say? That would be the new master up at the Northern Ruins."

"Northern Ruins?"

"Old sect compound, abandoned for centuries. Some group of demonic cultivators moved in about six weeks ago. Their leader fits your description. Black hair, young looking, powerful enough that none of the local sects want trouble with him."

Six weeks. That lined up with the timeline in Morvran's report. Tyrus had been building his base of operations while Slifer was dealing with Lady Chi and then undergoing his breakthrough.

"How many cultivators does he have with him?" Slifer asked.

The bartender pocketed the spirit stone smoothly. "Maybe forty or fifty that we've seen in the city. Could be more at the ruins. They come in for supplies occasionally, always pay in gold or spirit stones. Don't cause trouble in town, at least."

That was interesting. Tyrus wasn't being overtly aggressive toward the local population. Smart. Building power quietly while avoiding unnecessary conflicts. The original Slifer's memories suggested Tyrus had always been clever, just ruthless about it.

"These Northern Ruins, how far from here?"

"Half a day's flight for a Foundation Establishment cultivator. Maybe an hour for someone at your level." The bartender leaned in. "Word of advice, stranger. Whatever business you have with that man, be careful. Some of the local sect elders tried to confront him about taking over the ruins. He killed three of them in less than a minute. Didn't even seem like he was trying hard."

Slifer nodded his thanks and left the tavern. An hour of flight sounded tedious when he could just use Dimensional Slide again. But he needed to see the ruins first, get a sense of the layout and defenses.

He walked through the city streets until he found a map seller. The man had jade slips with detailed maps of the Crimson Wastes region, including the Northern Ruins. Slifer purchased one for another spirit stone and found a quiet corner to review it.

The ruins were located in a rocky canyon system north of the city. According to the map, they'd once been home to the Scarlet Wind Sect before that organization collapsed two hundred years ago. The buildings would be in poor condition, but the defensive formations might still be partially functional.

Slifer memorized the layout and the spatial coordinates of the canyon. He could visualize the location clearly now, which meant Dimensional Slide would work.

Time to finish this.

He found another quiet alley and prepared the technique. The qi conversion was becoming easier with practice. His Nascent Soul Realm cultivation made spatial manipulation feel almost natural.

The portal opened, and he stepped through.

This time the transition was nearly instant. He emerged in a rocky canyon with high walls on either side. The afternoon sun cast long shadows across ancient stone buildings that were crumbling but still standing.

The Northern Ruins spread out before him. What must have once been an impressive sect compound was now a collection of half-collapsed structures and overgrown courtyards. But there were signs of recent occupation. New wooden structures had been built between the old stone ones. Campfires burned in cleared areas. And he could sense multiple cultivators scattered throughout the ruins.

Slifer's spiritual sense swept across the area. Fifty-seven cultivators total. Most were at Foundation Establishment or Core Formation level. Three at Nascent Soul Realm. And one overwhelmingly powerful presence at Origin Realm, located in what looked like the ruins' main hall.

That would be Tyrus.

Slifer walked forward openly. He wasn't trying to hide or sneak up on anyone. This was going to be a direct confrontation, and there was no point in pretending otherwise.

He'd barely made it ten steps before cultivators started appearing from the ruins. They materialized on rooftops, behind broken walls, from inside buildings. All of them wore dark robes that marked them as demonic cultivators, and all of them looked ready for combat.

"That's far enough," one of them called out. A woman at Mid Core Formation, based on her aura. "State your business, old man. This territory belongs to Master Tyrus."

"I'm here to speak with Tyrus," Slifer said calmly. "Tell him his former master has come to visit."

That caused a stir among the gathered cultivators. Several exchanged glances. The woman who'd spoken looked uncertain.

"Former master? You're from the Black Rose Sect?"

"I am the Black Rose Sect." Slifer let a fraction of his Nascent Soul aura leak out, just enough to make his cultivation level clear. "Now go tell Tyrus that Slifer is here. Unless you'd like to try stopping me yourselves."

The woman's face paled. She turned and ran toward the main hall without another word. The other cultivators maintained their positions but looked significantly less confident. A Nascent Soul cultivator challenging their master was serious business.

Slifer waited patiently. Around him, more demonic cultivators were gathering. The three Nascent Soul Realm ones appeared and positioned themselves strategically. They were preparing for a fight, which was smart. But they also weren't attacking immediately, which meant they recognized they'd lose badly if they tried. After all, there was a difference between the tiers of Nascent Soul cultivators.

Movement from the main hall drew his attention. A figure emerged from the entrance, walking with casual confidence.

Tyrus looked almost exactly as the original Slifer's memories showed him. Black hair pulled back in a short ponytail. Sharp features that some might call handsome. Dark robes that marked him as a demonic cultivator. He carried himself with the bearing of someone who'd fought and won countless battles.

But there was something different about him too. His eyes had changed. They held a hardness that went beyond simple ruthlessness. This was someone who'd killed enough people that it no longer meant anything to him.

Tyrus stopped about six meters away and stared at Slifer.

For a long moment, neither spoke.

CHAPTER TWENTY-EIGHT

Slifer stared at Tyrus, waiting for the shock to register. The surprise that his former master was standing here alive when he should have been dead for over a year. The disbelief. The denial. Something.

But Tyrus just looked afraid.

"You found me," Tyrus repeated, his voice shaking slightly.

That was wrong. Slifer frowned. The man should have been questioning his own sanity right now. He should have been backing away in horror, demanding to know how this was possible. The original Slifer had died. Tyrus had killed him personally, left the body bleeding out on cold stone. There should have been confusion, terror at seeing a ghost made flesh.

Instead, Tyrus looked like someone who'd been expecting this conversation eventually. Like he'd known all along that Slifer might show up one day.

"You're not surprised I'm alive," Slifer said.

Tyrus's jaw clenched. His hands flexed at his sides, and Slifer noticed the way his weight shifted backward almost imperceptibly. The man was preparing to run. Behind him, several of his followers exchanged confused glances. They could sense the tension but didn't understand it yet.

"I heard the rumors," Tyrus said carefully. "About a year ago. One of my spies mentioned that you had somehow survived." His eyes darted around the canyon, looking for escape routes. "I didn't believe it at first. Thought it was some kind of mistake or deception. But then more reports came. You defeating Elder Olakin. You taking control of the Black Heart Sect. You closing a portal to the Nether Realm."

Slifer absorbed this information. Of course, word had spread. The cultivation world was like any other society in that regard. People talked. Stories traveled along trade routes and through sect networks. His rise to power hadn't been subtle, and every major event had witnesses who would share what they'd seen.

One of Tyrus's followers, a woman at Mid Core Formation, stepped forward cautiously. "Master Tyrus, what's happening? Who is this man?"

Tyrus didn't take his eyes off Slifer. "This is Sect Master Slifer of the Black Rose Sect. My former master."

The woman's eyes widened. She looked between them, clearly trying to reconcile what she was seeing. Slifer's spiritual pressure registered as Nascent Soul Realm to anyone who could sense it. Tyrus was Peak Origin Realm. The power difference should have been insurmountable. A Nascent Soul cultivator confronting an Origin expert like this was suicide.

"That Slifer?" the woman repeated as she took a step back in shock. "It's really him?"

"Yes," Tyrus said while subtly moving his hands in small circles, gathering spiritual energy in preparation for something.

Slifer watched the energy build around Tyrus's palms. Dark red qi coalesced into swirling patterns. The other demonic cultivators had spread out now, forming a loose semicircle behind their leader. They were preparing for combat, though most of them looked uncertain. Fighting a Nascent Soul cultivator should have been straightforward for their Peak Origin master.

But something about the situation had them spooked. Maybe it was the way Tyrus was acting. The fear in his eyes despite his overwhelming cultivation advantage. Or maybe they sensed something off about Slifer that their spiritual senses couldn't quite identify. Or, more likely, it was his reputation that was making them hesitate.

"I don't want trouble," Tyrus said, and Slifer almost believed him. Almost. "I've built a life here. These people depend on me. I'm not the same person I was back then."

"Neither am I," Slifer replied.

Tyrus's expression flickered with something that might have been hope. But it died quickly, replaced by resignation. "Then you understand why I have to leave. Right now."

The energy around his hands exploded outward. A massive wave of dark qi erupted from Tyrus's body, filling the canyon with choking pressure. The demonic cultivators behind him staggered, some falling to their knees under the weight of their master's power. The attack wasn't aimed at them, but the residual force was enough to overwhelm anyone below Nascent Soul Realm.

Slifer felt the wave hit his position. It pressed against his body like a physical weight, trying to force him backward. The technique wasn't meant to injure him; it was designed to disorient and immobilize, creating an opening for escape. Smart. If Slifer had been a normal Nascent Soul cultivator, the technique would have disorientated him for a moment, perhaps long enough for Tyrus to flee.

Instead, Slifer activated a Critical Block Card.

The invisible barrier materialized between them, perfectly positioned to intercept the qi wave. The dark energy struck the barrier and simply stopped. It didn't push through. It didn't spread around the edges. It just ceased to exist where it made contact, as if reality itself had rejected its presence.

The wave collapsed. Tyrus stood frozen, his hands still outstretched in the casting position. His eyes had gone very wide.

"I won't let you leave," Slifer said calmly.

Behind Tyrus, his followers were scrambling to their feet. The woman from earlier looked terrified now.

Tyrus's voice was barely a whisper. "What are you?"

That was a complicated question. Slifer was a middle-aged man from Earth who'd died choking on pie and somehow ended up in the body of a demonic cultivator. He was a transmigrator with a System that gave him cards and missions. He was someone trying to reform an entire cultivation sect while dealing with immortal assassins and dimensional threats. He was a lot of things.

But right now, he was someone who needed answers.

Tyrus didn't wait for a response. His body blurred as he moved with the enhanced speed of Peak Origin Realm. He shot upward, launching himself into the air with enough force to crack the ground beneath his feet. His trajectory was nearly vertical as he aimed for the canyon rim over a dozen meters above.

Slifer had been expecting this. He pulled out an Ethereal Chains Card and activated it with a thought.

Spectral chains materialized from nothing and wrapped around Tyrus's ankles mid-flight. The chains were translucent white, almost ghost-like in appearance, but they held firm. Tyrus jerked to a stop, his upward momentum arrested. For a moment he hung suspended in the air, chains stretched taut between his legs and some invisible anchor point below.

Then gravity reasserted itself and he fell.

Tyrus twisted as he dropped in an attempt to land on his feet. He managed it—barely—and slammed into the canyon floor in a crouch. The chains remained wrapped around his ankles, preventing movement. He immediately began channeling qi into his legs as he tried to burn through the ethereal bindings.

"Those won't break," Slifer informed him. "They're designed to hold cultivators up to Half-Step Immortal Realm."

That was stretching the truth slightly. The card's description said it could restrain up to Peak Ascendant Realm, which was technically a half realm below Half-Step Immortal. But Tyrus didn't need to know the exact specifications. The psychological impact of thinking the chains were even stronger than they actually were would help keep him docile.

Tyrus's followers had recovered from their shock. Several of them rushed forward, weapons drawn. A tall man with a scar across his face reached Tyrus first, and he brought a sword down in a vertical slash aimed at the chains.

The blade passed straight through the ethereal bindings without making contact. The man stumbled, his momentum carrying him forward. He nearly tripped over Tyrus before catching himself.

"Stand down," Tyrus ordered. "All of you, back away. This doesn't concern you."

The scarred man hesitated. "But Master, we can—"

"You can die pointlessly if you interfere," Tyrus interrupted. "Look at him. Really look. What do your instincts tell you?"

The man studied Slifer for a long moment. His expression gradually shifted from determination to uncertainty to fear. He took a step backward. "I . . . I don't understand. He's only Nascent Soul Realm, but . . ."

"But he makes you want to run," Tyrus finished. "Trust that feeling. All of you, return to the ruins. Wait for me there."

None of them moved. They exchanged glances, clearly torn between loyalty to their master and their own survival instincts. Finally, the woman from earlier spoke up.

"Will you be alright, Master Tyrus?"

"That depends on Master Slifer's intentions," Tyrus said. He was looking directly at Slifer now, his expression carefully neutral. "But either way, your presence won't help. Go."

They went. Slowly at first, reluctant to abandon their leader. But as they walked away, their pace increased until they were nearly jogging. Within minutes, the canyon was empty except for Slifer and his captive former disciple.

Tyrus tried one more time to break the chains. Dark red qi flooded his legs; it was so much power that the stone beneath his feet began to crack and splinter. The ethereal bindings glowed brighter in response but held firm. After several seconds, Tyrus released the technique and slumped slightly in defeat.

"Alright," he said tiredly. "You win. What do you want?"

Slifer walked forward until he was standing about three meters away. Close enough to talk comfortably but far enough to react if Tyrus tried something unexpected. Though, with the chains in place, there wasn't much the man could do.

"Answers," Slifer said. "I want to know what happened after you tried to kill me."

Something flickered across Tyrus's face. Guilt, maybe. Or possibly just annoyance at being reminded. "After I killed you, I fled the sect immediately. Took everything I could carry in my ring and disappeared. I knew that once the other elders discovered what had happened, they'd come after me. Killing an elder, even one who was dying anyway, isn't something most sects tolerate."

"But you didn't go far," Slifer observed. "You stayed in the region."

"I was waiting," Tyrus admitted. "I thought if I broke through to Origin Realm, the sect master would allow me to return to the sect and appoint me as a grand elder, and eventually I would become the sect master."

"But that's not what happened."

"No." Tyrus's expression turned frustrated. "Instead, you somehow survived, and within weeks, you'd consolidated power more thoroughly than you ever had. You defeated Elder Olakin. You survived a confrontation with the Black Heart Sect. You started reforming the sect's practices."

Slifer absorbed this. From Tyrus's perspective, it must have looked completely inexplicable. A man who should have been dead not only returning but becoming more powerful and competent than before. No wonder he'd run to another continent.

"So, you approached the Black Death Sect," Slifer prompted.

Tyrus nodded slowly. "I was desperate. My plan to retake the Black Rose Sect was ruined. I needed allies, resources, a way to rebuild my power base. The Black Death Sect was weak at the time, recovering from internal conflicts. I thought I could offer them something valuable in exchange for their support."

"What did you offer them?"

"Information," Tyrus said. "About the Black Rose Sect's defenses, formations, patrol schedules. About you, specifically. What techniques you used, what your cultivation level seemed to be, who your allies were. Everything I knew."

Slifer felt a flash of anger but suppressed it. Of course Tyrus had sold out the sect. That was completely in character for someone who'd already betrayed and murdered his master. But the anger was strange because it wasn't really his to feel. The original Slifer was dead. These weren't Slifer's disciples that Tyrus had endangered. This wasn't Slifer's sect that had been betrayed.

Except it was, now. Slifer had taken on the role. Made it his own. Those disciples depended on him. That sect was his responsibility. Which meant Tyrus's betrayal did matter, even if the original target was someone else.

"And in exchange?" Slifer asked.

"Protection. Resources. A position within their organization once they'd dealt with the Black Rose Sect." Tyrus's voice was flat, emotionless. He was just reciting facts now. "They promised me the position of Sect Master of the Black Rose Sect. Access to their cultivation techniques. A chance to rebuild."

"But you didn't account for the Inter-Sect Tournament."

"No one did," Tyrus said. "The Moon God King's plan was beyond anything I'd imagined. When Sect Master Vowron approached me and explained what was really happening, that the Sealed Realm itself was the prize . . ." He trailed off, shaking his head. "It was too big. The scope was terrifying. But by then I was already involved. Pulling out would have meant execution."

Slifer thought back to the tournament: The chaos when Black Death Sect disciples had flooded through the portal. The desperate battle as Morvran and the other Black Rose members tried to hold them back. Val transforming into her massive dragon form to fight off the invaders. And then Slifer himself confronting Vowron and trapping the Half-Step Immortal in the Jade Skyfire Cauldron.

"You were there," Slifer said, realizing. "At the tournament. Watching."

"Watching from a distance," Tyrus confirmed. "I wasn't part of the assault team. Vowron didn't trust me enough for that. But he wanted me present to provide intelligence if needed. I saw everything: The invasion. Your disciples fighting. You capturing Vowron."

He paused, and when he spoke again his voice had changed. There was awe in it now, mixed with fear.

"I saw you trap a Half-Step Immortal in a cauldron like it was nothing. I saw you stand in front of four supreme elders and somehow convince them you belonged there. I saw all of it, and I knew right then that staying on the Eastern Continent was suicide."

"So, you fled," Slifer said.

"I fled," Tyrus agreed without shame. "I'd already lost everything in the Sealed Realm anyway. Nomed and I had coordinated our efforts before the tournament. We'd planned to use the chaos to eliminate certain targets, consolidate power, position ourselves for when the realm opened. But then your disciples killed the Moon God King. That entire plan collapsed overnight."

Slifer's attention sharpened. "You worked with Nomed directly."

"Yes. Though, I never met him in person until the week before the tournament." Tyrus shifted his position slightly, testing the chains. They didn't budge. "We communicated through intermediaries. Encrypted messages.

Dead drops. The usual spy craft. He was the one who initially approached the Black Death Sect about the alliance."

"Why would he approach them?"

"Because he needed bodies," Tyrus said bluntly. "The Moon God King's ritual required massive amounts of spiritual energy. Outsider energy was best, but regular cultivators would work too if enough of them died in the right place. The Black Death Sect was perfect. They were already connected to the Nether Realm, already had demonic cultivators willing to die for power. Nomed just had to point them in the right direction."

Slifer felt cold. He'd known Nomed was a traitor. That much had been obvious from the System warnings and the disciple's behavior. But hearing the extent of the manipulation laid out so casually was disturbing. How many people had died because of Nomed's schemes? Hundreds? Thousands?

"After the Moon God King died, what happened?" Slifer asked.

"Nomed disappeared," Tyrus said. "Just vanished completely. I tried to contact him through our usual channels but got nothing. For weeks I thought he'd been killed in the fighting or captured by your sect. Then about two months ago, I heard rumors."

"What kind of rumors?"

Tyrus hesitated. For the first time since being captured, he looked genuinely uncomfortable. "Rumors that Nomed had been asking questions about immortal summoning rituals. That he'd been seen purchasing rare materials associated with blood magic. That he was looking for information about Greater Immortals specifically."

The cold feeling in Slifer's chest intensified. "He's trying to summon reinforcements."

"That's what the rumors suggest," Tyrus said. "Though, I don't know if he succeeded. The last confirmed sighting was three weeks ago in the northern mountains. After that, nothing. Either he completed whatever he was doing and went into hiding, or something went wrong and he's dead."

Slifer thought about the implications. A Greater Immortal in the mortal realm would be catastrophic. The realm's natural laws would suppress them somewhat as they had with Lady Chi. But a Greater Immortal was multiple tiers above a Lesser Immortal. Even suppressed, they would be far beyond anything the mortal realm could normally handle.

And if that Greater Immortal was working with Nomed, working against Slifer specifically . . .

"You said northern mountains," Slifer said. "Where exactly?"

"The Shadow Peak Region," Tyrus replied. "There's a graveyard there that used to belong to some dead sect from a thousand years ago. It's mostly ruins now, but it has defensive formations that still work. Perfect hiding place if you're doing something you don't want discovered."

Slifer committed that to memory. Shadow Peak Region. A graveyard. It was something to work with, at least. More than he'd had five minutes ago.

"Why are you telling me this?" he asked.

Tyrus met his eyes steadily. "Because I want you to leave me alone. That's all I want now. A chance to live quietly, away from the Eastern Continent and all its complications. I've built something here. These people, my disciples, they depend on me. I'm actually helping them. Teaching them proper techniques, protecting them from stronger sects. I'm doing good work, in my own way."

"You betrayed the sect that raised you," Slifer pointed out. "Murdered your master. Allied with the enemies who tried to destroy everything you claimed to care about. And now you want me to believe you've reformed?"

"I don't need you to believe anything," Tyrus said. "I'm just stating facts. I've changed. Whether you acknowledge that or not doesn't affect the reality. And honestly, the person I betrayed and murdered is standing right in front of me, apparently alive and healthy. So maybe the universe has a sense of humor about these things."

Slifer wanted to argue. To point out that he wasn't the original Slifer, that the man Tyrus had killed was gone forever and couldn't be brought back. But doing that would raise questions he absolutely couldn't answer. Like how he was alive at all. Or why his personality had changed so dramatically. Or what exactly had happened in those first few weeks after the original's death.

Better to let Tyrus think whatever he wanted to think.

A notification appeared in Slifer's vision, the familiar System interface materializing with its characteristic timing.

Urgent mission detected.

New Mission: Traitor's Fate

Your disciple Tyrus has been located and subdued. Choose his fate.

Option 1: Execute the traitor.

Reward: 50,000 Karmic Credits

Consequence: None

Option 2: Capture and convert the traitor to righteous cultivation.

Reward: 50,000 Karmic Credits, Tyrus restored to Disciple Management Panel

Consequence: Must spend minimum 30 days personally overseeing conversion.

Option 3: Release the traitor.

Reward: None

> Consequence: -50,000 Karmic Credits, increased difficulty for all future missions
> Time Limit: 1 hour

Slifer read through the options carefully. Execute, capture, or release. Fifty thousand credits for conversion and for execution. And releasing Tyrus would actually cost him credits, which was unusual. The System rarely penalized inaction.

The execution option was tempting. Clean. Simple. No ongoing complications. Fifty thousand credits were nothing to sneeze at. And from a practical standpoint, killing Tyrus made perfect sense. The man was a proven traitor who'd directly contributed to multiple attacks on the Black Rose Sect. Letting him live was a security risk.

But Slifer found himself thinking about Hughie. About Caelum and Amelia and Fenlock and all the other disciples who'd changed over the past year. They'd been demonic cultivators. Some of them had done terrible things. Amelia alone had probably killed dozens of innocent people in her quest for soul power.

Yet, they'd changed. With guidance and proper techniques and actual care, they'd become better people. They weren't perfect. Amelia still enjoyed torturing enemies a bit too much, and Hughie's berserker form was a constant danger. But they were trying. Making progress.

Could Tyrus do the same?

And more importantly, did Slifer want to be the kind of person who executed someone without giving them a chance at redemption?

The original Slifer would have killed Tyrus without hesitation. Would have made it painful and public as a lesson to other potential traitors. But Slifer wasn't the original. He'd been working hard for the past year to prove that, to build something better than what had existed before.

Killing Tyrus would be regressing. It would be choosing expedience over principle. And while Slifer wasn't naive enough to think that mercy was always the right choice, he also knew that cruelty for the sake of efficiency was how the original had operated.

He'd sworn to be different.

"I'm taking you back to the sect," Slifer said.

Tyrus went very still. "To execute me."

"To convert you," Slifer corrected. "You're going to learn righteous cultivation techniques. You're going to make amends for what you've done. And you're going to prove that you've actually changed and didn't just run away to avoid consequences."

"And if I refuse?"

Slifer got ready to use another card, this one called Binding of Eternal Servitude. He'd bought it back during the war with Lady Chi and never used it. The description was straightforward: it would bind a cultivator's will to Slifer's commands, making disobedience literally impossible. It was horrific in its implications. Slavery with extra steps. The kind of technique that demonic cultivators loved and righteous ones condemned.

He really didn't want to use it.

"Then I'll make sure you can't refuse," Slifer said quietly. "I'd rather not. I'd rather you choose to come willingly to actually try to improve yourself. But I'm not letting you run away again. You're going to face what you've done, one way or another."

Tyrus stared at him for a long moment. His expression was unreadable. Finally, he let out a long breath, and his shoulders slumped in defeat.

"Fine," he said. "I'll cooperate. But I want your word that my disciples here will be left alone. They had nothing to do with my past actions. They're innocents."

"They're demonic cultivators living in abandoned ruins," Slifer pointed out.

"They're refugees who had nowhere else to go," Tyrus countered. "The Northern Ruins were being destroyed by sect conflicts. I offered them sanctuary and training. That's all."

Slifer considered. It was probably true. From what he'd seen, Tyrus's followers had been genuinely confused by the confrontation. They hadn't known about his past or his connection to the Black Rose Sect. They just saw a powerful master who'd taken them in.

"Alright," Slifer agreed. "I'll leave them alone. Though, if any of them cause problems later, that protection is void."

"Fair enough."

Slifer deactivated the Ethereal Chains Card. The spectral bindings dissolved into nothing, freeing Tyrus's legs. The former disciple stood slowly, rubbing his ankles where the chains had been. There were no physical marks, but Slifer could tell from the way he moved that the restraint had been uncomfortable.

"How are we getting back to the Eastern Continent?" Tyrus asked. "It's hundreds of thousands of kilometers. Even with flight, that's weeks of travel."

"We're using Dimensional Slide," Slifer said.

"A spatial technique?" Tyrus's eyes widened.

Slifer didn't bother explaining. Instead, he pulled out a set of suppression cuffs from his storage ring. They were simple iron bands inscribed with formation script, designed to limit a cultivator's ability to channel qi. Not as elaborate as the Ethereal Chains, but good enough for transport.

DEMONIC SECT ELDER AND THE GREAT WAR

"Put these on," he instructed.

Tyrus hesitated but complied. The cuffs clicked shut around his wrists, and immediately his spiritual pressure decreased dramatically. He was still Peak Origin Realm in terms of raw cultivation, but without access to his techniques, he'd been effectively neutered.

"Ready?" Slifer asked.

"Not really, but I doubt that matters."

Slifer began gathering his qi and visualized his destination clearly: the main courtyard of the Black Rose Sect. The familiar stone patterns, the Wall of Elders in the background, the administrative building to one side. He'd stood in that courtyard hundreds of times over the past year. The spatial coordinates were burned into his memory.

Space began to fold. Reality bent around them to create that characteristic white void that existed between locations. Slifer grabbed Tyrus's shoulder to maintain physical contact and ensure they'd arrive together.

The technique ended. The canyon disappeared and was replaced by the endless white of dimensional transit. For a few seconds they existed in that liminal space, traveling thousands of kilometers in an instant.

Then they emerged in the Black Rose Sect's main courtyard.

It was late evening here, the moon casting long shadows across the stone plaza. A few disciples were visible in the distance, going about their daily routines. None of them had noticed the spatial distortion yet.

That changed quickly.

"Sect Master!" someone shouted. "The sect master has returned!"

Within seconds, disciples began appearing from every direction. They poured out of buildings, materialized from training grounds, and descended from flying positions. Word spread through the sect with remarkable speed. Within minutes, several hundred people had gathered in the courtyard and formed a respectful circle around Slifer and his prisoner.

Slifer saw Grand Elder Wyatt pushing through the crowd. The old man's face showed relief mixed with curiosity. Behind him came Morvran. And then Slifer's personal disciples appeared, drawn by the commotion.

Caelum arrived first, his hand on Starforge's hilt. His eyes swept the courtyard, assessing threats automatically. When his gaze landed on Tyrus, he froze. His hand tightened on his sword, and for a moment Slifer thought he might draw it.

Hughie appeared next, with Oliviare close behind him. He recognized Tyrus immediately. His expression went cold, colder than Slifer had ever seen. Li Fenghao must have been saying something because Hughie's lips moved silently in response, though Slifer couldn't hear what.

Amelia floated down from above, her wings spread wide. She landed gracefully near Caelum and followed his gaze. When she saw Tyrus, her face split into a grin that showed far too many teeth.

"Well," she said cheerfully, "this is going to be interesting."

Fenlock and Lenvari came running from the direction of the library. They skidded to a stop at the edge of the crowd, breathing hard. Fenlock's eyes went wide when he recognized the prisoner.

Val arrived last, transforming mid-flight from her massive dragon form into her small cherub size. She landed on Slifer's shoulder and peered at Tyrus with curious ruby eyes.

"Who's this?" she asked in her high-pitched voice. "Is it lunch?"

"Not lunch," Slifer said firmly. "This is Tyrus. He used to be a disciple here before he betrayed the sect and tried to kill me."

That declaration caused a wave of murmuring through the gathered crowd. Many of the disciples were new, recruited during the past year of reforms. They didn't know the story. But the older members remembered. Slifer could see recognition followed by anger dawning on their faces.

"You brought him back alive?" Caelum asked quietly. His voice was light, but Slifer could hear the strain beneath it.

"I brought him back to face justice," Slifer corrected. "And to give him a chance to make amends."

"Amends?" Hughie stepped forward, his usual friendly demeanor completely absent. "Master, this man killed you. Or tried to, anyway."

"I know," Slifer said.

"Then why is he breathing?" Amelia asked. She'd drifted closer, circling Tyrus like a predator sizing up prey. "I could fix that. Very quickly. Very painfully."

"No one is killing anyone," Slifer said firmly. "Tyrus is going to become a student again. He's going to learn righteous cultivation. He's going to prove that he can change."

The crowd's murmuring intensified. Slifer heard fragments of conversation floating through the air.

". . . give the traitor another chance . . ."

". . . the sect master has gone soft . . ."

". . . what kind of message does this send . . ."

Grand Elder Wyatt had finally reached the front of the crowd. He bowed respectfully to Slifer, then studied Tyrus.

"Sect Master," Wyatt said carefully, "are you certain this is wise? Many would call it weak to show mercy to someone who attempted an assassination."

"Many would be wrong," Slifer replied. "Mercy isn't weakness. It's a choice. And I'm choosing to believe that people can change if given the opportunity."

He looked at each of his disciples in turn. Caelum, whose mother he'd saved from poison. Hughie, who'd gone from mindless berserker to someone capable of love and restraint. Amelia, who'd learned to heal instead of only destroying. Fenlock, who'd built confidence and found romance. They'd all changed. He'd watched them grow.

"All of you were demonic cultivators once," Slifer continued. "Some of you did terrible things—killed innocents, tortured enemies, consumed souls—but you're different now. Better. Because you were given a chance to learn a better way."

He turned his attention back to Tyrus. The former disciple stood silently, his head slightly bowed. The suppression cuffs glinted on his wrists.

"Tyrus will get the same chance," Slifer said. "He'll have to earn your trust. Prove he's serious about changing. But he deserves the opportunity to try."

"And if he betrays us again?" Caelum asked. His hand was still on Starforge's hilt.

"Then I'll kill him myself," Slifer said simply. "No second chances after that. But until he proves untrustworthy, we treat him like any other disciple trying to walk the righteous path."

The courtyard fell silent. No one seemed to know how to respond. Finally, Morvran stepped forward and bowed.

"Shall I arrange quarters for him, Master?" Morvran asked. His tone was neutral. If he had opinions about this decision, he wasn't sharing them.

"Yes," Slifer said. "Somewhere with strong formations. I want him monitored at all times until we're certain he won't try to escape or cause problems."

"Understood. I'll see to it personally."

Morvran gestured to several death warriors who'd been standing at the crowd's edge. They moved forward and surrounded Tyrus in a loose formation. Not threatening, but clearly ready to restrain him if necessary.

Tyrus looked at Slifer one last time. "Thank you," he said quietly, "for the chance."

"Don't thank me yet," Slifer replied. "Earning redemption is harder than earning damnation. You'll find that out soon enough."

The death warriors led Tyrus away. The crowd began dispersing slowly as disciples returned to their duties, casting backward glances at the departing prisoner. Within minutes, the courtyard was nearly empty again.

Only Slifer's personal disciples remained. They stood in a semicircle, all of them looking at him with varying expressions. Hughie looked confused.

Caelum's face was troubled. Amelia seemed disappointed that she wouldn't get to torture anyone. Fenlock and Lenvari whispered to each other quietly.

"You don't approve," Slifer observed.

"I don't understand," Hughie corrected. "Master, you taught us that actions have consequences. That cultivation is about discipline and responsibility. How can we preach that while also forgiving someone who tried to murder you?"

It was a fair question. Slifer thought about how to explain it in a way that would make sense.

"Consequences and forgiveness aren't opposites," he said finally. "Tyrus is facing consequences. He's being forced to return to the sect he betrayed, to work under the supervision of the person he tried to kill, to learn cultivation methods that go against everything he's practiced for decades. Those are serious consequences."

He paused, gathering his thoughts.

"But consequences don't have to mean death. Sometimes the harder path is letting someone live with what they've done and making them work to become better. Death is easy. It's final. It solves the immediate problem but doesn't leave room for growth."

"What if he can't change?" Caelum asked. "What if this is just who he is?"

"Then he'll fail," Slifer said. "And at that point, we'll know that we tried. That we gave him every opportunity. But I'd rather try and fail than not try at all and wonder if we could have made a difference."

Amelia made a disgusted sound. "You've gotten sentimental, Master. A year ago, you would have just executed him."

"A year ago, I was a different person," Slifer replied. "We all were. That's kind of the point."

No one had a response to that. After a moment, they began drifting away to their own duties. Caelum lingered longest, still clearly troubled by the decision. But eventually even he left, heading toward the training grounds with his hand still resting on Starforge's hilt.

Slifer stood alone in the courtyard, thinking about what came next. He had Tyrus secured. He had information about Nomed's last known location. But that information was weeks old at best. Nomed could be anywhere by now. The Shadow Peak Region was huge, and a graveyard was hardly a precise address.

He needed more specific information. A way to track Nomed directly rather than chasing rumors and outdated intelligence.

Slifer pulled up the System Shop interface. He navigated through the various categories: Cards, Treasures, Techniques. There had to be something here that could help. Some kind of tracking method or detection tool.

He found it in the Divination subcategory.

> Name: Fate's Compass
> Rank: Mythic
> Description: A one-time-use artifact that can locate any person the user has met personally. User must possess clear mental image of target and provide sample of target's qi signature. Compass will point toward target's current location regardless of distance or concealment methods.
> Accuracy: 99.97%
> Duration: 24 hours after activation
> Range: Unlimited within current realm
> Cost: 85,000 Karmic Credits

Slifer stared at the price. Eighty-five thousand credits was enormous for a one-time-use artefact. It was more than he'd spent on most Heaven Rank techniques. But it would give him Nomed's exact location. No more chasing rumors or investigating graveyards. Just a direct line to wherever the traitor was hiding.

He thought about the urgency. A Greater Immortal in the mortal realm. Working with someone who'd already proven capable of orchestrating massive conspiracies. Every day that Nomed remained free was another day for him to prepare whatever he was planning.

Slifer selected the Fate's Compass and confirmed the purchase.

The System's confirmation appeared in his vision along with the satisfying *ding* of a completed transaction. The Fate's Compass materialized in his hand, a simple bronze disc with a needle in the center. It looked unimpressive for something that cost almost one hundred thousand credits.

Slifer closed his fingers around the compass.

Next week he'd activate it. Next week he'd find Nomed.

This week, he had a former disciple to monitor and a sect to run.

But at least now he had a path forward. Finally, after months of reacting to threats and dealing with crises, he could take the initiative, hunt down the source of so many problems, and end this particular threat before it could escalate further.

Slifer headed toward his quarters, the Fate's Compass secure in his storage ring. Around him, the Black Rose Sect continued its daily operations. Disciples trained. Elders administered. Life went on.

And somewhere far away, Nomed was planning something terrible.

But not for much longer.

CHAPTER TWENTY-NINE

For the next week, Slifer visited Tyrus every day.

Tyrus currently resided in a specially prepared chamber deep within the sect grounds. Not a prison exactly, though the suppression arrays and monitoring formations served similar purposes. Tyrus couldn't access his cultivation freely. Couldn't leave without permission. Couldn't communicate with anyone outside the sect.

Those restrictions were necessary. Tyrus had betrayed and murdered the original Slifer, had sold information to enemy sects, and had participated in conspiracies that had nearly destroyed everything the Black Rose Sect represented. Trust wasn't going to come quickly or easily.

But Slifer had decided to try anyway.

The first day had been tense. Tyrus had sat in his chamber with his back against the wall, eyes tracking every movement Slifer made. Ready to fight or flee at the slightest provocation. Not that either attempt would succeed, but the man expected torture, expected punishment, expected everything the original Slifer would have inflicted on a betrayer.

Instead, Slifer had brought tea.

"We need to talk," he'd said, settling cross-legged on the floor across from Tyrus, "about what happened. About why you did it. About whether there's any path forward that doesn't end with your execution."

Tyrus had stared at him like he'd grown a second head. "You're actually serious about this conversion thing?"

"I am." Slifer poured tea into two simple clay cups. "I've converted other disciples. Caelum used to be demonic and is now righteous. Hughie transformed from a ruthless cultivator into someone who values protecting others. Even Amelia is learning empathy, which nobody thought was possible."

"Those disciples didn't kill you."

"True." Slifer pushed one cup across the floor toward Tyrus. "But you killed who I used to be back then. Not this me. I'm . . . different."

That conversation had lasted hours. Tyrus talked about his reasons for the betrayal. The original Slifer's cruelty. The impossible demands. The casual way he'd sacrificed disciples for minor advantages. Tyrus described years of watching his master become progressively more monstrous, more willing to cross any line for power.

"You were going to sacrifice me," Tyrus had said quietly. "Consume my spiritual essence. You'd been preparing me for it for months. Making me cultivate specific methods that would make my essence more potent. I realized what was happening and struck first."

Slifer had listened without interrupting. The original Slifer's memories confirmed most of it. There had indeed been plans to sacrifice Tyrus. Not out of malice particularly, just cold calculation. Tyrus's cultivation had plateaued. His usefulness was declining. Why not extract the final bit of value before discarding him?

The original Slifer's ruthlessness was genuinely disturbing when viewed from the outside.

Day two had focused on understanding Tyrus's current cultivation methods. The man had reached Peak Origin Realm through demonic techniques that involved consuming other cultivators' qi—standard demonic path advancement, though particularly brutal even by those standards.

"I'm not proud of it," Tyrus admitted. "But it was the fastest way to gain power. I needed strength to avoid being hunted down by the sect's retribution squads. Needed to defend myself against anyone seeking revenge for killing an elder."

Slifer explained the reformed sect's approach. How cultivation advancement didn't require evil acts. How righteous methods could be equally effective without the karmic consequences. How the System offered alternatives that the original cultivation world had never considered.

Tyrus had been skeptical. "Righteous cultivation is slower. Everyone knows that. Demonic methods trade morality for speed."

"Everyone is wrong." Slifer pulled out several jade slips containing righteous cultivation techniques. "These methods are efficient if practiced correctly.

They don't require sacrifice or cruelty. And more importantly, they don't paint a target on your back from every righteous sect in existence."

By day three, Tyrus had agreed to try. Just try. No commitments, no promises. He'd study the righteous cultivation methods Slifer provided and see if they were legitimate or just propaganda.

The results had been surprising. Tyrus's talent was actually quite good when not being suppressed by the original Slifer's interference. Within two days of practicing the new methods, he'd stabilized his cultivation and refined his qi quality. The demonic energy in his meridians had begun converting to something cleaner, more balanced.

"This actually works," Tyrus had said, staring at his hands like they belonged to someone else. "I thought righteous cultivation was just . . . propaganda. Stories the righteous sects told themselves to feel superior."

"It's not propaganda. It's just different." Slifer had leaned back against the wall. "Demonic cultivation focuses on taking power from external sources. Righteous cultivation focuses on internal refinement. Both can reach the same heights, but the paths are different."

Day four had brought the first real breakthrough. Tyrus's loyalty counter appeared in Slifer's System interface. It started at negative forty-five percent, which made sense given their history. But by the end of the day, it had climbed to negative thirty. Still hostile, but less so. Progress.

The conversion process required daily conversations. Slifer shared stories about his disciples' transformations. How Caelum had struggled with abandoning demonic techniques he'd practiced for years. How Hughie found purpose in protecting others rather than just pursuing personal power. How even Fenlock, the gentlest of his disciples, had overcome the sect's brutal culture.

Tyrus listened. Sometimes argued. Occasionally agreed. The man was intelligent enough to recognize genuine change when he saw it. The Black Rose Sect really had transformed from what it used to be. The evidence was everywhere.

By day five, Tyrus had asked about the possibility of rejoining the sect formally if he were to convert. Not as a disciple necessarily, but as a member. Someone who could contribute without being treated as an enemy.

"That depends on you," Slifer had replied. "On whether you genuinely change. Not just pretending for safety, but whether you actually believe that the righteous path is worthwhile. Can you do that?"

Tyrus had gone quiet for a long time. "I don't know. Maybe. The old you deserved what happened. But I've done terrible things since then. Killed people who didn't deserve it. Consumed their cultivation to fuel my advancement. That's not something I can just forget or pretend didn't happen."

"I'm not asking you to forget. I'm asking if you want to change going forward. Past actions can't be undone, but future choices are still yours to make."

The conversation had ended there. Tyrus needed time to think. Time to decide if genuine change was possible or if he was too far gone down the demonic path.

By day six, the loyalty counter had climbed to negative fifteen percent. Still negative, but trending in the right direction. Tyrus had spent most of that day cultivating the righteous methods Slifer had provided, refining his qi and stabilizing his foundation.

Day seven was yesterday. Slifer had visited the chamber to find Tyrus meditating with perfect form, his spiritual energy flowing smoothly through meridians that were visibly cleaner than before. The demonic corruption that had stained his aura was fading. Not gone, but definitely diminished.

"I'll give it a try," Tyrus had said without opening his eyes. "It's either that or rotting away here for the rest of my life, so I might as well try."

The loyalty counter jumped to positive five percent. It was barely positive, but crossing that threshold meant something significant. The System recognized his genuine intent to change.

"Then we'll try when I return from this current mission," Slifer had promised. "I have something urgent to deal with, but it shouldn't take more than a day or two."

Tyrus had opened his eyes. "What kind of mission?"

"Hunting down the last remnants of a conspiracy that's been targeting the sect." Slifer hadn't elaborated. No need to explain about Nomed or the Moon God King's avatar or any of that complicated history. "It's been hanging over us for months. Time to finish it."

"Be careful out there. If you die, I'm back to being a prisoner with no advocate. I don't think the others will treat me as kindly as you have, especially Amelia."

Slifer had smiled at that. "Practical as always. Don't worry. I don't plan on dying today."

That was yesterday. Now he sat in his quarters with reports spread across his desk, preparing for what came next. The Fate's Compass rested in his palm. Though bronze and unassuming, it had cost eighty-five thousand Karmic Credits for good reason.

He'd activated it an hour ago and focused his intent on Nomed, recalling every detail of the traitor's face and spiritual signature. The compass needle had spun for a few seconds, then locked firmly in one direction: southwest, roughly two hundred thousand kilometers away, based on the spiritual resonance.

The tracking was precise. Unnaturally so. The needle didn't waver or drift: it pointed exactly at Nomed's current location with perfect accuracy. Worth every credit spent.

Slifer stood and walked to the window. The sect grounds below looked peaceful. Disciples practiced combat forms in the training yards. Elders supervised from shaded pavilions. Everything appeared normal and orderly.

But somewhere far away, Nomed was plotting something. Working with unknown allies. Planning attacks against the sect or worse. Every day he remained free was another opportunity for catastrophe.

Time to end that threat permanently.

Slifer closed his eyes and used another card to increase his spiritual sense temporarily to visualize the location. The compass provided direction and distance, but Dimensional Slide required more than that. He needed to see the destination in his mind. Needed to know exactly where he'd emerge.

The technique reached out with his spiritual sense, following the compass needle's direction. Two hundred thousand kilometers southwest. Through mountains and forests and cultivated territories. Past dozens of smaller sects and villages. Until finally reaching an isolated mountain range.

There. An abandoned monastery built into the mountainside. Stone structures crumbling from centuries of neglect. Prayer halls empty of worshippers. Courtyards overgrown with weeds.

But beneath the surface, something else existed. Underground chambers. Spiritual energy signatures that didn't match abandoned buildings. People hiding in the depths.

Slifer locked onto one chamber in particular. Large, roughly fifteen meters across. Two spiritual signatures present. One matched Nomed's energy perfectly. The other was . . .

Powerful. Extremely powerful. Half-Step Immortal Realm at least, possibly suppressed from something higher. The signature felt wrong somehow. Not native to this realm. Like it had been forced down from a higher plane and confined to mortal limitations.

A Greater Immortal. Had to be.

Slifer's jaw tightened. The urgent mission had said to eliminate Nomed. It hadn't mentioned a Greater Immortal ally. But that explained the ridiculous five million credits as reward. The System knew what he'd be facing. And it seemed Tyrus hadn't been lying at all.

For a moment, he considered retreating, gathering more resources, and preparing better defenses. Maybe recruiting help from Ace or the other sect masters.

But no. The compass only worked for twenty-four hours. If he waited, he'd lose the precise location. Nomed would move or hide deeper. The opportunity would be wasted.

Besides, he was a Nascent Soul cultivator now. With powerful System cards and enough defensive options to survive most threats. If the Greater Immortal was suppressed to Half-Step Immortal Realm, then this should still be doable.

He gathered his qi and activated Dimensional Slide. Space twisted around him, reality peeling open like torn fabric. The white void appeared, and he stepped through without hesitation.

CHAPTER THIRTY

The abandoned monastery sat in the mountains like a forgotten relic. Stone walls had crumbled in places, leaving gaps where wind whistled through. Prayer halls that had once echoed with chanting now stood silent, filled only with dust and bird nests. The main courtyard had weeds growing between cracked flagstones. Wooden beams sagged under centuries of neglect.

But beneath the ruins, in chambers carved deep into the mountain itself, something else entirely existed.

Yan Shenhua floated in darkness.

No, not darkness. Blood.

The sphere of blood surrounded him completely, thick and viscous, moving in slow currents that brushed against his skin. It was warm. Almost uncomfortably so. The liquid pressed against his closed eyelids, filled his ears, covered every inch of his body. He could feel it seeping into his pores as it carried spiritual energy directly into his meridians.

The blood came from demonic beasts. Lady Chi had left behind a substantial supply before her capture, stored in preservation arrays that kept it fresh for months. Each beast had been at least Ascendant Realm level, their life essence potent enough to aid in recovery. The blood had been processed with herbs and spiritual essences to create a mixture that could nourish an Immortal avatar damaged by dimensional crossing.

Yan Shenhua hated every second of it.

He kept his breathing shallow, controlled. Each inhale brought traces of the blood into his mouth and nose. The taste was metallic, tinged with the acrid flavor of processed demonic qi. It reminded him of battlefield hospitals in the Immortal Realm, where wounded cultivators soaked in similar concoctions to speed their healing.

This was beneath him. A Greater Immortal, reduced to floating in beast blood like some injured mortal. The indignity rankled. But necessity overrode pride. His avatar had sustained severe internal damage during the forced descent through dimensional barriers. The mortal realm's rejection of his power level had caused spiritual backlash that would take months to heal naturally.

The blood bath accelerated the process. What should have required twelve months of recovery could be accomplished in three. Every day saved was another day closer to finding Li Fenghao. Another day closer to finishing what he'd started two thousand years ago.

Yan Shenhua opened his eyes. The blood was too thick to see through clearly. Everything appeared red and hazy, like viewing the world through stained glass. He could make out the curved walls of the chamber, the formations carved into stone that regulated temperature and prevented the blood from coagulating. Spiritual energy flowed through those formations in visible streams, golden light threading through crimson darkness.

He raised one hand. The movement felt sluggish as he fought against the blood's resistance. His fingers emerged from the surface, breaking into open air. Blood dripped from his skin in heavy drops and pattered onto the stone floor below the suspended sphere.

Sixty percent capacity. That was his current estimate. The avatar had stabilized enough for basic combat operations. He could fight at Half-Step Immortal Realm level without risking catastrophic failure. Not ideal, considering his true body commanded power that could shatter continents. But sufficient for dealing with threats in this backwater realm.

The chamber was large, perhaps fifteen meters across and ten tall. Lady Chi had converted it from an old meditation hall. The walls were bare stone, unmarked except for the formations. A single doorway led out to the corridor beyond. No windows. No decorations. Just functional space for recovery and cultivation.

Yan Shenhua sank back into the blood sphere, letting it envelop him completely again. The warmth was cloying. Oppressive. But it worked. He could feel his internal injuries continuing to mend as microscopic tears in his spiritual channels knit themselves back together. The forced suppression from Greater Immortal to Half-Step Immortal had damaged his avatar on a fundamental level. Repairing that damage required both time and resources.

Time was the more frustrating constraint. Every day spent floating in blood was another day Li Fenghao could be consolidating his position, gathering power, preparing defenses. His brother had always been patient. Strategic. If he'd survived wounded in this realm for two thousand years, he'd have made plans. Established contingencies.

But Li Fenghao was also weakened. Had to be. The ambush two millennia ago had dealt catastrophic damage. A Greater Immortal's spiritual core didn't recover easily from that level of trauma. Li Fenghao would be operating at diminished capacity, probably suppressed even further by the mortal realm's limitations.

The thought brought grim satisfaction. After forty-seven thousand years of living in his brother's shadow, watching Li Fenghao receive praise and admiration for his "righteous" cultivation methods, Yan Shenhua had finally struck a decisive blow. That the blow hadn't been fatal remained his greatest regret.

Footsteps echoed from the corridor outside.

Yan Shenhua didn't move. His spiritual sense had already identified the visitor. Only one person came to these chambers regularly.

The door opened. Nomed entered carrying a tray with tea and simple food. The avatar of the Moon God King had adapted well to his current circumstances. He wore plain gray robes, his expression neutral. Nothing about his appearance suggested danger or deception.

Nomed set the tray on a small table near the wall. "Senior Yan. I brought updates from the surface."

"Speak." Yan Shenhua's voice came muffled through the blood, but clear enough to understand.

"The Black Rose Sect continues its reforms. Slifer has implemented new training methods. His disciples are advancing faster than expected. The Disciplinary Hall's point system appears to be working. Sect members are competing for rewards rather than fighting each other."

Yan Shenhua processed this information. "How many of his disciples have reached Ascendant Realm?"

"Four confirmed. Hughie, Amelia, and Fenlock. Caelum achieved it first, before the others. They're calling him the Golden Prodigy now. His sword cultivation has progressed to levels that shouldn't be possible at his age."

Interesting. Prodigies were common enough in the Immortal Realm, but this mortal realm produced them rarely. Natural spiritual energy was thinner here. Cultivation resources were scarce. For multiple disciples from a single sect to advance so quickly suggested either exceptional talent or external assistance.

"And Slifer himself?"

Nomed poured tea into a simple clay cup. The liquid was green, some herbal blend common to this region. "Still at Half-Step Immortal Realm. He hasn't attempted to ascend to the Immortal Realm despite having the resources to do so. Some elders speculate he's consolidating his foundation. Others think he's preparing for a particularly difficult tribulation."

"Or he's reached his limit." Yan Shenhua allowed himself a thin smile. "Many cultivators stall at Half-Step Immortal. It's possible this Slifer is simply less talented than his reputation suggests."

"Possible. But unlikely, given what he's accomplished." Nomed sipped his tea. "The other sect masters respect him now. Ace of the Heavenly Light Sect visits regularly. They closed a portal to the Nether Realm together. That's not something a mediocre cultivator accomplishes."

True enough. Yan Shenhua had encountered Nether Realm portals before. They required specialized knowledge and significant power to seal properly. If this Slifer had managed it at only Half-Step Immortal Realm, he possessed either extraordinary skill or powerful artifacts.

"Have you identified which of his disciples carries the ring?" That was the critical question. Li Fenghao's soul had to be contained in an artifact. A ring was most likely, given his brother's specialization in soul techniques and artifact refinement.

"Not definitively." Nomed set down his cup. "But I've narrowed it to three candidates: Hughie, Caelum, and the new disciple Oliviare. All three show advancement speeds that exceed their apparent talent levels. All three demonstrate knowledge they shouldn't possess."

"Tell me about each one."

Nomed settled into a seated position on the floor. The chamber had no chairs, no furniture beyond the small table. He seemed comfortable enough with the arrangement.

"Hughie is the most obvious suspect. He's a dual cultivator with berserker transformation abilities. His luck is extraordinarily abnormal. He's formed a relationship with a mortal girl who somehow gained cultivation talent overnight. That suggests outside assistance."

"And his personality?"

"Simple. Straightforward. Values friendship and loyalty. Gets emotional during combat. Not the type to effectively deceive others about a hidden Immortal in his possession."

Yan Shenhua considered. Li Fenghao had always been charismatic. Good with people. If he was coaching a host, he'd probably prefer someone malleable. Someone he could mold. But Hughie's emotional nature could also work against maintaining a long-term deception.

"What about Caelum?"

"More complex. He's the eldest disciple, the one most devoted to Slifer. His mother was poisoned recently. Slifer saved her using an expensive elixir. That bought complete loyalty. Caelum achieved something called Sword Soul Realm. His weapon is a demonic sword named Starforge, formerly Bloodthorn. The sword appears to have its own consciousness."

That caught Yan Shenhua's attention. "A conscious weapon?"

"Yes. It feeds on blood and demonic energy. Caelum can merge with it temporarily to gain tremendous power at the cost of physical strain. He's also converted to righteous cultivation under Slifer's guidance, despite his weapon's demonic nature."

A conscious demonic sword. That was unusual. Such weapons would typically corrupt their wielders, not cooperate with righteous cultivation methods. Unless the sword itself was more than it appeared. Could Li Fenghao have split his consciousness? Placed part of himself in both a ring and a sword?

No. That level of division would be catastrophically unstable. Even a Greater Immortal couldn't maintain awareness in multiple artifacts simultaneously without severe degradation.

"And the third candidate?"

"Oliviare. She's new. Hughie's girlfriend. A mortal who somehow gained cultivation talent through what Slifer claimed was a 'random fate talisman.' She went from zero spiritual roots to having enough talent to enter Core Formation within months. That kind of transformation is impossible naturally."

Yan Shenhua's eyes narrowed. "Unless an Immortal directly altered her spiritual foundation."

"Exactly." Nomed picked up his tea again. "Li Fenghao would have the knowledge to perform such a modification. If he's coaching Hughie, he might have assisted the girlfriend to secure Hughie's continued cooperation and loyalty."

The logic was sound. Li Fenghao had always been sentimental about mortal attachments. He'd argued for centuries that Immortals had a duty to uplift worthy mortals, to guide them toward enlightenment. It would be entirely in character for him to help a young woman simply because she'd caught his student's heart.

Yan Shenhua felt old anger stirring. His brother's righteousness had always been nauseating. Acting like cultivation wasn't about power, pretending that helping others mattered more than personal advancement. It was weakness disguised as virtue.

"Continue surveillance on all three," Yan Shenhua said. "I need definitive confirmation before I move. Li Fenghao won't reveal himself easily. He's had two thousand years to perfect his hiding technique."

"Understood." Nomed stood, collecting the tea tray. "There's one more thing you should know. The Celestial Court enforcers who captured Lady Chi. They're still in the region."

That was concerning. Celestial Court enforcers served as the Immortal Realm's police force, hunting down cultivators who violated realm-crossing laws. Their presence suggested they were watching for other violations. If they detected his avatar, they might interfere.

"How many?"

"Three confirmed: two Lesser Immortals and one who might be Greater Immortal level, though he keeps his cultivation suppressed. They're based in the capital city, maintaining low profiles. They haven't approached the Black Rose Sect directly, but they're monitoring the situation."

Yan Shenhua processed this. The Celestial Court couldn't stop him. His avatar technique was legal, approved specifically for emergency interventions. But they could make things difficult. Delay him. Force him to justify his presence here.

Worse, they might interfere with his final confrontation with Li Fenghao. The court maintained strict rules about Greater Immortals fighting in lower realms. If they deemed his vengeance mission too disruptive, they could forcibly eject his avatar.

"Have they made any moves toward investigating us?"

"Not yet. They seemed to be monitoring Slifer."

That made sense. The demonic sect master had shown tremendous potential and was likely being scouted by the Immortal sects. It would be best to deal with Slifer and his disciples before the Immortal sects made their move to recruit them.

"How long until you can provide definitive identification of the ring's bearer?"

Nomed was quiet for a moment. "Three weeks. Maybe four. I need to observe them in combat situations. Li Fenghao's coaching would show most clearly under pressure. If he's giving tactical advice during life-or-death battles, I'll be able to detect the inconsistencies."

"Make it two weeks." Yan Shenhua's tone left no room for argument. "I've already wasted two months recovering. My power should be recovered by then."

"I'll do what I can." Nomed bowed slightly. "Is there anything else you need?"

"No. Leave me."

Nomed departed, his footsteps fading down the corridor. The door closed with a soft click.

Alone again, Yan Shenhua floated in the blood sphere. The silence of the chamber pressed down on him. No sound except the occasional drip of blood from his hand when he moved. No light except the golden glow of formation arrays.

Two more weeks. Maybe three.

He'd waited two thousand years. A few more weeks shouldn't matter.

But they did. Every day increased the risk of Li Fenghao discovering his presence. Every day gave his brother more time to prepare countermeasures. The element of surprise was Yan Shenhua's greatest advantage. Li Fenghao thought he was safe hidden away in some disciple's ring, plotting his eventual return to power. He had no idea his brother had found him and had crossed dimensional barriers specifically to finish their ancient conflict.

Yan Shenhua clenched his fist beneath the blood. The liquid rippled, currents swirling around his movement. He imagined that fist closing around his brother's throat. Imagined the look of shock and betrayal on Li Fenghao's face when he realized Yan Shenhua had tracked him across realms and millennia.

Would Li Fenghao beg? Probably not. His brother had always been too proud for that. He'd face death with dignity, spouting some philosophy about the cycle of karma and accepting one's fate.

The thought brought no satisfaction. Yan Shenhua wanted fear. Wanted his brother to understand what it felt like to be second best for once. To be the one left behind while someone else received all the glory and praise.

Bai Lianhua's face flashed through his memory. Beautiful beyond words, with eyes that seemed to see into your soul. She'd chosen Li Fenghao. Not because of cultivation level or combat prowess. Those had been equal. She'd chosen him because of his character. His righteousness. His genuine desire to help others.

She'd looked at Yan Shenhua and seen ambition. Ruthlessness. The willingness to do anything for power. And she'd rejected him.

That rejection had festered for millennia.

Yan Shenhua forced the memories away. Ancient history. Bai Lianhua had departed for distant territories long ago, achieving Immortal Lord Realm and leaving both brothers behind. She was beyond reach now, operating in cultivation levels that made even Greater Immortals seem insignificant.

What mattered was Li Fenghao. Finding him. Killing him. Proving once and for all who was superior.

The chamber's formation arrays pulsed as they drew more spiritual energy into the blood sphere. Yan Shenhua could feel his injuries continuing to mend. Sixty percent capacity now. Give it another week and he'd be at seventy percent. Ninety percent in two weeks. And in three weeks, he would be at a level of Half-Step Immortal Realm power that even Lady Chi couldn't hope to survive a blow against.

Time passed. How long, Yan Shenhua couldn't say. Minutes felt like hours in the blood sphere. The chamber's isolation was absolute. No windows to show the sun's movement. No sounds from outside to mark the passage of time. Just floating in warm darkness and feeling spiritual energy seep into his broken avatar.

His mind drifted. Not sleeping, but not fully conscious either. A meditative state that Greater Immortals could maintain for years without effort. Awareness remained sharp, ready to react to threats, but the conscious mind rested, conserving energy for healing.

Images flickered through his thoughts. Memories from forty-seven thousand years of existence. His parents' farm, barely remembered after so long. The traveling Immortal who'd sensed his potential. Training alongside Li Fenghao in those early centuries, when they'd still been friends and brothers rather than rivals.

The day Bai Lianhua appeared at their sect. How both brothers had fallen for her simultaneously. The competition that followed, each trying to prove themselves worthy of her attention. Li Fenghao's eventual victory, announced with apologetic eyes and genuine regret for hurting his brother. Yan Shenhua had smiled. Congratulated them both. Attended their bonding ceremony with appropriate gifts and well-wishes.

And then he'd gone to his private chambers and destroyed everything within reach. Furniture shattered. Walls cracked. Spiritual techniques unleashed with such fury that the entire mountain had trembled.

No one had asked about it. Accidents happened during cultivation breakthroughs. Rooms could be repaired. Yan Shenhua had thanked the helpful disciples and rebuilt his quarters in silence.

The resentment had never left. It grew. Metastasized. Poisoned every interaction with his brother. Every compliment Li Fenghao received felt like an insult to Yan Shenhua. Every student who praised the Heavenly Cloud Sect's righteousness was implicitly criticizing the White Cloud Sect's methods.

The split between the allied sects had been inevitable. Yan Shenhua had welcomed it. Finally, a chance to prove the White Cloud Sect superior. To demonstrate that his approach to cultivation produced better results than Li Fenghao's philosophical nonsense.

Wars followed. Not total conflict, but border skirmishes and political maneuvering. For thousands of years, the two sects had competed for territory, resources, and prestige. Neither gained lasting advantage. They were too evenly matched.

Until the ambush. Until Yan Shenhua had spent centuries preparing the perfect trap, timing it for when Li Fenghao would be most vulnerable. The attack should have been fatal. Would have been fatal for any other Greater Immortal.

But Li Fenghao had activated some emergency technique: spatial manipulation at a scale that shouldn't have been possible in his wounded state. He'd vanished, leaving only traces of blood and the echo of dimensional tearing.

Yan Shenhua had searched for centuries. Questioned witnesses. Investigated rumors. Nothing. His brother had disappeared completely, as if erased from existence.

Until recently. Until that faint spiritual signature had been detected in this mortal realm, buried under layers of concealment but distinctly Li Fenghao's essence.

The hunt could finally be completed.

Yan Shenhua's eyes opened again beneath the blood. His spiritual sense extended outward, mapping the monastery above and the surrounding mountains. Nothing unusual. No threats approaching. Just wind through ruins and small animals making their homes in abandoned buildings. He withdrew his sense and prepared to return to meditation. Another hour of focused healing would—

The air in front of the blood sphere rippled.

Yan Shenhua's attention snapped to full alertness. That ripple was familiar. He'd seen it countless times before in different contexts and locations. It was the telltale distortion of space manipulation. Someone was using a dimensional technique. It wasn't a portal from the Immortal Realm—the signature was wrong for that. This was localized: a short-range teleportation between two points in the same realm.

The ripple intensified. A crack appeared in the air itself, white light bleeding through from some between-space. The crack widened, pulling apart reality like tearing fabric.

Yan Shenhua's blood ran cold. Not from temperature, but from recognition.

He knew this technique. He had seen it used hundreds of times over thousands of years. The specific pattern of qi manipulation. The way the dimensional boundary peeled open rather than simply appeared. The characteristic white light that filled the gap.

Dimensional Slide. Li Fenghao's signature movement technique.

The white crack expanded into a full portal, roughly human sized. Through it, Yan Shenhua could glimpse the void realm between spaces. Empty whiteness stretched into infinity, broken only by the faint shadows of things that didn't exist in normal reality.

Yan Shenhua remained perfectly still within his blood sphere. His mind raced. Li Fenghao had found him. Impossible. He'd been so careful. Used Lady Chi's old hideout specifically because it had no connection to the Heavenly Cloud Sect's mortal affiliates. Maintained complete silence about his presence. Nomed was the only one who knew, and the avatar wouldn't have betrayed him.

So how had Li Fenghao located him?

Unless Li Fenghao hadn't been looking for him specifically. This could be coincidence. An accident. Pure bad luck that his brother had chosen this particular location for dimensional travel.

Or perhaps Li Fenghao was simply using the abandoned monastery as a waypoint. A convenient empty location to materialize without witnesses.

The portal stabilized. A figure stepped through.

Yan Shenhua's eyes narrowed. His first thought was that this couldn't be right. The figure wasn't correct for Li Fenghao. His brother was tall, dignified, with features that suggested wisdom and strength. This person was . . .

Old. Very old. Elderly to the point where mortal mortality would be imminent. The man's back was slightly hunched. His face was deeply lined with a long white beard reaching nearly to his waist. Liver spots marked his hands and face. His hair was white and wispy, pulled back in a simple style.

But the robes. Orange robes. Plain, unadorned, but clearly of good quality. The color was distinctive. Yan Shenhua had never seen orange cultivation robes before. What sect used that color?

The old man stepped fully through the portal. It closed behind him with a sound like tearing paper. He looked around the chamber with an expression that suggested mild curiosity rather than surprise at finding an underground blood sphere.

Footsteps pounded in the corridor outside. Nomed burst through the door, then stopped abruptly. His usual composure cracked. The avatar's eyes went wide. His hand moved toward a weapon, then froze as if he'd thought better of it.

"Slifer," Nomed said. His voice was controlled, but underneath, Yan Shenhua could hear fear.

The chamber fell silent except for the slow drip of blood from the sphere.

CHAPTER THIRTY-ONE

The first thing Slifer noticed was the blood.

A massive sphere of it floated in the center of the chamber, roughly three meters in diameter. Dark red and viscous, it was held in place by spiritual formations carved into the floor. Something moved inside the sphere. A human figure was suspended in the center, floating in the blood like a grotesque cocoon.

The figure's eyes opened. They were sharp and calculating, belonging to someone ancient. Someone who had seen millennia pass and considered mortals beneath notice.

Footsteps pounded in the corridor outside. The chamber door burst open.

Nomed stumbled through, his usual composure completely shattered. His eyes went wide when he saw Slifer standing there. His hand moved toward a weapon, then froze.

"Slifer," Nomed said in fear.

Slifer looked around the chamber, taking in the scene: The blood sphere. The formations carved into stone. The preservation arrays that kept everything fresh. His nose wrinkled slightly.

"I heard you've been keeping tabs on me," Slifer murmured. He kept his tone mild, almost friendly. "Thought I'd return the favor and pay you a visit."

Looking at the bloody scene around him, Slifer realized something important. The Greater Immortal was likely a demonic cultivator. That blood sphere wasn't decorative. It was a recovery method. The kind used by demons who'd sustained serious injuries.

Finding out that the Greater Immortal hunting you was demonic was never good, but finding out that said Greater Immortal was weakened was useful information.

The figure in the blood sphere moved suddenly. The liquid parted as an old man emerged, blood dripping from his white robes and long beard. He looked ancient, perhaps in his late seventies or eighties physically. His face was wrinkled but dignified, with the kind of bearing that suggested someone accustomed to respect and obedience.

The robes were distinctive: pure white fabric embroidered with silver clouds that seemed to drift across the material. On his left breast, a symbol showed nine layered clouds. The White Cloud Sect.

So, he wasn't a demonic cultivator after all, but was from one of the three great righteous sects from the Immortal Realm.

Slifer found it ironic that this "righteous" cultivator was literally bathing in blood. The hypocrisy was almost funny.

The old man stepped fully out of the sphere, his feet touching stone floor. Blood continued dripping from his clothes and beard, but he ignored it completely. His attention was focused entirely on Slifer with the intensity of a predator evaluating prey.

"Who taught you the Dimensional Slide technique?"

The question came out aggressive. Demanding. Like he had every right to interrogate Slifer.

Slifer considered his answer carefully. He couldn't exactly say that he'd used the System to copy it from Hughie. That would lead to too many questions. It would make him sound less like a mysterious, powerful senior and more like someone taking advantage of his disciples.

"I learned it," Slifer said simply. Noncommittal. The kind of answer that could mean anything.

The old man's eyes narrowed dangerously. "Don't play games with me. That technique is the signature method of Li Fenghao of the Heavenly Cloud Sect. Nobody else knows it. I've spent two thousand years hunting anyone who might have learned it. So, I'll ask again: who taught you?"

Slifer remained silent. He was starting to understand the situation. This old man was hunting Li Fenghao. That's why he'd descended to the mortal realm. That's why he'd allied with Nomed. They were both searching for someone connected to Li Fenghao.

And they'd somehow decided that person was Slifer.

"Is Li Fenghao your master?" the old man pressed. He took a step closer, his spiritual pressure beginning to leak out. Half-Step Immortal Realm power pressed down on the chamber. "Is this why you've been able to achieve these impossible feats? Which item is he sealed in? A ring? A pendant? A sword? Tell me where he's hiding."

"I don't have a master," Slifer replied honestly. The System had trained him, but that wasn't the same as having a cultivation master in the traditional sense.

The old man's expression shifted to confusion. He extended his spiritual sense and examined Slifer from every angle. His frown deepened as seconds passed.

"I don't sense him," he muttered more to himself than Slifer. "If Li Fenghao were here, contained in an artifact, I would be able to detect traces of his spiritual signature. But there's nothing. Just your cultivation and some unusual fluctuations that don't match my brother's pattern."

Brother. That was interesting. This Greater Immortal was Li Fenghao's brother. That explained the obsessive hunt across realms and millennia.

"Enough of this." Nomed spoke up from near the doorway. His fear had transformed into something else—desperation. "Kill him, Senior Yan. We can search his storage ring and belongings afterward. If Li Fenghao is hidden somewhere, we'll find him once Slifer's dead."

Yan Shenhua nodded slowly. His expression of confusion gave way to one of grim determination. "You're right. I might not be at full power, but I'll force the information out of you. One way or another, you'll tell me where my brother is hiding."

He took a step forward as he gathered spiritual energy around his hands. The white light of his cultivation method mixed with traces of blood qi from the sphere. His power level spiked as it approached the absolute peak of what Half-Step Immortal Realm could achieve.

Slifer activated a card before Yan Shenhua could take a second step.

A beam of compressed energy shot across the chamber too fast for normal reaction. Too concentrated to be blocked by basic defenses.

The beam caught Nomed directly in the chest.

For a fraction of a second, nothing happened. Nomed's expression showed surprise. His mouth opened like he wanted to speak.

Then his chest exploded.

The beam punched straight through and obliterated his heart, lungs, and spine in an instant. Blood and viscera sprayed across the chamber wall behind him. The force of the impact threw his body backward, already dead before he hit the stone.

But the beam didn't stop there. It continued and caught Nomed's head, turning it into red mist. Skull fragments scattered. Brain matter splattered across the doorway.

What remained of Nomed collapsed to the floor. It wasn't even a corpse, really. Just pieces. His torso was a hollow ruin. His head was gone entirely. His limbs twitched once, nerves firing in death spasms, then went still.

The chamber fell silent.

Slifer lowered his hand. The Ascendant Strike Card had lived up to its description by delivering a one-hit kill against an assailant below Ascendant Realm. Nomed had been Nascent Soul or Origin Realm at best. He never stood a chance.

Yan Shenhua stood frozen mid-step. His eyes were locked on what remained of Nomed. The Greater Immortal's expression showed genuine shock. He'd been preparing to torture Slifer for information. Instead, his ally had been erased in front of him in less than a second.

"How—" Yan Shenhua started.

Slifer didn't let him finish. He activated another card: Deadly Strike. It had been purchased months ago and saved for exactly this kind of situation. It could kill anyone below the Immortal Realm, which meant it could damage a Greater Immortal who had been restricted by the heavens.

The attack materialized as a massive blade of golden light, fifteen meters long and bright enough to hurt if you looked at it directly. Slifer swung it in a horizontal arc aimed at Yan Shenhua's torso.

The Greater Immortal reacted on pure instinct. His hands came up and spiritual energy exploded outward in a defensive barrier. White light mixed with traces of spatial qi formed a shield just before the golden blade connected.

The impact shook the entire chamber. The golden blade crashed against the white barrier with enough force to create shock waves that cracked the stone walls. Dust rained from the ceiling. The blood sphere behind Yan Shenhua rippled violently as the formation arrays flickered.

Yan Shenhua was thrown backward, his barrier shattering under the assault. He tumbled through the air and crashed into the far wall, leaving a crater in the stone. Blood appeared at the corner of his mouth. Not much, but enough to show the attack had hurt.

The Greater Immortal climbed to his feet, his expression transforming from shock to cold fury. "What are you?"

"Someone who's tired of conspiracies targeting my sect," Slifer replied. He readied another attack. "You should have stayed in the Immortal Realm."

Yan Shenhua's spiritual pressure exploded outward once again. The chamber couldn't contain it anymore. The ceiling cracked further. The walls groaned under the strain. Some of the formation arrays shattered completely, their inscriptions burning away.

"You think killing the servant means anything?" Yan Shenhua wiped blood from his mouth with the back of his hand. "Nomed was useful but ultimately disposable. You, however, have information I need. If you won't talk willingly, I'll rip it from your broken mind."

He attacked with both hands extended. Twin beams of spatial qi shot forward, designed to pierce through defenses and strike directly at Slifer's spiritual core. The technique was called Void Lance, one of the White Cloud Sect's advanced methods. It could tear holes in reality itself.

Slifer activated a Critical Block Card.

An invisible barrier materialized between him and the incoming attacks. The twin beams struck the barrier and stopped completely. No penetration. No damage. Just absolute negation of the technique.

The beams dispersed harmlessly against the invisible shield, their energy dissipating into nothing.

Yan Shenhua's eyes widened. "What kind of treasure—"

Slifer launched himself forward and closed the distance before the Greater Immortal could finish his question. He drew his Heaven Rank sword, the Skyfade Emerald Blade, and activated Sunrise Slash while simultaneously using an Enhance Strike Card to empower the attack.

The sword technique manifested as a wave of brilliant light. Not just any light, but concentrated dawn energy that purified and destroyed anything demonic. The wave expanded as it crossed the chamber, growing from a simple sword arc into a massive crescent a dozen meters wide.

Yan Shenhua tried to dodge. His spatial cultivation allowed for short-range teleportation. He flickered out of the attack's path and reappeared six meters to the left.

But Slifer had anticipated that. He'd fought enough powerful cultivators to recognize spatial movement patterns. The Sunrise Slash technique included a tracking component. The light wave curved mid-flight and followed Yan Shenhua to his new position.

The Greater Immortal realized too late. He threw up another defensive barrier, this one reinforced with multiple layers of spatial distortion meant to deflect attacks into pocket dimensions. The dawn light burned through the spatial distortions like they weren't there. Purification energy was anathema to demonic cultivation, and Yan Shenhua had been soaking in demon blood for weeks. His body was saturated with it. The defensive technique relied on that blood qi for power.

It couldn't stop righteous purification.

The light wave struck Yan Shenhua directly and carved a deep gash across his chest from left shoulder to right hip. Blood sprayed, but it wasn't normal blood. This was black and corrupted, the kind that came from demonic cultivation taken too far.

Yan Shenhua staggered backward, his hand pressed against the wound. His face showed pain and disbelief in equal measure. "Impossible. That attack contained Sword Intent and space manipulation and purification energy all layered together. No mortal should be able to—"

Slifer pressed his advantage. He activated Void Piercer, the technique he'd developed during his enlightenment after saving Fenlock. The sword disappeared, phasing out of normal reality, then reappeared inside Yan Shenhua's guard, the tip aimed directly at his heart.

The Greater Immortal reacted with desperate speed. He twisted his body as he redirected his internal organs with spatial manipulation. The sword that should have pierced his heart instead punched through his right lung.

That would have been lethal for most cultivators, but Yan Shenhua was a Greater Immortal, even if suppressed. He'd survived worse wounds during thousands of years of existence.

He grabbed Slifer's sword arm with one hand while his other hand formed a complex gesture. Space qi gathered around his palm and compressed into a tiny sphere of absolute destructive force. This was Spatial Collapse, a technique that created miniature black holes capable of consuming everything within a three-meter radius.

Slifer saw the technique forming and immediately activated another Critical Block Card.

The invisible barrier appeared just as Yan Shenhua released Spatial Collapse. A miniature black hole formed, and reality folded in on itself with enough force to shatter mountains. Everything within range began getting pulled toward the center point, air and dust and loose stones all accelerating toward oblivion.

The Critical Block held firm. The black hole couldn't expand past the barrier's edge. It consumed air and energy and nothing else, trapped against the invisible wall.

Yan Shenhua released Slifer's arm and leaped backward, putting distance between them. The Spatial Collapse technique collapsed on itself without anything to consume and disappeared with a sound like reality tearing.

"What in the heavens are you?" Yan Shenhua demanded again. His breath came hard now, the lung wound affecting his stamina. "Those barriers. You've used five different ones, and none of them show any signs of weakening. That's not natural cultivation. That's artifact assistance. But I don't sense any treasures on you powerful enough to replicate that defense."

Slifer didn't answer. He was too busy analyzing the fight. Yan Shenhua was strong. Very strong. Even suppressed to Half-Step Immortal Realm, his techniques were refined by millennia of practice. His combat instincts were sharp. His spatial cultivation provided mobility and versatility that made him difficult to pin down.

But he couldn't damage Slifer. The Critical Block Cards negated every major attack completely. And Slifer's offensive techniques were landing, accumulating damage that even a Greater Immortal's recovery rate couldn't ignore.

The fight was tilting in Slifer's favor.

Yan Shenhua seemed to realize it too. His expression shifted from fury to calculation. "You're not normal. Not a standard Half-Step Immortal Realm cultivator. Your techniques are too diverse, too powerful. Your defenses are absolute. And that sword technique earlier contained traces of space manipulation identical to Li Fenghao's methods."

He straightened despite his injuries and gathered his spiritual pressure once more. "I don't understand what's happening here. But I know one thing with certainty: you're connected to my brother somehow. Maybe not directly, but the connection exists."

The Greater Immortal's aura began changing. The white light of his cultivation took on a rainbow shimmer, fragments of color mixing into complex patterns. His wounds stopped bleeding. His breathing steadied. Power that had been suppressed started breaking free.

"This avatar was limited to Half-Step Immortal Realm to avoid triggering the mortal realm's defenses," Yan Shenhua said. His voice carried absolute confidence now. "But I can temporarily release those limitations. For a few minutes, I can manifest my true power. The realm will reject me afterward and probably destroy this avatar in the process. But a few minutes at Greater Immortal Realm is more than enough to obliterate one troublesome mortal."

Slifer felt the change. The pressure in the chamber increased exponentially. The walls began cracking seriously now, their structural integrity failing under the strain. The ceiling groaned, threatening total collapse.

This was bad. A Greater Immortal at full power was beyond what he could handle. Even with all his cards and techniques, the gap between Nascent Soul and Greater Immortal was too vast. It wasn't about skill or tactics at that point. Just raw power overwhelming everything else.

But Yan Shenhua had made a mistake.

He'd monologued. Given a dramatic speech explaining exactly what he planned to do and how long it would take. Classic villain behavior.

Slifer activated three cards simultaneously.

The first was a Temporal Stasis Field. The technique froze time in a three-meter sphere around Yan Shenhua. The Greater Immortal's movements slowed to glacial speed, his power release interrupted mid-activation.

The second was Soul Binding Chains. Ethereal chains materialized from the floor and wrapped around Yan Shenhua's spiritual form. They didn't restrict his body; they bound his soul directly and prevented it from manifesting power beyond certain thresholds.

The third was a Reflection Barrier: a specialized defensive card that didn't just block attacks, but stored them temporarily and could release the energy back at the attacker.

The three techniques combined created a perfect trap. Yan Shenhua was frozen in time, his soul was bound by chains, and any power he managed to release would be reflected directly back at him.

The Greater Immortal's eyes showed awareness even in the time-frozen state. He understood what had happened. Understood he'd been caught mid-preparation because he'd wasted time explaining his plan instead of just executing it.

Slifer walked forward slowly. His sword remained drawn, still coated in traces of Yan Shenhua's black blood. It began glowing with accumulated energy. Every technique Slifer knew channeled through the blade simultaneously. Sunrise Slash. Void Piercer. Stellar Nova Strike. His Sword Intent. His Nascent Soul's power. His Enhanced Strike Cards. All of it was compressed into one final attack.

"You know what? I'm tired. Tired of fighting Greater Immortals. Tired of conspiracies. Tired of threats against my sect. So, here's my response to your dramatic buildup."

Slifer thrust the sword forward.

The blade punched through the Temporal Stasis Field like it wasn't there. It passed through the frozen defenses Yan Shenhua had been raising and penetrated the Greater Immortal's chest directly through his heart.

The Soul Binding Chains flared with light as they held Yan Shenhua's spiritual form in place, preventing him from escaping his body even as it was destroyed. The Reflection Barrier triggered and took the power Yan Shenhua had been gathering for his breakthrough and slammed it back into him.

The combined effect was catastrophic.

"This is merely an avatar! My true body will get revenge!" Yan Shenhua screamed as his body exploded from the inside out. Not metaphorically—it literally detonated as incompatible energies collided within his meridians. His chest cavity burst open, ribs shattering outward. His head snapped back, eyes wide with shock and disbelief.

The explosion continued. Arms and legs separated at the joints, blown apart by runaway spiritual energy. The torso split in half lengthwise, and organs spilled onto the stone floor. Blood sprayed everywhere, coating the walls in arterial patterns.

By the time the Temporal Stasis Field collapsed, there was nothing left to freeze. Just scattered pieces of what had once been a Greater Immortal avatar. The body had been destroyed so thoroughly that even the white robes were torn to shreds.

Slifer stepped back, his sword dripping with black blood. The chamber looked like a slaughterhouse: two bodies destroyed in different ways, blood and gore covering every surface. The formations were all broken. The ceiling was barely holding together.

The System interface appeared in his vision.

> *Ding!*
> Mission Complete: Eliminate the traitor
> Targets Eliminated:
> Nomed (Moon God King Avatar): Confirmed
> Yan Shenhua (Greater Immortal Avatar): Confirmed
> Mission rewards calculating . . .
> You have gained 5,000,000 Karmic Credits.
> Additional Rewards:
> Greater Immortal eliminated: 2,000,000 Karmic Credits
> Zero casualties (friendly): 500,000 Karmic Credits
> Combat performance (exceptional): 300,000 Karmic Credits
> Total Karmic Credits Earned: 7,800,000

Slifer stared at the numbers. A total reward of 7,800,000 credits. That was . . . that was more than he'd accumulated in the entire past year. The urgent mission hadn't just been about Nomed. The System had known about Yan Shenhua all along. The five million base reward was for both targets, not just one. And the bonuses pushed it even higher.

He was rich. System-Shop rich. The kind of wealth that opened up options he'd never seriously considered before.

But looking at the destruction around him, Slifer felt uneasy rather than triumphant. A Greater Immortal had descended to the mortal realm specifically to hunt Li Fenghao. That meant Li Fenghao was important enough that someone would spend forty-seven thousand years holding a grudge.

And Li Fenghao was currently sealed in a ring on Hughie's finger.

Which meant Hughie was in danger. Serious danger. If Yan Shenhua had found them, others might too. The Immortal Realm apparently knew Li Fenghao was down here somewhere. They'd send more hunters eventually.

Slifer needed to protect his disciple. Needed to figure out how to deal with the ancient Immortal trapped in jewelry. Needed to understand what that whole situation meant for the sect's long-term safety.

He walked toward the chamber's exit, stepping carefully around Nomed's remains. The corridor beyond was empty. Nobody else in the monastery. Yan Shenhua and Nomed had been operating alone.

The monastery itself would collapse soon. The structural damage from the battle was too severe. Stone groaned ominously. Cracks spread across walls and ceilings. Best to leave before it all came down.

Slifer activated Dimensional Slide and returned to his quarters in the Black Rose Sect.

The transition was smooth: one moment standing in a collapsing monastery, the next moment back in familiar rooms. Safe and secure. Protected by the sect's formations and surrounded by allies.

He sat heavily in his chair, finally allowing exhaustion to catch up. The battle had been short but intense. He'd burned through expensive cards, used techniques that taxed even his Nascent Soul cultivation, and killed two major enemies in quick succession.

But it was done. Nomed was dead. The Moon God King's influence was finally eliminated. Yan Shenhua's avatar was destroyed. The conspiracy against the Black Rose Sect had been broken.

So why did Slifer feel more worried than relieved?

Because Yan Shenhua's final words kept echoing in his mind. "This is merely an avatar. My true body will get revenge."

Except Slifer had cut that threat short and killed the avatar before Yan Shenhua could finish explaining. But the implication was clear enough: The real Yan Shenhua was still alive. Still in the Immortal Realm. Still hunting Li Fenghao. And now he'd know that his avatar had been killed by someone connected to his brother.

That someone being Slifer.

Which meant a Greater Immortal with forty-seven thousand years of cultivation and infinite resources would eventually come looking for revenge.

The thought was sobering. Terrifying, really. Slifer had just made an enemy of one of the most powerful beings in existence. Someone who commanded a major sect in the Immortal Realm. Someone with the patience and determination to hunt across dimensions and millennia.

He was going to need protection. Real protection. The kind that came from backing powerful enough to make even Greater Immortals hesitate.

Slifer thought about the Celestial Court, the organization that regulated Immortal Realm interference in lower realms. They'd offered membership before, back when they'd captured Lady Chi. He'd declined at the time, wanting to maintain his independence. But maybe independence wasn't worth dying over. The Celestial Court had Lesser Immortals, Greater Immortals, and who knows what else at higher ranks. They operated with the authority to arrest and punish even powerful sect masters. If Slifer joined them, he'd be under their protection.

Yan Shenhua couldn't casually attack a Celestial Court member. Not without risking war with an organization that spanned the entire Immortal Realm.

The more Slifer thought about it, the more sense it made. Join the court. Gain protection. Use their resources to deal with threats that exceeded mortal realm capabilities. Continue running the Black Rose Sect while having backup from higher powers.

It wasn't ideal. Membership would come with responsibilities. Missions. Obligations. He'd have to follow rules and answer to superiors. His independence would be curtailed.

But he'd be alive, his disciples would be protected, and the sect would be safe from casual interference by bored Immortals looking for entertainment.

Sometimes survival meant compromising on principles.

Slifer stood and walked to his window. The disciples in the sect grounds below continued their peaceful routines. They trained, and life went on. Nobody down there knew what had happened today, how close the sect had come to facing a Greater Immortal's wrath.

And they wouldn't know. Slifer would handle it quietly, accept the Celestial Court's offer, and join their organization. He'd become whatever they needed him to be. Because the alternative was waiting for Yan Shenhua's true body to descend and destroy everything Slifer had built.

He'd survived too much, come too far, changed too many lives. All of it would be pointless if a grudge-holding Immortal wiped it all away.

Time to make a decision. Time to secure the future properly, even if it meant giving up some freedom.

Slifer pulled out the jade communication talisman Han Shu had given him. The Celestial Court enforcer had said to contact them if he ever changed his mind about membership.

Looks like I'm about to take them up on that offer.

Later. He'd contact them later. Right now, he needed to check on his

DEMONIC SECT ELDER AND THE GREAT WAR

disciples, make sure everyone was safe, and confirm that the immediate threats were handled. Then he'd deal with the longer-term problems: The immortal in Hughie's ring. The vengeful Greater Immortal in the Immortal Realm. All the complicated messes that came from surviving in a cultivation world.

But at least he had over seven million credits to work with. That bought a lot of options. A lot of powerful techniques and treasures. A lot of ways to bridge the gap between mortal cultivation and Immortal threats.

Slifer looked down at his hands. They were steady despite everything. Despite killing two major enemies in the space of minutes. Despite making himself a target for beings that could shatter worlds.

He'd come a long way from the overweight basement dweller who'd choked on pie, from the confused transmigrator who'd woken up in an elderly cultivator's dying body, from the desperate survivor using System tricks to stay alive.

Now he was a sect master. A Nascent Soul cultivator. Someone who could fight Greater Immortal avatars and win.

The question was whether that would be enough for what came next.

Slifer hoped so. Because ready or not, the future was coming. And he had a feeling it was going to be complicated.

EPILOGUE

A month had passed since Slifer killed Nomed and destroyed Yan Shenhua's avatar.

The first week after that fight had been quiet. Suspiciously quiet. Slifer kept expecting retaliation from the Immortal Realm, some kind of response to a Greater Immortal's avatar being destroyed. But nothing had come. No angry immortals descended. No threatening messages appeared. Just silence. The good news was that Tyrus had formally begun his conversion to being a righteous cultivator. Slifer expected him to complete his transformation by the end of the month.

By the second week, Slifer had started investigating Li Fenghao's situation more thoroughly. The ancient immortal sealed in Hughie's ring had been content to remain hidden for the most part, but Slifer needed answers. Specifically, he needed to know if Yan Shenhua would be coming back for round two.

So, he'd sat down in his quarters one evening and called out to the ring.

"Li Fenghao. We need to talk."

There had been a pause. Then a voice had emerged from Hughie's storage ring, which Slifer had borrowed for the conversation. The voice was cultured and refined, belonging to someone who'd spent millennia perfecting their speech patterns.

"Sect Master Slifer. I've been wondering when you'd want to discuss recent events."

"Your brother tried to kill me," Slifer said bluntly. "Or his avatar did, at least. Before I destroyed it, he mentioned something about a thousand-year grudge. I need to know if he's going to send another avatar. Or worse, come himself."

Li Fenghao's response had been a long sigh. "Yan Shenhua will absolutely try again. My brother is nothing if not persistent. Once he sets his mind to something, he pursues it with absolute determination. It's one of his few admirable qualities, though in this case it's rather inconvenient for you."

"That's what I was afraid of." Slifer leaned back in his chair. "The avatar mentioned you two were brothers. What happened to make him hunt you for thousands of years?"

"A woman," Li Fenghao said simply. "Her name was Bai Lianhua. Both of us loved her. She chose me. He never forgave that choice."

Slifer had stared at nothing in particular, processing that information. "So, this entire mess, all this danger to my sect and my disciples, exists because one Immortal couldn't handle rejection?"

"I suppose when you phrase it that way, it does sound rather petty," Li Fenghao admitted. "But you must understand, we were young then. Only a few centuries old. Emotions ran hot. Pride mattered more than it should have. And once the conflict started, neither of us could back down without losing face."

"Where is Bai Lianhua now?" Slifer asked.

"Gone. She left us both behind a lifetime ago. She grew tired of the conflict and ascended to Immortal Lord Realm, then departed for territories beyond the Celestial Court's reach. Last I heard, she was exploring the Void Reaches, seeking enlightenment in isolation."

"So, she's not even part of this anymore, but your brother still wants you dead."

"Correct. The grudge stopped being about her thousands of years ago. Now it's simply about him winning our lifelong competition by proving himself superior and erasing the humiliation of her choosing me over him."

Slifer rubbed his temples. He'd been doing that a lot lately. "How likely is he to come after me specifically? I killed his avatar, but he doesn't know much about me beyond that I can use Dimensional Slide."

"Very likely, I'm afraid." Li Fenghao's voice carried genuine apology. "Yan is very vindictive. He'll focus everything on eliminating you and capturing Hughie."

"Great. Just great."

That conversation had confirmed what Slifer already suspected. He couldn't stay in the mortal realm and expect to be safe. Yan Shenhua would return eventually, and next time he might arrive with his full power. The only real solution was to ascend to the Immortal Realm himself and join an organization powerful enough to make Yan hesitate.

Which brought him to the Celestial Court.

Slifer pulled out the jade communication talisman Han Shu had given him weeks ago. The enforcer had said to contact them if he ever changed his mind about membership. Time to take them up on that offer.

He channeled qi into the talisman. It glowed with soft blue light as it established a connection across vast distances. A moment later, Han Shu's voice emerged from the jade.

"Slifer. I was wondering when you'd call."

"You knew I would?"

"The moment I heard about a Greater Immortal's avatar being destroyed in the Eastern Continent, I had a feeling you were involved. That kind of action draws attention. The wrong kind of attention."

Slifer winced. Of course the Celestial Court knew about the fight. They probably monitored all major spiritual disturbances in the mortal realm. "I'm interested in that membership offer. If it's still available."

"It is." Han Shu sounded pleased.

"What would membership entail exactly?"

"Ascension to the Immortal Realm, obviously. You can't enforce cosmic law from the mortal realm. Once there, you'd undergo basic training in court procedures and regulations. After that, you'd be assigned to a senior enforcer for field experience. Eventually, you'd work cases independently."

"What about my sect? My disciples?"

"Ah, yes. We anticipated that question." Han Shu paused, probably consulting notes or discussing with colleagues. "The Celestial Court is willing to extend protection to the Black Rose Sect in exchange for your service. Any interference from Immortal Realm cultivators would be treated as an attack on court interests. That includes grudge-bearing Greater Immortals looking for revenge."

That was exactly what Slifer needed: protection for the people he cared about and safety from threats he couldn't handle alone. "What's the catch?"

"The catch is that you'll be bound to the court for at least one thousand years of service. Enforcer work is demanding and often dangerous. You'll face situations that could kill even experienced Immortals. And you'll need to follow court regulations, which can be restrictive for someone accustomed to independence."

One thousand years. That was a long time by mortal standards. But in the Immortal Realm, it was apparently just a standard employment contract. Slifer thought about his disciples, about the sect he'd built, about everything he'd accomplished in the past year.

A thousand years of service in exchange for protecting all of that? It was worth it.

"I accept," Slifer said. "When do we start?"

"We'll need approximately one month to prepare everything. Ascension isn't instantaneous. We need to establish a stable gateway, register your transition with the Heavenly Dao, and arrange for the sect protection to take effect immediately upon your departure. Can you be ready in thirty days?"

"I'll be ready."

The conversation had continued for another hour as they worked out details and logistics. They'd also discussed what would happen to the Black Rose Sect after he left. The sect would continue operating normally under Morvran's administration. Slifer's disciples would remain as core members, training and advancing their cultivation. The court's protection would manifest as a formal decree, announced to all major powers in the Immortal Realm. Anyone who interfered with the Black Rose Sect and its affiliates would face court enforcement.

It was a good deal. Better than Slifer had expected, honestly.

The rest of that month had been busy. Slifer threw himself into sect administration, making sure everything was properly organized before his departure. He promoted several Core Disciples to elder positions and established clear succession protocols. With the System's help, he created detailed instruction manuals for cultivation techniques.

He also spent time with his disciples, though he didn't tell them about the ascension yet. That conversation would come later, when everything was finalized.

What he did notice, about a week in, was that something strange had happened with the System interface. There were unread notifications stacked up that were all marked with dates from several weeks ago.

Slifer pulled up the notifications properly for the first time.

Congratulations!
Your disciple Caelum has broken through to Ascendant Realm.
Reward: 50,000 Karmic Credits

Congratulations!
Your disciple Hughie has broken through to Ascendant Realm.
Reward: 50,000 Karmic Credits

> Congratulations!
> Your disciple Amelia has broken through to Ascendant Realm.
> Reward: 50,000 Karmic Credits

> Congratulations!
> Your disciple Fenlock has broken through to Ascendant Realm.
> Reward: 50,000 Karmic Credits

> Special Achievement: All Core Disciples have advanced to Ascendant Realm.
> You have gained 100,000 Karmic Credits.
> Total Karmic Credits Earned: 300,000

Slifer blinked at the numbers. All four of his main disciples had reached Ascendant Realm? When had that happened? He'd been so preoccupied that he'd completely missed these notifications.

He checked the dates. The advancements had occurred over the span of two weeks, starting right before he'd confronted Nomed and finishing right after. Each disciple had broken through independently using the resources and training he'd provided over the past year.

Three hundred thousand credits wasn't a massive amount compared to what he'd earned from killing Yan Shenhua's avatar, but it was respectable. More importantly, it meant his disciples were strong enough to defend themselves now. Ascendant Realm cultivators were sect masters in most organizations. They could handle serious threats without needing constant protection.

That made leaving easier. Slifer wouldn't be abandoning vulnerable students. He'd be leaving behind capable cultivators who could stand on their own.

The System had more notifications waiting.

> Hidden Quest Chain Complete: Reform the Black Rose Sect
> Original Objectives:
> Remove corruption from leadership: Complete
> Establish righteous cultivation methods: Complete
> Build alliances with major powers: Complete
> Eliminate threats to sect stability: Complete
> Gain recognition as righteous organization: Complete

Slifer focused on that last objective. "Gain recognition as righteous organization? When did that happen?"

More text appeared, explaining the situation. Apparently, about two weeks ago, the major righteous sects had held a conference. The Heavenly Light Sect, White Tiger Sect, Pure Soul Sect, and several others had formally recognized both the Black Rose Sect and the Black Heart Sect as righteous organizations.

The recognition came with official documentation, updated sect rankings, and invitations to join the Coalition of Righteous Sects. It was the kind of achievement that would have taken centuries of work under normal circumstances.

But these weren't normal circumstances. Slifer had defeated multiple demonic threats, reformed his sect's cultivation methods, and made powerful allies. Plus, having the Celestial Court interested in him probably helped. Other sects weren't going to oppose an organization that had court backing.

So, the Black Rose Sect was officially righteous now. No more demonic sect stigma. No more automatic hostility from righteous cultivators. His disciples could travel freely without worrying about being attacked on sight.

The System displayed the quest rewards.

You have gained 2,000,000 Karmic Credits.
Additional Rewards:
Completion time bonus: 500,000 Karmic Credits
Zero sect member casualties: 300,000 Karmic Credits
Performance (exceptional): 200,000 Karmic Credits
Total Karmic Credits Earned: 3,000,000
Special reward unlocked.
Name: Sect Master's Legacy Package
Contains: Advanced administration techniques, sect protection formations, disciple training manuals, resource management systems

---

Three million credits. That was substantial. Combined with the more than seven million from the Yan Shenhua fight and the three hundred thousand from disciple advancements, Slifer now had over eleven million Karmic Credits available.

He had the kind of wealth that could buy pretty much anything in the Shop that wasn't restricted to higher realms. Though, if he was ascending to the Immortal Realm soon, he'd need to spend those credits carefully and buy things that would help him survive as a new enforcer— techniques and treasures that worked at Immortal Realm power levels. They would undoubtedly be extremely expensive.

Slifer shelved those thoughts for later. Right now, he needed to focus on preparing the sect for his absence.

The Sect Master's Legacy Package turned out to be incredibly useful. It contained detailed manuals on every aspect of sect administration, like formation diagrams for protective arrays that could withstand Ascendant Realm attacks, training schedules optimized for different cultivation methods and talent levels, and resource allocation strategies that maximized efficiency while minimizing waste, and was written in clear language that even junior disciples could understand.

Slifer spent three days studying the package contents, then another week implementing the best parts. He established rotating elder duties so no single person bore too much responsibility, created oversight committees to prevent corruption from creeping back in, and installed the protection formations around the sect grounds, powered by spirit stone reserves that would last years.

By the end of the month, the Black Rose Sect was running like a well-oiled machine. Disciples trained efficiently. Elders handled administration competently. Resources flowed where they were needed. The sect didn't require Slifer's direct involvement for monthly operations anymore.

Which was good, because he wouldn't be around much longer.

The final day arrived faster than Slifer expected. One moment he was buried in preparation work, and the next moment Han Shu was contacting him through the communication talisman.

"Everything is ready on our end. The gateway will open at noon tomorrow. Make your farewells today. Once you ascend, you won't be able to return to the mortal realm for at least ten years."

Ten years minimum before he could visit. That was court policy, apparently. New enforcers needed to focus entirely on their training and duties without distractions from their former lives. Only after proving themselves capable would they be granted leave to visit lower realms.

Slifer gathered the sect's core members in the main hall that afternoon. All the elders, his direct disciples, Morvran, and various other important figures assembled quietly, sensing this wasn't a routine meeting.

"I'm leaving," Slifer said without preamble. "Tomorrow at noon, I'll be ascending to the Immortal Realm to join the Celestial Court as an enforcer."

The hall erupted in shocked conversation. Disciples turned to each other, elders exchanged worried looks, and Morvran's normally composed expression cracked into visible concern.

Grand Elder Wyatt spoke first. "Sect Master, this is rather sudden. Is there a particular reason for this decision?"

"I made an enemy of a Greater Immortal," Slifer replied honestly. "He'll come back for revenge eventually. The only way to protect the sect from that kind of threat is to join an organization powerful enough to make him hesitate. The Celestial Court fits that description."

"But who will lead the sect?" Grand Elder Lydia asked. "We've come so far under your guidance. Without you here, everything could fall apart."

"It won't fall apart, because you're all capable of running things without me." Slifer gestured around the hall. "I've spent the past month making sure of that. You have the training manuals, the administrative systems, the protection formations. Everything you need to keep the sect functioning smoothly. And Morvran will act as sect master, coordinating daily operations."

Morvran bowed deeply. "I am honored by your trust, Master."

"The Celestial Court has agreed to extend protection to the Black Rose Sect," Slifer continued. "Any interference from Immortal Realm cultivators will be treated as an attack on court interests. That means no rogue Immortals causing trouble, no powerful outsiders trying to take over. You'll be safe from external threats beyond what the mortal realm can produce."

That seemed to calm some of the worried expressions. Protection from the Celestial Court was no small thing. Most sects would pay fortunes for that kind of guarantee.

"What about your disciples?" Wyatt asked. "Will they be ascending with you?"

"No. They're staying here to continue their cultivation and help run the sect." Slifer looked at Hughie, Caelum, Amelia, and Fenlock. They stood together near the front, all four wearing matching expressions of shocked disbelief. "They've all reached Ascendant Realm recently. They're strong enough to defend themselves and contribute meaningfully to the sect's future." He turned to address the whole assembly. "I know this is unexpected. I know it's going to require adjustment. But I have complete confidence in all of you. The Black Rose Sect is strong now, stronger than it's been in centuries. That strength comes from the people in this hall. From your dedication and hard work and willingness to change. Keep doing what you've been doing, and the sect will continue to prosper." Slifer paused, letting his words sink in. "I'll be saying individual goodbyes this evening. For now, continue your normal routines. Nothing changes today. Tomorrow, after I'm gone, Morvran will assume full administrative authority. Any questions or concerns should be directed to him."

There were more questions, of course. About logistical details around succession protocols and communication methods and what to do if certain emergencies arose. Slifer answered what he could, redirected the rest to Morvran, and eventually dismissed the assembly.

His disciples lingered after everyone else left. They stood in an uncertain cluster, clearly wanting to say something but not sure how to start.

"Walk with me," Slifer said.

They followed him out of the main hall and through the sect grounds, Lenvari tagging along. The late afternoon sun cast long shadows across the training fields. Disciples continued their usual routines, though Slifer noticed several watching their group with curious expressions. Word was probably spreading already.

He led them to the meditation garden he'd claimed as his thinking spot. The same garden where he'd dealt with so many problems over the past year. It felt appropriate to have this conversation here.

They settled onto stone benches arranged in a circle. Val appeared from somewhere, chirping indignantly, and landed on Slifer's shoulder. The little dragon had probably been off hunting spirit-beast eggs—her favorite hobby lately.

"I didn't want to leave without explaining properly," Slifer said. "The assembly was necessary for administrative purposes, but you four deserve better than a formal announcement."

"You're really going?" Hughie asked. His usual enthusiasm was notably absent. "To the Immortal Realm? For how long?"

"Minimum of ten years before I can visit. After that, I don't know. The court contract is for one thousand years of service."

"A thousand years," Amelia repeated. "That's longer than most mortal civilizations exist."

"Welcome to Immortal time scales," Slifer said dryly. "Apparently, a thousand years is considered a reasonable employment contract up there. Though, to be fair, time moves differently when you're not aging."

Caelum had been quiet, but now he spoke. "This is because of Yan Shenhua. Because he'll come back."

"Yes." No point lying to them. "His avatar specifically mentioned revenge before I killed it. A Greater Immortal with forty-seven thousand years of cultivation holds grudges for a very long time. I can't protect you all from him while staying in the mortal realm."

"But you can from the Immortal Realm?" Fenlock asked.

"The Celestial Court can. They have the authority and power to tell even Greater Immortals to back off. As long as I'm working for them, and the sect is under their protection, Yan Shenhua can't touch you without starting a war with the court. He's arrogant and obsessive, but he's not suicidal."

Hughie slumped on his bench. "I still can't believe all of this started because Li Fenghao is hiding in my ring. If I'd known that it would lead to this mess . . ."

"You couldn't have known," Slifer said firmly. "Li Fenghao made his own choices. His brother's response is his brother's responsibility. You're just caught in the middle of a family dispute that's been going on for millennia."

"Speaking of which." Hughie pulled off the ring in question and held it up. "Should I get rid of this?"

"Keep it," Slifer said after a moment's consideration. "Li Fenghao's knowledge and guidance have helped you advance quickly. As long as Yan Shenhua doesn't know which disciple is hosting him, you should be safe enough under the court's protection. Just don't advertise the fact that you can use Dimensional Slide. That's the signature technique that would give you away."

Hughie nodded slowly and put the ring back on.

Slifer looked at each of them in turn as he said, "I want to talk with each of you individually before tomorrow. But first, I need you all to understand something important. This isn't abandonment. I'm not running away or leaving you behind because I don't care. I'm doing this specifically because I care too much to let you be endangered by threats I can't handle."

"We know that," Amelia said quietly. "It doesn't make it easier, though."

"No. It doesn't." Slifer stood, and Val adjusted her position on his shoulder. "Hughie, come with me first. The rest of you, wait here. I'll come back for each of you."

He led Hughie to a quieter section of the garden, out of earshot from the others. The young man followed silently, his usual energy completely subdued.

They stopped near a small pond with spirit fish swimming lazy circles below the surface. Hughie stared at the water, not meeting Slifer's eyes.

"I remember the day you came to me with Oliviare," Slifer said. "You were terrified that I'd reject your relationship, that I'd punish you for breaking sect rules. Instead, I helped both of you. Do you remember why?"

"Because you're not like the old sect master," Hughie replied. "Because you actually care about disciples as people, not just cultivation resources."

"Exactly. And that hasn't changed just because I'm ascending." Slifer put a hand on Hughie's shoulder. "You've grown tremendously this past year. You reached Ascendant Realm faster than most cultivators dream of, developed genuine skill with spatial manipulation, and found happiness with someone who accepts you completely. I'm proud of what you've accomplished."

Hughie finally looked up, eyes suspiciously bright. "I wouldn't have accomplished any of it without you."

"Maybe. But the effort was yours. The dedication was yours. The willingness to keep training even when it was difficult—that was all you." Slifer squeezed his shoulder. "Continue that dedication. Keep training. Keep protecting the sect. And take care of Oliviare. She's good for you."

"I will," Hughie said, voice thick. "Master, I know you said you can't visit for ten years, but is there any way to stay in contact? Letters? Communication talismans?"

"The court should allow letters, though they'll probably be monitored for security purposes. I'll write when I can. And if there's ever a serious emergency threatening the sect, the court will notify me immediately. That's part of the protection agreement."

Hughie nodded. Then he did something unexpected. He stepped forward and hugged Slifer.

It was awkward. Hughie was taller and broader now, having filled out during his cultivation advancement. Slifer was still in his elderly body, thin and somewhat frail looking despite his actual power level. The height difference made the hug even more uncomfortable.

But Slifer returned it anyway. Because sometimes disciples needed physical reassurance that they mattered.

After a moment, Hughie stepped back, wiping at his eyes. "Thank you, Master. For everything."

"You're welcome. Now go find Oliviare and treasure her."

Hughie left, and Slifer returned to collect Caelum. The sword disciple stood when he approached, his expression controlled but his eyes showing concern.

They walked in a different direction, toward the weapon racks where Caelum had spent countless hours training. The late afternoon sun glinted off stored blades, creating patterns of light and shadow across the ground.

"You've been unusually quiet," Slifer observed. "Even for you."

"I'm processing," Caelum replied. He ran his hand along a practice sword's blade, not quite touching the edge. "Master, I need to ask something directly. Was I a good disciple?"

Slifer raised an eyebrow. "Why would you doubt that?"

"Because I didn't have good thoughts about you for years. My loyalty only came after you saved my mother and proved yourself worthy of following. That's not the same as what a good disciple would do. They would choose you without needing that kind of persuasion."

"Caelum." Slifer waited until the young man looked at him. "Loyalty that's earned is worth more than loyalty that's given freely. You questioned me, challenged me, made me prove I deserved your respect. And once I did earn it, you became absolutely dedicated. Your loyalty has never wavered since that day in the village."

"But I should have—"

"Stop." Slifer held up a hand. "Don't waste time on what you should have done. Focus on what you did do. You've become one of the strongest disciples in the sect. You've helped train junior members in sword techniques. You've defended the sect against threats without hesitation. Your mother is safe and happy because of your efforts. That's what matters."

Caelum was quiet for a long moment. Then he bowed deeply, the formal bow of a disciple to master. "Thank you for everything you've taught me. About swords, about cultivation, about what it means to lead with honor instead of fear."

"You were always honorable," Slifer said. "You just needed someone to show you that honor and strength aren't mutually exclusive."

He pulled a jade slip from his storage ring and handed it to Caelum. "This contains sword techniques I developed specifically for your style, advanced forms that build on what you already know. Study them carefully. Some won't make sense until you reach Lesser Immortal Realm, but the foundation work will help you get there faster."

Caelum accepted the slip with both hands, treating it like the treasure it was. "I won't disappoint you, Master."

"You never have."

They stood in companionable silence for a moment, watching the sun sink lower toward the horizon. Then Caelum spoke again, his voice quieter.

"Will you be safe? In the Immortal Realm?"

"Eventually," Slifer replied honestly. "The initial training will be dangerous. Enforcer work involves handling situations that normal cultivators can't resolve. But I'll adapt. I always do."

"Then I won't worry. Well, I'll try not to worry." Caelum allowed himself a slight smile. "Take care of yourself, Master. The Immortal Realm doesn't know what it's getting."

Slifer returned to the garden and found Amelia standing apart from Fenlock and Lenvari, staring at nothing in particular. She'd been doing that more lately, just standing and thinking, processing the changes she'd gone through over the past year.

"Walk with me," Slifer said.

She followed without comment. They headed toward the Disciplinary Hall, the building where Amelia spent most of her time now. Her official duties kept her busy judging disputes and enforcing sect rules.

"You're different than when we first met," Slifer said as they walked. "Back then, you would have probably celebrated me leaving. One less authority figure telling you what to do."

"Back then, I was an idiot," Amelia replied bluntly. "I thought power was the only thing that mattered. That manipulation and cruelty were signs of strength. You proved me wrong repeatedly."

"I didn't change you. You changed yourself. I just provided opportunities for that change to happen."

Amelia shook her head. "You did more than that. You forced me to confront the consequences of my actions and made me see that treating people as disposable tools was wrong. Not because of some abstract moral principle, but because it was inefficient and counterproductive."

She paused at the Disciplinary Hall's entrance. "I still don't fully understand empathy. It doesn't come naturally to me the way it does for others. But I'm learning to simulate it well enough that most people can't tell the difference. And sometimes, I think I'm starting to actually feel it: small glimpses of understanding what others experience emotionally."

"That's progress," Slifer said. "More progress than I expected, honestly. When I first took you as a disciple, I wasn't sure if rehabilitation was possible. You've exceeded every expectation."

"Will you miss me?" The question came out uncertain, vulnerable in a way Amelia rarely allowed herself to be.

"Yes," Slifer replied simply. "I'll miss all of you. You've been the best parts of this past year. Watching you grow and develop has been more rewarding than any cultivation breakthrough."

Amelia looked away, but not before Slifer caught the slight reddening around her eyes. "I'll continue working on the empathy thing. Keep trying to understand people better. Make you proud."

"You already make me proud." He pulled out another jade slip and handed it to her. "This contains advanced techniques for mental cultivation. Methods to enhance your emotional intelligence without compromising your analytical abilities. Use them carefully."

She accepted the slip and bowed, the movement precise and formal. "Thank you, Master. For not giving up on me when everyone else had."

"Everyone deserves a chance to grow. You just needed someone willing to provide that chance."

Fenlock was the last one. He stood with Lenvari in the garden, the two of them talking quietly. When Slifer approached, Lenvari bowed respectfully and excused herself, giving them privacy.

"She's been good for you," Slifer observed as they walked toward the library, Fenlock's favorite location. "You're more confident since you two started working together."

"I am," Fenlock agreed. His voice was steadier now than it had been a year ago. The stammering uncertainty had faded as his cultivation had advanced and his confidence grew. "Master, I want to thank you for accepting us."

"I was just happy to see you find someone that wouldn't take advantage of you."

They reached the library and settled into Fenlock's usual study area. Scrolls and jade slips covered the desk, evidence of his continuing research into cultivation techniques and theory.

"I remember when we first met," Slifer said. "You were terrified of everything. Combat training, elder assessments, even casual conversation with other disciples. You've come so far from that frightened young man."

"Because you gave me opportunities to succeed," Fenlock replied. "Small challenges that built confidence gradually instead of throwing me into situations where I'd fail and give up. You understood that different people need different teaching methods."

"I understood that forcing you to conform to standard training would have destroyed what made you valuable. Your analytical mind, your attention to detail, your ability to spot patterns others miss. Those talents needed nurturing, not suppressing."

Slifer pulled out his final jade slip, this one larger than the others. "This contains everything I know about cultivation theory. Formation analysis, technique development, spiritual energy manipulation, all of it. You're the only disciple with the patience and intelligence to fully utilize this information. Study it. Add your own insights. Maybe someday you'll develop techniques that surpass even mine."

Fenlock accepted the slip with trembling hands. "Master, this is . . . this is too much."

"It's exactly enough. You've earned it through dedicated study and consistent effort." Slifer stood to leave, then paused. "Keep Lenvari safe. She's strong, but she relies on you for emotional stability. And keep researching. The sect needs scholars as much as warriors."

"I will." Fenlock looked up. "Master? Will you be happy there, in the Immortal Realm?"

That was an interesting question. Slifer considered it seriously.

"I don't know," he admitted. "This past year has been chaotic and stressful and frequently terrifying. But it's also been fulfilling in ways I'd never before experienced. I helped people. Made a difference. Built something meaningful. Whether I'll find that same fulfillment as a Celestial Court enforcer . . . I guess I'll find out."

After speaking to his disciples, Slifer went to find Morvran.

His servant stood outside Slifer's quarters with perfect posture as always, hands clasped behind his back, expression composed. But Slifer had spent enough time with Morvran to recognize the subtle signs of distress: The slight tension around his eyes. The careful control of his breathing. The way his fingers pressed together just a bit too tightly.

"Master, I—" Morvran began, then paused. "I want to say thank you. For everything you've given me."

"I should be thanking you," Slifer said. "You've been the foundation holding everything together. Every administrative decision, every logistical problem, every crisis that needed handling quietly. You did all of it without complaint. The sect wouldn't function without you."

"You gave me purpose." Morvran's voice was quiet but steady. "When you first recruited me hundreds of years ago, I was nothing, and now you've elevated me to sect master and given me real authority and responsibility. You've treated me like my opinions matter. Do you know how rare it is for someone of my station to be valued that way?"

"You earned every promotion through competence and dedication. I didn't give you anything you hadn't already proven you deserved."

"Still." Morvran's composure cracked slightly. "You changed my life, Master. I was content being invisible, doing small tasks, never aspiring to more. You showed me I was capable of so much more than I believed. You trusted me with important decisions. You listened when I offered advice. You made me feel like a valuable member of the sect rather than just a servant."

Slifer felt uncomfortable with the raw emotion in Morvran's voice. He'd never been good at handling sincere gratitude, even back on Earth. But this wasn't something he could deflect with humor or brush aside.

"Morvran, you're more than valuable. You're essential. This sect runs because of your work. The disciples are safe because of your vigilance. The reforms succeeded because you implemented them properly. I'm leaving tomorrow knowing everything will be fine because you'll be here managing things."

"What if I'm not enough?" The question came out barely above a whisper. "What if something happens that I can't handle? What if the sect falls apart without you here to guide it?"

"It won't. Because you're better at administration than I ever was. You understand people, you anticipate problems, you find solutions before crises develop. Those skills are more valuable than any cultivation technique." Slifer put his hand on Morvran's shoulder. "I trust you completely. That's not something I say lightly."

Morvran looked down, struggling visibly with his emotions. "I don't know if I can do this without you here."

"Yes, you can. You've done it for weeks whenever I'm in closed-door cultivation or dealing with external threats. You didn't need my guidance then. You won't need it moving forward."

"It's different when I know you're coming back. When I know I can consult you if something truly difficult arises. Once you're in the Immortal Realm . . ." Morvran trailed off.

"Once I'm in the Immortal Realm, you'll have the Celestial Court's protection backing every decision you make. You'll have loyal elders who respect your authority. You'll have my disciples, all at Ascendant Realm now, supporting your leadership. You'll have everything you need." Slifer squeezed his shoulder. "And you'll have the satisfaction of knowing you built something meaningful. This sect isn't just mine anymore. It's yours too. Every policy you crafted, every system you organized, every improvement you implemented—the Black Rose Sect's success is as much your achievement as mine."

Morvran finally looked up, his eyes bright with unshed tears he was too disciplined to let fall. "I will guard it with my life, Master. Every inch of progress we've made. Every reform we've established. Every disciple under our protection. I swear to you, the sect will be stronger when you return than it is today."

"I know it will. Because you'll be leading it." Slifer pulled something from his storage ring: a jade token carved with intricate formation arrays. "This is keyed to my personal cultivation chamber and all my private resources. If there's ever an emergency that requires techniques or treasures I've left behind, you have full access. Use them however you need to protect the sect."

Slifer's most loyal follower had broken through to Origin Realm, but to lead a sect like the Black Rose Sect, he would need to be at Ascendant Realm at a minimum. This chamber had the resources to let Morvran break through within a month or two.

Morvran accepted the token with both hands, holding it like the precious artifact it was. "Master, I don't deserve—"

"You deserve it more than anyone. You've earned my complete trust." Slifer dropped his hand from Morvran's shoulder. "Take care of them. All of them. The disciples, the elders, even the Outer Sect members who barely know my name. They're all counting on you now."

"I won't fail you." Morvran's voice strengthened with certainty. "On my honor and my life, I will protect what we've built here."

"I know you will. That's why I can leave without worrying."

They stood in silence for a moment. Slifer wanted to say something more, something profound that would encapsulate what Morvran's loyalty and dedication had meant over this past year. But words felt inadequate for that kind of sentiment. Instead, he did something that would have been unthinkable for the original Slifer. He pulled Morvran into a brief embrace, the gesture awkward but genuine.

"Thank you," Slifer said quietly. "For everything. For your service, your friendship, your unwavering support. You've been the best friend I could have asked for."

Morvran returned the embrace stiffly, clearly overwhelmed. "Thank you for . . . for being a master worth serving."

They separated, both slightly uncomfortable with the emotional display but neither regretting it. Morvran straightened his robes and resumed his professional posture, though his eyes remained suspiciously bright.

"I should let you finish your preparation," Morvran said.

"Right. Keep things running smoothly. I'll write when I can."

"I'll be waiting for those letters. And, Master?" Morvran bowed deeply, the full formal bow of a devoted servant to a respected master. "May your path in the Immortal Realm be clear and your cultivation swift. The Black Rose Sect will be here when you return, stronger and more prosperous than ever."

"I believe that completely."

The sun had set by the time Slifer returned to his quarters, exhausted emotionally if not physically. Val curled up on his desk, her small form radiating warmth.

"Just you and me tomorrow, huh?" Slifer said to the dragon.

Val chirped affirmatively. She'd be coming with him to the Immortal Realm. Their soul bond meant separation wasn't really possible anymore. Where he went, she followed.

Slifer went to sleep thinking about the future. About challenges waiting in the Immortal Realm. About his disciples continuing their cultivation without him. About whether he'd made the right choice.

Morning came too quickly. Slifer woke before dawn and went through his usual routine one last time. Cultivation exercises. Formation checks. A final walk through the sect grounds while most disciples still slept.

The Black Rose Sect looked peaceful in the early morning light. Gardens well maintained. Buildings clean and repaired. Training fields ready for another day of practice. Everything he'd worked to build over the past year was functioning exactly as it should.

DEMONIC SECT ELDER AND THE GREAT WAR

By midmorning, the entire sect had gathered in the main courtyard. Word had spread overnight. Everyone wanted to witness their sect master's ascension to the Immortal Realm.

Morvran stood at the front with the elders. Slifer's four main disciples formed a line beside them. Behind that, inner disciples, outer disciples, servants, and various other sect members crowded together. Hundreds of people, all there to say goodbye.

Han Shu appeared at precisely noon. He didn't use Dimensional Slide or any flashy technique. One moment the courtyard was empty except for sect members. The next moment the enforcer stood in the center, dressed in his formal Celestial Court robes.

"Ready?" Han Shu asked.

"As ready as I'll ever be." Slifer turned to face the assembled sect members one final time. "Thank you all for your support this past year. Continue the work we've started. Keep training, keep improving, keep making the Black Rose Sect something worthy of respect. I'll be watching from above, so don't slack off."

That got a few nervous chuckles from the crowd.

Morvran stepped forward and bowed deeply. "We will honor your legacy, Master. The sect will prosper under the foundation you've built."

"I know it will. You're all capable of great things."

Han Shu raised his hand, and spiritual energy gathered around him. The air above the courtyard began to shimmer, reality bending as dimensional barriers weakened. A tear opened in space, but this was different from Dimensional Slide's white void. This was golden light, brilliant and warm, and it carried pressure that made everyone's cultivation resonate.

The Immortal Realm.

Massive jade and gold gates stretching nearly a hundred meters high materialized around the tear. Inscriptions covered every surface: formation arrays working in harmony to stabilize the connection between realms. The gates swung open slowly, revealing a glimpse of the world beyond.

Slifer saw mountains that touched clouds. Saw floating islands suspended in a brilliant sky. Saw structures that made the Black Rose Sect's buildings look like children's toys. Everything was larger, grander, and infused with spiritual energy so dense that it was visible as rainbow mist.

"Time to go," Han Shu said.

Slifer looked at his disciples one more time. Hughie forcing a smile despite obvious distress. Caelum standing straight with perfect posture, hiding emotion behind formality. Amelia watching with cold eyes that couldn't quite hide concern. Fenlock gripping Lenvari's hand tightly, both of them struggling not to cry. Morvran looking proud while his overweight disciple, Dusty, held back a tear, but whether that was from sadness or difficulty forcing that oversized chicken leg down his throat, Slifer didn't know.

"Take care of each other," Slifer said. "And take care of the sect."

He turned toward the gates and began walking. Val rode on his shoulder, chirping softly. Each step felt heavier than it should, like he was leaving behind more than just a physical location.

But he kept walking. Because this was necessary. Because protecting the people he cared about required sacrifice. Because sometimes the right choice wasn't the easy choice.

Slifer reached the base of the gates and looked up at their towering height. Golden light spilled through the opening, warm on his skin. He could feel the Immortal Realm's pressure beckoning, inviting, calling him forward.

He took a breath, squared his shoulders, and stepped through.

The gates closed behind him.

ABOUT THE AUTHOR

Kalzara is the author of the Demonic Sect Elder series, originally released on Royal Road. He is an avid reader of LitRPG and cultivation novels so it was only a matter of time before he decided to write one of his own.

RESPAWN YOUR CURIOSITY

follow us on our socials

 podiumentertainment.com
 @podiumentertainment
 /podiumentertainment
 @podium_ent
 @podiumentertainment

www.ingramcontent.com/pod-product-compliance
Lightning Source LLC
LaVergne TN
LVHW041620060526
838200LV00040B/1357